Ce

D0516725

》》》》》》》》》》 《《《《《《《《《《

Fyodor Vasilievich Gladkov

CEMENT

TRANSLATED FROM THE RUSSIAN BY

A. S. ARTHUR AND C. ASHLEIGH

NORTHWESTERN UNIVERSITY PRESS

EVANSTON, ILLINOIS

》》》》》》》》》》 《《《《《《《《《《

Northwestern University Press

www.nupress.northwestern.edu

Copyright © 1980 by Frederick Ungar Publishing, Co., Inc. Northwestern
University Press edition published 1994 by arrangement with the Continuum
Publishing Co., Inc., New York. All rights reserved.

Printed in the United States of America

10 9 8 7 6

ISBN-13: 978-0-8101-1160-8

ISBN-10: 0-8101-1160-8

Library of Congress Cataloging-in-Publication Data

Gladkov, Fedor, 1883–1958.

[T͡Sement. English]

Cement : a novel / by Fyodor Vasilievich Gladkov ; translated by
A.S. Arthur and C. Ashleigh.

p. cm. — (European classics)

Originally published: New York : Frederick Ungar Pub. Co., 1960.

ISBN 0-8101-1160-8 (pbk.)

I. Arthur, A. S. II. Ashleigh, C. III. Title. IV. Series:
European classics (Evanston, Ill.)

PG3476.G53T813 1994

891.73'42—dc20   94-22785

                                                             CIP

∞ The paper used in this publication meets the minimum requirements of the
American National Standard for Information Sciences—Permanence of Paper
for Printed Library Materials, ANSI Z39.48-1992.

AUTOBIOGRAPHICAL NOTE

I WAS born in 1883, in the village of Chernavka, province of Saratov, district of Petrovsk, a member of a family of poor peasants. I spent my childhood in the village until I was nine years old. At this age I learned to read and write from an educated Old Believer—my parents belonged to the sect of the Old Believers. My grandmother and visiting preachers taught me apocryphal legends. I knew music only through ancient religious hymns, psalms and litanies. My grandmother (who had been a serf) and my mother, both expert in the art of story-telling and tears, very strongly influenced my childhood.

When nine years old, I left the village in order to go and live with my parents, sometimes among the fisher folk of the Volga and sometimes among the peasants of the Caucasus. In 1895, we settled in Krasnodar where my father was employed in a steam-mill. My mother went out to work by the day. I had a passion for study and read voraciously. I read all the classics. Lermontov, Dostoievski and Tolstoi intoxicated me. Pushkin and Gogol left me cold. I wanted to enter the High School but was not admitted : I had brilliantly passed my examination—but I was poor. Instead of entering High School I became apprentice to a druggist. I could not stand this, and left. Then I went to work in a lithographic shop, which I also left soon. I finished by becoming apprentice in a printing plant. There I stayed six months and then again took flight. I had a longing for the city. I finished my studies in 1901.

The end of my student days coincided with a long period of unemployment for my parents. I helped them with my miserable salary as tutor ; and also earned my first pence as a young writer through local journalism. My sufferings and chronic under-nourishment (I used to make my meals from the remains of the cafés of the Old Bazaar) brought about a severe illness. I spent two months in hospital. I had hardly left hospital when my father was imprisoned for uttering counterfeit money. He spent six months in prison before being sent to penal servitude in Transbaikalia. I followed my parents to Siberia. I became schoolmaster in a little lost hamlet among the Chaldons. My father was freed in 1905, but was subjected to obligatory residence in the district. Having bought him a small farm and some agricultural implements, I left for Moscow, without a penny in my pocket, with the romantic desire to study at the university. The first murmurs of the revolution began to sound. Instead of Moscow, I went to Tiflis, where I entered the Normal School. At the end of six months, I passed my examination as a day-scholar. I became initiated, at this time, into revolutionary activity. I went to Kuban. There I was active among the Social-Democratic groups. Sought by the authorities, I took flight to Transbaikalia, where I fell into the hands of the police. Result : three years' exile on the banks of the Lena. Then I returned to Kuban, where, as a Communist, I took part in the civil war from beginning to end.

I commenced to write while attending school, at the age of seventeen. The local papers published my stories. I was familiar with the ways of workers and of vagabonds. My stories were very favourably received. I entered into a correspondence with Maxim Gorki who showed me great consideration and sympathy. His influence over me was invaluable. Korolenko was equally kind to me and I corresponded with him for some time. My first important tale was accepted by the review *Zavieti* in 1913, but in 1914 this review was suppressed. I then sent the manuscript to the *Sovremenni* which was likewise suppressed. This tale only appeared after the Revolution.

FYODOR VASILIEVICH GLADKOV.

WORKS : Tales—*The Gulf* ; *The Wolves*. Novels—*The Courser of Fire* ; *Cement*. Plays—*The Horde* ; *The Deadwood*.

CONTENTS

CHAPTER   PAGE

   I. THE DESERTED FACTORY - - - - 1

  II. THE RED KERCHIEF - - - - - 26

 III. THE PARTY COMMITTEE - - - - 42

 IV. THE WORKERS' CLUB " COMINTERN " - - 57

  V. THE HIDDEN EMIGRANT - - - - 75

 VI. THE PRESIDIUM - - - - - - 90

VII. THE HOUSE OF HIS PARENTS - - - 105

VIII. BURNING DAYS - - - - - - 113

 IX. THE ROPEWAY - - - - - - 135

  X. STRATA OF THE SOUL - - - - - 150

 XI. IN THE VICE - - - - - - 172

XII. THE SIGNAL FIRES - - - - - 187

XIII. SLACKENING PACE - - - - - 199

XIV. THE RETURN OF THE PENITENTS - - 217

XV. SCUM - - - - - - - - 231

XVI. TARES - - - - - - - 263

XVII. A THRUST INTO THE FUTURE - - 284

Chapter I

THE DESERTED FACTORY

I

THE THRESHOLD OF HOME

It was all as it had been at the same hour of morning, three years ago; behind the roofs and angles of the factory the sea foamed like boiling milk in the flashing sunlight. And the air, between the mountains and the sea, was fiery and lustrous as wine.

The ringlets of March did not yet show on the sprigs of the hedges; and the blue smoke-stacks and cubes of the factory buildings, coated with concrete, and the workers' dwellings of the " Pleasant Colony "; the flanks of the mountains, gleaming like copper, molten in the sun and bluely transparent as ice.

Three years ago—and all was as yesterday; nothing had changed. These hazy mountains: their ravines and gullies, quarries and crags—exactly as in his childhood. In the distance he could see, upon the lower slopes, the workings he knew so well: the conveyor-shafts standing amidst the rocks and bushes; the bridges and cranes in the narrow gorges. The factory down below—just the same: a veritable city of towers and domes and cylindrical roofs; and the same Pleasant Colony on the hillside, above the factory, with its parched acacias and the little yard before each house.

If you were to pass through the gap in the concrete wall which separates the factory grounds from the suburb (once there was a gate here, and now but a gap) in the second block of cottages is Gleb's lodging.

In a moment his wife, Dasha, and their daughter, Nurka, will see him; will joyfully cry out and then cling to him, quivering with happiness. Dasha was not expecting him; nor did he know how much she had undergone during the three years of his absence. In the whole Republic there was not a road, nor footpath, which had not been stained with human

blood. Had Death here only gone through the street, passing
by the workers' hovels, or was his house also razed by fire and
whirlwind?

Gleb strode, in the wine-gold lustre, along the path on the
mountain slope, through the clumps of still wintry brushwood,
among the sparkling yellow flowers. It seemed to him as
though the very air sang and chirruped and danced on wings of
mother-of-pearl.

In the square, beyond the wall, a mob of dirty children were
playing, and paunchy, snake-eyed goats roamed, nibbling at
bushes or acacia shoots.

Astonished roosters jerked up their red combs, crying
angrily:

" Who is this? "

In Gleb's heart—swollen and throbbing—he heard the
mountains and quarries, the smoke-stacks and the dwellings
reverberate with a deep subterranean murmur. . . . The
factory Diesel engines. The cable-ways. The pits. The
revolving cylinders in the furnace-rooms.

One could see, between the grey buildings of the works, an
overhead cable-line stretching down to the sea, upon triumphal
concrete arches, each shaped like a gigantic " H ". The steel
cables are taut as violin strings, to which cling motionless
trucks; beneath them the rusty gauze of the safety-net, and
below, upon the pier at the edge of the sea, stretch the wings
of an electric crane.

Splendid! Once again, machines and work. Fresh work.
Free work, gained in struggle, won through fire and blood.
Splendid!

Like giddy maidens, the goats scream and laugh with the
children. The ammoniacal stench of the pig-sty. Grass and
weeds besmirched by hens.

What's this? Goats, poultry, and pigs? This used to be
strictly forbidden.

Concrete and stone. Coal and cement. Slag and soot.
Filigree-towers of the electric conveyor. Smoke-stacks higher
than the mountains. Net-work of cables. And, right next to
it all, stalls and live-stock? Damn the fellows! They had
dragged the village here by the tail, and it spreads like mildew.

Three women were walking towards him in single file, with
bundles under their arms. In front marched an old woman
with the face of a witch; behind, two young ones, like tramps.
One of them was fat and full-bosomed, her face wreathed con-

tinually with laughter; her lips could hardly cover her teeth. The other with red eyes and red swollen eyelids, her face deep buried in her shawl. Was she ill or weeping?

He immediately recognised two of them. The old woman was the wife of Loshak the mechanic; the laughing one was the wife of Gromada, another mechanic. The third was a stranger whom he had never seen before.

As he approached them on the narrow pathway he stood aside in the high grass and gave them a military salute.

"Good morning, Comrades!"

They looked at him askance as though he were a tramp and stepped past him. Only the last one, the laughing one, gave a screeching laugh like a scared hen: "Get on with you! There's enough scamps like you about. Must one say 'Good-day' to everybody?"

"What's the matter with you, wenches? Don't you recognise me?"

Loshak's wife looked morosely at Gleb—just as an old witch would do—then murmured to herself in her deep voice: "Why, this is Gleb. He has risen from the dead, the rascal!"

And went on her way, silent and sullen.

Gromada's wife laughed and said nothing. Only, from a way off, by the factory wall, she looked round, then stopped and screeched like a noisy magpie.

"Hurry up, man, to your wife. If you have lost her, find her. And if you find her, marry her again."

Gleb looked back at the women and did not recognise in them the friendly neighbours of old days. Most likely the women of the factory had had a hard time indeed.

Here was the old fence around the little yard, fourteen feet square, with the water-closet like a sentry box on the side near the street. The fence leaned a bit more from age and the north-east wind, and a greyish growth covered the pales. And when he went to open the gate, the whole structure trembled.

Now, in a moment Dasha would come out. How would she meet him after three years of separation—he who had passed through fire and death? Perhaps she thought him dead, or that he had forgotten her forever; or perhaps she had been awaiting him every day, from the very hour when he had left her alone with Nurka in this rabbit-hutch and had gone out into the night that was filled with foes.

He threw his military coat upon the fence, unstrapped his haversack and laid it upon the coat. Then threw down upon it his helmet with its red winged star. For a moment he stood still, shrugged his shoulders high, swung his arms wide (one must calm oneself—bring one's limbs to order), and wiped the sweat from his face with the sleeve of his tunic. But he could not dry his face; one would think it was not a face but a sieve. He looked again upon the doorway of the house, where the door ajar was creaking its riddle to him through its black chink.

And just as he tore off his tunic, and again swung wide his arms, the door creaked loudly and—

Is it Dasha, or is it not?

A woman with a red kerchief about her head, in a man's blouse, stood in the black oblong of the doorway, looking hard at him, knitting her brows. Her eyelashes quivered with amazement, and as though she were about to scream. When she encountered Gleb's smile, suddenly her brows lifted and the tears sparkled in her eyes.

Is it Dasha, or is it not?

The face, with the mole on the chin and the round nose; the sideways turn of the head when looking intently—this was she, Dasha. But everything else about her—he couldn't quite say how—was strange, not womanly, something he had never seen before in her.

" Dasha ! My wife ! My darling ! "

He made a step towards her, his boots scraping on the concrete path, and stretched out his arms to embrace her. He could not hold the beating of his heart nor the spasmodic contraction of his features.

Dasha stood in the doorway on the top step. Frozen in the conflict between her impulse towards him and the struggle against her own weakness. While the blood rushed to her face she could only stammer :

" Is it you ? Oh, Gleb ! "

And in her eyes, in the black depths of her eyes, like a spark of fire, burnt an unknown fear.

Then Gleb seized her—the crushing embrace of a husband, of a peasant—till her bones were cracking ; pressed his prickly, unshaven lips to her lips. And she gave herself to his will, and remembrance was lost in rapture.

" Well, then, you're alive and well, my little dove ? Have you been waiting for me, or have you been leading the life of a gay widow ? Ah, my dear ! "

She could not tear herself from him and stammered in the crooning voice of a child, " Oh, Gleb ! How was it . . . ? I didn't know. . . . Oh, Gleb ! "

But this sprang from her heart for a second only, and in this second Dasha felt the old power of Gleb once again upon her.

Ah, once, three years ago, when she was a young housewife, and the young bride bloomed as did the geraniums in the window-box—this power of her man was sweet and welcome, and it was good to feel herself deprived of her own will and secure with him.

But Gleb was not able to take her into his arms as a child and carry her into the room, as in the first days of their married life. Firmly but tenderly, Dasha lifted his arms from about her and gazed at him distantly with a surprised smile.

" What's wrong with you, Comrade Gleb? Don't be so wild. Calm yourself."

She trod a step lower, and began to laugh.

" You soldier ! You are altogether too excitable for this peaceful neighbourhood. . . . The key is in the door. You can boil yourself some water on the oil-stove. But there's no tea and sugar and bread. You'd better go to the Factory Committee and register for your ration."

She came yet another step lower. And her careworn face showed anxiety—a strange anxiety, not for herself.

This was more than an insult—it was a blow ! He had sought a human being, and run his head against a wall. He felt shamed and hurt. His arms were still extended, and uncontrolledly his smile still flickered.

" What the hell do you mean ? ' Comrade ! '—what's that ? Do you think I'm a damned fool ? "

Dasha had already gone down the steps and had reached the gate. There she stood, gazing at him, smiling.

Is it Dasha, or is it not ?

" I take my dinner in town, in the communal restaurant of the Food Commissariat ; and I get my bread ration from the Party Committee. Gleb, you'd better call in at the Factory Committee and register there for a bread card. I shall be away for two days. They've ordered me to go to the country. Take a good rest after your journey."

" Here ! Wait a bit ! I can't understand this. Since when did you become ' Comrade ' to me ? What have I wandered into, anyway ? "

" I'm in the Women's Section. . . . Can't you understand ? "

" And Nurka ? Where's our Nurka ? "

" In the Children's Home. Go and rest yourself; I haven't any time, Gleb. We'll have a talk afterwards. Take a good rest."

She walked quickly away, with long decided steps, without looking back, the red kerchief on her head teasing him, beckoning him and laughing at him.

When she reached the breach in the wall Dasha turned and waved to him.

Gleb stood on the steps, bewildered, watching Dasha's vanishing figure ; he could not understand what had happened.

He had returned home and had met his wife Dasha. It had been three years since he had seen her last. Three years, passed in the tempests of war. Dasha also had been through these three years. And what path had she followed ? He did not know. And now their paths again crossed, strangely. Before their marriage their ways went side by side and then fused into one path. Then circumstances tore them apart, and they journeyed on, each following a separate road, knowing nothing of the other. Had Dasha travelled farther than he ? Had they become strangers to each other, unable to meet again in their former love ?

Three years. What had happened in these three years to this wife without a husband ? These three years, which for Gleb had been a whirlpool of frightful events—what had they been for Dasha ?

Now he was back in the home which he had once left to go out into the empty night. Here was the same factory where he had worked as a boy, grimed with oil, soot and metal dust. Now the nest was empty ; and his wife Dasha, who had clung to him so desperately at the time of their parting, had not welcomed him as should a wife, but had passed on by him, like some cold and hostile ghost in a dream.

Gleb sat down on a step and suddenly realised that he was very tired. It was not the four miles he had walked from the station, but the last three years and then this incomprehensible encounter with Dasha, the unexpected anguish of which had profoundly wounded him.

Why this heavy silence ? Why does the air vibrate and the hens creep screeching through Pleasant Colony ?

These are not buildings, but slow-melting ice-blocks ; and smoke-stacks, light blue like glass cylinders. There is no more soot on the tops of them ; mountain winds have brushed it away. From one of them the lightning conductor has been torn—by the storm ? by rust ? or human hands ?

Previously one could never smell manure here ; but now the sharp-smelling dung of cattle is found in the grass which spreads down from the mountain.

That building just under the mountain slope is the workshop of the mechanics. In the old days, at this hour, its gigantic windows, with its countless panes, blazed in the sun's rays. Now one could see the black emptiness of the interior through the broken panes.

And the town on the hill on the other side of the bay—it also has changed. It has become grey. It is covered with mildew and dust, so that it merges into the mountain slope. No longer a town, one would say, but an abandoned quarry.

" Comrade Gleb ! . . ." The door which she left open, looking into the empty room. . . . The darkened, forgotten factory. He had once been a worker in this factory. And now he was the commander of a regiment and wore the Order of the Red Flag.

A rooster strolled over to the fence, raised his head and regarded him with a cold and evil eye.

" Who is this ? "

And the goats looked at him curiously with their serpent eyes, while with their maiden lips inaudibly they chattered nonsense.

" Shoo, filthy creature ! I'll shoot you, devil take you ! "

2

GLOOM

On the opposite side of the narrow street, from an open window in the tenement, sounded muffled drunken voices. It was the bass voice of the cooper, Savchuk, mingled with the hysterical voice of his wife, Motia, screeching like a hen.

Gleb left his kit lying near the fence and went over to Savchuk's place. The walls of the room were grimy with lamp soot. Overthrown stools lay upon the floor, upon which clothes were also strewn. A tin kettle lay upon its side and, like little white gleams, flour was scattered over everything.

With the sun in his eyes, Gleb could not immediately distinguish any person. Then he noticed two dirty convulsed bodies fighting, rolling on the floor.

Looking keenly, he saw it was the Savchuks. The man's shirt was torn to ribbons, his back was bent like the curve of a wheel, his ribs stuck out like hoops. Motia's skirt was around her middle and her full breast heaved violently as they struggled together.

Gleb seized Savchuk under his arms and squeezed his ribs until they cracked.

" Here, man ! Have you gone crazy ? Take a breather ! Stand up ! "

Savchuk's muscles quivered. He clawed the air so violently that his finger joints cracked.

Forgetful of her naked thighs, Motia, raising herself on one hand, gesticulated with the other and tried, gape-mouthed, to scream, but could not.

" Savchuk, stand up, damn you ! Be a man ! "

Again squeezing Savchuk till his bones cracked, Gleb at last got him upright and planted his calloused heels upon the floor.

" I'll give you one on the head, you old devil ! Are you out of your senses, you blockhead ? And stand up, you, Motia. Are your limbs out of joint ? Cheer up ! Don't be ashamed ; you can stay as you are."

And Gleb burst into friendly laughter.

Motia screamed shyly like a little girl. She pulled her skirt down and curled up her legs under it, rolling herself up like a hedgehog. She was like a little frightened child and hid herself in a corner, crying.

Without recognising him, Savchuk looked at Gleb with bloodshot eyes. Then he turned away, exhausted, and said, hiccupping : " The devil brought you here at the wrong time, my boy. Get out ! Be off, before I break your head for you ! "

Again Gleb laughed cordially.

" Savchuk, my old pal ! I came to pay you a visit. Won't you receive me, Comrade ? You know for how many years we humped our backs together in this hell of a furnace ! What mad dog has bitten you, cooper ? "

Again Savchuk regarded Gleb with his bovine eyes. He stamped his grimy foot upon the floor and waved his hands. His rags fluttered upon him like a scarecrow. This was no shirt, but a mass of tatters. The muscles flickered beneath the skin like knots in taut cords.

" What, you old devil ! Gleb ! My old brother, Chumalov !

What devil has dragged you back out of hell ? You old bastard! Gleb! Look at me! Look at my ugly old dial! And kick me in the belly, if you like ! "

And he enveloped Gleb in a sticky, sweaty embrace.

" Get up, Motia! Get yourself to rights ; now I'm weak and peaceful. We'll carry on another time. I'm going to sit down with good old Gleb and cry a little bit and open my heart to him. Get up, Motia! Come over here. Now, let's have peace ! Kiss Gleb, our friend and comrade ! "

Like oak-shavings, his hair and beard stood up in tufts ; like ragged bast shoes.

Motia, still crouching like a hedgehog, still wept, still pulling her skirt down to her feet.

Gleb laughed at her like a merry old friend.

" Well, Motia, Savchuk didn't show himself stronger than you. Don't worry now. You're a free woman and know how to defend your rights. Stop now—and then begin all over again ! "

It was as though these words had pierced Motia's naked heart. Like a lizard she slid on her knees towards Gleb and her eyes bored into his like flames.

" Clear out, and don't come near me ! There are too many fellows like you around, you damned torturers ! "

She crawled over to the spots of sunlight on the floor, and glowed like fire in the blue rays and rainbow-coloured dust. Her straggling hair fell over her bare shoulders and mingled with the rags of her blouse.

" I shan't go away, Motia. I want to be your guest. Won't you treat me to cakes, roast meat and tea with sugar ? You deal in it, don't you ? "

Gleb went on laughing, caught hold of her hands caressingly, submitting smilingly to her blows.

" Motia, remember what a prime girl you were ? I wanted to marry you, but Savchuk got away with you, the damned old cooper."

Savchuk roared, gnashing his teeth.

" She's not a woman, she's a toad. If you're a friend of mine, train a machine-gun on her. My life is no longer worth living, and she's given everything up to her hoarding. Why does she worry me about the house and all her troubles when I havn't any home of my own and no one wants my work ? This is no proper life, Gleb. I don't exist, Comrade. And the works are dead too, God damn it ! "

Suddenly Motia stood up, and appeared quite changed. She was transformed; beaten, worn out and ill.

"Yes, Savchuk, just look at me! My strength is gone. I am worn to pieces. In order to get a handful of flour, didn't I pillage our home? Didn't I almost strip myself? I shall soon have to drop all modesty and go naked. I had children—little boys—and was a decent happy mother. Where are they now, Gleb? Why am I no longer a mother? I want a nest; like a hen, I want chicks. But they have perished. . . . Why am I alive? Let my eyes burn out, Gleb; they were not made for the night, but for the shining day."

Her lips and cheeks quivered, and she looked at him with eyes dim with tears.

She kept on pulling her skirt down over her knees, and pulling up her blouse over her bosom, until she almost split the stuff.

Yes, this was a different Motia, suffering and angered. In the drooping corners of her mouth and in her pain-scorched eyes, there lurked a feverish and still unrealised force. Gleb remembered her still among her noisy brood of young children—one at the breast, one clinging to her skirts, and the others playing around her; and she in their midst like a busy clucking hen, while in her eyes there shone the quiet happiness and cheerful self-sacrifice of a mother.

Savchuk seized a stool and threw it violently over towards the table. Then sat down, like a worn-out beast, and banged his fist upon the table.

"We've come to the end of things, curse it! We're starving! Brother Gleb, I'm giving up. There's nothing but emptiness and the grave. I'm dying from too much strength, dear Gleb. I'm full of strength, and yet I'm afraid. Tell me, why am I afraid? I'm not afraid of death: that means nothing to me. I'm afraid of the gloom and devastation here. Look at it: this is no factory—it's a rubbish heap. It doesn't exist any more. And where am I then, Gleb?"

Motia looked at him, the grimy tears trickling from her tormented eyes; and Gleb saw in her face an anxious love for her husband.

"Dress yourself, you big animal! Aren't you ashamed of looking like a tramp? Your face looks like a dented old bucket. Mine is pretty well beaten up—but yours has been smashed by the devil."

And in this deep cry of Motia's there was only a feigned anger, for her voice was broken with tenderness.

Gleb burst out laughing.

" You're a funny lot, you are ! "

" Motia, come here. Kiss me, my little wife ! "

Savchuk lifted her up like a little girl and set her down close to himself.

From far behind the hill the tops of the dead smoke-stacks glittered like empty tumblers. And along the mountain slopes, clothed in dark brown bushes, the silent trucks, like dead tortoises, were perched upon the rusty cable-way.

" The factory. . . . Oh, Gleb, think what it used to be and what it is now ! Just remember how the saws used to sing shrilly in the cooper's shop—just like young girls in springtime. Ah, old friend, I was hatched here. I knew no life outside of this hill."

Savchuk was longing for the old whirr and din of the factory. He shed tears at the death of once active labour. In his yearning for the vanished life of dead machines, he resembled a blind man, with his wistful smile and lifted face.

Motia stood close beside him, like him : as one blind and weeping. A mother bereft of her brood.

" You can beat me, Savchuk, if you like, but my home is everything to me. Well, at least do your beast's job properly. Come, hit me ! "

" Motia, do you want me to be like all the others ? Must I make tubs for the peasants on the sly ? And didn't you go with your rags, selling our household remnants from village to village, you poor stray beaten dog ? "

He clenched his fists and ground his teeth.

And Motia stood, speaking as in a dream.

" We had a decent home, Savchuk, and our children were such dear little things. Your blood and my blood. Let's make a new home, Savchuk. I can't bear it ; I can't, Savchuk. I shall go along the highway to find homeless children."

They stood there : Motia on one side, Gleb on the other.

Gleb, deeply moved, laid his hand on Savchuk's shoulder.

" Say, Savchuk, my old pal. When we were kids we used to go to work together. And Motia was our companion then. You've been sitting here like an owl hooting your misery through the night, while I was shedding my blood, fighting the enemy. Now I've come back. And I've no home any more and the works are closed. Motia's a good woman. Let's get our strength back, Savchuk. We've been beaten, but we've learned how to hit back. Damn it, we've learnt it well, Savchuk! Give me your hand, you damned old cooper!"

Savchuk gazed at him wildly and shook his head. He didn't understand. He saw him through a blood-shot mist.

Motia leaned towards Gleb and, without shame, put her arms round his neck.

"Dear Gleb. . . . Savchuk is a good fellow. It's his strength which has driven him mad. Savchuk's all right, Gleb. I don't want anything except to have some children to take care of. Oh, what a fate, what a fate!"

"Don't make such a fuss of him, Motia, he isn't your lover!"

Gleb caressed Motia's hand and laughed:

"What a funny couple you are!"

3

MACHINES

Two paths led from Pleasant Colony to the Factory Committee: one along the main road past the factory buildings, and the other by intricate paths over the hills, through bushes and boulders and disused quarries.

From here one could see the complicated mass of the buildings. Towers, arches, viaducts, blocks of concrete, iron or stone: here appearing almost transparent like gigantic globes, and there heavy and rectangular in their simple construction. They were piled up, joined closely one to the other, or emerging suddenly from the mountain side at different heights. And in the gorges, along which ran the ruined narrow-gauge lines, strewn with boulders, and the abandoned trucks, encroached upon by dust-grey weeds, under the cliffs or upon the cliffs, little lonely houses arose here and there from out of the blue cement. Like gaily coloured terraces, the quarries fell in tiers down the slope and ended in a young wood below in a valley. Far away, behind the factory, where the headlands melted in the hazy distance, was the sea; and the horizon cut clearly the glassy blue, above the roofs of the works, and between the aspiring smoke-stacks. There one could see, stretching out from the town to the other side of the bay, and from the factory to the bay, two jetties, upon the extremities of which were lighthouses. And one could see the eternal half-circles of foam, rolling snowily towards the factory and the quays.

Just as three years ago. But in those days the factory and mountains quivered with an internal rumbling. The roar of the machinery and the electric whirring upon the mountain side animated the factory, its great buildings, smoke-stacks and quays, as with volcanic force.

Gleb strolled along the path, looking down upon the factory and the still, stagnant valley, hardly stirred by the babble of its brooks, and felt that he himself was also growing heavy, foundering and covered with dust.

Was this the factory he had known in his childhood, in the fire and fury of whose life he had been reared? Where he had roamed the lanes and highways, the ground vibrating beneath his feet? And is he really Gleb Chumalov, mechanic, wearing the blue blouse—he who now walks lonely along the weed-grown path, a strange apparition whose eyes are filled with bewilderment and mournful interrogation?

In the old days he used to be unshaven—wearing a curled moustache—his face engrained with soot and metal dust; now he was close-shaven, his skin clearer, his cheeks and nostrils chapped by the winds of the plain. Is this really he, Chumalov, no longer smelling of soot and oil, no longer stooping from toil? Is this really he, Chumalov, the lobster, the stalwart soldier, with green helmet upon which the red star blazes, and with the Order of the Red Flag upon his breast?

Something fantastic has happened. An upheaval, as though the mountain, uprooted from its base, had somersaulted into the infinite depth.

He walked on, gazing at the factory and the quarries, upon the sterile smoke-stacks; then stopped, thoughtful, and murmured in a voice broken by sighs:

" Damn these people! To what have they brought things, curse them! Shooting isn't good enough for the scoundrels! What a wonderful factory they have ruined, the wretches! "

He knew only one thing: that here was a gigantic tomb, a place of desolation and destruction; and that here was he, out of the army, with this great desolation hurting his heart. And this tomb horrified him and he knew not what to do.

He went down towards the factory, down towards the empty coal-soiled courtyard, overgrown with weeds. Once, high pyramids of anthracite rose here, shining like black diamonds. The yard was dominated by a steep cliff, in yellow and brown strata. It was crumbling, and the rubble was burying the last traces of human labour. Rails ran in a semi-circle on its margin.

Behind the parapet, 250 feet in height, the blue obelisk of a smoke-stack rushed towards the sky ; and behind this, rising like a mountain, the enormous edifice of the power-station.

Like a dead planet, the factory slept in these idle days. The north-west winds had splintered the icy windows ; the mountain torrents had laid bare the iron ribs of the concrete foundations, little heaps of worked-out cement-dust upon the ledges had again solidified.

Klepka, the watchman, came by. He wore a long blouse made from an old sack, down to his knees, without a belt. Torn shoes upon his bare feet. And the old torn shoes were covered with cement, as though he had feet of cement. He grew no older, and appeared to have been here for ever. He stopped for a moment, looked indifferently at Gleb and then went on—a ghost from out of the past.

" Hey there, you old ruin, where are you wandering to, you old carcase ? "

Astonishment and fear showed in the hairy face.

" Strangers are strictly forbidden to trespass here."

" Idiot ! Who has the keys of the factory ? "

" Keys ? There's no more use for them ; there are no more locks. They've all been taken. You can go wherever you want. There's goats in the factory . . . and rats . . . nothing but gnawing animals. As for men, there aren't any more . . . disappeared."

" Why, you're nothing but an old rat yourself ! Hiding in crevices like a crab . . . and slouching round like a loafer, you old bastard ! "

Klepka looked sourly at him and scratched his head, covered with tufts of cement-tipped hair.

" You, with your pointed helmet—the horn of the devil ! There's none to blame here . . . there are no more men."

And he moved on with trailing steps, his old shoes scraping each other.

A high viaduct on stone columns connected the courtyard with the main buildings of the factory. Here and there, the concrete walls had been rudely pierced—loop-holes for machine-guns. The factory had been used by the White Guards as a stronghold. It had been turned into stables, and barracks for prisoners of war. And, in the days of the intervention, these barracks had been nightmare tombs.

Now let us have a look at the interior of the factory.

There were no doors ; they had been torn from their hinges. Cobwebs, heavy with cement dust, fluttered like ashen rags. From the huge dark belly of the factory there breathed the stench of mildew, and air laden with the dust of old workings.

The twilight quivered with the sonorous echo of desolate oblivion. The bridges, stairways, galleries, levers, pipes, transmission belts—torn down and piled in filthy rubbish heaps. Over all, the heady acrid odour of cement. The massive bulk of the furnace chimney, from which the oven door had been wrenched. The air rushed up the shaft, roaring like a waterfall, with whirlwind sweep, pushing and sucking Gleb into its moaning mouth. In former days, a cast-iron door safely stopped the roaring vent, and the chimney thunderously sucked up the glowing refuse from the pot-bellied furnaces.

Gleb went down a metallically echoing staircase and walked with clanking steps by the dust-covered windows. The great tanks of the rotary furnaces dwarfed him to the stature of a doll. In the old days, their monstrous red-hot bodies revolved with a cosmic roar and howl, belching hellish flames, while below them crowded men, like agitated ants, dominated by fire. Vertical and lateral, thick pipes crawled in complex knots and spirals, like cast-iron cactus-growths, over the bodies of the stoves. And here, again, the power-belts creep along the walls and cleave the air.

" Swine ! Dirty swine ! What have they done with this great power ? What a state they've brought it to ! "

Passing down long black tunnels, Gleb came to the engine-room. The peaceful light, filtered from the sky, revealed the austere temple of the engines. The floor is of chess-board tiles. And the Diesel engines stand like black marble idols, bedecked with gold and silver. Firmly and solidly they stood in long regular rows, ready for work—just a touch, and their polished metal limbs would start dancing. The fly-wheels appeared to be alive in flight : Gleb almost felt the hot waves of air, laden with grease and sulphur, rushing to meet him. The engines stood in rows, like altars demanding their sacrifice. And the fly-wheels stand still, and yet whirl. He laid his hand upon the engine : they stood there firmly rooted in the earth, immovable. Mighty crystals—ready to explode.

Here, as in the old days, everything was trim and clean. Every part of the machines testified loving human care. As of old, the polished floor gleamed, and not a speck of dust obscured the windows through which flowed the blue and amber light. Here a man must be living on, doggedly ; and under his care the machines live also in tense expectation.

And this man, in a blue shirt and cap, suddenly sprang out from a gangway, between the Diesels. He wiped his hands with waste ; one could mark the whites of his eyes and of his teeth. A flat little cap pulled down over his nose ; and a nose as flat as his cap. His moustache sprouted, red and bristling. He was tough, prickly and keen as a fox.

" Hullo, old friend ! Is it you ? Now you're a brave commander ! Something told me you were still alive and kicking. I guessed you would come back and that we'd go the rounds again as before. Well, you've certainly cheered me up. Let's smear you with a little engine grease ! "

It is Brynza, the engineer, his old friend.

He was born here, and his father before him was a mechanic ; he grew up among the machinery and the machinery was his whole world. Gleb and Brynza grew up together, and together went as boys into the factory.

" Well, so here's our fighting man ! Let's have a good look at you. You're wearing a helmet now, I see ; but only your nose and the red star seem to have grown any bigger. I recognise your hands and feet, all right : they stick out far enough."

Gleb gave a shout of joy and opened his arms wide to embrace his old friend.

" Brynza, my old pal ! So you're still here ? So you're not loaded down with fodder bags, for hoarding grub, like most of the factory loafers. Or are you working at pipe-lighters ? Everything is so neat here one would think you were going to start on the job."

Brynza caught Gleb's hand and drew him into the narrow gangway between the engines.

" Look at these devils, friend ! You see how they look ? How clean they are ! It only needs one word : ' Start her off, Brynza ! ' and all this jolly machinery would start turning, and trumpeting out an iron march. Machines need discipline and a live hand, just like your army. When I'm with the engines, I'm an engine myself . . . and you can all go to the devil with your politics, yelling and brawling. Fight like hell ; smash each other's skulls ; bathe yourselves in blood ; play the very devil ! All that doesn't concern me. For me there's only one thing : me and the machine ; we are one."

" Brynza, I know your capable hands ; you've got hands of

gold . . . are there any goats round here? In the devil's name, let imbeciles and good-for-nothings play around with them. And as for the pipe-lighters, I know you wouldn't touch them. You old devil, you've buried yourself here with your machines and don't know a thing about all the changes that have taken place. A cannon-shot wouldn't rouse you."

Brynza suddenly stood perfectly still and stared fixedly at Gleb.

"Halt! Are you trying on your agitation and political meetings? You won't get me on that, brother. You're among the engines now, and not at a public meeting. You know that, don't you?—so shut up! How have I been dealing with the matter? Well, once there used to be work here, but now there are tramps on all the highways. Sometimes one of these loafers wanders in here, and gets a couple of good ones in the behind. The best place for these chatterers is up at the Factory Committee. The people have gone plain crazy with so much jabbering! Idleness and jabbering, they both amount to the same. You can't do anything here with big words. These are machines, and machines are not words; they're hands and eyes."

Gleb caressingly stroked the glossy surfaces of the engine. With moist and almost drunken eyes he gazed fixedly at Brynza.

"Why, old friend, you've got a real living, organised thing here! One hates to leave it. But how rusty the factory has got; and how stale the people have become. Why in hell do you stay here and work your hands to the bone on these machines when the factory is nothing more than a rubbish heap, and the workmen good-for-nothing loafers, or petty hagglers? Get out of this before you peg out."

Brynza shook with rage from head to foot. His face was contorted. It was as though his heart was bursting, and his blood was boiling in madness. With all his might, he brought down his fist on the shining flank of the Diesel.

"The factory must be set going again, Gleb! It must not die. It must live, or it will devour us. Do you know how machines live? No, you don't! You would go mad, if you really saw and felt it. But who knows this? I know it—only I!"

Brynza had never before shown such despair. He had lived with the machines, and had stood by them all his life. When at last the engines were silenced and the people deserted them, surging out of the factory to revolution, to civil war, to hunger and to suffering—Brynza had stayed on in the silence of the engine-room. He lived as the engines lived, and was every bit as lonely as these austere glittering machines.

"This factory has got to get going, Gleb! When there's machines, they've got to work. Ah, if you could only realise it! But whether you do or not, you must do all you can to help us start things going. Keep your mind on that, and don't forget it for a minute."

Gleb caught Brynza's hand and shook it with joyful excitement.

"Right, old friend! If it's a factory, it's got to get to work. Here's my hand : we're going to start her going! We'll get her started if it kills me! Keep your Diesels ready. We'll put our backs into it!"

4

MATES

In the basement of the factory office-building, in a narrow dimly-lighted corridor, smelling of damp cement, numbers of workmen crowded and jostled. Here were the odours of the steam bath and of strong tobacco. Amidst these fumes of dirt were men, soiled also with the grey dust of the quarries and the highways; soiled as the foliage and the factory buildings. They were dull and troubled, gloomy like the evening shadows. There was a clamour as of a market-place, pierced occasionally by bellowing laughter, making the very walls tremble. They swore and wrangled about rations, about food-supplies for the communal restaurants, about paraffin, clothing-cards, pipe-lighters and goats; and about the poor working-people upon whose shoulders sat every kind of rascal.

The door of the office of the Factory Committee was open; and there also was the same rancid smell and smoke, and the sweaty smell of the crowd gathered there.

No one recognised Gleb as he elbowed his way through the crowd. They looked at him sullenly, coldly; with ill-concealed hatred they glanced at his red-starred helmet and the Order of the Red Flag upon his breast. But they did not turn to look after him as he passed them by; in a flash they had forgotten him, in their indifference. Aren't there enough commissars floating about here, and all kinds of people, with or without portfolios, strolling about the office?

Before the door was a youth, arrayed in a woman's white bonnet, with a corset laced over his coat, wearing an artificial moustache on his shaven lips. He was dancing. The dense crowd jostled him closely, but he warded them off with his elbows and screamed in shrill feminine tones, with mincing affectation.

"Let me introduce myself. . . . Ah, excuse me ! . . . Now, citizens, I'm a respectable proletarian girl ! Ah, don't touch me—don't tickle me ! "

And then broke into song :

> "Oh, little apple, where are you rolling?
> Into the office he goes strolling."

The admiring laughter and oaths of the crowd drowned his song.

"Hey, you low-down swine ! Mitka—you devil ! This concertina player : he's just the same as ever ; nothing can stop him—neither the devil nor the priest nor the Soviet ! "

In the doorway stood, infuriated, a little haggard man. He had only one eye, which gleamed angrily. It was Gromada, the mechanic. Gleb was shocked to see how frightfully wasted he had become in the past three years.

"Don't brawl, Comrades. You should be ashamed of such goings-on. We can't properly understand each other——"
Mitka cut him short :

"Ah, Comrade Committee-man, excuse me, I beg. Tie your nerves up in a knot and pin them to your navel. I feel dead, worn out, exhausted ! I'll lay the corsets on the floor with my hat in front and the braces as harness. With this equipage I shall drive in great state to the demonstration. Hurray ! "

And, continuing his antics, he made a way for himself with his elbows through the crowd towards the door. The crowd followed him as though entranced by the spectacle.

Gleb entered the committee-room and stood by the wall behind the workmen. At the table sat the hunchback mechanic, Loshak, old, rusty and black as ever, next to Gromada. Loshak's breast and his head, wearing a cap shiny and soiled by much handling, rested upon the table like a block of anthracite. Of his face one could only see his flattened nose and bloodshot eyes. He was motionless as a stone idol, while Gromada, agitated, spat, jumped up, again seated himself, gesticulating and shouting.

A broad-hipped woman, quivering like jelly, was screaming.

"You good-for-nothings! Who put you on our backs, you rotten lot? We poor people are dying so that you can fill your bellies. Look at their fat faces! My husband sticks at home scratching the goat while I have to come and jaw with this fat-bellied lot!"

Some of the workmen clapped her on the back; they were almost choking with laughter.

"Go on! Curse away, Mother Avdotia! Swear for all you're worth! You've got plenty of strength with a rear elevation like that!"

"Be quiet, you swine! What has your Factory Committee been put here for? Is it taking care of us, or bothering its head about us? Are they doing anything for the working-man?"

She took a step backwards, then kicked her leg high in the air, letting her heavy boot strike the table with a loud thud. Her raised skirt revealed her blue and swollen leg.

The crowd thundered laughter and applause.

"Bravo, Mother Avdotia! You've given us some perform-ance. Pull the curtain higher and let's see the main act!"

Loshak sat like a blank-eyed idol of wrath. Gromada sprang up, his arm upraised—a thin wreck, gnawed by con-sumption.

"Citizeness! Comrade! After all, you are a working woman. The Factory Committee is doing its duty. . . . Er—in every possible way——. You must understand. . . ."

"Speak, Mother Avdotia! Answer for all of us!"

"To the devil with you, you rascals! What does she mean by it? Here is Comrade Lenin's portrait on the wall, and this slut makes herself half-naked!"

"Hold your tongues! Where are the boots your committee gave me? Look at them. I've only walked to the cossack vil-lage with my sack and afterwards the three of us went to the dining-room where we got grub that's only fit for pigs. Look how the uppers are sewn, and the toes here! What's the good of boots like that? I've a mind to make you eat them!"

She drew her foot out of the boot and stamped it on the floor; while the gaping boot revolved drunkenly on itself and fell by Loshak's chest.

But Loshak sat still as a block of anthracite. Quietly he took the boot and placed it before him.

"Go on, woman, have your say: we shall hear you."

Gromada could stand it no longer. He jumped up, waving his arms wildly. The last drops of his blood flickered in his livid, earthy cheeks.

"I can't stand this, Comrade Loshak! This citizeness talks without any logic—and so on, and so on. . . . It's shameful on her part; the Factory Committee is not a pack of thieves! We cannot tolerate a provocation like that."

"Have patience, Gromada. A good steam bath does no harm. We'll get this fixed to rights. Now, you poor little orphan child, explain to us for what kind of work did you get those boots?"

"Don't you try and come it on me, you damned hunchback! Whether I worked or not, I've got them coming to me."

"Shut up! Use your brain instead of your tongue. I am asking you: for what specific work do you claim to get your cornflour and milk, all nicely sprinkled with sugar? Well?— Give me the other boot. They were given to you for nothing, by the State. And we're requisitioning the pigs for soup with which to fill your empty belly. Explain yourself; if you can you'll get them back. Come on, speak out!"

Avdotia leaned back upon those behind, causing the whole crowd to shift step.

"Gently, devil take you! Look out, brothers, don't hurt her!"

With the same air of melancholy calm, Loshak took the boot (its sole hanging like a cow's tongue) and held it out to her.

"Here you are, my good woman; take it! Get your husband to repair it and then you can wear them. And come back another time, so as to give us all a laugh. When the factory start's working we'll send you to the quarry: you'll blow the rocks up without dynamite."

Fat Avdotia took the boot and, sitting on the floor, began to force her fat varicose leg into it, while continuing to vent a medley of muttered comment.

"Listen, blockheads," she said. "Listen how the Soviet power puts everything right. They took the grain from the peasant so as to make war on the bourgeois; and they took the factories from the bourgeois—factories like ours. And now there's no work! They took the bourgeois' goods away from them and said: 'Divide this among yourselves, workers, so that nothing gets wasted.' All right, go ahead. . . . But when the factory works, it will be different. Why don't you go home, you wooden heads!"

Gleb got up to the table at last, saluted, and began to laugh.

" How are you, lads ? It's a long time since we met. I've got back at last, but there's no factory here now ; it's a regular slaughter-house. What a hell of a mess you've made out of the works, my friends ! You ought all to be shot, my dear Comrades."

Gromada sprang up, knocking his chair over.

" Gleb, dear old Comrade ! Don't you see who it is, you old humpback ? It's Gleb Chumalov, our Gleb ! Once dead and now living ! Look at him, Loshak."

Like a black idol, Loshak remained seated, fixing on Gleb the same sad gaze with which he regarded day after day the workmen, the fat Avdotia, all the hurly-burly of the crew, bubbling from morning to night, in the Factory Committee's office.

" Good, so I see. So you have reported here : you were a mechanic, and then went as a soldier. That's all in our favour. Now listen, soldier, you must help get things straight. You see how our workers are going to seed. You see what's become of the works. And as for the repair shop, they're just turning out pipe-lighters there. A hell of a situation."

Slowly he stretched his abnormally long and heavy hand across the table to Gleb. Somehow it seemed strange to Gleb that this immense hand belonged to Loshak.

Workmen from the various shops came up and gazed in amazement at Gleb, as though he were a risen corpse. They looked in astonishment at each other, murmuring their surprise, and jostled each other in order to seize him by the hands.

Then suddenly it was still, except for the deep sighing breath of the men. The confusion and hubbub had disappeared with Mitka and Avdotia.

" Well, Comrade Chumalov ! We've got a job for you now, all right ! You see how it is. . . . We've chased the masters away. . . . And now look how it is : everything's disappearing. One pinches the fittings, another takes copper, and another steals belts. We call ourselves the masters now—it looks like it ! "

From whom came these plaints ? It was hard to tell : it was indeed a chorus of protest ; and it seemed to each that he alone complained.

Gleb gazed at the crew, and cheerfully nodded his helmeted head.

" Ha ! coopers, smiths, electricians, mechanics—I see we're all here, brothers ! "

That little meagre man, Gromada, came through the crowd carrying a chair, which he noisily set down.

" Let's have room, Comrades ! Give place to our Comrade Chumalov. He's our warrior from the Red Army and, as he's also a worker in our factory, we must make the most use of him on every occasion. If Comrade Chumalov hadn't landed in the Red Army, you must all know, after serving with the Greens,[1] there would have been a good many now who wouldn't have taken the step of joining the C.P.R.[2] See, Comrades, that's exactly what Comrade Chumalov means to us."

Again voices from among the workers :

" So you're living, brother ? . . . That's good. . . . Enjoy yourself a bit now you're here. . . . What are you going to do here ? . . . Tobacco—we'll look after that. . . . The factory's hopeless—dead and finished."

But Gromada was again waving his bony arms and shouting in his piercing, wheezy voice.

" Comrades, our class fights to control the means of production ; but it's a shame that we have such a bent for demagogy. We've been victorious on all fronts and liquidated everything ; can't we do anything when it comes to productive work ? "

Gleb was silent. He looked at the pale, wasted faces of the workmen, at the dying Gromada, that small man whose name signified business, at Loshak, who was bent down as though under the weight of his angular stony head. Sitting there, silent and weary, he felt that his life was about to take a new path. Everything seemed clear and simple ; everything was going on as usual. And yet, deep down in him, moved a dim sadness.

His wife, Dasha, who had passed by him, strange and distant, wounding him to the heart . . . the empty house . . . the empty factory with its dusty cobwebs . . . all was strange to him. The army, which was so dear to him. . . .

" Yes, friends, your life here is not pleasant. How could you—in the Devil's name—have brought everything to such hideous ruin ? We were fighting over there, getting killed,

[1] Peasant troops which acted independently during the Civil Wars. They generally, but not invariably, supported the Red Army.—Tr.
[2] Communist Party of Russia.—Tr.

shedding our blood . . . but what were you doing here, brothers? What were you fighting for? The factory looks a beauty now, doesn't it? And what are you doing now? Have you all lost your senses? What have you been doing here?"

Gromada wished to say something, but could not master the big words. The workmen also wished to cry out, each louder than the other, but their shouts were still-born, perishing in sighs. And only one of them was heard, right at the back, unseen, crying with a hoarse laugh:

"And if we had all stuck in the factory, damn you, we'd have died like flies. Is the Devil himself in this factory?"

Gleb ground his teeth, and struck his knee with his clenched fist.

"Well, and what if you had died! You might have gone west, but the factory would still be running!"

"Ha, we've heard that old song before. You'd better go and tell them about it who told us the tale. Tell them how they've fogotten all about us now; be damned to them!"

From the depths of his hump rumbled Loshak's bass voice.

"You've come back to the factory—that is good, Gleb, you'll be starting work now. We'll have to get things put to rights. That's good!"

With eyes burning with enthusiasm, Gromada gazed at Gleb, seeking to use big words beyond his power.

Gleb took off his helmet and placed it on the table in front of Loshak.

"I returned home; and my wife passed by me without stopping. Nowadays one doesn't recognise one's own wife at the first glance. There are wood-lice in my house, and no bread. Write me out a food-card, Loshak, like a pal."

Hardly had Gleb uttered these words than the laughter of the workmen crashed through the silence.

"Ha, ha! he's a great speaker, but his belly's empty. Just the same as us. You should have started with this question. Come on, boys! A brother has come to us. He's living at the same address as we are—his stomach's empty."

"Comrades: Comrade Chumalov is one of us. He is ours. . . . He's been in the battles . . . er, and so on, and so on."

"Well, what about it! The old belly's still got to be filled. Let's go home, brothers."

Gleb stood up and put on his helmet.

"Brothers! . . ."

He had cried this word in tones too loud for the place in which they were cooped ; he had shouted with all his strength as he used to do when in the army. The workmen stopped and drew together, immobile.

" Brothers, it's true then : the belly must be filled. I've been fighting over there and I'm going to fight here. We're going to fight to get the factory started. I shall peg out, or explode or go mad, but will get this factory going. I may get burnt alive, but the smoke-stacks will be smoking and the machinery will be turning. I'll bet my head on it ! "

The workmen stood shuffling their feet and blinking in confusion and surprise.

" Get it going, Gleb ! That's what I say. Go to it, boy ! Here's my hump on it ! Fine ! "

Gromada, burning as with fever, ran laughing round the table.

Gleb shuddered, a spasmodic choking in his throat. Through the window he saw, passing along the concrete path, leaning heavily upon a stick, a stoop-shouldered old man with the appearance of a gentleman. But no, this is no old man it is a tall man with a silver beard. It is the engineer, Kleist. Again he stood in Gleb's path, as he had done before.

Chapter II

THE RED KERCHIEF

I

THE COLD HEARTH

GLEB did not take his rest at home. This deserted dwelling, with its dusty window (even the flies no longer buzzed against the panes), unwashed floor and heap of ragged garments, had become strange, uninhabitable and stifling. The walls seemed to press in on him and there was not room to move. Two steps to the right—and there was the wall; two steps to the left—again the wall. As night drew on, the walls came closer and the air was so thick that one could grasp it. Worst of all were the mice and the mildew. And no wife, no Dasha.

Gleb rested in the deserted works, in the quarries overgrown with bushes and grass. He roamed about, sat down, reflected. . . .

At night-time he came home and found no Dasha. She was not waiting for him on the threshold as she used to three years ago, when he returned home from the workshop. In those days it was cosy and cheerful in the room. Muslin curtains hung before the windows, and on the window-sill the flowers signalled welcome to him like little flames. The painted floor glittered like a mirror under the electric light, and the white bed and silvery table-cloth sparkled like frost. And a samovar. . . . The chinking jingle of the china. . . . Here Dasha lived in every corner : she sang, sighed, laughed, spoke of to-morrow and played with her living doll, their little daughter Nurka. But even then, sometimes, for a moment, her brows would knit ; through her love, her stubborn character would sometimes reveal itself.

That was a long time ago. It was the past. And the past had become a dream, dreamed recently.

And this gave pain, because it was the past. And one felt nauseated with this abandoned and mildewed home.

Where the mice have fouled there can be no rest. Where the cosy fire has died now swarm the stinking vermin.

Dasha came home after midnight. She no longer feared passing the dark corners of the deserted factory.

The little tongue of flame in the lamp burnt, dim and strange, in a bulb dirtied by finger-marks; and the rosette-shaped lampshade, attached to a cord of tarnished flex, hung like a frozen flower.

Gleb was lying on the bed. Through his drooping eyelashes he was drowsily regarding Dasha.

No, this was not Dasha, not the former Dasha. That Dasha was dead. This was another woman, with a sunburnt, weathered face and stubborn, opinionated chin. Her face seemed larger under the fiery red kerchief with which her head was bound.

She was undressing at the table. Her hair was bobbed. She was chewing a crust of her rationed bread and did not look at him. He watched her face, tired but tense and stern as though she were clenching her teeth. Did he embarrass her? Or was she trying not to disturb his repose? Or did she not sense the change that had come into her life with his arrival? His Dasha was strange and remote.

He decided to test her.

" Explain this question to me, Dasha : Firstly, I was in the army. Secondly, I've been fighting, and haven't had a home of my own, nor an hour to myself. Now I've come home, in my own house, and you are not part of it. I've been hanging round waiting for you here like a deserted mongrel, and I haven't slept at nights. After all, you know we haven't seen each other for three years."

She was not frightened at his voice : remained just as she was when she came in. She spoke without looking at him.

" Yes, three years, Gleb."

" That's so, and you don't seem very happy about it. What does that mean ? Do you remember the night when we parted ? I was all bruised and beaten and hadn't properly come to myself yet. Do you recollect how you nursed me upstairs in the attic, as though I was a little child ? How you cried when we parted ! Why are you so cold now ? "

" It's true, Gleb, that I'm different now. I don't stay around the house so much. I'm not the person I used to be."

" Just so. That's what I was saying."

" That home of ours, I've forgotten about it. I don't regret it. I was a little fool then."

" Well, well! And where shall we have a home then? In this rathole? "

Dasha gazed attentively at him from under her lowered brows. She twisted the red kerchief in her fingers. Then she leant forward, her fists upon the table (there was no longer a tablecloth upon it and it was black and greasy with dirt).

" Do you want flowers on the window-sill, Gleb, and a bed overloaded with feather pillows? No, Gleb; I spent the winter in an unheated room (there's a fuel crisis, you know), and I eat dinner in the communal restaurant. You see, I'm a free Soviet citizen."

She no longer looked at him as of old, when she was his sweetheart. Now she was vigorous, unsubduable, knowing her own mind.

Gleb sat up on the bed and in the eyes which had looked upon blood and death there flashed alarm. A devil of a woman! One had to treat her differently.

" And Nurka? I suppose you've thrown her to the pigs too, with the flowers? That's a pretty business! "

" How stupid you are, Gleb! "

She turned and moved away from the table as though she had become unaware of him.

Outside in the darkness an owl was crying in the valley— all alone like a child. . . . And under the floor, hungry rats scampered amongst the earth and shavings.

" Good. Nurka is in the Children's Home. I shall go there to-morrow and bring her back here."

" All right, Gleb. I've nothing against it: you're the father. But I'm up to my eyes in work. So you'll take care of the child, won't you? "

" Won't you have an affectionate word for her? "

" Now, Gleb, give me my share of the bed. I've nothing under my head."

" All right. If that's how it is, let's start an argument. It's my turn to speak."

" What do you think you're talking about, Gleb? There's no argument or speaking to-night. Shut up! "

Gleb rose from the bed and walked to the door. Again he felt the room was too small for him: the walls were closing in upon him and the floor creaked and shook under his feet.

He looked at Dasha. Skilfully and quickly she unmade the bed and piled the bedding on her arm. Without glancing at him, she prepared for herself a flat and uninviting sleeping place in the corner. And it seemed to Gleb that, as she flung off her petticoat, she smiled sneeringly in his direction.

Well, the question must be answered : did she love him like a woman, as before, or had her love died and had she followed it into the past ?

He could not understand what was uppermost in her : a woman's guile or hostile caution ? An enigma : was she tempting him as a man, or was she snapping the last threads that bound them together ?

She had abandoned the fireside, left the home ; and the warm fragrance of her woman's flesh seemed to have faded together with snugness and the household tasks. Whom had she warmed and caressed with her body these past three years ? A healthy and vigorous woman, mingling day and night with men in her work, could not live like a sterile flower. She had not hoarded for him her loving womanly tenderness ; she had dissipated it in chance encounters. Was not this the reason of her coldness and aloofness ? So thought Gleb, and his tortured soul shone in his eyes with a bestial fury.

" Yes, citizeness, it was so. . . . We parted weeping ; and now we meet again, without a word to say. For three years I used to think : ' My wife, Dasha . . . who is here . . . is expecting me, and so on. . . .' At last I get back . . . to this cursed place. It's as if I had been married only in a dream. There were men, all right . . . but not I. Isn't that true ? "

Dasha turned towards him in amazement and cold drops again glittered in her eyes.

" And you—didn't you have any women without me ? Confess, Gleb, I don't know yet whether you've come back healthy or rotten with disease. Confess, now ! "

She continued to smile. She spoke carelessly, as of a tedious subject. And at these words of Dasha, Gleb shook with fury, and then slumped weakly upon himself. This carefully kept secret of his nights—Dasha knew it ! She knew him so much better than he knew her. And because, without any closer contact, she could see right through him and wring out his strength as one wrings out a rag, he, the warrior, weakened and wavered, humiliated.

Then he recovered, hardening his heart ; he even smiled and gulped.

" Well, then, so be it ; I confess ; there were occasions. The peasant at the front carries death with him. . . . But the women are different. A wife has a different lot, different cares."

Dasha had undressed but had not yet laid down. She was leaning against the wall. She was unashamed. Under her shift, gently rose and fell her rounded breasts. She looked askance at Gleb, measuring him sharply, with a pained and understanding gaze. She answered him casually.

" That's a nice thing : a woman has other cares ! It's an evil lot—to be a slave, without a will of one's own, always playing the second part. What kind of an *ABC of Communism* have you studied, Comrade Gleb ? "

But hardly had she spoken these words, than the blood rushed to Gleb's head : his suspicions had not been idle. She . . . Dasha . . . his wife. . . . Somebody's nights had been intoxicated with her ; and her own blood had become drunken through the intoxicated blood of another.

With a heavy determined step he approached her. With a dark look, with the look of a beast, he looked into her face, which was smiling broadly and mockingly.

" Well, then, it means—words or no words—that it's the truth ? Eh ? "

A hot shudder burst from his heart, tearing at all the muscles of his body.

She—his wife—Dasha. . . .

Outside there was an oppressive silence, stars, crickets, and night bells. Over there, beyond the factory, lay the sea in a phosphorescent shimmer. The sea sang in an electric undertone, and it seemed as though this deep reverberation did not come from the sea, but from the air, the mountains and the smoke-stacks of the works.

" Well, then, tell me, with whom were you carrying on ? Who was it you squeezed in your arms at night ? "

" I'm not asking you about your women when you were at the front, Gleb. Why are you concerned about my lovers ? Come to your senses."

" Now, remember, Dasha. I'm going to find out about this. I'll find out your secrets. Bear that in mind."

She stepped forward, the whites of her eyes were shining.

" Don't stare at me, Gleb. I can frown just as hard as you can. Stay where you are, and don't show off your strength."

Enemies? She, with her eyes smouldering; he, sturdy, bold, his jaws clenched till his cheeks sank in.

Was it Dasha looking at him with the cruel gaze of an unconquerable woman, or had he never understood her real soul, which in these three years had revealed itself, obstinate and indomitable?

Where had Dasha absorbed this power?

Not in the war, not with the food-scroungers, bag on her back, not in the ordinary duties of a woman; this strength had awakened and been forged from the collective spirit of the workers, from years of deadly hardship, from the terrible heavy burden of the newly acquired freedom of women. She crushed him with the audacity of this strength, and he, a Red War Commissar, was confused and lost.

It happened all of a sudden: he seized her in his arms and hugged her till her ribs cracked.

" Now then, what is it to be—life or death? "

" Take your hands off, Gleb! You won't put your hands on me. You're only an ordinary human being, Gleb."

Her muscles were writhing like snakes under Gleb's hands and she was desperately trying to spring free.

" Now tell me where you've bestowed your love while your husband was away? Come on, tell me! "

" Let me alone, you brute. I'm going to hit you! I'll fight, Gleb! "

Frenzied, drunken with the heat of his own blood, he carried her to the bed and threw himself down with her, tearing her shift, hungrily clasping her, as a spider will a fly. She was turning and twisting, fighting silently with clenched teeth and without shame, tearing away from him her naked bruised flesh. With a final effort she flung him off on to the floor and leapt like a cat to the door. She looked away from him, breathing deeply, and setting her clothes straight.

" Don't touch me, Gleb! It will only end badly. I've learnt to take care of myself. These ways don't go with me, Gleb. It's true you're a soldier, but you can't overcome brains."

Gleb, stunned, felt as though ulcers were burning in his soul. The pain was greater than any bodily hurt.

He must not beat her. One has to fight at the war, but at home one must find other ways. Where was the enemy hidden in her, who was so strong and elusive?

He sat on the floor, leaning against the bed, tamed, grinding his teeth with bitter remorse.

Dasha's eyebrows quivered; she laughed and went into the corner to her own bed.

" Turn the light out, Gleb, and lie down. You need rest. It's being overtired that is making you crazy."

" Dasha, darling, where is our love? Has hard work turned you into a devil, and have you ceased to be a woman ? "

" Lie down and calm yourself, Gleb. I'm worn out from work. To-morrow I'm ordered into the country again, to organise the Women's Section, and there are bands of roughs throughout the district. There is no assurance against death. Don't be silly, Gleb."

She moved to the table and turned out the lamp; then she lay down, covered herself with the clothes and was silent. Gleb could not hear her breathing.

He sat in the darkness and waited.

Suffering and insult. A burning in his soul. Dasha at once so near and so distant.

He waited for her voice and for her love. He expected her to come to him and gently, as of old, to press his head to her bosom, whispering like a mother, like a friend.

She was lying there a stranger, her heart shut against him. And he was alone with his longing and his pain.

He went up to her quietly, sat beside her and put his hand on her shoulder.

" Dasha, love me as you used to. You know I've been through fire and blood. I have had no caress for a long time."

She took his hand and laid it on her breast.

" How foolish you are, Gleb . . . so strong, but so foolish. . . . No, not now, Gleb. I've no strength for caresses. Calm yourself. . . . The time will come for you and me. . . . My heart is steeled against love-making; and you, you're passionate and I've no words for you yet. Lie down and go to sleep."

He looked forlornly at the blue window. The sky was studded with stars and somewhere, most likely in the mountains, distant thunder rumbled with a rolling echo from the depths. The wood was singing in the steep valleys under the breath of the north-east wind.

He got up, shook his fist and fell heavily on the bed.

" I shall find a way . . . or it won't be me. Take care ! I have never given in yet, not till to-day. Remember that."

Dasha was silent, cold, near and . . . a stranger.

2

THE CHILDREN'S HOME

In the morning, Gleb, still asleep, felt that the room was not a room but an empty hole. A breeze was blowing between the window and door, whirling in gusts, redolent of spring. He opened his eyes. It was true ; the sun was blazing through the window. Dasha was standing at the table, adjusting her flaming headscarf. She glanced at him and laughed. An amber light shone in her eyes.

" We don't sleep as late as this here, Gleb. The sun is beating down like a drum. I've already worked out a report for the Women's Section on the children's crêches and the estimate for the linen and furniture. I've got it worked out, but where's the money coming from ? We're so beggarly poor. Our Party Committee should be given a jolt, so they'll squeeze something out of the bourgeois. I'm going to kick up a row about it from now on. And you, remember you haven't seen Nurka yet. Do you want to go with me to the Children's Home ? It's close by."

" Good. One—two—and I'm ready ! Dasha, come over here to me for a moment."

Dasha smiled and stepped up to him with a question in her fresh morning face.

" Well, here I am. What next ? "

" Give me your hand. . . . That's it ! That's all. You are the same woman as before, and you are a new Dasha also. But perhaps I'm no longer the mechanic of the old days ? Am I perhaps a new Gleb, grown like a new crop of corn ? Well, we shall learn. Even the sun shines differently now."

" Yes, Gleb, the sun and the corn have changed. I'm waiting. . . . Make haste."

All the way to the Children's Home Dasha walked in front, along the path among the bushes and brushwood, disappearing at moments till the red headscarf showed again like a flame. Gleb felt that she was avoiding him purposely. Was she teasing him or was she afraid ?

Dasha, in whom lay a riddle. A woman remains a woman, but her soul travels slowly.

The Children's Home, "Krupskaya", was there in the mountain gorge among clusters of trees, the red roof bristling with chimneys. The walls were of unworked stone, well-built and firmly cemented. The windows were large as doors, wide open, and from the dark interior a birdlike din of voices came. From among the green bushes round the yard also came cries and chattering. There were two storeys, each with balconies, and with massive steps ; with verandahs ornamented with Grecian vases. On the verandahs, like melons ripening in the sun, were the heads of children. Even from a distance one could see that their faces were like skulls. Boys ? Girls ? Impossible to say. All wore long grey shirts. The nurses in grey too, with white caps, also stood drinking in the sunshine.

On the right, behind the buildings and above them, was the sea, intensely blue and flecked with dazzling sparks. A motor-boat like a black water-beetle was churning away from the coast leaving a triangular wake behind. The town and the distant mountains looked very distinct and near. The burning air vibrated with a humming of golden strings. It was the bees darting starlike and the flies buzzing.

Without understanding why, Gleb felt wings unfolding in his soul. All this, the mountains, the sea, the factory, the town and the boundless distances beyond the horizon—the whole of Russia, we ourselves. All this immensity—the mountains, the factory, the distances—all were singing in their depths the song of our mighty labour. Do not our hands tremble at the thought of our back-breaking task, a task for giants ? Will not our hearts burst with the tide of our blood ? This is Workers' Russia ; this is us ; the new world of which mankind has dreamed throughout the centuries. This is the beginning : the first indrawn breath before the first blow. It is. It will be. The thunder roars.

Dasha stood on the steps by the tall vases, waiting for him, breathing deep draughts of air.

" What beautiful air, Gleb, like the sea. Nurka lives on the second floor."

She walked on a few steps. She seemed as though she were going home, as though she were quite at home here.

From the verandah Gleb saw more children down below among the bushes and the clumps of ill-clad trees of early spring. The children were straying about like the goats at the factory, fighting with each other, crying. Some groups were turning over the soil, digging greedily and hurriedly like thieves, glancing fearfully behind them. They would dig and dig and then turn and tear the booty from each other's grasp. The one who was stronger and cleverer would roll clear of the heap of little bodies and run aside with his loot, gnawing greedily, chewing and choking, tearing at it with his hands as well as with his mouth. Near the fence some children were swarming over the muck heap.

Gleb clenched his teeth and struck the balustrade with his fist.

" All these poor little wretches will starve to death here, Dasha. You ought all to be shot for this job."

Dasha raised her eyebrows in astonishment, glanced down and laughed.

" You mean their scratching in the earth ? . . . That's not so very terrible. Much worse things happen than that. Had there been no one to look after them they would all have starved like flies. We have the children's homes, but we have no food. And if the staff were left free to do as they liked they would bite the children's heads off. Though some of them are fine—real hearts of gold . . . trained by us."

" And Nurka—is she in this state too—our Nurka ? "

Dasha met the white-faced Gleb's gaze calmly.

" In what way is Nurka any better than the others ? She has had her hard times too. If it hadn't been for the women the children would have been eaten alive long ago by lice and disease and finished off by starvation."

" You mean to tell me that Nurka has been saved by a lot of screaming women and suchlike ? "

" Yes, Comrade Gleb. Exactly—in that way and no other."

Coming down the mountain they had noticed the children on the verandah, but when they arrived the children and nurses had disappeared. Probably they had run off to tell of the arrival of visitors.

The sun was shining in the hall, and the air was thick and hot, smelling of sleep. The beds stood in two rows, covered with pink and white counterpanes, torn and patched. Some of the children were in grey smocks, some in rags. Their faces were wan and their eyes sunk deep in blue sockets. The nurses passed through the hall, in and out. There were little pictures on the walls, the children's club work.

The nurses in passing stopped deferentially.

" Good day, Comrade Chumalova. The matron is just coming."

Dasha was not reserved here. This was her household.

" Here I am, Nurka ! "

A little girl in a smock, small, the smallest of all, was

already running towards them, jostling the other children, with cries and laughter. And all the other children pattered after her with their bare feet, and their eyes like those of little hares.

" Aunt Dasha has come ! Aunt Dasha has come ! "

Nurka ! There she is, the little devil ! Impossible to recognise her ; a stranger, yet with something so familiar about her.

She rushed up to her mother, flew to her like a bird, shrieking, laughing and dancing all at once.

" Mummie ! Mummie ! My Mummie ! "

Dasha laughed too, lifting her in her arms and kissing her. Like Nurka, she cried out :

" My Nurochka ! My little girl ! "

This was the old Dasha again ; the same as ever, as when she used to wait for him with Nurka when he was coming home from the factory. The same tenderness, the same tears in her eyes, the same musical voice with the wistful quaver in it.

" Here's your father, Nurochka ; here he is. Do you remember your Daddy ? "

Nurka opened her eyes wide, frightened. She looked at Gleb with timid curiosity.

He laughed and stretched out his hand. But he felt his throat contracted, as if it were bound by a string.

" Well, kiss me, Nurochka. How big you are ! You're as big as Mummie . . . so big ! "

She shrank back and again looked piercingly at her mother.

" It's Daddy, Nurochka."

" No, it's not Daddy. It's a Red Army soldier."

" But I am Daddy, and a Red Army soldier too ! "

" No, this Daddy is not Daddy. Daddy looks like Daddy and not like an uncle ! "

Dasha's eyes laughed through her tears. Gleb's laugh strangled in his throat.

" Well, all right. For this first time I'm not your Daddy. But you're still my little daughter. Let's be pals. I'm going to bring you some sugar next time. Even if I have to dig it out of the mountain, I'll bring it. But why is Mummie any better than I am ? You're here, and she's somewhere else."

" But Mummie is here ; she's here in the daytime, and when it isn't daytime. But Daddy isn't. I don't know where Daddy is. He's fighting against the bourgeois."

" Aha, you got that off well. Give me a kiss ! "

The children danced around, staring at Gleb and hungrily waiting for Dasha's voice and hand. The girls, with their hair cut like boys, kept stretching out their hands towards Dasha, clasping violets. Each wanted to be the first to put the flowers into her hands.

" Aunt Dasha ! . . . Aunt Dasha ! "

Somewhere off in one of the rooms the " Children's International " was being strummed on a piano and discordant children's voices were shouting :

> " Arise, ye children of the future !
> Freedom's youth of all the world ! "

Dasha laughed and patted the children's little heads ; they were evidently accustomed to this caress and were waiting for it as for their ration of food.

" Well, youngsters, what have you had to eat and drink ? Whose tummy is full and whose empty ? Tell me ! "

And they all shouted their answers in a general uproar. They were scratching their heads and their armpits. One dirty little wretch kept hawking and swallowing the mucus ; his eyes bulged and he groaned, scratching his filthy chest under his shirt. Gleb went up to him and raised his shirt. Bloody scratches and scabs ! But the boy screamed, terrified, and ran to hide behind the beds in the corner, so that only his head and protruding eyes were visible.

" Ta, ta, ta ! There's a hero for you ! Look at him behind the barricades already ! "

And the boy and Dasha and the children all burst out laughing ; and the sun laughed too in at the open windows as large as doors.

Dasha walked on with Nurka's hand in hers, without a single glance at Gleb ; and this hurt him. Dasha and Nurka were as one—and he was a stranger to them—a stranger and separate. Dasha, hand in hand with Nurka, was truly a mother, and more so here than at home. And he was alone, here and at home . . . childless.

Yes, here too, life had to be conquered.

They visited the different floors and the dining-room, where the dishes were standing and the children sitting round ; they went into the steamy kitchen, smelling of food, where were more children, and then into the bare-looking clubroom, whose walls were covered with mildew and drawings.

Here, clustered around a short-haired maiden with a brown

birth-mark that covered all one cheek, the children were singing the " International " in deafening, discordant voices.

> " Arise ye children of the future !
> The builders of a brighter world ! "

Domasha and Lisaveta, their neighbours, were here too.
Gleb glimpsed in them also something new, something he had
not seen before. They too seemed quite at home here.

Domasha was in the kitchen, helping with the cooking.
She was very hot and bustled about, sleeves rolled up, quite at
home. She greeted Dasha with kisses.

" Oh, look ! Here's our boss ! You won't half have to bully
that scurvy Narodbraz ;[1] it's work that's needed, and not
wiping their noses on handkerchiefs. And you must wake up
the Prodkom[2] too. How can we feed children on worms and
mouse-droppings ? But I see your dear husband is hanging
around you again. Clear him out ! What do you need him for ?
Mine hasn't come back, thank the Lord. The Devil take him.
Stallions are cheap these days, you can pick and choose !
Now then, don't you gape at me—I'm not scared. . . . Don't
try to come it over me with your precious cap ! As for the
Prodkom, I shall go myself, and to the Narodbraz too on the
way. They'll be getting my boot in the jaw. . . ."

Dasha slapped her on her broad shoulders and laughed.

" So you're gabbling away again, you old goose. You're a
terror, Domasha."

" Pooh ! They all need to get it in the neck . . . the blasted
devils. They do nothing but look at their bellies. I'll take
their trousers down for them."

Gleb was choking with laughter.

" Here's a bitch of a woman ! She doesn't even stop to take
breath ! "

They found Lisaveta in the store-room with the housekeeper. She and the housekeeper were both tall, fine-looking
women ; they were cleanly dressed and looked like nurses.
The housekeeper was dark, with a faint moustache, an Ar-
menian type ; Lisaveta was fair and her face was puffy, swollen
through hunger and trouble. They were weighing up goods,
tallying and entering them.

Lisaveta greeted Dasha in her proud manner, and it was
only her eyes that smiled.

---

[1] People's Education Committee.
[2] Food Committee.

" Dasha, go to the linen-mistress. The linen's all in rags when it comes from the wash. The children can't change. We shall have a demonstration to-morrow to show their nakedness. Whose head ought to be punched ? The children go to the mountain to fetch wood, and it's all been gathered by the workmen. There's nothing to cook the grub with. Who ought to be slammed for that ? "

Dasha made notes of what Domasha and Lisaveta said; wrinkles puckered her forehead above her nose.

" Comrade Lisaveta, you are instructed to investigate everything in the home and report afterwards to the Women's Department. The ground's got to be dug, that's true. And it's true too that we have to make a row."

Lisaveta only glanced once at Gleb and then took no further notice of him.

And he saw still more women, with white headscarves and without, who smiled at Dasha deferentially and flatteringly.

At Gleb they looked askance, nervously. Who was he ? Perhaps it was one of those troublesome inspectors who had to be watched carefully so as to discover their weaknesses.

Gleb kept wanting to take Nurka's hand again ; he kept whispering :

" Nurochka, come, give me your hand. You give it to Mummie—why not to me ? "

She turned away and hid her hands. But when he kissed her as if by chance and took her into his arms, she suddenly submitted and looked at him for the first time, steadily and thoughtfully.

" Your Nurochka is a lovely little girl."

It was the matron speaking, a little woman, alert like a mouse, freckled and with gold-filled teeth.

Dasha looked past her at the walls and windows and her face grew stern and hard again.

" Now stop that, that about Nurochka. . . . They're all equal here, and they all ought to be lovely."

" Yes, certainly, certainly. We do everything for the proletarian children. The proletarian children must have all our attention. The Soviet power takes such great care."

Gleb could scarcely control his irritation.

She's talking through her hat. We'll have to see what sort of elements we have here.

There followed complaints, complaints, complaints.

And Dasha answered in a voice which Gleb had never heard with words that struck like blows.

"Don't grumble, Comrade. Show what you can do and don't grumble. Grumbling doesn't cut any ice."

"Certainly, certainly, Comrade Chumalova! It's so easy and pleasant, working with you."

Gleb clenched his teeth.

Dasha went everywhere, looked at everything, asked questions. Then, losing patience, she walked into the staff's rooms.

"Aha! Why are there chairs, easy chairs and sofas in these rooms? Oh, and there are flowers and pictures, statuettes and all sorts of things! But I told you not to take anything away from the children. It's disgusting! Don't you think the children might like to roll about on sofas and carpets sometimes? And they're fond of pictures, too. This can't go on!"

"Well. . . . Yes, Comrade Chumalova. You are right, certainly. But educational practice. . . . Pedagogy. . . . And besides, it's harmful—encourages laziness. And you see . . . dust . . . and infection. . . ."

There was a steely gleam in the matron's eyes, while Dasha without looking at her went on in the same hard voice, with red spots burning on her cheekbones:

"To hell with your practice! Our children have lived in holes like pigs. . . . Give them pictures, light, fine furniture. Everything possible must be given to them. Furnish the Clubroom, make it beautiful. They must eat, play, have a lot to do with nature. For us—nothing, but for them—everything. Even if we have to cut ourselves to pieces, even if we have to die, we must give them everything. And so that the staff shouldn't get lazy, they can sleep in dirty attics. . . . Don't throw dust in my eyes, Comrade. I understand very well—other things as well as your practice."

But the alert little woman, with her freckles and gold-filled teeth, laughed admiringly, while the steely gleam shone still in her eyes.

"And who doubts it, Comrade Chumalova? You are an exceptional woman, far-sighted, with keen perception. Under your direction everything will go well, everything will be splendid."

When they were leaving, Dasha again embraced Nurka and caressed her, and the children clung to her with shrill bird-like cries.

And Nurka looked long and thoughtfully at Gleb.

" Would you like to come home, Nurka ? To play there like you used to . . . with Daddy and Mummie ? "

" What home ? My bed is over there. We've just had some milk, and now we're going to march to music."

For the first time she shyly and softly threw her arms round Gleb's neck, and the light of a question shone in her eyes, those eyes like her mother's.

All the way from the Home to the highroad Dasha remained silent. The tenderness still shone in her face, slow to fade. On the highroad she spoke, more to herself than to Gleb.

" We of the Women's Section have a lot of work to do. It's not the children we have to train, it's those damned women. If it weren't for our eyes and hands they'd steal everything, down to the last crumb. And they're servile, like slaves ! Ugh ! Enemies everywhere—oh, how many enemies ! People like that, with gold-filled teeth, it's natural in them. . . . But our own. . . . Our own, Gleb ! Like slaves ! What do you think about a requisition, Gleb ? "

Chapter III

THE PARTY COMMITTEE

I

COMRADE SHUK SPEAKS OUT

THE Palace of Labour was a heavy square, brick building, two storeys high, standing on the quay, not far from the long jetty which, supported on black piles, stretched out into the bay. A concrete wall ran out in irregular lines from each side of the facade, separating the quay from the railway. Through the holes and gaps in the wall one could see the rusty and worn rails meeting and separating like iron nerves. The grain sheds stretched along all the way to the station; and far away, at the foot of the mountain, like ancient towers, the summits of the elevator appeared, overgrown with moss. The elevator glowed a fiery red under the mountain and itself looked mountainous like a huge inaccessible temple.

Carts rattled noisily over the paving past the wall. The grey quays with their giant rings for the mooring of steamers, the metallic gleam of the rails shining amongst the litter of broken trucks, divided the bay into quadrangles of stone, with deserted moles and breakwaters. In the distance through the spring mist the harbour danced in bright flecks of light and the white sails of fishing-boats flashed dazzlingly like sea-gulls; fat-backed dolphins were diving and leaping and the silvery fishes glittered in the sun.

Desolate harbour, hungry sea. . . . In what waters, to what shores, are wandering the captured ships?

Near the Palace of Labour, in front of the high pyramid-like steps of the entrance, was a flower-garden with chestnut trees. But there were no longer any flowers, the chestnut trees were misshapen, and the fence had been broken up for fuel. Instead of flowers were scattered sunflower seeds, and brown mushrooms made shadowy patches under the trees. But one could plainly see high up above the roof the letters R.S.F.S.R. shining and disappearing like white daisies on the red flag.

Two corridors crossed each other—one led straight ahead to the Assembly Hall (the red flags gleamed like blood through the open doors), the other running from right to left ended in two dark caverns : on the right was the Party Committee and on the left the Council of Trade Unions.

The tobacco-laden air was thick with over-heated steam ; the walls were dirty, splashed with dishwater, and the plaster was broken. There were coloured placards, men with black or yellow leather coats, some with portfolios, and men—just men, in rags, booted or barefooted (although March had only just come, it was warm). Near and far in the corridors and rooms, singing voices could be heard, the stamping of boots, the patter of bare feet, and the clatter of the rifles in the department of the Cheka.

Gleb went down the corridor to the right. Two men were standing at the glass door of the Party Committee room. Their profiles showed distinctly against the ground glass of the panes. One was bald, with a Turkish nose. His upper lip was short and his mouth half-opened in a smile. The other was snub-nosed with a low forehead, sharply furrowed down the middle, and a large chin which stuck out like a fist.

" It's too bad, it's disgraceful, my dear Comrade. Absolutely disgraceful ! "

It was the snub-nosed man speaking, or rather he was not speaking, but barking.

" Bureaucracy is ruining us. . . . Bureaucracy. We've scarcely had time to bury the bodies of our Comrades . . . their blood is hardly dry . . . before we're sitting in private rooms and easy chairs with lovely riding breeches like generals. And the formalities—docketing papers, marking doors ' no admittance ' . . . soon we shall get to ' Your Excellency.' We had Comrades. Where are they ? I feel that the working-class is oppressed and miserable once more. . . ."

" You're wrong, Comrade Shuk. That's not the case. Your point of view is radically wrong. One can't argue like that. That's not important. We have many enemies, Comrade Shuk. We need merciless terror, or the Republic will linger between life and death. That's what one must consider. I understand you, Comrade Shuk, but the Soviet has to have a firm, efficient, well-tested administrative machine—even if it is bureaucratic—so long as it works reliably."

" You too ! It's the same with everyone. Everyone says the same things. Where does the working-class come in ?

Ah, Comrade Serge. . . . It hurts. . . . And there's none you can talk to."

" There's only one thing that matters, Comrade Shuk, and that's work among the masses. Work, work, work. . . . The masses have got to penetrate the whole administrative machine of the Republic right up to the top. Comrade Lenin's well-known saying about the cook must be turned into an accomplished fact. That's the thing that matters. And you're making a mistake. You're trying to force an open door."

" Come off it, Serge ! . . . You may be a devoted Communist but you're blind. . . . The working-class needs a bit more sympathy, and as for enemies—the Devil take them ! We've managed to deal with them hitherto, and we can carry on the same way. But what about the Party officials and workers ? They've no sooner got into high positions than they change from friends and comrades into scoundrels. . . . That's where the trouble is, Serge ; that's the enemy, Comrade ! "

From the complaints he was barking out, from the angular profile, Gleb recognised his old friend, Shuk, the turner from the Southern Steel Trust Factory. He had not changed ; he was shouting and grumbling just as he did three years ago.

Gleb went up and clapped him on the shoulder.

" Hullo, my friend ! I see you're shouting and cursing. When are you going to stop cursing ? You ought to be organising things, putting your back into it, and you're just whining, you old snub-nose ! "

Shuk, astonished, opened his eyes. He was dumbfounded and confused. He drew in his breath and whistled.

" Gleb ! Dear old pal ! You old warrior ! Well, I'll be damned ! "

He flung his arms round him, stifling him in heat and sweat.

" Is it really you ? Oh, my friend, we'll go together at once and tell them all off. We'll put them all in their places. . . . What planet have you sprung from ? Here, Serge, here's my oldest pal. We've seen trouble and blood together."

" Don't talk hot air, Shuk. Grumbling wins no victories with us."

" Do you hear, Serge ? He'll skin the lot of them, he will ! That's the kind of chap we need, Serge. He'll knock down thirty-three mountains."

Gleb and Serge shook hands, just touching each other's

fingers for a second, warily, like strangers. And Gleb felt in Serge's fingers the softness and timidity of a young girl.

An intellectual ! . . . Soft-handed. . . . Refined.

Gleb looked into his face. His hair was red-brown, a smile lurked in the tilted corners of his mouth and in his red-brown eyes. There was a sneer in the smile, but a hint of kindness and inquiry was visible also.

" I know you already, Comrade Chumalov. I have seen you before in the Registration Office. They were talking about you on the Presidium. You've come just at the right time."

" There, you see, my friend ? Our generals smell an enemy. You'll have to treat them in military fashion, otherwise they'll make your life a burden to you. They wanted to catch me too, but I'm too clever for them and I know what I'm about. . . . I'm going to show them up, the whole lot of them."

" Well, explain then, Shuk. What's the row about ? "

" I've no faith in them. They talk all the time about the workers. But actually they care for nothing but their own bellies. Profiteers ! Posers ! Swankers ! "

" Well then, Shuk, let me have a look at your generals too. Lead me to them, Shuk ! "

"Go to the Secretary, Comrade Chumalov. He's at a meeting but he left orders that you were to be summoned by telephone. His name's Shidky."

"No, you take him along, Serge. It's your job. I'll come along and see if they can catch him with bare hands."

" I'm busy, Comrade Shuk. There's the Agitprop[1] meeting on now, and then the Department of Education has a sitting, and then I've got to speak."

" Oh, Serge ! You may be educated, but you're worse than a monk for obedience and humility."

Gleb and not Serge entered the room first. And because the room was small, or because there were only women in it, Gleb felt that he filled it and had not room to move. It seemed to him that his helmet touched the ceiling and was scraping against the plaster.

Comrade Mekhova, Secretary of the Women's Section of the Party, sat near the window, with a pencil in her hand, dressed in a blue smock. Her hair curled from under her red headscarf like wood shavings and glistened in the sun. On her upper lip was a light down like a boy's, and her eyebrows

[1] Agitation and Propaganda Committee.

moved expressively. She lifted her round eyes with long lashes quickly to Gleb and her eyebrows quivered like dragon-fly's wings. Her dimpled cheeks were plump and rosy as a school-girl's.

Dasha was standing near the table speaking loudly and energetically. She cast a rapid glance at Gleb but showed no recognition of him. Her face was like a stranger's, businesslike, inaccessible. Near her and along the walls women were sitting. They all wore headscarfs and were listening to Dasha's report.

Comrade Mekhova was looking away, as though she were not listening, warming herself in the sun like a cat.

Shuk started to laugh and took hold of Gleb's sleeve.

" A dangerous place, friend Gleb. The women's front! They'll bite us to death, hack us to pieces and deafen us with screeching. Look out for yourself! "

Serge smiled confusedly.

Gleb raised his hand to his helmet.

The women at once broke out shouting at Shuk, and in the din it was impossible to understand whether they were in a rage or just pretending for a joke.

" Here, look ! A committee of devils. Not one of them will bear any more children as long as she lives. The whole blasted gang of them is going to boycott us—the bitches ! "

Dasha threw up her head, stopped speaking and clasped her hands on her chest. She was waiting for the men to go away. She again flashed a glance at Gleb. In it Gleb could see nothing but stern aloofness.

Comrade Mekhova banged the table with her fist.

" Enough ! Take your places, delegates. Order ! Pass along, you men comrades there—don't interrupt us. Go on, Dasha."

Dasha had begun to speak again when Mekhova interrupted:

" Comrade Chumalov, on your way back will you call in on me ? I want to speak to you."

" All right."

The sunlight danced on her eyebrows. Her eyes were round and clear, like a child's, but in their depths were signs of an indefinable grief.

" It's not about business matters. I want to make your acquaintance."

" All right."

Dasha was reporting about the children's crêches in the town.

2

A CONCRETE PROPOSAL

As soon as the door of Shidky's room opened, there issued a blast of sweaty stuffiness and tobacco fumes.

In this room the sun did not shine in golden patches as in Mekhova's, but came through the window in thin green threads the tips of which touched the table. The spirals of light burned ; the dust danced.

This room was also small and the people were bathed in the smoke-filled sunlight. Shidky and Shibis, the President of the Cheka, wore their leather jackets unbuttoned. They were both clean shaven. Shibis' face had a light coating of dust ; behind white eyelashes his eyes glinted metallically. He was seated at the table opposite Shidky and seemed to be resting. His cheeks were cut by deep vertical wrinkles ; his nose was decidedly Asiatic with sensitive nostrils. When he raised his eyes, he pierced you with his gaze, while at the same time those sensitive nostrils twitched.

On the window-sill, his feet planted against the jamb, sat a bony, lanky youth. It was Lukhava, President of the local Council of Trade Unions. His shirt was black as was his bushy hair and his face was coffee-coloured. His eyes were feverish. He listened silently, leaning his chin on his knees.

Gleb swung his hand to his helmet in a wide salute, but Shidky paid no attention. So many Party members came to him, there was no time to welcome them all. He merely looked at him, surprised, and sniffed.

" All right, then. We've got some woodcutters. . . . And there's the District Forestry Department. We've got supplies."

He punctuated each phrase with a fist banged on the table.

" Now, what's next ? The main thing is the delivery of the wood. The stuff is beyond the mountains along the shore. Our wood supply is going to bits. We must find dependable and rapid means of delivering fuel before the winter is here. To hell with tinkering and makeshifts, we must take the bull by the horns and do the job on a big scale. We must put all our energies into this, it will be an enormous concentration of effort. The District Forestry Department hasn't carried out its job; all kinds of swine are there—each one looking after Number One—carrion who ought to be shot. The workers will be rioting soon ; they're already starving. We must have fire-wood: or are we going to make bonfires of our own workmen and children? There'll be a meeting of the Economic Council in a week's time, and we must be ready. Speak up, Lukhava. You're usually such a firebrand, but to-day you're mute."

The young man at the window did not hear Shidky's words. A fever burned in him.

Shibis looked at no one, and it was impossible to tell from his face, under its mask of dirt, whether he was thinking or merely resting, bored with it all.

Shidky banged his fist upon the table.

" To hell with it! We all ought to be shot as fools and muddlers! We're up a blind alley, lads."

Lukhava hugged his knees to his chest with his bony hands, and by this movement turned so that he could face them. He burst out into a boyish broken laughter, which he endeavoured to restrain.

" Have you lost your head, Shidky? What blind alley are you talking about? Hell, if you're in a blind alley you've got to break your way out, using your head. Otherwise you ought to be shot, and Shibis would take on the job without any trouble. There's no blind alley. There are only problems, and I've solved this one for you."

" Your concrete proposal? "

Shidky's nostrils quivered as he greedily sniffed the air, giving him an expression of joyous ecstasy.

" We shall have to use the power from the factory."

Serge raised his hand, asking for the floor.

" By the way, I wanted. . . . About the proposal of Lukhava. . . ."

The hard lines on Shidky's cheeks broke into a smile of indulgent and affectionate raillery.

" Serge has a practical proposal, Comrades. State it! "

" With regard to the proposal made by Comrade Lukhava, I wanted to draw your attention to our Comrade Chumalov's presence. Our discussion of this question might be shortened if Comrade Chumalov, as a workman in the factory, gave us his opinion. At this moment, I must——"

With a quick gesture, Shidky stopped him in the middle of a phrase.

" Whoa, there! Serge, you're beginning to froth as usual and getting red all over your bald patch."

" I must go at once to the meeting of the Agitprop and then subsequently to the Department of Education."

Shibis smiled and said drawlingly, looking piercingly at Serge :

"Intellectual ! That 'then subsequently' in his mouth sounded like a chant. At night he can't sleep because of so many damned problems. The intellectuals are always the donkeys in the Party ; they always feel themselves guilty and oppressed. It's a good thing that we keep them on a string, well in sight."

Serge blushed deeper and became confused ; tears glittered in his eyes.

"But you also are an intellectual, Comrade Shibis."

"Yes, I'm an intellectual, too."

Shidky still smiled with affectionate irony.

"Well, Comrade Chumalov, step nearer. You'll have to stand, there are no chairs."

Gleb came up to the table and stood at attention.

"I've been demobilised as a skilled worker and am at the disposition of the Party Committee."

Without taking his eyes off Gleb, Shidky held out his hand and his nose wrinkled with friendly laughter as they gripped.

"Comrade Chumalov, we have appointed you secretary of the factory group. It is disorganised now. Smugglers and speculators—they've all gone mad over goats and pipe-lighters. The factory is being openly robbed. You probably know all about it. You'll have to put it straight, and get it in working order—military fashion."

Gleb again saluted.

"All right, Comrade Shidky ! "

Lukhava leant his chin again upon his knees. He was chewing a cigarette in the corner of his mouth and gazing at Gleb through feverish half-closed eyes with a keen provocative questioning which went deep into Gleb's soul. And it was really in answer to Gleb's words that he called coldly and carelessly to Shidky :

"Send the comrade to the Organisation Department. We can't waste the time of this session with trifles."

He continued looking at Gleb, screwing up his eyes in the cigarette smoke. Gleb threw back his head, his eyes directly encountering Lukhava's, but he said nothing. He felt only a sort of dull blow on the breast. Lukhava's eyes agitated him with a dim provoking suggestion.

Shibis glanced keenly at him under his heavy brows.

"Yes, you're a skilled mechanic. Also a military commissar.

Why did you leave the army already when the factory has been put out of business for years ? "

Gleb turned to Shibis, but his answer was for all of them.

" Put out of business, you say ? Yes, that's so ! A rotten place, a dump-heap, a desolate abomination. And what a factory it was : it was a huge thing, a beauty, known all over the world. You must grab the workmen by the scruff of their necks and drive away the goats. What about production ? It's the most important thing of all, even if it kills us to make the factory go. Without it the workmen won't be workmen, just goat-herds."

Again he met Lukhava's gaze and again met the tantalising suggestion and a smiling enmity. Gleb in turn looked fixedly at him and once more from Lukhava's gaze he felt that dull blow in his breast.

" The heroes of the Order of the Red Flag, besides their bravery, must also have an understanding of the actual facts of the situation."

Shibis was leaning back in his chair, cold and restrained, and under the dusky mask of his face it was impossible to know whether he was following the discussion or was merely resting and bored with it all.

Shidky sniffed ; the lines in his cheeks deepened with a smile. He raised his fist for another blow on the table.

" I have not yet given you the floor, Lukhava. Sit down. Let's resume our discussion on fuel."

Lukhava's words, as provoking as his smile, and the insinuation in his half-closed eyes, made Gleb shudder and his heart was flooded.

" Comrade Chumalov, we haven't a single stick of kindling. We're starving. The children in the Homes are perishing. The workers are disorganised. How can you talk of the factory now ? What rot ! It's not a question of that. What have you got to say about delivery of wood from the forests ? In what way can you use the factory for that ? What have you got to say about Lukhava's proposal ? "

" Fuel ? Well, let's take fuel first. In a month we shall have wood here on the spot. I'll be responsible for that."

" Well, tell us how we can get the thing done practically, without a lot of phrases."

" Yes, we'll get down to bedrock."

Gleb paused for a moment, gazing thoughtfully at the window.

" There's only one way. We'll use the ropeways up to the mountains ; and then the trolleys down to the jetty. Load them up and run them to the town and to the station. We'll have a campaign for voluntary Sunday labour in all the unions. I've nothing more to say."

Shuk, puffing and blowing, perspiring copiously, embraced Gleb, smiling joyously.

" You sit there, like a lot of old fat-bellied tubs . . . mucking about hopelessly. And then, look ! Gleb starts on it. He's really starting things and making them hum. That's the stuff, show them all up, old pal ! "

No one listened to him, and his familiar figure disappeared in the crowd, a nonentity. He was always before their eyes, but they never saw him, and his cry which came from the heart was unheard.

Shidky, his cheeks patterned with the wrinkles of his smile, was not writing, but was drawing straight lines and long curves on the paper. And his face became quiet and customary, so that he suddenly appeared old and haggard.

" I think you wanted to speak on this point, Lukhava ? "

Lukhava jumped eagerly up from his place, passed before Gleb and then returned to his window.

" I was thinking more or less on the same lines as Comrade Chumalov. He put it better than I. We should unquestionably accept his proposal and invite him to the sitting of the Economic Council to report to them on it."

Shidky threw his pencil on the table ; it bounded off and fell at Gleb's feet. He sprang up, his hands in his pockets.

" It's Utopian, Comrade Chumalov ! Stop gabbling about the factory all the time. The factory is a tomb of stone. It's not the factory we want—it's wood ! There is no factory—only an empty quarry. The factory for us is a question of the past or the future, not of the present. We're talking about the delivery of wood now only."

" I don't know what you mean by Utopia, Comrade Shidky. If you don't pronounce the word factory, the workmen will say it. What are you jawing about : the factory is the past or the future ? If the workers are banging their heads against the factory every day—as they are—then the factory is there, and it's waiting for workers' hands to run it. What's all the joke about with you, Comrades ? Have you been to the factory ? Have you seen the Diesel engines and the workmen ? The factory is a whole little town and the machines are all ready to run. Why have the workers been robbing the factory? Why do rain and wind eat into the concrete and iron? Why does destruction go on? And the rubbish heaps pile up? Why have the workers nothing to do except fool around with empty bellies? The worker isn't a broody hen : you can't ask him to sit down on the eggs and hatch chicks! And you keep on telling him that the factory isn't a factory, but an abandoned quarry, and he spits on you then and curses with all his might. How could he treat you otherwise? he's right in stripping the factory and dragging it bit by bit to his home ; it would all go to the devil anyway. You've been filling his head with all sorts of beautiful language, but what have you done to make him a class-conscious proletarian instead of a cheese-paring haggler? That's the way you have to put the question, my dear Comrades."

The discomfort which had been oppressing Gleb, both in his home and in the factory, was the same here, and he could not keep silent. It was poisoning his healthy blood with fury.

Shidky shuddered and his eyes widened.

" You're making an idol of the factory, Comrade Chumalov. What do we want the factory for, when we've got bandits and famine here, and when our Soviet institutions are swarming with traitors and conspirators? Who wants your cement, man, nowadays, and all your workshops? Do you want it for building common graves? You're preaching the conquest of industry while the peasants are moving like a Tartar horde against the town."

" I understand that just as well as you do, Comrade Shidky. But you can't start industry with naked hands and build it up on naked men. To hell with all your petty tinkering! We must go straight for reconstruction and the re-establishment of production. That's the question before us! Otherwise we might as well give up everything, and just sit down and wait for the peasants to come and slaughter us."

Shibis got up and walked to the door. One could not tell what he was thinking. By the door he stopped and said monotonously, with long pauses between each sentence for effect :

" Our Special Department is poor. While we're speaking about the factory why can't we also discuss the situation among the soldiers, and the offensive against the bourgeoisie? These are all fine words, but I haven't time to relish them. Later on, perhaps."

He opened the door and went out without looking back. Shidky looked at the door, smiling knowingly.

"Don't let's argue, Comrade Chumalov. The main question is not to get the factory working, but the organisation of the masses. Isn't that right?"

Shidky laughed and firmly pressed Gleb's hand.

"Will you give Shuk a little training, too, Comrade Chumalov? He's like a hungry rat without it."

Gleb put his arm round Shuk's shoulder, drawing him towards the door. In vain Shuk endeavoured to embrace him.

"Gleb, my dear Comrade! But we'll make things go now, we'll move mountains and fill up craters!"

Behind them they heard Shidky's voice once more.

"Comrade Chumalov, it wouldn't hurt if you had a straight talk with Badin, Chairman of the Executive Committee. And you ought to go and have a good row with Lukhava, so as to become good friends afterwards."

In the doorway Lukhava pressed Gleb's elbow. There was fever in his eyes and in his words.

"I heard about you from Dasha. We're going to consider your plan all together, and use it as the basis for our work. We must go to work on facts and not on words. The future is in our brains, but we must realise it with our muscles."

The two men regarded each other fixedly. Once more Gleb felt the other's words and gaze were stabbing him deep.

Dasha? Lukhava? Was Lukhava perhaps the answer to this confusing puzzle?

3

THE WOMAN WITH THE CURLS

Gleb went back to Mekhova. He accidently leaned on the table and it boomed like a copper bugle. Mekhova, suppressing her laughter, looked at him in astonishment and without geniality.

"Moderate your attack, Comrade Chumalov. This isn't a heavy gun. We're working here in peace-time surroundings."

"Sorry, I've got used to having space for my elbows, and here it's narrow as a hen-coop."

"Well, get used to taking shorter steps. We'll soon put you in your place here, and you'll get your Soviet work to do; then you'll have to get going like everyone else with the monotonous hard work of the administrator. You'll soon forget the smell of powder and deeds of daring. You'll get soft and faded, Comrade. I believe they've appointed you secretary of the factory group. Well, we'll see how you manage that crowd. You can't get near the women : they all stink of pigs, goats and dung. Every house is a little shop and a warehouse for stolen goods. In another six months the factory will have vanished bit by bit. And what a factory ! "

" Oh, and we're just thinking of setting the factory going again. We're starting the Diesels and dynamos and we're building ropeways to the top of the mountains for the transport of wood fuel."

" Oh, you all say the same thing. To hear you, you're all a lot of wonders, but in truth your whole idea is to make yourselves a little more comfortable and become Soviet bourgeois. Time passes very dully here. It's livelier in the army. I wanted to join the army but they wouldn't let me go. It's only your wife that doesn't feel the dullness : she finds something worth doing in every trifle."

Dasha, standing by the wall, smiled chaffingly. She showed impatience in every movement.

" I can't understand your conversation, Comrades. What's it all about, and what's the good of it ? Get out, soldier, you're in our way. Clear out while you're still safe ! "

And she smiled amusedly.

"There, look at her ! That's a stern business-like woman ! "

"It's true, Dasha sabotages her household pretty thoroughly."

Mekhova laughed, shaking her curls.

" Doesn't she carry out her wifely duties ? What a disgrace ! The revolution has completely spoilt the woman."

Dasha burst out laughing, but it was not the charming laugh of his old sweetheart.

All the women were laughing now. They had just pushed Shuk out into the corridor and were crying to him through the door : " Your mastery is finished, you shaven goats ! You look like a lot of women since you shaved your beards off. And the women look like men ! You'll never get the good old times back."

Again Mekhova looked closely at Gleb, and it seemed to him as though she were greedily savouring him.

" You haven't really got acclimatised yet ; you're still full of the war and the army. One would think you were going back to-morrow to re-join your regiment. Do tell me about your exploits. When did you receive the Order of the Red

Flag ? If you only knew how I love the army ! You know there was a time when I fought in the trenches. It was at Mannich."

She smiled, and her smile was not for Gleb, although she was looking at him. A partly concealed joy sparkled in her eyes.

" It was wonderful ! They were unforgettable days, like the October days in Moscow—for the whole of my life. Heroism ? It is the fire of revolution."

" That is so, Comrade Mekhova. But here also on the industrial front we must also have heroism. A difficult situation : destruction, muddle, hunger. Right ! The mountain has fallen, crushing man like a frog. Now, for a real big effort, shoulder to the wheel, and shove the mountain back into its place. Impossible ? That's precisely it. Heroism means doing the impossible."

" Yes, yes. That's what I wanted to speak about with you, Comrade Chumalov. Heroism is exactly that : one big effort altogether, and then nothing is impossible."

She laughed again and her eyes sparkled more than ever.

" Shoulder to the wheel ? Yes ! Splendid ! You use the right words ! With every fibre of one's being. We must talk together about this, Comrade Chumalov. I live in the Soviet House."

Dasha smiled and looked curiously at Mekhova and Gleb. Then she went up to Gleb, turned him round by the shoulders and pushed him towards the door.

"Now be off from here, soldier ! You've nothing to do here."

Gleb turned round, seized her in his arms and began to carry her out of the room. The women burst out laughing ; Mekhova also laughed. This shameless caress before all these people made Dasha shriek out and she flung both her arms around him. For a moment Gleb felt the old loving heart of Dasha and heard her dear woman's laugh, which cannot be defined, for it flows from the blood into the blood.

" Comrade Chumalov, do you know what your Dasha is ? Hasn't she told you her adventures ? She's been through a great deal, perhaps more than you yourself have experienced."

Dasha started, then leapt out of Gleb's arms.

" I don't want you to talk about me, Comrade Mekhova, whether good or bad. No more jesting, Comrade Mekhova, and leave me in peace."

" Oh, I didn't know that this was a forbidden subject."

Why was she so startled ? Why did she shut Mekhova's mouth ? Why, when everyone knew about her years without him, would she tell him nothing ?

Lukhava, standing in the doorway, gazed at Gleb with burning eyes.

Gleb passed him, trying not to jostle him. But Lukhava caught the sleeve of his tunic and stopped him.

"Comrade Chumalov, call a special meeting of the group. I want to come and make a report. Come and see me to-morrow at the Council of Trade Unions; we'll lock ourselves in and discuss the whole matter. For a big plan one must have precise details. I'm not only speaking of the fuel, but also of the factory. I've been thinking about it. We're going to fight by all possible means. Do not forget that this will be a real struggle, calling for all our strength. And don't forget that the time may seem inopportune. It's a fight for the future, and therefore appears Utopian and absurd. Of course we know that only by audacity and strength can the future be made the present. So let's get down to work."

He gripped Gleb firmly by the hand and quickly passed through the door of the Women's Section.

Mekhova joined Gleb in the corridor.

"Stop, Comrade Chumalov. You haven't told us what you've arranged in there with Shidky. I'd like to be informed at once. In this hole, we're beginning to rot and the daily routine is turning us all into moles. The revolution doesn't mean that. If you're going to shake the Soviet and the Party out of their rut you must have pretty good teeth. I'll be with you, Comrade Chumalov. Whatever you do I'll be with you. I have a feeling that you won't get into the rut, you were in the army. There's one other thing, Comrade: you mustn't worry Dasha. . . . Oh, I've been acting foolishly. . . . She'll come to you of her own accord, you'll see if she doesn't. Now, what do you intend doing?"

"Everything in order to get the factory working—unless we break our backs."

"Well, go on; that's all I wanted."

She smiled at him, her eyes and golden curls shining, and hurried back.

In the street Shuk met him, joyfully waving his arms.

"Well, how do our chiefs look now? I shall show them up, brother. I shall get in every corner and cranny to hunt out the evil spirit. They know me well. I go round there every day—scoundrels—I give them no rest. Now, with you we'll turn all the mountains over, we'll chase out all the bureau-crats!"

Chapter IV

THE WORKERS' CLUB "COMINTERN"[1]

I

THE C.P.R. GROUP

THE Workers' Club "Comintern" was housed in the former Director's house, a strong, German-built structure in rough stone in three colours : yellow, light blue, and green. The two storeys of the building arose from the ribs of the mountain, which were covered with holly and other bushes. Its plan was severe, sober and puritanical like a church, but lavish in verandahs and ornate balconies. There were outbuildings in the courtyard, which were also plainly but solidly constructed, and flower beds and playing grounds. Within, there were innumerable rooms, obscure corridors and staircases, with oak pilasters crowned by stained glass lamps. In each room was silken wall-paper, rich panels and pictures by great painters, gigantic mirrors and furniture of different periods.

In front of the house, along the mountain slope, lay a flower and fruit garden, dirtied and partly devoured by goats. It was surrounded by an iron fence on a stone base. To the right, beyond the mountains, rose the immense blue chimneys of the works ; on the left, more chimneys ; and high up were the quarries and the broken-down ropeways.

Once there dwelt here a mysterious old man, whom the workers had only seen from a distance and whose all-powerful voice they had never heard. It was strange how this venerable and dignified director could live here without fearing the emptiness of his thirty-roomed palace, without a nightmare terror of the poverty, dirt and stench of the bestial existence of the workers herded in their foul barracks.

Then came war and revolution—the great catastrophe. Saving himself from the wreck, the director, helpless and

[1] "Comintern" is a contraction of the two words, "Communist International."—Tr.

wretched, fled for his life. The engineers, technologists and chemists fled with him. Only one remained behind, the engineer Kleist, one of the constructors of the factory. He remained shut up in his study in the main administration building, across the main road, a little lower down, opposite the palace, which was his last creation.

There came a fine spring day, when ardent light played upon the sea, the mountains and the clouds, when the diffused glare of the sun stabbed the eyes. The workers had come together in the repair shop. Amidst shouting, the shuffling of feet and clouds of tobacco smoke, the mechanic, Gromada, proposed: "Let's take the palace of the director, that old blood-sucker, and turn it into a working-class club, and call it the 'Comintern.'"

So the ground floor of the building was used for the club and for the groups of the Party and of the Young Communist League, and the upper part housed the library, recreation rooms and the Cheka.

Where once reigned an austere silence, where once no worker was allowed even to walk on the concrete paths around the mansion—now in the evenings, when the window panes glowed in the fire of the sinking sun, came the brazen bellowing of the trumpets of the club musicians and the explosive thundering of drums. They had carried all the books from the houses of the vanished officials into the director's library. They were beautiful books, with shining gilt covers, but mysterious: they were written in German.

Gromada was elected club manager, and when he was reporting on the library, at a meeting of the workers, he said, "Comrades, we have a wonderful library, whose books have been confiscated and nationalised from the bourgeoisie and the capitalists—but they're all of German origin. Now, according to proletarian discipline we must read them, because we must remember that, as workers, we belong to the international masses and therefore, must command every language. The library is open to all, whether they can read or whether they cannot. I call upon you, Comrades, to come there to achieve culture and not to sabotage. . . ."

So this was the workers' club "Comintern"; no longer the director's residence, but a communist centre.

The workers continued to live in their tenements. The houses of the officials remained deserted, awesome with their scores of echoing empty rooms.

The workers were manufacturing pipe-lighters in the repair shop. In the evening they would go up the mountain, searching for their goats. The women were walking to the Cossack village, and then to other neighbouring villages, buying and selling food as a speculation.

And the first floor echoed with the thunder of the trumpets and the crashing of the drums.

Meetings of the Party Group were held regularly each Monday. Various questions were discussed such as : (1) The stealing of butter and beans in the communal dining-room ; (2) Regarding the feeding of pigs with food for the communal dining-room ; (3) The religious practices of the members of the Party ; (4) Robbing the factory, for purposes of barter and speculation.

Gleb opened the Special meeting of the Group in the club.

It was a spacious room, with panels of Karelian birch and hand-made furniture of the same wood. The rays of the evening sun gilded the walls and the furniture.

They brought in rough benches from the recreation room.

Gleb sat at the raised table, from where he could see all their faces ; and they all looked alike. It seemed to him that although they were really different, yet there was a common trait in all of them, which made them into one. What was it—this something, living yet vague, that strains one's gaze and strains one's mind in an effort to define it ? One wanted to find a word for it, but there was no word for it upon his tongue. Then suddenly he understood : it was hunger.

Many of them saw Gleb for the first time and greeted him idly and indifferently as though he had never been away. His last time in the village was on that sunset evening when, at the factory gate, the officers had dragged him from the ranks of the passing workers and had unmercifully thrashed him and others of them.

There were some of them who shook him heartily by the hand, with a forced smile, guffawed and, hardly knowing what to say, spoke in vague ejaculations.

" Well ? What then, brother ? How are things ? How is it——— ? "

Then they went to their places. Once seated, however, they again stared at him with smiles they could not repress.

Then came Gromada—the little man with the big name— laughing and choking in his consumptive voice.

" It's a bit different now, Comrade Chumalov—eh ? True !
Now we'll get a move on ! How we Communists have gone
all astray over goats and pipe-lighters. . . . But don't allow discussion. Speak plainly and don't stand for any contradiction ! "

He turned towards the workers, his enthusiasm almost
suffocating him.

" You see, you loafers ! Here's a man, who's been through
death and so on. . . . I declare—. It's not my turn to speak, of
course, but I'm just announcing in advance that it's he, Comrade Chumalov, who made me what I am—it's he who got
me into the ranks of the C.P.R."

They listened to Gromada, laughing. It was not usual for
Gromada to speak thus. And Chumalov smiled at him as at
an impulsive youngster. Laughing and coughing, the workers
sprawled amidst the dense fumes of tobacco.

" Go on, Gromada ! Go to it, let it rip ! We're going to
win, all right ! "

Loshak sat in the far corner. Black and hump-backed, he
was like a block of anthracite among the dusty cement-
covered rags of the workmen. He sat silently, the smallest
of them all, but visible and oppressing them all with the
mournful, silent question in his eyes. He gazed far away
beyond them all, but at any moment he might come down upon
them crushingly with words as black as himself, like his face,
stiffened by smoke and metal dust, and then everyone would
be appalled by his weight.

The women were fidgety, fingering their ragged clothes,
smiling broadly and chattering like sparrows. As their guide
and leader, somewhat apart from them but fully in view, was
Dasha. Her red headscarf burned like a calm flame. Now and
again she would come nearer the women and they would
cluster together, whispering and giggling.

They were all waiting for Lukhava to come in with his
report on the struggle against disorganisation and the full
crisis. The door opened and Savchuk entered, tattered and
barefoot, with bloodshot eyes.

Enormous, his muscles heavy with useless strength, he sat
down heavily on the floor near to the door, his back against
the wall, sticking out his bony knees covered with bruises
and scabs. A turgid anguish burned in his vanquished eyes.

Dasha threw open the heavy windows.

" What people they are, in this group ! All the work is done
in a cloud of smoke ! Smoking is work for idle brains ! "

She had scarcely opened the windows when a volume of
noise poured in, making the room resound. On the first floor
balcony the trumpets blared and the drums thundered deafeningly.

Straying from their den-like homes, forgetful of the factory
—its noise, smoke, dust and machines—themselves covered
now with the dust of the mountain winds, the factory workers,
with sacks on their backs, were creeping up the mountain side.

Along roads and footpaths, on hills and steppes they
journeyed to villages and to Cossack hamlets as in the days
of primitive barter, driven by hunger and blind greed. These
toilers of the factory, who once had awakened not at the crow-
ing of the cock but at the metallic screech of the whistle, had
learned during the past years the charm of pigsties and goat
pens, the acrid savour of manure and the warmth of henhouses.
And these men who once worked amidst the din of machines
now gave ear to the cackling of the farm-yard and concerned
themselves with pigs, hens, goats—and about the little neglected
pig which had devoured somebody's food ration.

The electricity supply to the works and the workers' dwellings had ceased ; the whistle was choked with dust ; silence
and stagnation reigned amidst this pastoral idyll, except for
cluckings and gruntings.

But here in the " Comintern " Club, at the factory group
meeting, the Communists were rubbing their eyes ; and their
soiled hands and clothes smelt of the excrement of fowls and
beasts. They were sitting crowded together and the blare of
the trumpets and the unaccustomed words recalled from the
past a forgotten life. Gleb also belonged to the past as though
he had come but yesterday, smelling of oil and molten iron
and the sulphurous vapours of cooling slag. And so once
more : the factory . . . production . . . the ropeways . . .
the workshops !

Hardly had Dasha left the window when Serge entered with
his shy glance, bald patch and locks falling to his shoulders.
He went up to Gleb, bent over him and whispered importantly
to him.

Gleb stood up and skilfully flung his cap on to the window-
sill.

" Comrades, Comrade Ivagin is here instead of Lukhava.
Comrade Lukhava is down among the stevedores ; they're
raising a hell of a riot about their rations. We'll open the meeting now—but keep quiet, damn you ! Now I'm going to tell

you something ; I had heard a rumour of it and now the radio announces it. Foreign countries, the Entente, are going to trade with us and are sending ships. I don't think we'll feel offended at that ! Certainly not ! We shall be very glad ! We can do our bit too."

And he laughed at his own joke.

Gromada began to gesticulate and his eyes glittered with joy.

" Comrades, as we are workmen of a magnificent factory, but have encumbered ourselves with pigs and goats, and so on . . . er, yes. . . . Come out of your lairs, Comrades. I propose that we liquidate all surpluses in favour of our Children's Home. And as we are the working-class——"

Dub-a-dub of the drums ! A buzzing tumult of voices amidst smoke and dust.

" The pigs . . . there's always plenty of people out for someone else's property ! Whose been dragging stuff from the villages and farms ? He thinks a lot of himself. . . . Not enough to go round. . . . Gromada's wife wore out her clothes going round the villages. . . ."

" Liquidate ? . . . To hell with it ! Decide, Chumalov— Let the Group decide ! "

" Ah, Brothers ! . . . There's nothing to eat, you know ! What ! A devil of a fight, eh ? . . . Now, Brothers. . . ."

Gleb struck the bell and called the meeting to order.

" Silence, Comrades ! So far there are no restrictions about pigs and goats, if you want to fool around with them you may. When the time comes we'll deal with them in a real proletarian way like we did with the bourgeoisie."

And thus with a joke and a laugh he induced order and calm.

" Comrades, I propose we elect a Chairman."

Hardly had he uttered these words than the women in their part of the hall, with Domasha and Lisaveta at the head, jumped up and down, shot up their hands, shrieking out one name, but each vying with the other as to who could call loudest.

" Dasha ! Dasha Chumalova ! Dasha ! "

The men were also shouting, but without at first being able to yell down the voices of the women.

" Gromada ! Chumalov ! Savchuk ! "

The name of Savchuk was drowned in a roar of laughter.

Gromada jumped up by the table, wildly waving his arms at the women and screaming to the men : " Comrades ! I don't mind about the women—they have equal rights, the creatures. . . . Ah, yes. And the young ones, they must be the leaders, of course. But let them wait a little longer. We need a beard on the Chairman."

" And where's Chumalov's beard ? And what about your whiskers, has the cat licked it off ? "

The women were bawling at the top of their voices.

" Dasha Chumalova ! Dasha ! Gromada's not even capable of passing her a glass of water ! Savchuk's beard is just good enough for a hearth brush, and Motia knows his fists well enough ! "

" Savchuk ! Chumalov ! Loshak ! "

Gleb banged the bell repeatedly.

" We'll have a vote on it, Comrades. Dasha Chumalova is first on the list. Although she's my wife, I have no objection to a woman taking the chair. Who is for——"

But before he could call out Dasha's name the women again began to scream.

" Dasha ! Why don't you give way to the women, you good-for-nothings ? "

Gleb was the first to raise his hand, and with him the women and Serge. The other workers raised their hands one after the other as though unwillingly, coughing and sniffling :

Savchuk, without raising his hand, roared from out of his corner : " Drive 'em out, these women ! Send them all home ! Phew, I can't bear them ! "

Again Gleb rang loudly to still the clamouring.

" Now we'll vote for Gromada. . . . Very few. Now vote for Loshak . . . only a few. Take your place, Comrade Chumalova."

The women began to applaud like a lot of hens flapping their wings.

" Bravo, Women ! We've won ! Show these bearded and shaven goats what you can do, Dasha ! "

Dasha stepped with firm tread to the table and stood beside Gleb.

" Comrades, I ask for silence and a real proletarian spirit. Give me the agenda, Comrade Chumalov. Comrade Ivagin has the floor for his report. You have fifteen minutes to speak, Comrade."

Serge, astonished, could only laugh with a gesture of dismay.

" This is too strict a ruling, Comrade Chumalova."

" Don't pad it out, Comrade Ivagin. If you're going to talk, go to it or we shall go on with our business ! "

" She thinks enough of herself! I told you so. We didn't want a woman. . . ."

" Kick them out! Let them all go home, the noisy hens! I'd pick 'em up by their petticoats and sling them out of the window."

" Silence, Comrade Savchuk! I'll have you put out for this anarchy. Remember you're Communists, Comrades! "

Dasha is right. A little time is enough; what can be said in a report to workmen? Serge has too many words in his head. She knows best what he wants at the present time. Cold text-book phrases are strange and unintelligible, abstract and remote as Serge himself, in his words and in his nature.

" Comrades: A terrible economic debacle . . . a formidable crisis . . . a most difficult test for the working-class. The liquidation of the military front. . . . All our strength must go to the industrial front. The Tenth Congress of the Party have drawn up a new economic policy. The proletariat is the only force . . . revival of the industry of the republic . . . concessions and the world market. . . . (Phew, these stupid intellectuals!) We must stand for the country of the proletariat . . . increase our strength tenfold, and with iron ranks. . . . We have broken the blockade. . . . The working class and the Communist Party. . . . (Finish now, Comrade Ivagin!) Recovery of fuel supply. . . . Use of the factory power. . . . On this matter, Comrade Chumalov can speak better than I."

" Comrades, the report is before you. Silence, please, Comrade Gromada! "

" It's about the Comrade Speaker. . . . But his father doesn't belong to the working-class elements. . . . Lukhava is a stronger speaker. . . . Though the Comrade is sympathetic his argument is good for nothing. We've been filled with enough words. What is the C.P.R. doing about it? "

" Comrade Gromada, you seem to have no idea of order. Comrade Chumalov has the floor."

The audience became silent. Well, let's see what Gleb Chumalov is going to say. The main strength is in him. To-morrow depends on his words.

" Comrades, don't let us play around with words. We've played around enough already with pigs and pipe-lighters. Enough. The factory isn't a factory any more, but a cattle barn. We're a lot of fools. Is this business, Comrades? There's two sides to every man: You can either let the devil grab you, or you can swing him by the tail. It all depends on just how much of a fool you are. Our hands aren't meant for goats and pigs, but for something else. We know this : As our hands are so are our souls and our minds. To hell with all foolishness ! As Comrade Ivagin said, there is now a new economic line. What is this new economic policy ? It means hit the devil in the jaw with a great effort at reconstruction. Cement is a mighty binding material. With cement we're going to have a great building-up of the Republic. We are cement, Comrades : the working-class. Let us keep that in mind. We've played the fool long enough ; now we've got to start real work."

In the hullabaloo it was impossible to understand what the Group were trying to say. In flushed faces, white eyes grew bloodshot. Gromada jumped up, arms wildly waving ; Savchuk sprang out from his corner howling.

Gleb raised his arm asking for attention. His jaw-muscles quivered. Dasha rang the bell furiously for silence and shouted :

" Comrades ! Communists ! You're still a rabble ! Keep discipline. I had not given you the floor, Savchuk ! "

" Well, Comrades, let's consider it closely. Ask yourselves. What's lacking in the factory, Brothers ? There's no fuel ! And the workers have no fuel ! We've come to the point where there's nothing left. Winter's coming and will give us hell. Let's set up a new ropeway on the mountain sides. And we'll bring wood to the town. Let's get at the Economic Council and tell them : Give us petrol and benzine, you hounds ! What have you done with the oil reserves ? We've got the orders for the stores. And if they try to trump us, we'll play our trump card, through the Cheka to the Revolutionary Tribunal. The ropeway—that's our first step. Through the Trade Unions we'll organise voluntary Sunday labour. We'll set our engineers at drawing up plans and to oversee the construction work. Let the damn goats go to the devil ! "

Savchuk made his way to the table, and banged his fist upon the papers with which it was littered.

" Ah, the bloody idlers, swineherds ! "

" Come to order, Comrade Savchuk ! "

" Why are you shutting me up, woman ? How can I keep quiet when there are swineherds here and makers of pipe-lighters ? "

" Comrade Savchuk—for the last time ! "

" Oh, you bitch ! Comrade Gleb, give your wife a kick in
the ribs. Ah, she's not my wife. . . . And you good-for-
nothings. . . . Goatherds ! Where are your hands and your
throats ? Say, what's the Cheka doing about Engineer
Kleist ? Gleb, what kind of friend is Engineer Kleist, who
delivered you up to be killed ? I can't stand for that ! Let
them bring Engineer Kleist here ! "

" Right ! The specialist. . . . Engineer Kleist. . . . Have
him arrested and sent to the Cheka ! He's shut himself up like
a rat in a hole. He sneaks around like a thief. . . . Didn't
he try to have your blood ? "

Engineer Kleist. This man had Gleb's life in his hands and
he threw it to the executioners as though it were a dirty bit of
waste, Engineer Kleist. . . . Isn't Gleb's life worth that of
Engineer Kleist ? But this was bygone, and now their two
lives had met again.

The hunchback Loshak met Dasha's eye at that moment
and silently raised his hand.

" Comrade Loshak has the floor."

All heads were turned to the corner where the humped
mechanic sat. His words always hit like stones and did not
spare his hearers.

" Yes, we want to do the work, but we've been yelling a lot
of nonsense. It's my turn to speak now. We've been like a
whole lot of bladders : we've swollen and burst. Put the
right man on the job and things will move. That's where the
point is, you idiots. And as for Engineer Kleist, he may be a
louse but—— I want to say this : it's true that he turned Gleb
over to them, but how did he treat Dasha ? How did Engineer
Kleist treat Dasha, when he rescued her from death——? "

Dasha suddenly leaned forward over the table and shoved
Loshak by the hump.

" Comrade Loshak, I'm not a subject of this discussion.
Shut up, or keep to the subject of the report. If you've nothing to say get back to your place ! "

Loshak glanced at her, made a gesture of discouragement
and went back to his seat.

Dasha again ! Again this mystery. . . .

Gleb contained himself with a strong effort. He pondered,
wrestling with his own thoughts.

" Well, Comrades, if that is so, let me fight my own battle
with the engineer face to face ; and now let's leave that
question."

The tired workmen were wiping the sweat from their foreheads with their shirt-sleeves.

Dasha lifted a piece of paper to her eyes and glanced over it around the room.

" Comrades, we must seriously consider the question of the Party Committee. We are ordered to dispatch a certain number of members of the Group for work on the communal farm. It's a Party order."

Again it was as though a bomb had exploded amidst the Group.

" No, we won't let ourselves be ordered. Ordering us here and ordering us there ! It's just throwing us as food to the bandits. This is no ' Order to dispatch,' it's sheer murder. We're not beasts to be sent to the slaughter-house."

" But, Comrades, you're a Group of the Party and not a bunch of speculators. I'm only a woman but I tell you : I have never even for an hour trembled for my fate. You all know that well."

" If you like, dispatch yourself by order and take all your damned hens with you."

" What a woman ! She's trying to bridle the whole Group ! Drive the women out of the Group ! "

Then the voice of Savchuk. But even he could not dominate the tumult.

" Dispatch Gromada ! He's buried himself in his Factory Committee ! "

" And Loshak, Brothers ! The Factory Committee members have had an easy time all right."

Gleb walked calmly and with heavy steps from behind the table to the middle of the room. His face was drawn and the clenched muscles stood out.

" Choose me, Comrades—Communists ; and choose my wife. She has called you speculators and she was right. I've been in far worse hornets' nests than the one you're speaking of. For three years I've looked death in the face. Those goddamn goats keep you glued to the spot ! "

" Well, and what about it ? You're not dead yet, Chumalov ! Who hasn't seen blood these last years ? "

" That's it ! And why haven't they killed me ? I'm as tough as the immortal Kashchai.[1] I've fraternised with death as an equal. And if you've seen anything of blood you must know that death has sharp teeth. Better than a mincer ! There, have a look at and admire it ! "

[1] A famous figure in Russian folklore.—Tr.

With a great gesture he tore off his tunic and his soiled shirt and flung them on the floor. By the light of the oil-lamp they could see his muscles, from neck to waist, moving flexibly under the skin, emphasised by shadows.

" Who'll come and touch them. Here! Come and feel them ! "

With his fingers he tapped his chest, neck and side. And wherever he tapped scars showed purple and pallid.

" Shall I take down my trousers ? Do I have to ? Oh, I'm not ashamed ; I am wearing the same sort of decorations lower down. You want other people to go to work instead of yourselves, so that you can sleep in your goat-pens, eh ? Good ! I'm going there ! Choose me for this job ! "

No one came near Gleb. He saw about him wet eyes, saw how suddenly they subsided into silence. They looked at his naked body, all knotted and scarred. Dismayed and shocked by his words, they steamed with sweat and were silent, glued to their seats.

" Comrades ! This is a shame and disgrace. . . . To what extent, Comrades, are our souls decayed ? "

Gromada was choking, writhing and gesticulating convulsively ; the storm of feeling within him could find no words for expression.

A bearded workman rose from a bench and struck himself violently on the chest. He was tremendously agitated.

" Write my name down ! Hurry up ! I'm going ! I'm no bloody coward ! Yes, I've got three goats and a pig with a litter. Yes, and I've carried a traders' sack along the country roads. . . . What can be said ? We've been rotting in our holes, lads ! "

Heavy hands were being raised in silence behind him.

And Dasha, gazing at Gleb with dull eyes, raised her hand.

" Comrades, is our Group worse than the others ? No, Comrades ! We have good workers, good Communists ! "

And she was the first to begin to clap ; her teeth glittered in a smile.

When all was calm again and things were going easily, Dasha amazed them by introducing a motion that was not on the agenda.

" Comrades, the houses of the officials who ran away : they are empty. I propose that we start crèches for the children there. This cursed household work. . . . We want free proletarian women."

" Hear, hear ! Ah, these women—they peck like hens and crow like cocks ! They're sure handing it to us, brothers ! "

" No objections ? Motion's carried ! Let's sing the ' International.' "

2

AUGUST BEBEL AND MOTIA SAVCHUK

It was only a ten minutes' walk on the slope from the Club to their house. Gleb and Dasha, touching shoulders, swung their clasped hands.

Dark purple distance behind the factory ; the sea and the outskirts of the town were misty and troubling in their air of desolation : flashes of life alternated with black shadows upon them. A fiery cord was stretched from the lighthouse to the factory. and then broke into knots. One could see falling stars swoop down far over the sea. And the sky over the broken outline of the mountains had the iridescence of a peacock's train.

Gleb and Dasha walked on in silence ; they wished to speak but could not.

Mysterious lights flashed and disappeared among the mountains behind the town and in the summits above the sea. They blazed out, turned round to darkness and then blazed again.

Dasha touched Gleb's hand.

" Do you see those fire-signals ? Those are the signals of the White-Green forces. There'll be a lot of trouble with them yet. They will give us a lot of work and considerable blood will be shed."

Thus she spoke, but in her words there was another spirit, certainly not that which looked for protection and a caress from his masculine strength. They were not the words which Gleb wanted. What kind of life had Dasha led without him ? What force had given her a distinct personality ? This force had crushed the former Dasha, and the present Dasha was bigger and finer than the old. And it was this force which lay immovable and impregnable between them.

Dasha walked with a firm quick step. Although the path could not be seen, she could see clear in the night like a cat.

" Tell me, Dasha. What was this business of yours with Engineer Kleist ? "

Dasha remained silent, her eyes seeking Gleb's face through the darkness.

" Don't you know ? "

" But what have you told me about your life ? A mere acquaintance can know all about it, but of course I'm your husband ! "

Gleb could not see Dasha's smile.

" Well then—. I was working with a counter-espionage group—. And Motia begged Engineer Kieist. . . . He gave his word and made himself responsible for me. . . . I was mixed up in the affair of the Greens."

" The Greens ! Don't you know you might have lost your life in that affair ? And you got away safely from their clutches ? Tell me about it."

" Oh, it's a long story. I'll tell you all about it when we have more time. We've something else to do just now, Gleb. I can't get into my stride all at once. . . ."

She stepped a pace or two away from him and increased her speed. In these hurried movements Gleb scented her alarm. He remembered that she had behaved in a similar way when they were walking to the Children's Home.

" Little Dasha, something is worrying you, I can see that. Someone's got the better of you ? It's not difficult for a fine fellow to put it across you women."

" Gleb, you're really not a blackguard so far as I know. You've just said this out of foolishness ; but take care of your tongue another time."

In their unfriendly room, with its mildewy smell, she sat down at the table and took some books from a paper parcel. She chose one, moved the lamp nearer and rested her head on her hand.

" That's nice ! What wisdom are you reading now ? "

Without raising her head from the book she muttered " August Bebel : *Woman and Socialism.*"

" Splendid !—and those other books ? "

" They're by Comrade Lenin. Take them if you wish. We Communists have to pump ourselves full of knowledge."

Dasha was reading assiduously. She murmured, gulped, struggled with difficult words and raced over the easy parts. Then stumbled again, looked away a moment, thinking and scratching her eyebrows, then began reading again.

Through the open window flew many nocturnal insects, playing, weaving living threads around the lamp, burning themselves at the glass chimney and falling to the table where they lay like strewn grain. Like the gnats, the stars flew in

through the window from the dark night. The troubled cry of
a screech-owl sounded among the mountain thickets, questioningly : " Yes—No ? Yes—No ? " A dim low light entered also
from the window of Savchuk's dwelling across the way.

Gleb got up and walked out bare-headed.

The Savchuks were already going to bed. On the table were
the remains of supper. All that was needed was to stack them
up, wash them and turn in. Motia, in her chemise, was occupied at the table. Savchuk, barefooted, his hair disorderly as
usual, seemed to be carrying his heavy stagnant body with an
effort. He opened the door to Gleb and stood shuffling near
the bed.

" And what the devil brought you here at this time of night,
you old villain ? During the day you howl like a dog and at
night you skip like a flea ! "

This was Savchuk's usual irritable and affectionate bark.

Motia was shyly pulling up her chemise over her chest,
covering her large full breasts.

" You're one of us, Gleb. . . . I'm dressed for the night
now. You won't go chattering. . . ."

" Don't be ashamed, Motia. I know you're a woman with-
out that. I'm not going to take you away from Savchuk.
He's pretty reliable ; you couldn't move him with a shell.
Well, tell me what kind of time have you been having with
Savchuk anyway ? "

" Savchuk ? He's a growler, but good. . . . I've got him
under my thumb all right ! "

" Don't talk such rot, you bitch ! Who did I thrash yesterday ? Have you forgotten ? "

Motia's eyes sparkled. She sprang up like a cat.

" You're talking nonsense yourself, you old bear ! D'you
remember who I slammed in the jaw ? "

Gleb laughed. They were funny, these Savchuks !

" Well, how are you getting on, Savchuk, my old Comrade ?
From to-day on you are strictly forbidden to lay hands on
Motia. Get your hands ready for another kind of work."

Motia sprang up with a cry of joy and rushed over to Gleb—
no longer ashamed of her bare breasts.

" Yes, yes, Gleb ! Oh, how badly we need work ! If only
there was work already. . . . Gleb, dear Gleb, wouldn't we
have a quieter, healthier life then ? When we did have work
there were children . . . when the work died, the children
too . . ."

She turned to the table with tears in her eyes.

" Well, Gleb, you scoundrel, if my hands find nothing to do, you won't be alive to-morrow. I'll go to the coopers' shed to-morrow and hear my lasses sing their songs. Your wife's a hell of a woman : she can twist the whole Group round her little finger ! "

Motia's eyes flashed as she looked deep into Gleb, as only a woman can.

" I can't understand Dasha. How could she abandon Nurka like a dog into strange hands ? A woman without a child and a home is a savage. She wanted to get me into her gang, but I'm not such a fool. I'd rather die than leave my home."

Savchuk banged his fist on his knee.

" A devil of a woman—your wife ! Oh, how she's got hold of that Group, ha, ha ! "

Gleb was awaiting precisely Motia's words. They were the very ones he was expecting. Did she understand him ? Did she know the turn his life had taken in these recent days spent with Dasha ? Only women can thus penetrate the thoughts of others. She looked at him with bright eyes in which there was a half-formulated suggestion, while, without attending to Motia's words, he answered Savchuk.

" That's true. Without me Dasha has grown into a fine fearless woman. And how she could do it without me, I don't know. She's proud and doesn't brag about her deeds."

Motia's eyes lit up with anger, and she seemed to check herself.

" Don't come here with such words, Gleb. Don't insinuate. You left Dasha to torture and to death, and now you can't expect to get hold of her straight off. Don't be sly. I know you're playing a sly game, eh ? I'm no fool. If she's what she is you can't help it. You put her to the test—because you're like that you damned men——. Well, and now you've burnt your fingers, isn't it true ? I shan't tell you anything, if she hasn't. Don't try and dig up ground with your hand if your claws aren't long enough."

Gleb became confused and started laughing to hide it.

" You've got a sly nose, Motia, and that's a fact ! Well, what's true is true. The old Dasha is no more, and what's happened to her I don't know. I feel that there is something deep in the woman. Perhaps she has made a mis-step as women will ? Then let her say so ; I'm not a monster ! "

Motia again raked him with her eyes, and Gleb saw that she perceived his hidden craft.

"Oh, Gleb! Aren't you ashamed to try and pump me? Go home and go to bed. Don't be too artful—it's in vain. Only why did Dasha—? I love your Dasha very much, Gleb! Only, why did she send Nurka to stew in that Children's Home? Nurka was staying with me. Why didn't she leave her here? How can a woman live without husband and children? What fools you men are! You don't notice this in women."

In the passage, when Motia saw Gleb to the door, she pressed his hand in the darkness with the shy laugh of a young girl.

"Oh, Gleb, you're one of us. . . . A real friend of ours. You don't know what joy is mine. . . . You don't know. I'm going to be a mother, you know—a happy mother, Gleb!"

And on the threshold she sighed with a sudden pity for Gleb.

"Oh, Gleb, what an unhappy lot! You won't be able to live close to Dasha any more. But you deserve it, you men—throwing your women to the dogs like that!"

Gleb found Dasha the same as he left her, reading, her head on her hands, her stern occupied face, muttering diligently over her book. As he entered she threw him an inquiring glance.

"Well, what have you learned from our Comrades the Savchuks?"

Gleb went up close to her, his face working with pain. He embraced her and spoke in unusual tones. This was not the Gleb who had passed through the tempests of war, but a man worn out by love and anxious thought.

"Dasha—. Tell me then, my little dove, tell me. . . . Be kind as you used to be. . . . It's so hard for me, Dasha. You're like a stranger to me. As though you hid a knife in your bosom."

Dasha said nothing, but Gleb felt her tremble, and there was a response to him in the depths of her. He felt her head and shoulder press against him; he felt her once more become the dear and yielding woman of old. But she leaned against him still, fighting with herself, without yet regaining mastery.

"Well, and supposing something has happened, it's not of the greatest importance. It could happen to anyone in the bad times."

She freed herself from his arms, sighing deeply. Then she

looked attentively into his eyes, as Motia had, and said in a low voice, broken with sorrow :

" Yes. . . . it was so—. It did happen, Gleb . . . and more than once."

It was as though a monstrous hand had thrown Gleb and Dasha asunder ; as though a huge abscess had burst within his breast. An animal fury filled his face with blood, and a bestial strength his fists.

" Then it's true, is it ? It did happen ? You've laid in the ditch with a lot of tramps like a filthy drab ! You dirty bitch ! "

Blinded with rage, his eyes goggling, his heart swelling too large for his breast, with crouching steps, he flung himself at Dasha, his fists raised. But she had risen quickly from her chair and stood steadily, seeming taller than usual. With a voice that was not like a woman's, seeming to spring deep from her breast, she curbed at once Gleb's bestial wrath.

" Come to your senses, Gleb ! Aren't you ashamed of yourself ? What is it now ? "

She became silent, frowning darkly. And when, checked by her cry, he stopped suddenly with quivering lips, she said quietly in a low voice, slightly hoarse : " I wanted to test you, Gleb. You can't behave like a man. You cannot listen to me yet as you should. What I just said to you was just to help me to see more clearly. You went to Motia's to spy—I know it. I know well what you are. . . . You're a Communist, it's true. But you are also a brute man, needing a woman to be a slave to you, for you to bed with. You're a good soldier, but in ordinary life you're a bad Communist ! "

And she began to prepare the bed.

Chapter V

THE HIDDEN EMIGRANT

I

THE SECRET ROOM

THE windows in their massive oak frames were never opened, and the dust from the quarries, filtering through the crannies, lay in a velvety pile on the window-sills.

In the morning, when the mountains glowed with a violet light, and the sun's rays slid obliquely between the window-bars and through the panes, rainbow-coloured crystals of quarry dust sparkled. The technologist, Engineer Kleist, used to stand long before his window looking at these tiny whirling worlds, dreaming of past geological epochs. A tangible thick silence surrounded him.

And as by happy chance this room was lost at the end of a winding corridor, where dreamy silence reigned at daytime and where night brought black emptiness and ragged shadows, the engineer's study seemed joyfully inaccessible, far away as that quarry in the valley overgrown with wild roses and ivy.

After the factory had been abandoned, and the dark blue gaps left by the stolen doors and windows faced questioningly the volcanic masses of the hills and the quarries' terraced stone steeps with their smashed and rusty ropeway—then life was bound to stop and decompose into two elements : chaos and calm. Why not then be the technologist of a dead factory, when by so doing he was not bound in any way and time passed with steady balance ?

The main thing was not to open the oak frames of the window, but to apprehend the profound significance of the spiders' constructions between the double panes. At some unfixed point between past and present, Engineer Kleist had suddenly observed a deep beauty and meaning in the complex architecture of the cobwebs in the airy space between the windows.

He would stand for long periods at the window, round-shouldered, long-legged, with silvery hair *en brosse*, gazing at the pearly webs, at the multitude of their luminous planes, intersecting and inclining at various angles, the illimitable radiation of ladders, the interlacing and twining, with their power of prodigious tension.

No one called at his study. Who would want the technician when the factory was silent as a grave and the cement lying in damp sheds had long ago petrified into blocks hard as iron, when the cable-ways were damaged, the cables broken, the trucks derailed and flung down the slope, rusted from rain and lying amidst grass and refuse ? No one wanted the engineer when the mechanics wandered idly along the highroad and footpaths, around the empty buildings and through the yard, carrying away wood for fuel, the metal parts of machines in order to make pipe-lighters, and the belting from the transmission gear.

Down below in the semi-basement, in the half-darkness of the uninhabited rooms, could be heard the stamping, thundering and shouting of the Factory Committee. It seemed to Engineer Kleist that this was a tavern, an evil inn, sheltering rioters and brigands. Through the dusty obscurity of his window, he saw workmen running up or down the concrete steps. He noted their faces : mournful and dusted over greyly with hunger and suffering and stamped with the lines of implacable obstinacy. These men pursued their own frightful and incomprehensible game and had no care for him.

Everything had turned out right for him through his carefulness and cleverness in setting a simple mathematical problem. From his far-away corner he watched the workers with a sneering and febrile hatred. All these creatures exhausted by hunger and lack of employment in their revolt against this condition had produced the revolution, that great tragedy, that devastation. It was they that had ruined his future and burned up the world like a handful of waste ; and they had forgotten the few remnants of the past in this hidden room.

The steps and terraces of concrete outside his window glowed and shimmered under the glaring sun. It seemed as though they were being brought to white heat and were on the point of breaking into flame. One would think that water was flowing over the heated surfaces and hissing and swelling in bubbles and steam. But these are only the steps of the workers crackling on the loose cement and pebbles on the concrete steps. Down there, they were running about like ants from door to door, in and out of the Factory Committee.

Why was a Factory Committee needed now ? There was none previously and yet the factory was known around the world ? What business could they have to do, these workmen condemned to idleness amidst the remnants of a once highly organised and immense undertaking ? Why so much anxious scurrying if to-morrow is the same as to-day and if afterwards there will follow merely a series of similar senseless days as alike as the infinite series of reflections in double mirrors ?

Every day at one o'clock sharp, Jacob, the office-messenger, arrived carrying a little brass tray. He entered silently, stern, grave and stooping. His grey moustache with its sharp, pointed ends and the bluish bristles on his red scalp seemed transparent as glass. He would put down a glass of tea and two minute tablets of saccharine wrapped in paper and he would step backwards two paces, and stooping low pick from the floor with his finger tips a couple of crumbs which he would carefully place in a wire basket under the table. The walls were white and clean, and in their oak frames the architectural drawings looked as severe as in the old times.

" One o'clock already, Jacob ? "

" One exactly, Herman Hermanovitch."

" Very well. You may go. Don't let anyone up to me."

" Very good, sir."

" Dust the windows, Jacob, but don't open them."

" Very good, sir."

Engineer Kleist stood at the window with his back turned to Jacob. His silvery bristly short hair gave him a slight air of being vexed ; his neck muscles moved like elastic bands, and his old jacket hung from his shoulders in straight folds sticking out below like a little tail.

Somewhere, far beyond his corridor, faint voices were raised now and then, and one heard the clicking of the Abacus.[1] New people had already been sent here by the Economic Council.

Who were they ? What were they doing there ? Engineer Kleist did not know, nor did he want to know. He had his study, forgotten by everyone and guarded by Jacob, where only the past existed, traversed by the present but untouched by it. The present was rushing along the highroad with the automobiles and carts and the masses of men and workers who had broken loose and now shouted and swore senselessly

[1] The Abacus, or counting-board, similar to that used in our nurseries, is still in use in Russian offices.—Tr.

—a thing which previously the management had strictly forbidden.

He regarded the round mass of the mountain, striped by the edges of rock strata, clothed with shrubs and juniper bushes. Higher up the slope stood the mansion built of rough stone, standing like a massive block, fiery red from the sun, its towers and arches conferring upon it a sober puritan dignity.

" What's over there now, Jacob ? What do you call that ? "

" The Workers' Club and the Communist Group Head-quarters, Herman Hermanovitch."

" They've brought with them a new unintelligible language. There is something murderous in it like the revolution. Please let no one enter this room, and on no account open the window. You may go."

The engineer gazed at the house of the director (" Communist Group ") admiring its strength and great size. This house had been built by him, Engineer Kleist.

On the left, to the side of the slope, among green patches and stones the iron and concrete smoke-stacks of the factory shot upwards ; from the window they seemed higher than the mountains. He could see the cupolas and arcades of the factory buildings behind the ropeway, beneath the chimneys. These, too, had been built by Engineer Kleist. He could not have fled abroad without having destroyed his creation. The masterpieces of his hands stood in his path more immovable than the mountains, more indestructible than time ; he had become their prisoner.

This room, with its polished floor, still retained the simplicity and the atmosphere of a workroom. Rough drawings on the wall and on the massive oak desk ; the grave dignity of the heavy, carved Gothic furniture. Time had stood still here, and the past had here congealed and become tangible.

2

ENEMIES

Had an error crept into the logical constructions of Engineer Kleist, or had life for a while ceased to conform to the laws of human reason ? Whichever it was, the closed circle which was the isolated world of Engineer Kleist broke suddenly like a piece of rusty wire.

Only an hour before, when Jacob's customary visit had affirmed the unchangeableness of the unvarying course of time, the scheme of Engineer Kleist's life could easily be expressed in a severe graphic plan : a circle and a tangent. In moments of blessed repose, safe behind many walls, he would sit at his writing-table over the old projections of the factory buildings, and respecting the traditional decorum of his office, drew unconsciously on his English scribbling-pad, always the same design : circle and tangent—a figure that held good for all combinations.

Then suddenly everything was exploded and scattered in minute particles. The figure suddenly became nonsense. The tangent became a stone smashing the shell of his existence. And as it all happened so simply and quietly, Engineer Kleist was seized by deadly terror.

He had gone into the lavatory and had stayed there rather longer than usual. Owing to the inferior food he often suffered with his bowels. Coming back through the corridor he saw that the door of his room was open. Neither he nor Jacob ever allowed this.

Shortly after Jacob had left him he had noticed some workers standing outside on the terrace looking out towards the quarries ; then they had turned and gazed at his window. Even then he had felt a kind of light electric shock within him, an inquietude which lasted only a moment, and then he had forgotten it. And now his door stood wide open and again he felt the shock. But this time it burned and was accompanied by nauseating foreboding.

Preserving his air of frigid importance and accustomed poise he entered the room with even steps. On the threshold he stopped and could not at first grasp what had happened. Assuredly a brutal and unexpected change had taken place in his lonely world. The window was open and the dust streamed over the table and window-sill. Through the airy aperture of the window the copper slopes of the mountain, dappled with spring foliage and piles of stone, could be seen distinctly and appeared magnified. Far away, on the high slope of the quarries, stood a little house with two windows, whose angles and gables were sharply outlined against the sky. Wreaths of smoke and wisps of cobwebs were transparently mingled in the air current.

A clean-shaven man with a helmet, military tunic and blue puttees, stood by the window, pipe in mouth. He had prominent cheek-bones and hollow cheeks.

" Well, a nice mess you've made here in your den, Comrade Technologist ! "

With his cloth helmet he was sweeping down cobwebs and killing the crawling terrified spiders.

" You were well barricaded in here, Comrade. But much too lonely a place, at the end of all things."

Engineer Kleist walked towards his table with uncertain steps. There had been a time when this man, beaten and battered, had been condemned to death, and had grimaced at him with his bloody mask.

And now, unexpectedly, he was here, and so strangely and dreadfully calm.

" Yes. . . . I never open the window."

" Right, Comrade Technologist ; it's a poisonous draught that comes from us. . . . These Bolsheviks, be damned to them, have turned everything upside down, ripped the guts out of everything and scattered it to bits. The damned fellows ! "

" Why didn't Jacob announce your visit ? "

" We're sending your Jacob to the coopers' shop to saw wood. We can't stand flunkeys. You ought to remember me ? "

" Yes, I remember you. Well, what about it ? "

" Oh, a devil of a business. In our hands is the dictatorship of the proletariat ; but we're struggling bare-handed against economic ruin. The workmen, the factory and our transportation are all without fuel ; the cable-way is smashed ; the factory is almost a ruin ; and the technologists are hiding in their holes like rats. Why are there cobwebs here ? Why are cobwebs covering yourself and the factory ? That's how the question must be put, Comrade Technologist."

" Let us suppose that I have already put this question to myself and have answered it to my satisfaction. What do you want from me ? "

" Well. . . . I bumped into this barricade of yours, right into this little nook. . . . Let's turn the place over, thought I. It's a hell of a habit of mine, Comrade Technologist."

" I don't indulge in idle conversation. I neither understand nor wish to understand what you are saying. Be kind enough to leave me in peace."

Gleb stepped to the table, smiling, protruding his lower jaw. He took his pipe out of his mouth and looked intently at Engineer Kleist. Did the reflection of the spiders dance in his eyes, or were threatening spectres standing about Gleb ? Engineer Kleist's face went grey.

" Comrade Technologist, doubtless you remember that fine evening when you so kindly picked me out and tanned me all over ? It was a pretty heavy dressing you gave me. A lesson like that, if it doesn't kill you, is good for one. I've come to visit you to talk about the good old times. I like to meet old friends."

He stuck his pipe in the corner of his mouth, stretched himself and began to laugh.

" Now I'm going to ask you a riddle, Comrade Technologist. Quite a little one but pretty interesting. One spring day there were four damn fools. The god-damned Whites pinched these fools and brought them into this very room. Their faces were hardly faces by that time, but looked like old shoes. The question is : why were those battered things dragged here, and how did four dead fools become transformed into one living one ? Just a trifling riddle and the answer is a tough one, eh ? "

Gleb went on laughing, charmed with his jest.

" It's just a joke I'm telling you—something to laugh at, Comrade Technologist. It's a long time since we met."

He went to the window and leant out, shouting loudly :

" Hi, Brothers ! Wait a moment, I'm coming out ! I've just asked the Comrade Technologist a riddle. A bloody fine riddle—full of wit ! "

His voice could be heard far away, making his whole frame shake. And the answering shouts of the workers sounded nearer, although the words could not be distinguished. The sound like water hissing on the red-hot terraces continued, exploding in bubbles and steam. Gleb came back to the table and stood looking at Engineer Kleist with a mocking smile. He was waiting for an answer. But no answer came, and with military step he walked from the room without turning his head.

Engineer Kleist sat there a long while, exhausted after this encounter. Through the open window could be seen the ridges and clefts of the mountains. The open door yawned on to the corridor. Kleist felt sick, miserable and painfully agitated. Jacob returned, respectfully grave, and remained standing in the centre of the room. He seemed lost, and his face was crumpled with alarm. Kleist turned his feverish gaze upon him and asked very quietly and sternly :

" Is it you, Jacob ? Can't you tell me how all this has happened, Jacob ? "

" It's no fault of mine, Herman Hermanovitch. Nothing is forbidden to them here, there are no limits—nowhere, and in nothing. They have the might, Herman Hermanovitch, and their strength is law."

The presence of Jacob was pleasant. There was something soothing in his cold devotion.

" So it's really the Communist Group, then, Jacob ? "

" Chumalov, the mechanic, has been returned from the front. And now he's the head. He bosses everything, Herman Hermanovitch, and gets everything into his hands. Is there anything now to be done against them ? They've overrun everything, Herman Hermanovitch ! "

" And you too couldn't resist them, Jacob ? "

" I wasn't able to, Herman Hermanovitch. It's distressing that your peace has been disturbed."

Engineer Kleist was silent as though he had not heard Jacob's last words. Calmly and with a pre-occupied carelessness he lit his cigarette.

" You remember, Jacob, don't you ? There were four of them. It was painful and cruel. You remember the night they were shot. . . . I know well that they were killed."

" They were beaten and tortured to death, Herman Hermanovitch."

" Yes, Jacob, that was a frightful deed, that one can never forget. But one thing must be considered here : I acted with due reflection, under no outside influence. Fear ? Dread ? Vengeance ? No, it was not that. There is only one compulsion and that is time—the power of events. And with the same amount of consideration I did everything possible to save the life of this workman's wife."

He could not check the palsied shaking of his head. He could not hold his cigarette steadily between his fingers.

" Stay with me a little, Jacob. . . . I don't feel very well."

" You should go home, Herman Hermanovitch. You need rest."

" Where, home ? Abroad ? Don't you think, my brave fellow, that we are now both of us passing our last few hours here ? "

" How can you believe that, Herman Hermanovitch ? Our workmen are rowdy bawlers, it is true ; but they are peaceful and incapable of murder. Be calm, Herman Hermanovitch."

But Jacob also was trembling convulsively.

And hardly had he uttered these words when Engineer Kleist threw himself back in his chair and his face became ashen.

" Do you remember, Jacob ? I delivered this man over to his death, but his death has rebounded on to me. Accompany me, Jacob."

He rose, and stooping, with horror in his eyes, passed by Jacob. With senile, twitching gestures, Jacob took the engineer's hat and stick and with short, hurried steps followed him into the darkness of the corridor.

3

RETRIBUTION

Engineer Kleist ascended the slope of the mountain, passing along a path littered with boulders and strewn with refuse, through wild brush and thickets of evergreen, thorn and juniper. The shadows of the night seemed to flow up upon the slope from the hollows below. They were thicker still down below on the high road and among the concrete buildings of the factory. The gardens and walls barred the way to the shadows and they thickened into a heavy black fog. The purple clouds of the ash-trees and witch-elms, still leafless and partly transparent, showed faintly, and the poplars swayed high their branched heads like enormous smoky torches.

At the foot of the mountain, the hard masses of the factory. Beyond, above its roofs and towers, the sea appeared like lustreless crystal. Above, the opal sky was gemmed with stars. One could no longer distinguish the town on the other side of the bay but points of light, large and small, twinkled in the black shadows of the mountain. Everything seemed far off and strange. For Engineer Kleist, only the iron concrete giants which he had built were near to him and intimate. The only things in the world at that moment were the wrought power of these immense buildings and he, their creator, Engineer Kleist. At this terrible hour when the extinguished factory slumbered, menacingly silent among the shadows of its yawning courts, a tomb of rusting machinery, Engineer Kleist was gliding like a wandering shadow along the railway lines and flights of steps, by the walls and towers, and his silence was one with the silence of the factory.

This evening for the first time he saw in the yawning breaches of the factory walls the grandiose death of the past. His graphic formula was proving true : the wheel of events was running inexorably along the appointed track.

The strange encounter with Gleb Chumalov signified to Engineer Kleist that this track had come to an end and that his life had approached its limit.

The factory should have been blown up when it was possible and he should have perished with it. This would have been an excellent counter-blow according to the law of compensation.

If one were to meet him now on his way he was quite ready. What would have to be done was really quite the simplest thing : just to take him and shoot him through the head. The preparatory stages had already been accomplished. He only wished to spend a few more moments among these buildings where his life had crystallised into powerful and austere edifices.

Out of what world was the new culture which this workman Gleb Chumalov brought with him ? He, resurrected from blood, was fearless and unconquerable and strength lay in his dread eyes. And when Gleb had smiled to-day at their meeting, there was an unplumbed profundity in that smile—a knowledge which Kleist could not seize. And his strange helmet was part of this indefinable significance and the face and the helmet were one.

An obstinate sinister face—an obstinate sinister helmet.

This helmet stressed the menacing present. Beyond the helmet and face of Gleb Chumalov there was nothing at all.

No way out. Engineer Kleist was ready. It was better to be murdered here among these buildings than at home. These giants and he were inseparable ; to kill him meant to destroy within him the shrine of his spirit.

Beyond the far hills and the town the sky was slowly dying out like cooling iron ; and the battlements of the mountains were like the black turrets of a gigantic factory. There was a distinct harmonious stillness. Somewhere not far off a block of metal whistled and screeched under tired hands. A frightened cuckoo cried in the distance and somewhere in the same direction was the shivering and clattering of falling iron.

Gleb stood on the top of the tower, which was woven like a cobweb of steel girders. Once the coal had been loaded here into trucks, destined for the power-house. The trucks were conveyed by the lift down into the black abyss of the shaft and were drawn along by cables on rails which ran through tunnels to the power-house. Now the stage was empty and behind the parapet gaped a black and dark gulf.

He was clasping the iron rods of the railing till his fingers hurt. He regarded the iron and concrete blocks of buildings, the high chimneys soaring to the stars, the twanging tense cables with their motionless trucks. He clenched his jaws, grinding his teeth.

The factory roared like the fires of hell. The earth shook with the fury of machines; the air was flecked with flashes from the flaming windows, from the dazzle of the blast furnaces, from the bursting of countless purple moon-like bubbles, and dynamite explosions in the heart of the mountain. There, in the bay, great ocean steamers were moored alongside the quays, their insatiable bellies swallowing millions of tons of fresh cement. From the factory to the docks and from the docks to the factory the trucks were gliding like flying tortoises, whistling and moaning. Thousands of workers like legions of demons, red with the glare of the fire, were demolishing the mountain, reducing it to rubble and to dust; the days were lit by sulphur smoke and whirling dust and the nights by flaming windows and roaring fires.

This was in the past. Now there was stillness—a giant tomb. The ropeway, the steel rails and the roads to the factory were overgrown with grass. The metal was scabbed with rust and the iron and concrete walls of the buildings showed gaps and the erosions caused by mountain torrents.

Engineer Kleist walked on, stopping frequently to contemplate the high rectangular building, the mausoleums of a past epoch. He gazed thoughtfully. He walked on, then stopped again, pensively contemplating.

Gleb bent over the railing and attentively viewed the vague shadow of the engineer.

Here was a man whom he could strangle with his hands at any moment with the greatest delight, and that hour would be a happy one in his life. In a spirit of revenge, this man had once turned him over to a gang of officers for torture and death. Gleb would never be able to forget that day.

The factory workers had been lined up on the main road in front of the office building. There were not many of them left; many were in hiding and many had gone off with the

Red Army. He and three of his comrades had had no chance to run away, having remained right through the street fighting. One of the officers, carrying a whip, was reading out names from a paper. As each man stepped from the ranks he struck him with his whip and handed him over to the other officers. And they in their turn beat him with their whips and with the butts of their revolvers. Vaguely, with the surface of his consciousness, Gleb could hear the anguished screams of the workmen. He could not distinguish for a moment whether they were cries of protest or whether the officers were beating them. Then he saw for a moment, through tears of blood, that they were flying in all directions and that the officers were running after them with whips and revolvers. And when the four of them, with their bloodied faces, were dragged into the office of Engineer Kleist, the latter looked at them for a long time, pale, his jaw working. The officers were talking to him in short crisp sentences in military fashion, and he kept silent, concealing his agitation. He looked at Gleb fixedly and in his eyes Gleb saw compassion mingled with disgust. Then he said in low tones, croaking hoarsely :

" Yes, this is he. . . . And those—. Yes, yes ; those are the very ones."

" Have you anything more to say, Mr. Kleist ? "

" What may happen further is outside my powers, gentlemen. It is a matter for your discretion."

Then they were thrown into an empty shed and beaten and beaten until late in the night. In moments of consciousness Gleb could feel the blows—some slight and remote, seeming not to hurt him ; some smashing and terrible, almost crushing him to pulp. But even these blows seemed strangely useless and painless as if he were nailed up inside a cask which someone was aimlessly and impertinently kicking.

When he came to himself it was pitch dark and silent. He began to crawl round the shed, terrified and half-dead. He jostled against the bodies of his comrades, cold, rigid and slimy with blood. Crawling along by the walls he found a large hole through which he crept. Hidden by night and the thick shrubbery he struggled home, and since then no one had seen him.

Never, for all eternity, could he forget this.

Gleb had remembered this during the day when he was in Kleist's room. He thought of it now while he was watching the engineer wandering like a lost shadow in the wide space beneath.

"Good evening, Comrade Technologist, a fine old ruin, isn't it? There are many such all over the Republic but none that can beat this."

Engineer Kleist stopped as though turned into stone, then recovered quickly and looked attentively, not at Gleb, but at the black gaps of the smashed windows in the machine shop.

This man was everywhere! He did not pursue Kleist, but was planted in his way, terrifying him like a spectre. The iron web of his world was torn and it was impossible to weave a new one. He could not evade the red-starred helmet and the strength of this man. Since when had he acquired this dreadful power over him? In former days this workman was lost in the mass of blue oily blouses, without a face or voice of his own. Like all the others, indistinguishable, he fulfilled the tasks assigned to him. An insignificant unit in the mighty and complicated process of production. Why could Engineer Kleist, once so strong and dominating, no longer resist the crude, barbaric power of this man? From what point sprang this new development? Was it from the moment when he gave him up to destruction or from that hour to-day when he saw him in his office, risen from the past.

It was as simple as a blow. That which he had been awaiting and with which his whole day had been filled had arrived. It opened before him like a narrow bottomless abyss.

"Come up here, Comrade Technologist. Seen from up here the grave is deeper. You've been rambling? So have I, every day. But what's the sense of it? Be kind enough to step up here, Comrade Technologist."

The logic of events knows only merciless endings and implacable beginnings. There are no accidents: accidents are an illusion. With a nauseating pain in his heart, swooning with terror, Engineer Kleist slowly ascended the creaking, vibrating stairway—time was whirling in suffocating darkness—and yet in the hour of his fate he preserved his accustomed dignity and silent calm.

"Take care, Comrade Technologist; I say there's a deep hole here, damn it. If you stumble into it there'll only be small pieces of you left. Some shaft this is, that you've built. This is part of your work."

Engineer Kleist answered coldly and sternly.

"We built it to last for ever: solidly and with thought. But you have turned it all into chaos and ruin."

"Well, but you made a mistake somewhere, Comrade

Technologist. You built it up, pile on pile, and all for yourselves. An impregnable fortress, eh ? But it did not hold ;
it fell. But all your care was not worth much. Where now is
your work which was to last for centuries ? "

Gleb, puffing his pipe, loomed like an enormous iron statue
in the twilight. And because he was so calm and simple and
spoke with such deep and primitive significance, Engineer
Kleist felt that he could not escape this man, and that the out-
come of the next few moments was contained within his hands.
The engineer stood as if paralysed, leaning against the parapet,
his head shook in little palsied jerks.

" Just look at the factory, Comrade Technologist : what a
giant and what a beauty ! Ah, to make this graveyard live
again ! To fire the furnaces once more, and make all these
cables and power lines live again ! It is a miracle of construction ! "

Erect and soldierly, his chest thrown out, Gleb grasped the
iron railing and for a long time looked down upon the black
blocks of the factory. He felt crushed by their massive grandeur and by the profound silence. Were his ribs actually cracking under his tunic or was it the grinding of his teeth ? Engineer Kleist heard a deep, moaning sigh.

" A graveyard . . . a common graveyard . . . curse it
all ! "

Why did the engineer stand here, gaunt and stooping ? Why
was he so silent and like a condemned man ?

Something in common with the factory, something vexed
and oppressing was in Gleb. Ah, the past ! The remembrance
of the suffering and death of his comrades, that was his torture.
The unforgettable ! Should he fling him downwards into the
deep gulf ? Two tightly-stretched cables plunged from the
roof down to the dynamos. One would say that they were
serpent's tongues and that the shaft was a hungry maw claim-
ing its prey.

Gleb gave Kleist a side-glance ; but he felt no desire for
revenge.

" So, Comrade Technologist ! You've been a good one at
building memorials. When you die, here is a grave already
prepared for you. Do you see this hole ? We shall let you
down there in a truck and bury you under the highest smoke-
stack."

Almost losing consciousness, Engineer Kleist started erect,
wrenching himself away from the railing. His whole body

ached acutely and seemed to be about to dissolve into misty space. A wild cry stayed in his throat, changing into a hoarse choked moan. He clenched his jaws convulsively with such force that his head ached with the tension.

" You. . . . Chumalov ! For God's sake do quickly what you have to do ! "

Gleb stepped nearer to the engineer; he was feverish, tense.

" Comrade Technologist, we've acted the fool long enough. We need heads . . . and hands. We've got to start things going ! Coal and oil ! Warmth and bread for the workmen. The industrial revival of the Republic. . . . Over the mountains are great stacks of felled wood. We can bring it not by horse-power but by the mechanical power of the works. Thousands and millions of logs. . . . Loaded trucks . . . voluntary Sunday work ! Thousands of muscular bands and backs ! "

He seized Kleist by the shoulders and shook him in joyful excitement ; in his hands the engineer shook nervously like a scarecrow. His hat fell from his head and swooped like a night-bird into the darkness below.

" Enough, Comrade Technologist ! We're going to put you in harness. We have proved our strength. Your brains and hands are worth gold to us. A technologist like you—why, you're one of the greatest in the Republic ! "

And in this, his last exhausting struggle for life, Engineer Kleist realised in the depths of his being that these dreadful hands ingrained with death had sternly and firmly attached him to life. Stupefied, he could not grasp the meaning of this shattering event ; he stood there, emptied of all thought, bare-headed, with galloping heart.

Gleb struck the balustrade with his fist and the iron lattice-work resounded.

" Well, Comrade Technologist, get your brains in hand and we'll get to work. We'll build bigger things even than these. A new world, Comrade Technologist ! "

Engineer Kleist, stooping, shuffling his feet, groped with trembling hands in the space between him and Gleb. And then collapsed.

Gleb descended the stairway, his heavy boots resounding on the iron steps.

Chapter VI

THE PRESIDIUM

I

THE FIRST LINKS

A BEARDED messenger in a military blouse and grey hat, as worn during the Imperialist War, sat outside the door of the office of the Chairman of the Executive Committee of the Soviet. He glared at Gleb like a wolf from under his heavy eye-brows. His hairy hand was clasped by habit around the brass door-handle. In this way he guarded the door of the Chairman's office every day, from ten in the morning until five in the evening, without leaving his chair, even when the Chairman went forth on business. Whether they were busy persons carrying brief-cases or unknown petitioners timidly stretching their necks like birds, it was all the same : each had to pass by this silent morose guard, with wolf-like gaze under heavy grey eye-brows—dumb and unapproachable. And each meekly awaited his turn in line, unless the urgency of his affair was vouched for by the Secretary of the Executive.

In the queue, people were standing in uniform coats, with or without portfolios, with or without papers, patient or furious ; but all knew that it was impossible to force their way past this old devil with the wolf's gaze.

The Remingtons were clicking metallically inside near the door and a hoarse rasping voice was crying : " It's a shame and a disgrace, Comrades. . . . Bureaucracy and formalities are devouring us. You should all be sent to hell ! or be shot like rabbits ! "

Gleb walked up to the door, and he and the messenger silently eyed each other.

" Well, you mop-haired old devil, take your hand off the knob."

The people in the long queue began to murmur. What was this ? Was Gleb any better than anyone else ? Why was he trying to get in first ? If they were patient enough to wait their turn, why shouldn't he do the same, according to the rules?

It was quiet now in the office. The door was close shut and a piece of paper was stuck on it saying: "No one can enter unless previously announced." Lower down another paper: "The Chairman of the Soviet Executive Committee only receives persons coming strictly on business." And lower down still: "Admission out of turn on urgent business, only through the Secretary of the Executive Committee."

A diabolical arrangement! To make it work properly it has to be broken.

Gleb made his way to the Secretary's office. Here was stuffiness and confusion and another long queue. A typist was tapping busily and slamming the drawers of the filing cabinet. Girls were installed at old stained tables, turning over papers and nibbling at their rations of black bread. They were indifferent to this customary sweaty tumult. As usual, the blonde-haired china doll was looking into her pocket-mirror and patting her hair with her fingers. Was that why the Secretary, Peplo—with his grey locks and youthful face—was smiling while he gazed at the grey faces around him? His irrepressible smile reveals his even white teeth, trimmed with little bubbles of spittle.

Peplo knows everybody. He calmly listens to the tumult. The Secretary knows everything; he sits there smoking and never appears hurried. All business is the same, and it does not need wings.

Then in one corner, and again in another, a loud hoarse voice dominated the uproar of the rowdy crowd.

"You ought to be all kicked out, you blasted drones! You've got the working-men into a hell of a harness! One should have horns on one's head and fists of steel to smash your fat bureaucracy. I'll make you sing small! I'll teach you to persecute the working-class. . . ."

The cries died down unanswered, and Secretary Peplo continued to smile broadly. Doubtless they were all accustomed to these outcries. The machine was functioning at full speed and the protests and anger of the citizens did no more than help grease the wheels.

Shuk, covered with perspiration and with tears in his eyes, was striding up and down like one possessed, stooping under the weight of his wrath.

Gleb took him by the arm and pulled his hat down over the back of his head.

" Keep your pecker up, Shuk ! Don't bark so much and wave your arms about like a windmill ! "

Shuk devoured Gleb with his swollen eyes ; he trembled with joy, raised his hand and stopped in his tracks.

" Hullo, Gleb, my own dear friend ! How it saddens me to see the working-class so ill-treated ! But I won't give them any peace while I'm living in this miserable world. I've really got nothing to do here, but I'm stirring up the work a bit. . . . I've been to the Economic Council to-day—it's a mess ! I've been to the Food Council—another mess ! Everywhere it's a mess ! And here, damn it all, what a mess too ! So you see, I'm going around swearing like a trooper."

" Shuk ! You're crazy, Comrade ! One must act—talking's no good."

" I. . . . You want me to—. But, God damn it—! I'm going to expose them all. I'm going to stand them up against the wall."

" I must give you some work to do, Shuk, or you'll be firing nothing but blank cartridges all the time. You're wasting yourself. Don't forget : I'm going to find a job that will suit you."

" No, Brother Gleb, dear Comrade. They'll find out about me yet. I'm going to remind them of 1918. . . ."

He shook his clenched fists towards the ceiling and went away with heavy step.

Without awaiting his turn, Gleb broke through the crowd to Peplo, the crowd booing and murmuring at him.

" Comrade Secretary, will you please send in my name to the Chairman of the Executive——"

Peplo regarded Gleb with a broad smile.

" First get into the queue here, and then you will join that one over there."

" To hell with your queue, Comrade Secretary. I have very urgent business. Will you announce me without delay ? "

Peplo, pink-cheeked and amazed, shook his curls.

" Urgent ? What business ? About what ? "

Cries were raised among the crowd : " I've urgent business too—! Important business—! D'you call that fair ? "

Peplo was looking at Gleb with a smile in which there was a glint. He was not listening to him but to the others. Gleb drew himself up and his eyes began to look like Shuk's. He raised his fist and jostled his way rapidly to the door. In the corridor, he pushed the hirsute guardian on one side and broke into the office of the Chairman of the Executive. The fiery sunshine bathed him in a red light. The dazzling rays were painful to his eyes. The walls of the room shimmered white.

" What's the matter, Comrade ? Why do you rush in here when I'm not seeing anybody ? I am busy."

Gleb could not see who it was speaking behind the curtain of sunrays, but it was clear that here was no fool. The Chairman had a loud, metallic voice. Gleb moved out of the sun's glare and everything resolved itself into the ordinary and familiar. The writing-table, and a man dressed in black leather who leant with his chest against the desk ; his face was deeply sunburnt as though it were of bronze. Another in Circassian dress, with dagger and revolver, was standing near the table, his hand on the back of a chair. His hand was clenched so tightly upon the chair back that the fingers were dead white and quivering. The muscles of his face were twitching and his eyes protruded. His nose was Caucasian, aquiline. He was one of those young heroes of the " Devil's Hundred " who during the war performed such wonders, and upon whose swords the blood was never dry.

Gleb saluted and sat down near the table, opposite the Chairman. They regarded each other with a silent stare. The Chairman's forehead projected vertically over his eyes like a spade. He did not look at the man in Circassian dress and he momentarily forgot Gleb. He spoke distinctly and monotonously into his dark hairy hands that rested on the table before him.

" Borchi, don't forget : if within a month from now you haven't obtained the supplementary deliveries of grain and in September don't obtain the return from the peasants of the seed-grain advanced to them, I'll have you shot. I'm not talking at random, you know that very well. As Chairman of the Executive Committee of your district you're responsible to me for everything. Remember that."

Borchi endeavoured to answer, rolling his eyes and clenching his teeth.

" Comrade Badin. . . . I'm also a Communist. I protest ! "

His voice was steady at first, but broke hoarsely. The Chairman continued coldly and heavily :

" Yes, it's precisely because you are a Communist that I'll stand you up to be shot if this plan is not carried out. In your district of Kurkal you're bickering and wrangling and giving in to the influence of the Kulaks."[1]

---

[1] The rich peasants in the villages who resisted the delivery of grain to the Soviets and endeavoured to exploit the poor peasants.—Tr.

"Comrade Badin, you must listen to me. . . . It's only a question of putting off the repayment of seed-corn until next year. You must understand the situation. Forced requisitions of produce have taken place four times since last Autumn. The peasants will die of starvation. And by such measures we're increasing the numbers of the White-Green bands. They'll cut our throats to the last man. We'll be chopped up like mince-meat."

"All right, then. Be chopped up into mince-meat. But the task set you must be carried out exactly and to date."

"Comrade Badin! I demand that this be put on the agenda—. I shall prove to the Executive——"

Badin sat straight up. The folds of his leather tunic glistened.

"Borchi!"

He rose and slowly turned his head to the Cossack.

"Chairman of the District Executive Borchi!"

He smiled, and it seemed that from his iron smile his jaw-bones would crack.

Borchi recoiled a step and drew himself up. His moist eyes gleamed. His voice was hoarse.

"Comrade Badin, the campaign will be carried out. I shall do everything. But it will be a butchery, Comrade Badin."

"Don't be afraid, we'll send you Saltanov, the chief of the local militia, as assistant."

He re-seated himself. In a moment he had already forgotten the Chairman of the District Executive Committee, Borchi. And Borchi, dauntless swordsman of the Devil's Hundred, crushed and tamed, threw him a final glance, in which was the last note of his opposition, and walked rapidly from the room, defeated. Badin supported the weight of his heavy brow upon his hairy hands.

"What do you wish, Comrade? Be brief."

"For a working man to get to see you, Comrade Chairman, is more difficult than to capture a trench."

"What do you want? Speak to the point."

The gaze of the two men met, hostile, each measuring the other's strength. The stone-cold immobility of the Chairman depressed Gleb, and he doggedly and truculently broke the calm of the administrative routine with words hard as cobble stones.

"The next time I'll grab that bewhiskered guard of yours by the legs and chuck him out of the window. Such high-faluting ceremony is not becoming to us."

" Comrade, I shall have you arrested at once, for threats and rowdyism. Who are you ? "

He got up and leaned with his hands upon the table, making it creak under his fists. Scarcely had the Chairman uttered these words than Gleb, his face working, shoved away his chair and bent over to Badin ; grasping him by the shoulders he filled the room with his voice :

" Comrade Chairman of the Soviet Executive, a workman of the factory is speaking to you ! Have the kindness to be seated ! You have no right to chase workmen out of your office ! "

Badin's thick lips stretched in a smile, displaying his glittering teeth. He sat down again ; taking out a packet of cigarettes he lit one and offered the packet to Gleb.

" I'm listening. Tell me shortly and precisely what you want. What is your name ? "

Gleb sat down too. He rejected the cigarettes, but took out his own Red Army man's pipe.

" Both the Group and a General Meeting of the workers have decided to bring the wood by mechanical traction—the ropeway—over from the forest. The factory technologist will provide the drawings and the working plans. Two or three Sundays' voluntary work from each of the unions and we'll have loads of wood for the trucks. Just reckon up how much wood we shall be able to get down here between now and next Autumn ! Forced requisitions of wood are no use ; the peasants run away and join the bandits' gangs. The lighters are rotten—let them go to the Devil !—they've been broken by heavy seas. There—my name is Chumalov, the mechanic, commissar of a regiment."

Badin stretched out his hand to him and smiled.

" Yes, this is a serious business that we shall have to go into carefully. Tell me, isn't Dasha Chumalova your wife ? "

Gleb, who was busy with his pipe, glanced sharply at Badin's face ; his eyes then travelled to his hand. With a sweeping, rounded gesture that nearly caused the seams of his tunic to split, he gave Badin his hand.

" That's not the question, Comrade Chairman. What do you think about getting the factory to work again, if we can get the question on to the agenda of the day ? "

Badin gazed at Gleb ; little gold points flashed in his eyes. He leaned back in his armchair. His eyelids twitched slightly.

Gleb Chumalov, the husband who disappeared. Dasha,

who is not like other women. Dasha, to whom he once held out his hand. There was not a woman who would not yield, docile to his eyes and hands ; but here he had come up against one like a steel spring which had recoiled upon him, defeating him utterly. And because this woman, leader of the proletarian women of the place, was obstinately working at her job, organising the fighting groups of the women, and thus conquering for herself a place among the men, Badin did not know how to approach her as he did the others. Every day he was wondering how he could approach Dasha and break down her resistance at one blow.

And now he found himself face to face with a man who unexpectedly had placed himself between Badin and this woman.

" Don't let's discuss the question of the factory for the present, Comrade Chumalov. It's not in our power to get it started. As to the question of setting up the ropeway, I shall bring it forward at the next meeting of the Economic Conference."

In astonishment Gleb let his pipe drop to his knees. Then he re-placed it and again met the gaze of the Chairman. What was in the depths of these eyes ? He could not imagine what it was. Suddenly a troubled and black flood seemed to pass through them.

" But why isn't it in our power ? It's a disgrace ! The factory doesn't even provide light for its own alleys. Not to speak of the workmen's dwellings. There's decay everywhere, no doors and windows. And where there are doors there are no locks, just bits of string or wire. How do you expect the factory not to be plundered, bit by bit or all at once ? Who's helping this ruin, you or the workers ? Orders have been issued for liquid fuel for the factory, but where is the stuff ? The workmen want to know who's guzzling their petrol. You see what a mess it is ? There's so much potentiality, power and raw material—. But the stores are empty. Organise the preparatory work ? You shout about wasters and loafers and you're breeding sluggards yourselves. This Economic Council of yours should be put up against a wall, as well as the responsible workers and the technical rabble, as incorrigible enemies of the Soviet power. That's the way to deal with the question, Comrade Chairman."

" Comrade Chumalov, we understand how to put this question just as ably as you. But we must start out from the actual facts of the situation. We cannot settle these questions, which have a general national importance, without an understanding with the Gosplan.[1]"

" I understand the national significance, Comrade Chairman. I'm speaking with regard to its national significance. And in your palavering at the Economic Council why haven't you dealt with the matter from that point of view ? "

" We shall do so at the right time, Comrade Chumalov. Everything depends on the perspectives of the new economic policy. And that moment is not very far off."

" Comrade Chairman, will you telephone to the Economic Council ? "

" Why, when it's useless ? "

" Telephone, please, to the Economic Council, Comrade Chairman. We shall speak seriously with them. I want to see before your eyes what this Economic Council really is."

" All right, then ; we'll talk to them about the ropeway."

Badin lifted the receiver. Again black trouble flowed through his cold sneering smile. Gleb did not look at him, puffing clouds of smoke from his pipe and ramming down the ashes with his finger tip.

Two forces. . . . The Chairman of the Executive and the workman Chumalov. The two forces had collided and a spark flashed ! What was burning back of the eyes of this man ? A beast ? A hero ? A jealous male ?

" Every responsible worker, Comrade Chumalov, is the more valuable in proportion to his capacity for concentrating on the immediate job in hand. My rule is : not generalities— but the immediate job. No fairy-tales, but a chunk of bread. Do you know we are threatened by bandits ? They have us surrounded, the wolves ! The struggle against them consumes the forces which we should devote to the restoration of economic life. We must have a new fighting method and a new disposition of our forces. Your project for getting the factory working is absurd ; you don't account for the present economic situation. If you succeed in setting up the supply of wood to the town, you will have accomplished a splendid deed."

Gleb took his pipe out of his mouth and looked fixedly at Badin. Why didn't this fellow understand the simplest matters ?

" You're so busy about little questions, Comrade Chairman,

[1] State Planning Commission, a body which co-ordinates on a national scale Soviet production and its future development.—Tr.

that you lose sight of the big ones. You're running after fleas with a sledge-hammer! Let's get to the root of the matter. The Red Army's covered thousands of miles and smashed the Entente, while your little crowd have only been breeding sluggards. What have you actually done to re-establish production? Nothing! The question has to be posed definitely but broadly, at once—immediately—without the least delay."

With a great gesture, Gleb seemed to outline in the air the rotundity of a giant cupola.

"I know this as well as you do, Comrade Chumalov. We talk about this at every Party Conference and at the Congresses of the Soviets and the Trade Unions. Productive forces; the economic development of the Republic; electrification and so on. But where are your actual possibilities?"

"They are here!"

"Let us see them!"

"Here they are. What is the worker doing now, do you know? And how's the peasant living, do you know? So far, we've only trampled the peasants' fields, but now they'll have to be ploughed. While the factory chimneys are not smoking the peasant will be a bandit."

The Chairman laughed and the curiosity died out in his eyes.

"There's nothing new in that, Comrade Chumalov. It will be discussed at the Tenth Congress of the Party."

"No, it's not new . . . but it's worrying you all the same, eh?"

This workman is as obstinate as he is naïve and short-sighted! Just like one of those demagogues who interfere with the normal course of the complicated task of administration. These dreamers possessed with a vision of the future a glittering romance which for them extinguishes the ruined present.

The Chairman of the Council of People's Economy entered, his brief-case under his arm, dressed in yellow leather from cap to boots. He had the soft face of a eunuch, with gold pince-nez perched on an effeminate nose. Without any greeting he sat down at the table facing Gleb and froze into an attitude of strained and unnatural repose. He moved neither head nor hands, and even his eyes were glassy like those of a wax-work figure. Everything about him was life-like, but he was only a manikin.

"Listen, Shramm: what can the Economic Council do if in a few days the question is raised of the partial re-starting of the cement factory?"

It seemed as though Shramm did not hear the question of the Executive Chairman. Not a muscle of his face quivered ; and when he spoke his lips scarcely moved. He did not answer Badin's question but spoke slowly, without pausing, in a gramophone voice, as though he were reciting an official report.

" The Economic Council has carried out a tremendous task. It has made an inventory of the State's property, from the most complicated machinery down to old horse-shoes, and has conserved it. We do not allow a single nail to be taken from stock, nor the machines to be touched, in spite of the heaps of schemes and proposals emanating from various enterprises and private persons."

" That's all very well. But now your Council of Economy will have to transform itself from a niggardly housewife into an enterprising industrialist. Your apparatus will have to get working at a higher pressure from now on."

Shramm's face remained dull as before, strained and lymphatic as a eunuch's.

" The Council of Economy receives its tasks and plans from the Bureau of Industry only."

The Executive Chairman gave him a hard black look and leaned forward with his weight upon the table.

" You're hiding behind the back of the Bureau of Industry in order to shelter your Economic Council. But do you even know what's going on on the two floors of your premises ? From your written reports it seems that you are doing nothing but auditing and inventories, over and over again. You've an uncountable number of departments and sub-departments with a staff of two hundred persons—but you haven't given us the smallest amount of real creative work. What are the intentions of the Economic Council for the immediate future with regard to the factories, workshops and other undertakings ? "

" The Economic Council takes the position that the most important thing is firstly to conserve the patrimony of the State without tolerating any doubtful undertakings."

" How is the District Forestry Committee working ? "

" I have nothing to do with that, or, rather, only indirectly. They are under my control, but they have their own apparatus."

" What data have you on the work of the Forestry Committee ? "

" The plan of what wood has to be felled."

" And the delivery of the wood to the districts ? "

" That is not the business of the Economic Council; that is the affair of the District Fuel Committee."

" Well then, Shramm, listen. The town, the suburbs and the transportation system must be provided with wood for the winter. We must at once get the dynamos of the factory working and install the ropeway to the top of the hill. The Economic Council must carry out this task as quickly as possible, using the machinery of the factory."

" That is not my business; that's the business of the Bureau of Industry. We cannot carry out this plan unless they sanction it."

" It is our business and not the Industrial Bureau's, and we shall execute it without their sanction."

For the first time a mournful expression came to Shramm's face, passing like a thin cloud, but his eyes remained glassy and unblinking as formerly.

" How much oil is assigned to the factory ? "

" The deliveries are very bad. According to our statistics thirty per cent. is lost through waste. We have been compelled, with the authorisation of the Bureau of Industry, to draw upon the oil reserved for the factory, which is in the tanks of the refinery, for the steam mills. With regard to the electrification of the factory and the construction of the ropeways: these items are not included in the plan of work for the year which has been approved by the Bureau of Industry. This question should first be sent for examination to the State Reconstruction Department and to the Industrial Department so that they can go into the details and draw up their estimates. Moreover, I shall myself energetically oppose these schemes, the adoption of which would only lead to the plundering of the people's money and property."

The Executive Chairman's eyes flashed.

" You're not going to speak against it. We shall know how to force you—understand ! You will make your report at the next sitting of the Economic Council. And now another question : do you know that the property of the people of which you have charge is being openly plundered ? "

The blood rushed to Shramm's face and a shadow passed in his eyes.

" This is unknown to me. According to the recently verified inventory everything is in order."

Badin smiled in the same way as he had smiled at District Chairman Borchi.

" Undoubtedly you are right, seeing that the Economic Council is formally committed to the point of view of the conservation of the people's property."

Terrified, Shramm looked at Badin and could not grasp what the Executive Chairman was saying.

Gleb shook the ashes of his pipe into the ash-tray. The first knot, quite a little one, had been tied. The others would come after. He got up and stretched out his hand to Badin. He saw a smile in his eyes and this time it was a quiet smile without glinting points.

" Comrade Executive Chairman, this is going to rip our guts out and break our backs, but we'll get the job done ! "

" Carry on, Comrade Chumaiov. The question of restarting the factory will be considered within a definite period."

Gleb stood to attention before Shramm.

" Your Bureau of Industry we'll send it to the devil with a kick in its behind ! We understand how to work it ! We'll send the whole Economic Council and you with them to clean out the water-closets ! Mildew and red-tape grow lush in this marsh ; but we know how to dry the marsh up ! "

The Chairman of the Economic Council looked at him in amazement. The blood fled from his face and the shadows in his eyes faded. His face again became soft, strained and still.

" No threats, please, Comrade. We do not accept any projects from outside. Those schemes which are sent to us, we file for posterity without examining them. We are enemies of all questionable enterprises and plans. We must cure our Comrades of their leaning to all kinds of adventures, which will be the best safeguard against disorganising enthusiasms."

Gleb broke out laughing. Sticking his pipe into his mouth, he looked at Badin and again met a smile in the depths of his eyes.

" Our boots stink of the dust of the highways, Comrade Chairman of the Economic Council, and they are hob-nailed. Our hands are acquainted with rifles and hammers. You must realise this as a Communist. You are a Communist, but you have no knowledge of a workers' policy. You've neither smelt powder nor the sweat of working men. I don't care a damn for your apparatus. . . . You've got swarms of rats there who have sharpened their teeth on Soviet bread, easily earned. You've everything nicely cut and dried—according to hour and minute—nicely camouflaged. But we've got a good scent and good bulldog's teeth too."

The shadows passed over the eyes of Shramm again and he bowed his head.

" Comrade Badin, I demand . . ."

But Gleb did not wait to hear the answer, he went through the sunrays to the door.

And now to Shibis ! No one is more needed now than Comrade Shibis.

2

EYES AT SEA BY NIGHT

In a small office with an open window (the powerful light that streamed in was too much for the size of the room) Shibis and Gleb sat at a heavy desk. Shibis seemed to be smiling and yet not smiling—as though his face was behind gauze. It seemed a frank face, with humorous eyebrows, as though ever ready to burst into laughter. At the same time he was shrewd enough and always a little reserved. Now joy was quivering in his face and spinning webs of little wrinkles round his eyes.

" Comrade Chumalov, you can speak at once if your business is urgent, or you may wait a few moments. I just have a minute free. Say what you wish. Are you getting on well with the factory ? "

" At present we're only just thinking about it and the work is still distant. We're still in the yelling stage."

Shibis was not listening. He screwed up his eyes at the impact of the warm light.

" I'm looking at the sea now. From here it looks like a soap-bubble. It's curved and the colours are so and so. . . . D'you see it ? That is no dream, it is reality. It makes you long to have a bathe or stretch out on the beach. That would be nice and so simple : like getting into another dimension and becoming invisible . . . and throw pebbles into the sea. And in the woods it's nice too. But look at the sea, how it's heaving and blue. Well, I'm here and the sea's over there. That's the way it will always be with me. Can you realise what it means : ' Forever ' ? This smells a bit of psychology, eh ? What's your idea about psychology ? "

"Let it go to the devil ! Take an hour off and have a swim ! What is there to stop you ? "

On Shibis' face there was no smile, only the grey mask. He raised his eyes and the mask dropped. And he looked at Gleb with a child's glance, eye to eye, from the depths of him. Did it only seem like this to Gleb, or had Shibis forgotten himself for a moment? A tear glittered in his eye, a child-like tear behind which was an indistinct black dot. This black point hovered, playing and leaping within the tear-drop. Gleb could not understand why this black point struck his heart so painfully, but he felt that Shibis' own personal devil was in this revolving dot, and nowhere else. Was that why Shibis screened his eyes with his long lashes, so that none might see this demon?

Gleb raised his eyebrows, waiting for Shibis to speak.

Child-like tears and behind them a leaping demon. Such eyes do not sleep at night; they can see through walls. Shibis had a language of his own which would never be uttered; images of the night swarmed in the cells of his brain. He spoke with strange incomprehensible words which dissolved into a child-like smile.

" Comrade Shibis, I don't know what you'll say about it, but these swine in the Economic Council are asking to be shot."

" That's so. And those of the Forestry Committee and of the Foreign Trade Commission also; and others too. . . ."

" Well, shouldn't we shoot the whole Soviet Executive ? "

" Yes, the Economic Council is a nest you can't take with bare hands. You'll come to grief with your factory and your ropeways. You must hit hard and straight."

" What do you think about the Chairman of the Economic Council, Comrade Shibis ? I've just been telling him what I think of him in the Executive Chairman's office, but I struck over the mark and hit the Bureau of Industry."

Shibis again looked long at the sea, the mountains and the clouds which floated like heaps of snow in the azure ; and the same boyish smile spread gently over his face.

" Have you seen people being shot, Comrade Chumalov ? "

" Yes, at the war. I remember how at first it shocked me to see their eyes rolling and to hear them howl like dogs."

" Yes, that's right ! Their eyes jumped all right and their bodies were dead and very dirty. Some of them die while they are still alive, in silence. Whom do you propose we should get after the Economic Council and the Forestry Committee ? Don't forget that some of these blockheads make the most intelligent and practical workers. They know how to see and how to take. . . ."

Gleb's tunic tightened over his chest, disturbing his breathing. He rose, suffocated with laughter. Then sat down again and laid his fist on the table before Shibis.

" Comrade Shibis, you're priceless ! "

Shibis threw him a glance veiled by his lashes and became distant, reserved again.

" Shramm is a strong Communist and would die for his department ; he'd let himself be knocked over like a ninepin. He's a Communist who's had his inside taken out, and they've stuffed him and made a scarecrow of him which doesn't even frighten the sparrows. But it's an obstinate scarecrow who thinks himself above all error. A scarecrow is the ideal, but in its rags how much harm is hidden ! Fools are worth more because they know how to stir up clear water. D'you know what it is to feel yourself indispensable ? Ha, to feel it is one thing and to know it is another ! Don't let that idea grow upon you or you will find yourself alone in the world with the whole universe upon your shoulders. What makes the world uncomfortable is that night is constantly crawling over it. Learn to give the thought of indispensability its proper place, and the nights won't frighten you any more with their phantoms."

Gleb, vaguely alarmed, considered Shibis, whose skull appeared to be swelling, cracking under the pressure of his thought ; Shibis' hands were too big for the table and wriggled like snakes.

" Comrade Shibis, have you anything to say against Shuk ? Is he a harmful fool in your estimation ? "

" Right ! Now we've finished with the affair. Send him to me to-morrow. We'll send him to work for the Economic Council and the Forestry Department as messenger. Well, off you go. Tell them to give you a permanent pass to let you into this office."

He turned away without shaking hands and pressed an electric bell. At the door Gleb turned round and his eyes encountered the face of a stranger. He felt he wanted to say something important but couldn't remember quite what it was.

" Have you ever seen Lenin, Comrade Shibis ? "

" It is of no importance whether I have or not."

Gleb laughed incredulously, readjusting his helmet.

" You're talking nonsense, Comrade Shibis. You have seen Lenin."

Chapter VII

THE HOUSE OF HIS PARENTS

I

THE BOOKWORM

ON the grey moulding over three peeling columns, the words " People's House " stood out clearly in stone.

Once you had passed the columns you would note in the corridor a large door of cracked oak on which was a white square of paper. Serge mounted the warm steps and peered shortsightedly at the paper. His father's handwriting. There was something senile and yet youthful smiling at him in the fantastic flourishes of the characters. In a deep sighing undertone a sad memory of his childhood overflowed his heart like a wave. Snow-white blossoms of the almond trees under the window in the garden ; his pale, silent mother kissing him and trying a new blouse on him. . . . This was long ago and like the misty images of a dream. He had not seen his father for years, not since he had left home for good.

The librarian, Verochka, his former pupil, bewildered and confused as ever, had encountered him in town (of course, she would !). She could never speak to him, but her eyes and nervous tremor seemed to await his words. And then she could only whisper as usual.

" So it's you ? Serge Ivanitch. . . . I was looking for . . ."

In her hands a piece of paper fluttered like a bird.

" Have you come from father, Verochka ? "

" From Ivan Arsenitch. Yes, yes. . . . Oh, if you only knew ! "

She was smiling and could not turn from him her round eyes glittering with wonder.

" Are you still in the library, Verochka ? Hasn't my old man bored you to death yet with his chatter about so many deep and useless subjects ? "

But she could not answer him, and just threw him her astonished smile.

And in the senile-childish handwriting of his father he read :

" MY SON,—When I think that consciousness defines life, it is a great victory of my immortal thought over the caprice of destiny. When one takes into account the priority of existence over consciousness, one realises that man is but nothing in his pride. Why this is so you will discover when you find the courage to call on me in my temple of books. I want to see you over some trifling matters which are, therefore, very troublesome (for trifles are always troublesome). I am sitting in my temple among my books, which are stirring and swarming like cockroaches. I am smiling and reading Marcus Aurelius. A bookworm and, by the accident of chance,—YOUR FATHER."

Serge smiled affectionately while reading the note.

Troubled by a vague presentiment he went to the library. He saw in imagination his father's head, bald like his own, but with rebellious ash-coloured hair surrounding it like a halo, and his beard which stuck out at right angles to his chin. There was something child-like in this head and something weak and restless in his inadequately expressed wisdom.

Serge saw through the cool dark corridor which stank repulsively of mice, through a partly opened door, a vast hall bathed in dusty twilight with far-away rows of books on shelves. He heard the murmuring rustle of pages.

In this hall once upon a time there had been a cinema. The floor sloped slightly. There were only two narrow windows. That was why there was always this dusk as in a temple. There was also the tranquillity of a temple, ancient and saturated with decay. No walls could be seen : only books from floor to ceiling, in flowing parallel rows. Why were there so many books ? Could a man read them all during his brief sentient life ? Were they squeezed so tightly on the shelves because man had grown alarmed at their numbers, threatening to devour his life, and he pining for the light of the sun.

Verochka smiled behind a pile of books on the counter, enraptured and amazed.

" Serge Ivanitch ! Is it possible ? Ivan Arsenitch. . . . Just a moment. . . ."

In the centre of the hall, like an altar-piece, was a large bookstand, full of books, and near it with his streaming grey hair was Serge's father, clad in a long linen smock. He looked at his son from afar, raising his eyebrows. As Serge approached his father, stepping cautiously over the inclined floor, he noticed that he was barefooted; his feet were disfigured and dirty, covered with bunions and scars.

"You love me—I can see it. Come to me at my altar and sit down. You had eyes like those even when you were a child—the eyes of one possessed."

He spoke and laughed in a confused whisper. He looked at him sharply and steadily, with an anxious questioning gaze.

"Do you know what it is to be possessed, Serge? It is stoicism; an unbounded curiosity about life. Such people suffer because there exists a sad necessity in the world: namely, sleep."

Serge smiled at his father's friendly words; and, as always when in his presence, felt joyfully excited. He seemed gigantic and inexplicably near to him.

His father was laughing very low and keeping his anxious questioning gaze upon Serge. He had something of the curiosity of a person who verifies the solution of a problem. With his trembling fingers he was stuffing bits of his beard into his mouth, and laughing mockingly. Serge felt that he had something serious and grievous to tell him.

"Don't you feel depressed in this cavern, father?"

"The fate of all books, Serge, is to be the prison of thought. Each book is a noose for human liberty. Isn't it true that all these shelves look like iron bars? Aspiring to immortality, the human spirit produces a book—its own tomb. An inexorable doom, Serge: man is in permanent rebellion, and rebellion is no more than a leap from one prison to another; from one's mother's womb into the womb of society, into the shackles of obligatory rules, and from there—into the grave! Marcus Aurelius was no fool: he knew how to sense freedom while rattling his chains, and possessed sufficient wisdom to look through the walls of his prison."

"Father, I think that real liberty is only in the creative union of our will with dialectic necessity. Man is immortal in the dynamics of creative collectivism."

His father looked at him attentively with the stern smile of a sceptic.

"Why don't you inquire about your mother? How would you feel if she were to die to-day?"

Serge remained silent for a moment, looking into his father's eyes.

"Is she very bad? I'd like to see her, if only for a minute."

"She's dying from a sorrowful love for her children. She's dying, little Serge."

His eyebrows quivered in a smile that was full of anguish.

"But I'm not going to die. Be calm. Real life, my son, means freedom from dependence on sequence. As the world is only relative, real happiness consists in losing oneself in the moment. Not only Marcus Aurelius, but even Lucretius Carus himself, could have made a friend of me."

Serge felt a beneficent calm and tranquillity in his soul. In the intervals of his tense and strenuous days, poisoned by sleepless nights, he could blissfully abandon himself in this bookish silence, let his soul rest without thought, remain undisturbed and alone. His nights in his little room in the House of the Soviets were torturing nightmares, haunted by headaches; for the House of the Soviets never slept, and for twenty-four hours it was full of tobacco smoke and telephone bells, and every fibre of one's mind was woven into the electric network of the Republic. There were no days and nights in the House of the Soviets—there was just a little room in which one felt the agony of over-strain, the austerity of effort and self-immolation.

"My dear Serge, your mother is very ill. Go to her. Yes, yes. Even if you don't talk to her, just look at her as you used to when a child and you will give her great happiness."

Serge became more and more troubled. In the confused words of his father he felt an intolerable anxiety which imbued his words with a special meaning. It had always been so: neither in the days of his childhood nor of his youth had Serge ever come close to his father's soul, which seemed to dissolve into the depths of his eyes, leaving nothing behind. His father had always seemed like a young child, and passed his days in the twilight of the library. He looked with dismay and perplexity at the money he received for his work; he was a stranger in his own home, laughing shyly when the mother spoke to him, always in a hurry. The mother filled the whole house from kitchen to bedroom; and even in the night amidst his dreams, his mother's face, worn with care and with eyelids moist and swollen, appeared and disappeared.

"Come on, father. I want to see her now."

"Yes, yes, little Serge. You have delighted me very much . . . very much. But listen: How will you look and behave if you meet your brother, Dimitri? Your brother, your brother. . . . Don't ask me about him; I fear him more than I fear you. At any rate, I fear no one and nothing because I am full of curiosity, my dear; and as you know, curiosity is nothing other than wisdom. Frightfulness, my dear Serge, is not in the depths of things, but only in the simple elements of movement—in a passing glance, in a gesture or a cry. In this, my friend, is the crucifixion of man : the curse which rests upon him."

2

AT THE MOTHER'S BEDSIDE

The orchard, surrounded by its fence, lay in a brownish mist. Bare branches and twigs were crossed and interwoven into flexible knots. Only the almond trees bloomed with thick swarms of white flowers.

This garden had been planted by his father's own hands when Serge was still a boy. He walked along by the fence, looking through the chinks, and saw the well-known trees and neglected paths and the arbour of lattice-work covered with clusters of wild grapes. He had hammered it together while he was still a high-school boy. And the stone house seemed near and yet distant, like a memory of childhood.

"Was it a long time ago, my little Serge, since you were living and growing up here ? Do you remember your attic ? "

The old man laughed, gripped Serge's hand and then at once released it. His scarred feet tripped on in short steps. And Serge realised that his father was glad to see him and was ashamed of his own joy. And suddenly Serge noticed for the first time the slovenly and neglected appearance of his father and the empty profundity of his eyes.

"Your revolution is one of the happiest revolutions in history, Serge."

The garden shimmered in the sun as though drunken by the sweet exhalations of the spring soil and the bursting buds, and by the dancing almond-blooms. There was the window of that attic where he had spent his childhood and school years.

At the end of the path, which was covered with last year's leaves, under the snowy foam of the almond-tree—which from afar appeared rainbow-tinted—stood a tall, one-armed man with shaven skull. He wore a white blouse which revealed his bare dark chest, and Cossack breeches. His bony eye-sockets were cut deep into his face ; a long nose protruded like a beak over his short upper lip.

" Father, I feel that meeting Dimitri will not bring us any good. Once we parted as friends and now we may meet as foes."

The one-armed man looked at them from afar with a sharp, bird-like glance, and his long, thin face grinned like a skull. He beckoned with his right hand—the only one—and shouted in a strong, singing voice in the manner of a cavalry soldier :

" With all my heart and soul, welcome to the knight of the Red Star under the peaceful paternal roof ! Ha, ha, my little Serge ! Hullo, dear friend ! "

A joyful laugh resounded under the flowering almonds, but there was something strained and insincere about his words. He did not come to meet Serge but stood there, in his yellow leggings, firmly rooted to the earth.

Serge waved his free hand in response and with a nervous tremor and clouded eyes went up the steps of the porch.

As in the old days, his mother's little room was darkened by lowered blinds and encumbered with clothes and chests-of-drawers and trunks. As always, there was the same warm stuffy smell of long years of intimate snugness. And every time that Serge thought of his mother, he could sense this odour so strongly that he had the hallucination of its actual presence.

This smell was an inseparable part of the tranquillity which slumbered within these old-fashioned walls which were saturated with the history of his days. Furniture and household objects were piled up in the corners owing to the recent billeting of other people in the dwelling.

From the downy white pillows a parchment skull, with black plaits pressed down upon the hollow cheeks, was gazing at Serge. He approached the bed on tip-toe. In the twilight of death he gazed long into the strange face of his mother : strange as if he had never seen her before. He took her hand and felt a strong vibration pass from her body to his.

This hand, trembling with love, and this skull framed in plaits, were alien to him, and yet near and dear even unto tears. Serge inhaled the immortal odour of his old home, and did not know what to do amidst these piled-up effects ; he did not know what to do with this fading hand.

His mother looked dumbly and fixedly at him from the clouded depths of her dying eyes.

Serge himself was silent and with an inward shudder awaited his mother's whisper. He was not expecting a voice or a shriek but a whisper. But there were only eyes behind the eyelashes which were stuck together.

And Dimitri was standing close to Serge. A jeering, amused light was in his eyes. He was full of life, with such great bones that his skin appeared too tight; there was something of the bird of prey in the curve of his brow and the line of his gristly beak.

The vibrating cord snapped and the mother's hand dropped on to the bed.

The father was smiling, his clear gaze unshadowed.

" How strange that you are my children. How strange that you two are both strangers—to each other and to me."

Ironic and distant, Dimitri's eyes flashed jeeringly.

" As you see, Serge, father jests as formerly, like old Diogenes in his tub. He nourishes himself only on flies and his own words. He is as free from sin as a sparrow and I love him very much."

Serge felt the weight of his brother's gaze and asked him brusquely :

" Where have you been until now ? We haven't heard a thing of you for years ? "

" I shan't tell you. Otherwise I should only lie or tell you the wrong thing. I was a colonel on the German front and then invalided home. Now I'm a citizen without definite occupation."

Dimitri suddenly raised the hand of his mother and kissed it, the kiss shaking the sick woman like a blow. She looked at him with dumb terror and could not turn her eyes from his face.

Dimitri's eyes glinted still and he squeezed Serge's shoulder.

" It's a long time since I saw you, Serge. . . . Since the years of our youth. . . . Let us embrace."

But Serge turned from him with a vague anxiety and moved towards his father.

Dimitri burst out laughing, made a military half-turn to the right and walked out, the blue-shaven back of his head glistening.

Two deep wrinkles blackly lined the broad brow of the father. With trembling hand he pulled at his beard which he wanted to put into his mouth, but always it escaped him.

Pale, with dim eyes and an anguished smile, he leaned with his back against the wall.

" What's the matter with you, father ? "

" Be stoically hard and don't give way to temptations, Serge. But there are times when even a stoic is a slave of his feelings. Learn how to study people from behind your shield, Serge . . . from behind your shield. . . ."

The mother, in a mad effort of pain, raised herself on her elbow and again subsided on to the pillows. In her eyes were humility, silence and terror.

Serge, shaken, slowly left the room, descended the porch steps and, hastening now, walked down the avenue to the gate.

On the street near the fence, he collided with Dimitri. His brother, his hand in the pocket of his wide Cossack breeches, looked at him sharply, screwing up his eyes.

" My best wishes, Serge ! We shall see each other again, won't we ? In other surroundings, Serge ? And then we can talk together at our leisure. Best wishes ! "

He bowed affectedly and bared his teeth. But his eyes did not laugh ; their sharp glance was stabbing Serge.

Chapter VIII

BURNING DAYS

I

WORKERS' BLOOD

In these days the sun was not burning; the sky was white-clouded. There was not enough air for one's lungs; and the town and mountains, the people and the docks, were all whipped by the wind which went rocking in whirlwinds of pebbles. The days burned only in the hearts of men, hearts that throbbed heavily.

Gleb, with his helmet pushed back on his head, was running to the Council of Trade Unions, to the Party Committee (Call immediately an Aggregate Meeting of the Party for the whole town !), to the Railway Men's Union (Comrades, hasten the dispatch of tank cars to the petrol refinery !), to the Factory Administration, to the power-house where Brynza and the Diesels waited all ready for work.

Shidky was clapping Gleb heavily on the back and burning with enthusiasm.

" God damn you, old Chumalov ! Harness yourself to the factory instead of the dynamos and you'll be able to make it work all by yourself. We ought to send you to Europe—you'd start a hell of a row there ! "

" That's an ideal ! Let's get Europe all worked up ! "

" The main thing, Chumalov, is not to forget that you are above everything a Communist. All our reconstruction isn't worth a damn unless it's burned in the red fire of revolution. Remember this and keep a sharp look-out."

" Yes, we're going straight ahead, Shidky. We're doing our level best ! The only thing is not to do it too well, not shoot beyond our mark ! That's the danger ! "

" I love you, Chumalov, you're a real man ! "

Gleb, nostrils quivering, breathed shortly with emotion.

He ran to Lukhava. But as usual Lukhava was not at the Trade Union Council, he could not stay within the walls of

his office. Every day from morning till night he was running
from one union to the other, to the various workshops, entering into all the details of production and into the life of the
workers ; organising special meetings, settling disagreements,
cursing the wasters and inscribing on the Red Roll of Honour
the heroes of toil. He haunted the offices, mills, workshops,
the economic services, the food department, fingering papers,
ordering, requesting, jostling, arousing fear and evoking
storms of enthusiasm. He was never worn out, never knew
the meaning of exhaustion ; in his eyes a fervid inextinguishable fire burned.

That's how he entered into the souls of the workers.

Gleb used to leave him notes :

" Hurry along the Railwaymen's Union Committee."

" Put the screws on the Economic Council for sabotage and
red tape."

" Give a kick to the Factory Committee of the oil refineries."

And Lukhava ran hither and thither, bronzed, fiery-eyed, his
hair streaming like black flames.

At the factory the electricians had commenced the repairs
to the installation. In the workmen's quarters, electric light
bulbs, taken from the factory store, had been fixed in the empty
sockets. The lamps glittered and cast genial reflections in the
windows ; at the sight of them the women and children were
moved to smiles and the grey mask of hunger on the faces of
the workmen melted away in a happy presentiment.

No more pipe-lighters were being made in the repair shops.
Different work was going on now : in a whirlwind of iron
clanging, gnashing, whistling, hissing and murmuring, the
machines were coming back to life. Workmen in blue shirts
stained with copper passed each other in the courtyards going
from workshop to workshop, building to building. But
neither Loshak nor Gromada were there. They had other cares:
the Factory Committee. In the Factory Committee office,
down in the basement under the factory offices, in the rooms
reeking of cement and cheap tobacco—tobacco rank enough
to make the Devil kick up his heels—people were crowding
and trampling from door to door, and the walls and windows trembled with the echoes of shouts and bellowing
laughter.

Factory Committee. . . . Increased rations. . . . Distribution of forces. . . . Ropeway. . . . Whirlwind of machinery
in the machine-shop. . . . Liquid fuel. . . . To-morrow the

dynamos will be working and by to-morrow night the factory will awaken. . . .

Gleb—he was the workers' representative on the Factory Management—rushed hither and thither, dripping with sweat, laughed, caught up tools, cut, sawed, drilled and could not keep pace with the mad tempo of his heart.

He often called on Brynza who would receive him with cries which filled the great engine-room.

" Ho, ho, Commander ! it's moving ! The machines are ready ! Fuel, my Commander, we must have fuel ! That and nothing else ! Now you've risen out of hell, the merry-go-round will start. I know it will ! Your head's a machine like my Diesels. Fuel—petrol and benzine ! That's all we need ! If you don't let me have some in two days I'll blow myself up and the Diesels too. And when I fly sky-high, I'll drag you with me by the feet ! "

Among the machines his assistants—who all looked rather like him—were moving about, cleaning and making the metal resound. Brynza nodded to them and winked under his peaked cap, joyfully showing his teeth.

" You see : the brothers have started work with a big push ! The idle chatter and trifling of the past years are forgotten, my friend. That's what the power of machines means. So long as the machines are alive, we can't get away from them. The yearning for machines is stronger than that for a sweetheart."

And suddenly his great voice filled the whole shop :

" Fuel, fuel ! Ten tanks—that'll be enough for the first go. Ten tanks ! Or I'll cut you in pieces, Commander ! "

Together with Engineer Kleist, the technicians and the workmen from the quarries, they walked along the valley, through the grass-grown yards. Grave, silent and sunkeneyed, Engineer Kleist was examining the old ropeway.

Two technicians of the old staff of the factory from traditional habit were walking two steps behind the engineer, rushing up to him with servile alacrity at the first silent nod of his head. The engineer did not look at Gleb but Gleb knew well that the engineer realised only his presence and lived only in his power. When Kleist talked to the technicians Gleb felt that he was really speaking to him, and that he was expecting from him words he would not be able to contradict.

They decided to repair the whole transportation system of the factory and to carry the ropeway from the highest stage in the quarries up to the crest of the mountain, about 800 metres.

And once again seated in his office (both windows were now wide open), Engineer Kleist said, after having worked on the plans and estimates :

" If we have a guarantee that the specifications will be fully approved and that sufficient labour is furnished us, the work can be completed within one month."

Gleb bent down towards the engineer and slapped his hand upon the papers.

" Comrade Technologist, the work must be accomplished within four days. Five thousand workmen are at your disposition. Material will be given you by the factory management upon your instant demand. If there's any sabotaging I'll smash them to bits : we've taken worse Bastilles than this. Not a month, but four days only, Comrade Technologist ! Take good note of it, and hit straight for the target."

Engineer Kleist looked closely at Gleb. For the first time a pale smile lit his face.

The coopers' shop was simply a useless shed. The glass roof had been smashed by mischievous stone-throwing children. Sticks, metal junk, broken hoops and all kinds of rubbish lay on the framework and on the few panes that remained. The work-benches, belting and circular-saws were covered with rust and with dust from the mountains and high roads, brought by the wind, that good grave digger. And over everything was a blue misty light. Three years ago, were not the work-benches, saws and unfinished barrels blue and icily transparent through this light ?

Gleb came here also and stopped on the threshold. In former times the golden shavings burned in fiery spirals, and the coopers, themselves covered with shavings and surrounded by flying sparks, were gay, intoxicated with the wine-like smell of wood and with the siren-song of the saws.

Gleb did not step forward ; this was enough to turn one's head—there was so much to do. But the day would come when this place would have its turn also : the shavings would glitter again and the sawdust fly, and the saws sing again their songs of youth.

He wanted to go away, called by work, work—work everywhere, but stopped, a laugh leaping to his face. Savchuk ! He was sitting with his back to Gleb, at his old bench, examining it, trying the treadle with his foot, testing the bench with his fist, trying its solidity until it wheezed and coughed like an old man.

" Ha, ha ! You're groaning, you old bastard ! Well, straighten yourself out. You've not forgotten how to work, eh ? "

He walked barefooted up to the saws and struck their ice-like discs with his big paw. They rang with remote reverberations as though in a dream.

" Ha, ha, my nice round girls ! You've grown pock-marked with no man to handle you. Let's see what kind of songs you'll sing ! Just wait a bit—some men will be here soon. We're going to breed barrels from you. Not barrels for women to pickle cabbage in, but barrels to go beyond the seas to all parts of the earth. Not carrying cabbage but cement. Ah, my lonely ones—you'll get your bridegrooms."

This damned Savchuk ! Big as a bear, and you can't get round him with either curses or kisses ! Yet here in this shed he's lamenting and whispering like a lovesick boy. Does this look like our Savchuk, going on like this—the hairy devil with legs like a cart-horse and fists as big as wheelbarrows ? "

Gleb didn't dare to laugh and disturb Savchuk. When a man's healthy strength is awakening and his blood is rising, he must not be interfered with. It is the deepest and most important moment in his life.

Gleb walked quietly out of the workshop. Outside in the sun once more, he struck his palm upon his helmet and was convulsed with laughter.

" That God-damned Savchuk ! You'll be the death of me with laughing ! "

During that day when the stones and rails seemed melting in the sun and the empty factory shimmered in its rays, a panting locomotive, belching steam, came hauling along towards the factory a train of tank cars with benzine and oil. Workmen in long blouses came out to welcome it, shouting and waving their hands.

2

A LEAP OVER DEATH

The Executive Committee of the Soviet had received a telephone message that Borchi, Chairman of the District Executive Committee had horse-whipped Saltanov, Chief of the District

Militia, who had been sent to aid him in the requisition of grain. Also that Saltanov had fired at Borchi.

It was reported that Saltanov, with a detachment of Red soldiers, was attacking the Cossacks and townspeople, was clearing the grain out of the granaries and driving the last of the cattle from their stalls. Then when the wagons, under a convoy of Red soldiers, were travelling towards the District Executive Headquarters, the band played the " International," while the peasant women followed the carts, striking their heads against the wheels, and mingling their wails with the noise of the cows and sheep. It was then, during the music, that the encounter between Borchi and Saltanov had taken place.

Badin was reading the transcript of the telephone message with his usual calm stony face and Secretary Peplo stood near the table awaiting his orders with his usual broad pink smile.

" Here's a nice bunch of fools ! One fighting the other ! Have a carriage got ready at once, Comrade Peplo. I'm going to look into this affair myself."

" Right ! "

" Will you please telephone to the Party Committee for Comrade Chumalova to come here at once. She has been asking for horse and cart to go to the same place. I will drive her there."

" Good ! Shall I inform Comrade Chumalova that you will make the journey with her ? "

Secretary Peplo gazed at Badin with blinking eyelids, smiling sweetly.

The Chairman lifted his gaze to Peplo's face, and the Secretary recoiled a step from the table, but the smile did not fade from his face.

" Right ! "

Badin sat, heavy as though cast from iron, his chest against the table, his head sunk between his shoulders as though it were heavier than his body.

Scarcely had the Secretary left the room when Badin got up, swung his arms high, then walked up and down the room. The metallic heaviness of his head and shoulders was gone ; he stood erect, big-boned with flexible muscles and head obstinately set.

In the Women's Section, Mekhova caught Dasha in the corridor, and placing her arm within hers, walked with her to the exit.

" Look here, Dasha : wouldn't it be better to send another delegate in your place ? You're ordered somewhere every week and the others are only having a soft time at home. Attacks on the road are becoming more and more frequent. We must take care of you ; we can't easily replace you. Every time you go away I'm worried about you."

" Comrade Mekhova, you should be ashamed to talk like this. I'm not a little girl any more and know my own business. What kind of a Women's Section should we have with our hearts in our boots all the time from fear ? "

Polia looked at her anxiously and stopped. Dasha patted her hand affectionately and walked sharply into the street, swinging her portfolio—which she had made herself—which contained everything : papers and bread.

At the front door of the Executive Headquarters stood a carriage, black and lustrous. The bearded coachman was blowing his nose to pass the time and wiping it on the ample lapel of his coat.

On the boulevard, befouled with rubbish and trampled by people and beasts, two boys in torn overalls, with blue swollen faces, were rolling about in the dust. The dust whirled above them like dirty smoke disappearing in the brown branches of the acacia trees. Dasha stopped near the carriage, looked down the boulevard, and then up at the open window of the Executive Chairman's office. Then she again looked down the boulevard.

Who were these children ? What were these strays doing here ? What is the Militia doing, and why is the Children's Commissariat so blind and helpless ? Or has it strayed far like these miserable children ?

She crossed the cobbles and approached the railing of the boulevard. There she stood for some minutes watching the wrestling of the dirty little imps.

" Kiddies, who wants bread ? I know your little bellies are empty. Come here ! "

The boys pricked up their ears like little startled puppies. The woman was smiling in a homely way and was not at all frightening. There was a red scarf on her head and she held the piece of bread in her hand. The red scarf inspired fear (for long had they known that this scarf stood for power), but the bread was new and, even at some paces away, they could smell the moist malt odour.

" Yes, yes. . . . We know. . . . You call us like that, and then you'll send us into the Home."

One of the two boys shook his tatters and took to his heels like a running scarecrow. Dasha started laughing and broke the bread into two pieces.

" But do come here, little piggies ! I'm not going to take you to the Home. Here, there's a piece for each of you. But what little cowards you are ! "

She was so jolly and friendly (if it weren't for the red scarf !) and the golden bread should be sweet as honey.

The boys glanced sideways at each other, and approached slowly and furtively, stretching out their hands from as far away as possible. She gave them each a piece of bread. She wanted to pat the tangled hair of the second one. But he shrieked and rushed away in terror.

Nurka was in the Children's Home, but was she happier than these naked little beasts ? Dasha had once seen Nurka with the other children digging in the rubbish heap behind the dining-room of the Food Commissariat. It had seemed to her then that her daughter was already dead, and that she, Dasha, was no longer her mother ; that Nurka had been abandoned to hunger and suffering through Dasha's fault. It seemed that her occasional caresses in the Children's Home were not the fondling of a mother, but of a sterile blooming. She had carried the little girl in her arms right to the Children's Home and her heart was ravaged with pain.

Badin was standing near the carriage now, his black leather coat shining. He looked straight at Dasha from under his bony forehead.

" Get in, Comrade Chumalova, and we'll be off."

He did not wait for her but clambered in, and all the springs creaked under his weight. Dasha sat beside him and felt the unyielding pressure of his hip. Badin took more notice of her ; he was reserved, cold and severe as usual.

" It's impossible to make this journey in an automobile. Even in this carriage we shall only go at a snail's pace in the mountain. Are you afraid of bandits ? I'm only taking my revolver with me. Perhaps I should have arranged for some Red Cavalrymen to accompany us ? "

Dasha glanced at him. Was Badin himself afraid ? But she could not make out. His face was firm and immovable as always—a face of bronze.

" Just as you wish, Comrade Badin. If you are afraid, order an escort. But I'm accustomed to be sent away without an escort."

" Right then ! Off we go, Comrade Yegoriev ! "

Comrade Yegoriev, frightened, turned round two or three times looking at Badin, longing to say something, but unable to get it out. Then he clucked to his horse, blew his nose and gathered up the reins.

While they were driving through the town they were silent and it was unaccustomedly pleasant and gay for Dasha to swing along so comfortably and easily.

On the street they saw Serge. He inclined his red bald spot to her, and his ruddy curls shook like wood shavings. Shuk met them also and stood still astonished with a confused expression on his face.

Badin's thick lips curled with a disgusted smile.

" I can't stand that type."

" Comrade Shuk ? Really ? But he's a good turner and a conscientious Communist. He doesn't like our generals and bureaucrats and worries a lot about it.

" Shuk is simply a good-for-nothing and a disrupter. Such fellows should certainly be driven out of the Party."

" No, Comrade Badin. Comrade Shuk is good and he speaks the truth. And when he finds something out, you're all angry. Is that right ? Isn't it true that all you responsible Party workers see the working-class only from your private workrooms ? "

" You're mistaken. The private office of a responsible militant is nearer to the working-class than are such wranglers as your good Comrade Shuk; because everything passes through these offices, from complicated questions of state to the smallest details of daily life. It was in the private bureau of a responsible Party worker that I made the acquaintance of your husband."

He laughed, not with his customary laugh, but like the roll of a drum ; and his words and his laugh were alike. This laugh of Badin's always disquieted Dasha.

The town was already behind them. They were driving through the ravine ; on the left the mountain slope was covered with vineyards ; on the right was a wood still bare and blue, dusky, with burst buds decking the branches like cobwebs. The trees were moving : the front rows retiring, and the succeeding rows going forward with Dasha ; and it seemed that the wood was revolving, in commotion, accomplishing some immense labour hidden from human eyes.

" Well, and how is your homelife getting on ? On the one hand marriage duties : a common bed and dirty linen. On the other hand Party work. And I believe that you have also offspring. You'll have to choose between the Women's Section and home cares. No doubt your husband is already making specific demands. You've a big-fisted lad there."

Dasha shrank back in her corner. A wave of disquiet flowed from her heart to her head.

" My husband lives his life and I live mine, Comrade Badin. We're Communists first of all, and not loafers."

Badin's laugh again drummed out. He placed his hand on Dasha's knee.

" You speak like all women Communists, but the bed is the bed all the same. Although it sounds more sincere from you than from most ; from you it comes from the heart. I know already how difficult it is to find common ground with you."

Dasha pushed his hand from her knees and drew herself as far away as she could.

" Comrade Badin, Communists can always meet on common ground in their common work."

Badin again became reserved and heavy as iron. He stirred away from Dasha and she caught a flare in his eyes which affected her painfully.

" Sit more comfortably. I'm not going to eat you."

He twisted his lips in an offensive smile.

" I'm not afraid of your teeth, Comrade Badin. We know each other well."

They journeyed in silence, each looking away on his or her side of the carriage, along the ravine, where the morning was darkened by cliffs and thickets, where brook murmured and coloured boulders lay. But Dasha sensed how Badin's blood leaped, and how he hid the clamour of his heart with a broken cough. She knew he was fighting within himself, without having the strength to throw himself violently upon her. She knew that he was not yet tamed ; when he was close to her a frenzied beast stormed in his eyes. If at this instant he was not going to throw himself upon her, he would seek another moment when he would be stronger than she. She felt her blood throb with suspense and could not conquer her anxiety, her fear for her own strength. If it were to happen now, she could not resist his muscles of a maddened bull ; the unsteady swaying of the carriage over the rutted road prevented her bracing herself firmly to resist him.

The ravine was three miles long, and then came a smooth,

wide road through the valley. At the end of it lay the Cossack town, at the foot of the hills among gardens and orchards.

The mountains rose with cliffs and steep, brown slopes to the sky. Cliffs and rocks flamed in the sun ; the twisting ridges and heaps of stone and slag seemed to flow like streams of molten metal. Down below the hovering misty darkness quivered over the woods and thickets. Above the mountains and woods streamed the blue sky, and the clouds stood in it like ice-bergs. The wood down below seemed to have been hurled from the steeps : impassable, and the night crept, fertile and moist, through the dense forests, sighing and rustling with dim foreboding.

One could not see the road ahead : it was broken by rocks and boulders, to right and left, above and below. In front of them they saw a wood, entangled with lianas, with ferns and bushes growing among crags—a wild place. It appeared to move away when they reached it, this wood with its mossy stones and cliffs moistened with the tears of subterranean rivulets ; to the right and left it moved away, plunging down precipices and climbing cliff-terraces—a terrible height ! Dasha did not see the crest, she shut her eyes and crouched in her corner like a little girl. And beyond there were other twilight ravines, full of a dread speaking stillness, where mysteries lay hidden or bandits' lairs were concealed.

Comrade Yegoriev turned round on the box, his beard flicking his shoulder. His eyes shone moistly out of the shaggy thicket of eyebrows and beard :

" You were wrong, Comrade Chairman, not to have had a Cavalry escort. The robbers are bound to kill us here. Speculators get murdered here nearly every day. You've made a mistake, Comrade Chairman."

Dasha remembered having seen eyes like this before. Such slimy eyes crawled in the shadows of counter-revolutionary cellars.

Badin, restrained, bursting with blood and quivering from its bestial throbbing, sat deep in the cushions of the phaeton. He was as though made of stone, fearless and calm ; but under his heavy brows, in his steady eyes, deep in those eyeballs of dark mother-of-pearl, excitement burned from the throbbing of his blood. Was it danger intoxicating him, or the heady fumes of Dasha's nearness? How could Yegoriev fear the roving bandits when Badin was here, so invincibly strong and brave ? The stony weight of Badin was oppressive and painful to Dasha, who sat motionless. Yet it was pleasant in these dark hours to feel the reliable support in this man of steel.

Badin smiled and stared at Yegoriev's beard.

" Cowardice is more dangerous than bandits, Comrade Yegoriev. Carry on with your job and hold firmly to your reins and whip. The road is not so bad."

Yegoriev bent as though under a blow. He no longer raised his voice to urge the horses on; just tightening the reins he turned his head from side to side, gulping his saliva with difficulty.

They drove on another mile. Suddenly, Dasha felt Badin's muscles become tense; it was obvious he was fighting with all his strength against his emotions, his secret impulse. He breathed deeply, and pressed her into the corner of the carriage with the full weight of his body. One arm was round her shoulders, the other on her breast.

" Comrade Badin. . . . You dare not, Comrade Badin! Take your hands away! For shame! "

He smiled drunkenly. He breathed heavily through his nostrils, and his face was pale.

" On the contrary, I do dare, and don't see any great shame in it. We're a good virile couple and it's not becoming for us to pretend and babble hypocritical words. Let me be! You know very well I never give in when there's a fight! And what I want to do, I do! In a struggle, I use all means."

Dasha struggled convulsively to free herself from his hands, but Badin pressed her more closely, suffocating her, causing her to shriek out. He pulled her closer to himself and for a moment she saw his enormous black head and maddened bony face. Then his face stifled her with savage kisses and the strong odour of a man's sweat.

Then suddenly she felt the blood of his hands, lips and nostrils surging upon her; then followed a languor, a wave of feminine weakness, of confused delight and fear. She could feel only her heart hammering ceaselessly in her breast. And one other thing she knew: she must fight furiously, strike, break his hands to catch him by the throat and strangle him, to get free from these iron, inhuman arms.

Suddenly the carriage gave a leap, flinging them about on the seat. The forest seemed to turn and flash up into the sky; and it seemed as though the cliff were crashing down upon them.

Dasha saw Yegoriev sway for a moment from side to side and then roll like a sack down upon the front wheel. At the same instant Badin tore himself from Dasha, and leaped forward seizing the reins. The horses began to struggle and rear between the shafts.

" Halt ! Hands up ! We've got you, you bastards ! "

From behind boulders and out of the bushes came creeping Circassian tunics and shaggy fur caps, rifle in hand.

Dasha saw only these caps and the eyes beneath them. She noticed their rapacious gleaming. Then she saw, near to them, a blond Cossack, hatless, with foaming lips, dashing towards the horses. His upper lip quivered, displaying swollen gums and small reddish teeth like nails.

Dasha had only time to shout convulsively :

" Drive on ! "

And she jumped from the carriage upon the Cossack, falling with him into the stone-filled ditch by the road.

Then an unbearable weight crashed down upon her, as though a whole crowd had fallen upon her and were dancing with their heels upon her flesh, forcing her into a narrow cleft. There was a sharp sour smell of wet wool and puttees. They were beating her ; she did not remember whether there were shots nor whether they pursued the carriage. It was as if she had been thrown into water, which was boiling in a red-hot tank ; and she knew only a roaring gulf and a crushing weight.

When she came to herself she was standing, leaning against a rock, and the whole band stood before her in a compact group, yelling at her, giving out stench of wet wool. She was being shoved about, her arms twisted and her hair pulled.

" Woman ! A bloody woman ! A woman ! The bitch ! Kick her in the guts ! "

There was no carriage ; only far away up the valley one could hear horses galloping and stones clattering down the slopes. As soon as Dasha heard this distant sound she recovered ; her mind and heart revived. Comrade Badin is there, and far along the road. Badin was unhurt.

On the other side of the road, opposite Dasha, with one leg raised against the cliff-side (a bare foot showing among leg-wrappings), Yegoriev lay on his coachman's coat ; his crushed hat lay in the road. His hair and ear and a part of his beard were congealed in blood.

Behind a rock a horse was snorting and kicking and

champing its bit. Other Cossacks ran hither and thither with sweaty dismayed faces.

" Bring her over here ! What the devil are you all doing here ? "

A moustached, fur-capped Cossack stopped by the rock and stood erect, his hand to the salute.

" A woman, Colonel. Let's hang her and have done with it ! She's the one that smashed Limarenko. Give us permission, Colonel."

" Bring her here and don't talk so much ! Instead of her I shall have all you cowards hanged ! You're only good for fighting women, you swine ! "

Growling, stumbling over their rifles, the group dragged Dasha along like a doll—she did not walk, but trailed along in their hands—over the stones and ruts, on to the grass, and placed her before a horse which was madly snorting, its eyes bulging, and prancing. Dasha felt the moist hot odour of horse flesh ; she felt shameless hands crawl greedily over her hips and thighs. The weapons rattled and voices cried together :

" Yes, it's really a woman, Colonel ! Let's crush the louse ! "

Dasha stood erect and looked straight at the Colonel. He regarded her steadily, swaying gently to the movement of his horse. He was wearing a Circassian cloak, a silver belt, silver epaulettes and a flat Kuban cap of Astrakan. His face was dirty and long unshaven ; his long black moustache fell over his lips and chin. His nose was snub with a shiny rounded tip ; and his bulging eyes flashed with laughter or with insult.

" Let her go ! Two paces to the rear ! "

And as it became lighter and freer around her and the air no longer smelt of moist wool, Dasha realised that she stood alone between this mounted officer and the band. She looked attentively at the Colonel. Her scarf had been torn off and trampled in the mêlée. Fighting with all her strength against the trembling in her knees she stood firmly planted in the earth.

" Your hair's bobbed. Are you a Communist ? "

" Yes, a working woman."

" Who was with you in the carriage ? "

" Comrade Badin, Chairman of the Polkom."[1]

" Polkom ? What language is that ?

" Russian. What else ? "

[1] Polkom, meaning the Executive Committee of the Soviet, is one of those composite words which have become so common after the revolution and which are formed by combining the first syllables of two or three words.—Tr.

" You lie. The Russian language is not like that. It's your jargon—Yiddish or thieves' slang."

" In Soviet Russia we haven't many thieves. We shoot them without mercy."

Someone guffawed behind her like a horse.

" The damned female. She chatters like a magpie ! "

" I'll hang her to one of these branches and then she'll chatter another tune."

Neither Dasha nor the Colonel ceased their steady gaze, one at the other.

" And are all your Communists like this Chief of yours ? Is it the proper thing to abandon comrades in danger ? "

" That never happens. I acted of my own accord."

The Colonel twisted his moustache. His cheeks quivered slightly and puffed out. He smiled.

" Your own accord ? Were you reckoning on our stupidity ? "

" It's your business to puzzle it out. I did it—and that's all ! "

The Colonel was swinging his riding-whip and looking at her with a smile of a Kalmuk idol.

And all the time Dasha felt an extraordinary relief. She breathed regularly and calmly ; her mind was empty—no thought, no pity and no fear for herself. It was as though she had never been as free and young as now. She was wondering why that lonely pine-tree on the cliff attracted her so ; just at the very top of the mountain—Oh, how high ! Why did she see for the first time this dense vapour over the mountain slopes, purple in hue ? But neither the pine-tree nor the purple air was really important ; there was something else, deep down, near, winged, to which she could not give a name.

" You speak frankly and without fear, you short-haired girl. You carry it off pretty gaily. This is the first case of its kind I have had. Usually when you Communists fall into my hands, you squirm like a lot of worms. Perhaps you count on my letting you go because you're a woman ? Don't imagine that for a moment. I'm going to hang you. I shall not shoot you, but just have you hanged."

" It's all the same to me. I was prepared for it."

The Colonel puffed out his cheeks, and his moustache was alive like a spider.

" I am your implacable enemy, and I destroy every Communist without mercy. However, I must admit that you carry yourself well. Now I want to see how you'll be under the noose."

Without taking his eyes off her he lifted his whip above his head.

" Baistriuk ! "

A bearded Cossack in a black shaggy fur cap walked out from the group. His beard did not hide his lips, which were red ; his eyes were green. He was mute, meek, heavy.

He took hold of Dasha and his hand was also heavy and clammy. It seemed it was not his hand leading her but that she carried his hand ; the hand seemed enormous to her as though at any moment she might fall beneath the burden of it.

That pine-tree on the mountains in the opaque fiery air. Oh, how high ! There was a sweet intoxicating smell of spring ; the young leaves were uncurling and changing their colours like glow-worms into rainbow hues. The brook played with the stones as though they were rattles. And this heavy intolerable hand was dragging her down. Dasha's mind was so clear, although without thoughts ; instead, purple, shimmering air. Everything was so clear, so transparent and winged. And because the hand was pressing like a dead body upon her and because the pine-tree on the peak was beckoning her, Dasha wanted to remember something, but could not : something extremely important which could not be put off. How sweet was the spring air ? The pine-tree in flight leaned over the precipice, stretching its wings. Oh, how high ! Yes, yes. . . . This was the essential : Comrade Badin was alive, Comrade Badin, a valuable militant. And she, Dasha, is only a blade of grass ; she was—and is no more.

Near her the hairy man was sniffing and blowing his nose. She did not see him ; she saw only the air and the purple depths.

There was the rasping of a rope somewhere . . . far away . . . at the back of her neck . . . it did not touch her senses or hurt her at all.

Yes, yes, Gleb . . . but that happened so long ago. Dear, stupid Gleb ! He's so big and near and foolish. He flashed across her mind, but she felt no regret. Oh, how far away : the purple depths, the pine-tree and the rain of fire among the spring trees.

Again the rope came sliding through her consciousness, and again the heavy hand like a dead body pressed upon her shoulder.

Yes, she was walking back under the sky. In front was the brown slope and behind the dim forest; and behind that, in the airy distance, up to the very sky, was the green mountain.

The Colonel was again looking at her stubbornly like a bull. His moustache hung wet like a rag upon his lips and chin.

Except for herself and this man on horseback no one was there.

" You're pretty brave, you with the short hair! You played your part well. Especially as you're a woman. You can go. Not a dog will touch you."

With his whip he gave a swinging cut to his horse. In a couple of bounds it had disappeared in the thicket.

3

THE PUFFED-UP CHICKEN

Dasha could never remember how she came out of that valley. She did not remember whether she met anyone upon the road or whether she was alone, whether she ran like a scared hare or crawled with the last remnants of her strength. She remembered only one thing, bright and joyful: little grey-tufted birds flew away and then returned again. They twittered as she passed, flew away and back again. Perhaps this didn't really happen then in the valley, but only now—the little grey birds with tufts.

In the wide spaces before the mountains, spreading out in gently sloping lowlands, she felt that she was alone among these hills and bare misty distances. The road ran glowing and ash-coloured; and all the land seemed imbued with a primitive dread. The slopes crawled towards her like a blind intangible emptiness, transforming her into a grain of invisible dust.

The mountains behind her climbed, terrace upon terrace—precipices, cliffs; green slopes and valleys were slit with black ravines, shaggy with trees.

The ravine was deserted. Among these isolated silent hills, checkered with squares of ploughed land and pasturage, with the ash-coloured road broken by hills like camel-humps—she became helpless, lonely, condemned, abandoned to this limitless solitude.

The valley . . . the unbearable heavy hand. . . . Yes, yes, the pine-tree on the far-away mountain top.

Dasha ran on blinded with fear, her throat dry, her lungs scorched, her heart oppressed, suffocating.

In the distance, behind the swaying hills, on a high eminence, the Cossack town sprawled. It was all gardens, and above the gardens stood the belfry of the church like a white column with one black eye at the top. Behind the Cossack town and the hills the ridges of the mountains were dimly seen.

Dasha clambered up the hill, her strength was running out of her. The Cossack town was there in the distance, inhospitable, strange and morose. It was blind, but saw with the eyes of the steppes, like a she-wolf. It was the Cossack town, bearded and in fur cap, which had laid its deadly hand on Dasha and cast her into a lonely wilderness. It was blind, shaggy, earthy and its eyes were filled with wild blood.

Dasha stumbled over a stone and fell foremost into the dust of the road. A keen pain in her knee brought her again to her senses ; and lamed, she turned aside and sat down on the grass near a ploughed field. The roadside grass was decked with little yellow dandelions—very young flowers and so little, reminding one of chicks just hatched. They seemed to be running to Dasha's feet.

When Dasha saw these flowers a tenderness overcame her. Her heart beat rapidly, she cried out and burst into tears. Then she grew calm and silent. She could not arise ; she had no strength. All the time she gazed at the dandelions, thinking of nothing in particular, listening to the silence of the earth.

She could not tell whether it was the stillness twanging in her ears like a taut string, or whether it was a lark singing. She looked at the transparent feathery clouds. Chords vibrated far away. This was perhaps the clouds singing or the golden dandelions laughing.

Suddenly there appeared from behind the hill a troop of Red Cavalrymen, rifles slung on their backs, at a smart gallop. In front of them rode a dark man in black leather, riding at breakneck speed. Dasha started and jumped to her feet.

Comrade Badin !

The Red Cavalrymen were all shouting at once, grinning and waving their arms.

Dasha shouted back and ran towards Badin.

He reined in his horse and jumped from the saddle.

" Dasha ! "

She seized Badin's hand with both of hers, laughing and crying.

The Red soldiers surrounded them, shouting indistinguishable phrases.

One of the riders looked at her for some time silently. He had prominent cheek-bones, a large mouth and deep-sunken eyes. He dismounted and touched Dasha on the shoulder.

" Comrade, here's a horse for you. Mount. Let me help you up ! "

Dasha began to laugh, she began to pat the Red soldier's hand as she had Badin's.

" Thank you, Comrade. You're all such good people. You've turned out a whole regiment to come to my aid. Comrade Badin is out of breath."

The Red soldiers were standing in a cluster, their horses' flanks touching, looking at her surprisedly and laughing. The large-mouthed one put her up on the saddle, grinning from ear to ear, and still silent pulled the stirrup from the foot of another soldier and jumped on to the croup of the horse behind him.

Badin rode beside Dasha. The whole of the way he was attentive to her least word, helped her over difficult places, and saw that the girth, saddle and bridle were in order. Dasha noted his care and smiled gently to him.

" Well, what happened to you ? Tell us."

" Oh, nothing, Comrade Badin. They were a bit tough at first and then they let me go. They haven't much use for women. They whipped me—that's all."

She laughed again.

Badin looked at her sagaciously, with shrewd eyes and a clear smile—a smile that no one had seen before on the face of the Chairman of the Executive. Right up to the Cossack town they rode side by side.

In the village square in front of the Church and the headquarters of the District Soviet Executive, carts and unharnessed horses stood in rows and cattle were swishing their tails and restlessly nodding from side to side. Cossacks trampled and shouted as on a market day ; the women cried out piercingly. Boys, bareheaded or with fur caps, were spinning tops and playing leap-frog. Somewhere, either in the yard of the Executive or hidden in the crowd, a drunken voice sang hoarsely and sadly :

> " Puffed-up chicken,
> Naked and bare-foot."

The voice could not sustain the burden to the end.

It moaned, sobbed, choked, repeating the same words hoarsely over and over as though possessed.

Borchi, in a Caucasian mantle, dagger in belt, with his big rolling Asiatic eyes, sat at a table, diligently scribbling. He raised his head and glanced at Dasha and not a muscle moved on the face of this warrior of the Devil's Hundred. He just bellowed :

" Ah, you had luck, death passed you by this time ! "

Badin walked up to the table with a heavy stride, just as in his own office. He was once more cold and reserved.

" Comrade Borchi, call Saltanov here."

Borchi, with a subtle feminine grace, walked to the door.

" Comrade Saltanov, the Chairman of the Executive asks for you ! "

And then returned to his place still gracefully.

As soon as Saltanov had entered and approached the table, Badin, looking straight at him, said coldly between his teeth :

" Comrade Saltanov, you are relieved from the task which was imposed upon you and you are placed under arrest. To-morrow you will go to the town with Borchi. I shall then without delay pass the matter over to the Revolutionary Tribunal."

Saltanov gave a military salute and looked steadily at Badin with staring, laughing eyes. He took two steps backwards.

" I have conscientiously and precisely performed all the orders I received from the Executive of the Province."

Badin turned away and silently glanced at Borchi.

" Comrade Borchi, you will wind up this whole business to our best advantage. The hostility of the locality must be broken down. When you return from the town you will have to sift the matter to the bottom. Let's go to the Square."

When the three of them, Badin, Borchi and Dasha, came out upon the square where the loaded carts were standing, the Cossacks, peasants and women looked at them with their deep-sunk eyes. The loaded carts had been standing here for twenty-four hours. The peasants would not leave them and at night time they sat round bonfires like gipsies.

Badin jumped up on a cart and looked coldly at the crowd.

" Citizens, Cossacks and Peasants ! "

The women began to bustle about, shouting round the carts and drowned his words. As though maddened by the women's howls, the peasants began to shout. They waved their arms and their faces seemed to swell to the size of water-melons and to be about to burst.

Borchi also jumped up on the cart, waving his arms, shouting like a commander, deafeningly and wildly.

"Silence, Children of the Devil! Listen to what the Chairman of the Executive has to say to you! What's all this row about, we haven't any vodka. If we had we'd beat the drums."

He grinned broadly. And this cry of Borchi's went like a wave over the crowd and stopped the uproar. Borchi was a Cossack of the same village, one of their own. In the front row you could see white teeth glistening over beards.

"Citizens, Cossacks! For unlawful acts the chief of the District Militia has been arrested. Harness your horses and go back home with your goods. You will be excused the supplementary requisition of grain which the Government had levied in order to aid the Red Army—to help your own sons who are fighting the nobles and the generals. I tell you this straight: our anxiety is not about the war now. We don't want blood flowing in our fields. Our main anxiety is about people's economy and reconstruction. But it's not our fault, it is our misfortune, if the nobles and generals won't leave us a moment's peace. We're not worrying about blood, but about the land. We don't want soldiers, but workers in the fields. We want peaceful work and plenty of cattle. The grain requisition is over; you won't hear about it any more; but we want to see the granaries full and all your fields ploughed. We want crop-rotation. . . . Manufactured goods for the hamlets and villages."

Badin spoke about taxation, the co-operative movement, the demobilisation of the Red Army, iron, manufactured goods and groceries. And also of Comrade Lenin who had dedicated his life to the peasants and workers.

The crowd shuffled on its feet, snorting and sniffing, forming a dense herd at the feet of the two Chairmen. Badin stopped short, raised his hand, desired to say something further, but a staccato clamour arose from the crowd where the peasants and women mingled in confusion. In groups or singly, they beckoned with their hands and with joyous faces climbed upon the wagons.

As soon as they became quieter and the sweaty faces were farther away and the cart-wheels creaking, Borchi showed his white teeth, laughing.

" Now, Comrade Badin, I beg you to release Comrade Saltanov from arrest. We were both a bit beyond ourselves. We shall be wiser in future."

Badin became cold and distant.

" Comrade Borchi, all quarrels and mistakes by responsible workers must be made to serve as a lesson not only to themselves but to all other Comrades. What I said will be done. Get a reliable Comrade to act as a substitute for you while you're away. To-morrow you will go with me to the town."

Near to them a drunken Cossack swayed on bandy legs. He was a very drunken Cossack with a thin beard and blood-shot moist eyes ; he was waving his hat and shouting in an exhausted hoarse voice :

> " Puffed-up chicken,
> Naked and bare-foot,
> Went for a walk on the square.
> He was caught !
> He was pinched ! "

Borchi stopped in front of the drunken man and, without moving an eyelid, looked fixedly at him with the eyes of a warrior in the Devil's Hundred.

The little peasant began talking incomprehensible nonsense, staggered and fell to the ground. Once or twice he clutched in the air with his black swollen fingers and began to babble, terror-stricken.

" Well, well, well, Ataman—Executive. You are our father. . . . We're just corpses . . . sons of bitches . . . well, dear, dear, dear ! "

And he laid himself down, resigned to the worst.

Dasha spent the day and evening with the women of the Cossack town. Badin was with her too. They both spoke with the women. There were many of them there on this day of rejoicing. And Dasha performed her task successfully. Work among the women of a Cossack town is the devil of a job !

Dasha had never seen Badin as he was that evening. Whenever she met his gaze the golden flowers by the roadside shone in her memory. In those eyes Dasha saw silent ecstasy and an unquenchable fire of love for herself. He did not leave her for a minute all the evening, tender and shrewd.

And in the guest room of the Executive Committee, Dasha (how it came about she never knew) spent the night with him in one bed, and for the first time during the past years his stormy blood brought to her in the night hours the unforget-table passion of a woman.

Chapter IX

THE ROPEWAY

I

THE MASSES

It was not the support of individuals that Gleb felt, but rather the combined power of the masses about him.

Bathed in perspiration he worked like a bull, turning over with a shovel the chalk and clay which was to become cement. This brute strength of his came not through his intelligence but from the profundities of his strong body; it did not explode within him but flowed upon him in great waves through the thunder of the earth, across the stones and rails, from this enormous ant-like crowd who with shouting and moaning were rising from the depths with spades and hammers, emerged from smoke-stacks and the factory buildings, from the breaches quarried in the rock, from the smoky depths up towards the obelisks supporting the power-cables.

White, woolly balls of cloud were rolling in the blue sky; and on the green slopes of the mountains the first spring flowers sparkled in swarms. In an opal mist, the bushes blazed among the stones and in the fissures. Here, to the right and left, are the huge mountains; over there, the sea, blue as the sky, rimless, with a horizon higher than the mountains. Between the sea and the mountains the air vibrated from the glaring of the sun.

But all this was unimportant. What was important was this: the rushing tide of toil of the ant-like masses. There they were before him; it was impossible to count or touch them separately or distinguish individual faces.

This countless crowd were living flowers. Red scarves were dancing; these were the women like mountain poppies. Blue, white and brown shirts and jackets played in the light.

There it was: that of which Gleb had been thinking only a short time ago; that which he had wanted to create in an agony of labour.

Engineer Kleist, leader of the technologists, long and gaunt, leaning on a thick stick, was directing the work of the masses. Sedate officials and technicians, and alert foremen were constantly near him, almost dropping with fatigue and requiring instructions. Engineer Kleist, grave and stooping, would calmly and coldly throw them his quiet orders.

Engineer Kleist was a devoted technician of the Soviet Republic. . . . The workman Gleb Chumalov could now become a friend of Engineer Kleist.

The engineer stopped near Gleb, preoccupied, and several times attentively surveyed the work on the mountains which was now in full swing, and Gleb noticed in his eyes flashes of pleasure and excitement.

With an habitual gesture, Gleb pushed his helmet down over the back of his neck, dried the sweat on his face and smiled merrily, showing all his teeth.

" Well, what do you think of it, Comrade Technologist ? Do you remember, you said that this job would take a month to get going, and now look, it's only the third day and we've already got the works going. A wise lot, eh ? "

Engineer Kleist smiled drily, and without losing his air of importance, yet breaking through the hard business tension to some extent, said :

" Yes, yes, with such a spate of energy it's possible to do wonders. But it is an uneconomical expenditure of strength. There is no graduation and organised division of labour. This enthusiasm is like a cloud-burst : it doesn't last long and it's not very healthy."

" But it's a memorable fact, Comrade Technologist. With enthusiasm we can break up mountains. In the midst of ruin that's the only way to begin. When we have put life into all this again we can proceed to study the rational process of production."

Kleist detected the laughter in Gleb's eyes and shrugged coldly. Leaning on his stick he went on up the hill towards the shiny obelisks of the electric cables.

There was an intolerable odour emanating from the sun-scorched stones and burnt grass. One's mouth and eyes were smarting with dust.

In the mountains bells were ringing.

It was good. All was vast, immeasurable. The sun was alive like a human being, near, pulsating ; and one's blood coursed in rhythm with the sun.

Thousands of hands raised in thousands of efforts; the clamour of spades and picks; thousands of bodies in unanimous action moved mightily as one body. A living human machine which shook the stones to their depths.

Up in the heights: an iron track to the sunlit summits.

Clear-cut rails ran down over the sleepers into the gulf below to the bottom of the slope where were the Works; and then again up to the summit to the electric cable-towers, to the rings of the blue obelisks. In another hour, steel cables will be drawn taut, stretched in the sun like incandescent wires; and the trucks—up and down, up and down, travelling—singing their metallic song.

Polia Mekhova, big-eyed and curly-headed, walked slowly up the mountain, wearily leaning on her spade. She was stumbling and uttering little cries, bending like a grass-blade and laughing.

Lukhava was standing on a stone abutment, among the towers of the power-station. He stood with bare breast, in an unbelted black blouse. He seemed to be on the point of waving his arms and shouting.

Polia was laughing with exhaustion and the sun, the spade in her hands was playing with pebbles.

"Oh, how tired I am, Chumalov! Hold me up, a weak woman!"

She threw an arm about his shoulder and leaned with her breast against him. Her breath came in little panting moans; now and again she chokingly laughed.

Gleb was leaning on his shovel and she was leaning against his breast; and they were both laughing into each other's faces, sensually, without speaking. Under her full breasts he heard her heart beat. He saw in the drunken play of colour in her eyes and the moist glint of her teeth, her readiness to abandon herself to his strength. And at each pulsation of her heart, through her breasts, and in the play of those eyes and teeth, he heard a voice deep down in himself saying teasingly:

"Well? Well?"

Walking firmly with a pick-axe on her shoulder, Dasha came along. She was followed by a crowd of women, head-scarves showing like red poppies, laughing and crying out. They were going towards the power-station in order to repair the roads.

"There is my Dasha. . . . The leader! And to think that once she was just a nice little wife."

He caught her on her way in an embrace, pressing her closely. She began to laugh, wrenched herself free, and smilingly threatened him with her pick-axe.

" Take care, Comrade Mekhova," she cried. " Gleb can break you with one finger; I've had some! If anything happens call to me for help! "

The cold lustre was no longer in her eyes; a warm, caressing ray of wonder and joy was in them now. She walked away, without turning back, her pick-axe on her shoulder, amidst the gay chorus of women's voices.

" My Dasha is a wonder! A real jewel of a woman! One must admit that."

" She loves you very much and is proud of you, Chumalov. Dasha is a real Bolshevik. I have a great fondness for her."

Tears glistened in Mekhova's eyes.

It would never die out in his memory. He continued to look at Dasha, greatly moved, a flood of tenderness rising in his breast.

That evening she had not spoken as during the ten days previously. She had clumsily and briefly related to him the adventure in the ravine. While speaking, she observed him closely, and in the light of the electric lamp one could mark in her face confused questioning and exaltation.

When Dasha related how she had jumped off the phaeton, and how the bearded soldier had led her off to be hanged—she related it quite simply with a smile—Gleb began to tremble at this throbbing light within her eyes contrasting so vividly with her commonplace, simple speech. It was not fear for Dasha, nor anger and jealousy against Badin; it was a confused guilty feeling with regard to Dasha herself, mingled with wonder at her devotion. And one thing he now resolved: from this hour he would never reproach her with a word, nor as husband offensively importune her with force or caresses. He dearly wanted to, it was true, but he could not.

The days they had lived together since his return until now had been poisoned by shame and his own helplessness before her. This had suddenly come to him, without reflection, during her words, in which there was no horror at what had happened, not a cry nor a boast. He listened to her silently, shuddering, and could not remove his gaze from her face. Then, hands in pockets, he walked up close to her, but did not touch her.

" Dasha, we're all fools and rascals. We ought to be hanged, not you. You're a wonder, Dasha. Don't be angry with a poor son of a bitch like me."

He moved away and laid down on the bed. In the darkness, lying apart, he on the bed and she on the floor, Dasha began to stir her rags and said caressingly :

" Gleb, are you asleep ? "

" Little Dasha, you're a fine brave one ! And no mistake ! When I think about that rope I shudder and my heart is bursting."

She laughed under her bedclothes, wished to say something but stumbled over it ; then without being able to help it, laughed again.

" And if I were to tell you, Gleb, that I slept with Badin then ? I suppose you would make a scene. You often wanted to beat me."

Gleb was astonished. Dasha's jest, in which he heard anguish and a troubled verity, did not move him. Her words were a blow, but it did not hurt. In the last days had his jealousy burned itself out—or had Dasha become something more than a wife to him ? His heart felt only tenderness towards her, as towards a new friend whom he had not known before.

" My head is hot as a furnace, little Dasha. . . . I'm thinking about that rope and your adventure, and all my inside is aching. Well, and supposing it did happen—well, let it happen. We're animals, and you can swear at me as much as you like. One must approach people from another angle. Let it be. . . . The time will come when we shall learn how to understand people thoroughly. Now I'm aching inside and that's all, little Dasha."

Again Dasha laughed under the bed-cover.

" Well, go to sleep ! I don't know—it seems as if life is going backwards to my young days, only it goes by another path."

She lay quiet for a moment, then stirred again and said :

" Gleb, are you asleep ? "

Gleb had not the time to answer before she rose from her pallet, walked barefooted over to him and slipped under his bed-covers.

Savchuk, at the head of the construction gang, was fastening the rails to the sleepers, thundering with his hammer like a madman in an intoxicated fit of work. His face was red, his eyes bloodshot and the thick veins in his hands and neck were knotted around the muscles under his sweaty skin, swollen like ropes.

Gleb shouldered his pick and, leaving Mekhova, went over to the front row of the workmen.

" Strike, Savchuk, strike ! Put your back into it ! "

" We're hitting as hard as we can ! You started things going, so get to the head, old pal ! We'll find fuel for the factory too."

" Hurray, Comrades ! We'll make the old mountain move ! Hurray ! "

He raised his pick on high, and the veins in his neck swelled with his roaring. And the crowd burst out yelling, brandishing their picks, shovels and hammers as an army would their weapons.

" Hurrah ! Hurrah ! "

From on high Gleb saw the mighty uproar rolling like a wave down the slope of the mountain. The people at the bottom were small as ants. They also were waving their hands and spades and were probably shouting as well.

Mekhova was gazing at Gleb, her eyes wide open.

The last sections of the track were being riveted to the sleepers. The cables lay like snakes and gave out a metallic tinkling like violin strings. The wheels were absorbing electricity for flight.

Red soldiers, leaning on their rifles, were keeping watch in the mountain pass. Above and around them the shrubbery stretched down in green foam. Rifles and helmets bespoke vigour and attention as the Red Army comrades vigilantly surveyed the cliffs and the dark descent on the other side of the mountain.

Exhausted, red-faced and with knees trembling, Serge stepped out from among the workers. He walked over to Mekhova and subsided tired on a boulder.

" Well, my dear Intellectual. Weren't you going to say that the roots of Communist labour are not always sweet ? "

Mekhova patted him on the arm in a friendly way.

His face lit up with a gay, child-like smile. The sweat ran down his nose and chin and fell on his hands in hot drops. He took Polia's hand and gave it a hard and friendly squeeze.

2

A DEATH STRUGGLE

As one approaches the end, work always becomes more strenuous and intoxicating. The last strokes are the most vigorous and exact. When Lukhava's warning cry came from the power-house tower, the front rows of the workers gathered together in wonder and alarm.

Far away on the tops of the mountains the air seemed to burst and scatter in splinters. Owing to the noise of the work that was being carried on no shots were heard at first. On the pass, the Red soldiers were running here and there, jumping over boulders and firing in disorder.

Lukhava, waving his arms, was shouting at the top of his voice.

" Be calm, Comrades ! Let each man remain in his place. There's an attack of bandits from the other side of the ridge. Don't stop work ! No panic ! "

The fusillade was shattering the air, which seemed to fall in fragments to the earth.

Work stopped suddenly. Thousands of people streamed down the slope. Half-way down, panic started: their terror broke out, and the crowd like an unrestrained torrent rushed madly downwards, falling, rolling over, piling up in heaps. To the right and left also, groups were running, and also single figures, lying down, then getting up and running on again.

Gleb climbed on to a ledge of rock and waved his pick.

" Halt ! Stop where you are, damn you ! Communists, come here ! If any of them show cowardice hit them with your picks ! "

The leaders of the Construction Workers' Union were rushing towards Gleb over the sleepers and stones. After them came others running. Lower down, at first one by one, and then in chorus, voices were shouting :

" Halt ! Halt ! "

To the right and left the flood continued, rushing, jumping and rolling past rocks and bushes.

The firing sounded as though the stones of the mountain were bursting.

Gleb threw away his pick and jumped off the rock.

" Savchuk, Gromada and you, Dasha ! Run down and

make them take their places ! Grab them by the scruff of the neck ; give them a good hard kick from behind—the cattle ! "

Savchuk, Gromada, Dasha and more and more people, now started bounding down the slope like falling boulders.

" Communists, come over here to me ! Get rifles, Comrades, and then on to the power-station. Quick, get a move on ! We'll serve them up a fine portion of iron beans, Comrades ! "

He was the first to run for a rifle. Behind him ran the Communist Party members and behind them a number of non-Party workmen.

Above on the slope, the metal workers and electricians were working calmly and silently ; only in their eyes was there a note of alarm.

People were taking out rifles and cartridges, breeches clicked. The shirts on their backs were soaking. They were gathering up sweat with their fingers and shaking it off, wiping it off with their sleeves. And the non-Party workmen were dashing to the rifles, but they were repelled. Mitka, the feller and concertinist, with his blue-shaved skull, was choking and furious.

" Don't get too excited ! Don't lose your heads there, you bastards ! I've been expecting something like this for a long time ! "

Elbows revolving, he squeezed his way to the front, grasped a rifle ; then winked, his big white teeth showing in a grin.

" That's the stuff! Let's get after them, Comrade Chumalov! We'll spill the guts of them ! "

The workmen were running hither and thither, snapping home the magazines of their rifles ; squatting down suddenly, then crawling on all fours.

The burning air, thrown back by the hot boulders, grasped one by the throat. There was a smell of sun and burnt grass. Polia was climbing the stony slope next to Gleb. He felt her soft shoulder and the sharp flavour of a woman's sweat.

" What are you coming for ? You've got to think twice before you get into a job like this."

" Why shouldn't I come ? Why may you go and I cannot ? "

" I'm used to this kind of a game. You're not experienced enough yet."

Polia laughed loudly.

Before them Red soldiers and armed workmen were running to and fro, suddenly stopping and kneeling down to fire. Far away, over the sea or behind the mountains, it seemed that sirens were crying.

" Those are bullets, Gleb. It's a long time since I heard them last."

Gleb walked on, his rifle at the ready. Polia walked close by him, also carrying a rifle. There seemed to be nothing but two immense eyes in her face. Her long curls flamed in the sun.

Gleb was no longer a workman, but had once again become the Red War Commissar. In crisp, clear phrases he ordered a detachment to go round and attack the bandits on the left flank, driving them out of the little wood on to the slope under the fire of the Red soldiers on the pass. He himself would direct the operations from a spot on the mountain where he would be in sight of both detachments.

" Do you hear, Comrade Gleb? They're close. They're shooting from the summit. They want to create a panic and destroy the ropeway."

Gleb did not answer. He was boldly climbing the steep side of the mountain, frequently turning and looking back at the ropeway. Mekhova would not leave him. She hitched her skirt above her knees.

" See! Our fellows have got them wedged in tightly now! We'll drive them all together! This ought to have happened long ago, in order to get all these rats out of their holes. It's all right : we'll give them a good thrashing now! "

Polia's face was all eyes.

The mountain crest blazed like a lighted cupola, and an iron geodesic tripod burned brightly in its rust on its highest point.

They climbed on up the steep slope of the summit, from whose heights they could see the sloping ribs of the mountain, with wooded clefts and ridges ; and in the far distance the ice-caps of other mountains against the horizon.

They lay down close to the tripod, and the heights and distances vanished. Under their hands was gravel and rocks. There was a sulphurous odour of burnt grass and heated cement.

" I can't see anything, Gleb. Where are they? "

Polia raised herself to her knees and leaned forward towards the tripod.

Suddenly an iron support tinkled sharply.

Gleb brusquely pulled Polia down by her skirt. There was a sound of tearing and a fastening of her skirt gave way. Polia burst out laughing and sat down next to Gleb.

" You've torn off a hook, you clumsy bear ! "

" You sit still ! If they get sight of you you'll be shot ; I don't like corpses ! "

He looked at her with bloodshot eyes. Then crawled behind the tripod.

To the right of the crest were the blue and yellow ruins of a wall. Scattered about were ruins of other ancient buildings. Among them grew brown bushes and wild roses.

Gleb lay flat on his belly, craning his neck to see.

A swarthy Cossack, bare-headed, his hand on the trigger of his rifle, was crawling stealthily up among the debris. When he squatted down among the stones he was quite hidden.

" I'm going to shoot him, Gleb. I can't stand waiting ! "

Polia's hands were trembling. One saw only the immense eyes in her face.

" Don't you dare or I'll smash you. Lie down ! "

Polia showed her teeth, laughing silently.

Gleb began to crawl over the stones towards the ruins, in the cover of the bushes. Then Polia saw him running bent low among the boulders. He was noiseless and grey—indistinguishable—the colour of the stones.

The Cossack stopped suddenly, jerked his head up, scared, raised his rifle ; then squatted down, disappeared from view.

Was it Polia's heart beating like this ? Or was it the shots popping in the woods ? Were the mountains shaking, or was it the tumult in the depths of her by which she was riven ?

Had he run away or was he hiding and watching ? Would he let Gleb come near him, or would he kill him ?

Polia's teeth were chattering. She clenched her jaws until it hurt, but her teeth would not stop chattering and her jaw-muscles were grinding under her ears. If one could only jump up, run, shout out, shoot blindly, in flame and smoke !

She did not hear the shot ; only a hot gust of air passed over her, rushing to the depths below ; and the abyss resounded with falling stones. An animal voice was hoarsely growling and choking amidst the clatter. It was not Gleb : Gleb could not cry out in this way. The beast was growling and choking, and the loose stones clattered down like broken glass.

Polia, rifle in hand, ran towards the rocks where Gleb was.

He had left no footprints, but she knew where he had passed. The rock before her burst into small pieces, and dust rose in a flame-like cloud. Splinters of stone struck her face, scorching her cheeks and brow.

On the other side of the rock, trampling the bushes, Gleb and the Cossack were locked in a wolf-like struggle. A rifle, suddenly cast away, clattered at Polia's feet. Gleb, with curving, creaking spine, and hunched shoulders, his face swollen with effort, was trying to tear a rifle from the hands of the Cossack.

With maddened bulging eyes, his face smeared with foam and sweat, the Cossack, strong as a bear, was twisting the rifle round and round; and one could see his muscles stretched and straining into knots under his tunic. He panted and grunted, grinding out oaths and insults, dragging Gleb with him down the slope towards a stony precipice. Behind them bullets were striking the stones and rubble, sending up clouds of dust.

At the moment when Mekhova was aiming the butt of her rifle at the Cossack's head, Gleb succeeded in getting his right arm round his neck and was grinding his face against the rifle, while with his other hand he seized the Cossack's wrist, bending it back until it broke.

The Cossack ground his teeth with pain and fury, howled and made a supreme effort to break Gleb's hold. Gleb, shuddering with strain, tightened his hold upon the Cossack's neck. Polia's instinct told her that in another moment Gleb would give way and the two of them would roll over the brink. Madly Polia, with all her might, smashed the rifle butt down on the Cossack's ribs. He grew limp, bellowing like an animal.

" I'm done for ! I can't—! I surrender ! You've got me ! "

Gleb slid his hand from the Cossack's neck and caught his other wrist in an iron grip. With ferocious, bloody eyes of a trapped animal, the Cossack looked at Gleb. His eyes were darkened with fear and deadly hatred. A sticky slime, mingled with blood and spittle, oozed from his nose and mouth. His eyes bulged ; he was jerking his head from side to side and choking with saliva and blood. Panting like a hunted beast, he hoarsely bellowed :

" Let me go ! I'm finished—. Done for ! "

Her hand on Gleb's shoulder, Polia pulled him back.

" Get away from here, Gleb, quick ! Don't you see that we're a target ! "

Gleb looked at her over his shoulder stupidly, and let go the Cossack's arms. His chest was heaving violently, almost bursting his tunic and raising his shoulders to his ears. His hand went to his holster, but his revolver was not there.

The Cossack, exhausted, was spitting bloody slime and hoarsely muttering. Suddenly he started and, twisting his lips and showing his bloody teeth, leapt towards the edge of the ravine.

" You swine, filthy hounds ! You wanted to beat a Cossack, didn't you ? Catch the Cossack now ! "

He whooped, as the Cossacks do at riding displays, and with one bound plunged over the brink of the abyss.

Gleb ran to the edge and watched the Cossack's body turning over and over far below, striking from rock to rock and re-bounding, until he lay crushed at the bottom.

Polia was again drawing him back from the precipice.

Suddenly Gleb heard the pattering of bullets upon the rocks, among showers of small stones and dust.

He ran behind a pile of boulders stooping low ; but Polia marched on calmly and silently, like a blind person.

With an angry gleam in his eyes, Gleb bounded back to Polia, raising his fist.

" I'll hit you in a minute ! Smash you like a toad, you damned doll ! "

Polia looked at him quietly, steadily, unseeingly—like a blind person ; then she started and struck him lightly on the hand with the barrel of her rifle.

" Put your hand down, blockhead ! And pick up the weapons you dropped on the way."

And she walked back to the tripod on the summit.

Men were running from the coppice in all directions, stumbling, firing, falling and rolling over. The tumult of shots, smoke, fire and yelling voices came from just beyond the summit where the Red soldiers were concealed. Polia was lying on her stomach, shooting also. The rifle kicked her shoulder painfully, but in wild excitement she was snapping the breech, aiming and firing among the figures in the distance who were running and jumping here and there like hares.

She was dimly conscious of Gleb running past her up the slope and of the dull echoes of his shouted commands from the other side of the summit.

3

THE FIRST TRUCK

The wheels in the power-house were humming ; their metal spokes swung round, beating like black wings at various slopes and angles. Like cobweb threads, the steel cables wound and unwound themselves on the rims of the fat coils. The electricians, labourers and young Communists, headed by the bronzed Lukhava and Engineer Kleist, were looking in silent admiration at the electric flight of the wheels, and listening to the resurrected music of the machinery.

An avalanche of people came running down the valley, a mile deep, over the cement and slate—gnawed by the wind and rain—among the boulders and through the gullies. The mass was boiling, heaving, roaring with its thousands of voices. It seemed to sway in muscular convulsions, spasmodically, like the convulsions of the body of a gigantic centipede.

From the highest point of the cable-line down to the bottom, where lay pyramids of stones, the human cataract was divided in two parts, between which four taut cables stretched over a track of cinders, humming strange tunes.

And, cleaving these two human torrents, far down, was moving a square tortoise, clinging to the cables by pulleys which gave out a flute-like whistling.

" Hurra-a-a-ah ! Hurra-a-a-ah ! "

You would not have thought that this was the roar of a crowd, but rather the roaring of a storm in the funnel-like crater of a high mountain.

The detachment of armed workers was now descending from the summit of the mountain in ragged formation. The Red soldiers had resumed their posts up there, and were keeping watch on high like vigilant birds. Gleb and Mekhova were leading the armed workers. Behind them the body of a comrade was being carried on rifles.

The workers' detachment came down to the machines and stacked their rifles. Their faces bore the trace of recent emotion, and were covered with dust and sweat. They laid down the body of their dead comrade—his head was a bloodied mass —on the concrete at the feet of the crowd. Pressing against each other, crying discordantly, the crowd rushed up to the detachment, surrounding it closely. Laughing and yelling, they jostled the workmen and seizing Gleb, swallowed him up in their midst. Then, with arms and legs flying, he was flung into the air like a dummy, falling back into the thick mass. Again seized, amid laughter and uproar, they tossed him again above their heads ; and again . . . and then again. . . .

Another crowd, silent and stern, faces drawn with grief, was gathered round the corpse. It was impossible to trace in this blood-clotted head the features of Mitka, the concertina-player, who by force had grasped a rifle and had thrust himself into the Communist detachment.

Amidst the tumult of the crowd, the girls of the Young Communist League were bandaging the wounded.

" You've been sweating, Comrades ! You do look pretty ! Well, we've let them have it ! They've dug their own graves, not ours ! "

"Ho, ho, workers! We'll smash them to Hell, the bastards ! "

A voice was choking with joy :

" I'll crush them all ! Bring up a thousand more generals— we'll send them to the right-about ! Oh, my little brothers, with breeches or without—! Let's sing the ' International ' ! We got them then ! The women, the dear little mothers—how I love the Women's Section ! Bring the whole Women's Section here so I may embrace them all ! "

More people were approaching, cheering. And again Gleb was enthusiastically tossed up in the air. Then they crowded round the corpse, murmuring with grief.

Mekhova was elbowing her way through the crowd, shouting all the time : " Comrades ! Comrades ! "

Her face was all eyes.

Engineer Kleist approached Gleb, his face working nerv-ously ; with his usual gravity he silently pressed his hand.

And Dasha, in passing Gleb, laid her hand on his shoulder and looked at him with wet eyes in which was a new and wondering joy.

" Gleb ! "

" Little Dasha ! "

But she went on and was lost in the torrent of the crowd.

And now, the most important thing of all—the masses. The thunder of toil. The winged flight of the wheels. That night the eyes of the factory opened, like electric moons ; and the dead opaque bulbs in the workmen's dwellings suddenly re-lit their twined threads. The factory ! It trembled already ; already its hidden power was resounding in its underground depths and its windows looked out yearningly, like a human.

The masses had awakened the mountain which had died in wilderness and mildew. The ropeway was crying out with its iron voice. Black clouds will eddy from the smoke-stacks' mouths, and the tortoises of the air will fly down to the docks and back to their heights, devouring the chalk in the quarries. The goats . . . the pipe-lighters . . . the mouse-like squeaking of the little hand-tools . . . this will be finished.

Lukhava stood near the machines, waving his arms and crying out to some people below.

There was an iron clanging somewhere; the wheels stirred and then stopped again.

Gleb ran down the steps to the engines. A large flat truck, covered with grey dust and smelling of decay, stood on a level with the platform.

He ran up, and with the habit of military command, shouted to the crowd:

" Place our Comrade's body in the truck. He shall be carried down with honour. Let everybody see—all who are here—let them see it right to the end."

Many hands raised the body. Silently and with care they carried it down the steps and put it on the truck.

" Comrades—! My lads! His pick! And his rifle! Lay them by him, Comrades! "

Gleb stood out on the abutments, between the blue obelisks, and raised his arms in a great gesture.

" Let her down now! All together! Ready! "

And to the noise of the wheels, the truck went down the slope, riding like a bird, easily and airily.

Again Gleb raised his arms on high.

" Comrades, listen! A sacrifice to labour. . . . With our united strength. . . . No tears or sobs! The victory of our hands . . . the factory. We have won. . . . We shall make ourselves heard with fire and machinery. The great work of building up the Workers' Republic. . . . Ourselves, with our brains and bodies. . . . The blood and suffering of the struggle —These are our weapons for winning the whole world. Let it go now, Brothers! "

And he began to sing, waving his arms. Then the crowd took it up, ever louder. The mountains seemed to be torn by the clamour; the air eddied as in a storm. The earth trembled as with an earthquake.

And the truck floated and swayed in the air like a little bird amidst the tempest and shattering thunder.

Chapter X

STRATA OF THE SOUL

I

QUIET MOMENTS

LEAVING the factory dining-room and passing through the tired crowd, Dasha and Gleb, worn out, came out upon the high road and then turned off down a wild path invaded by bushes, wild vines and tangles of ground ivy. They had only just entered a wood of young oaks and witch-elms, whose bluish semi-transparency pulsated with the murmur of spring, when they were joined by Polia Mekhova.

"Comrades, I'd like to walk with you as far as your little den. I would like to rest a few moments with you in quietness."

Dasha and Gleb glanced at each other simultaneously. Something flashed in the eyes of both. A question? Astonishment? Annoyance? They gave no sign by word or movement.

Dasha took Polia by the arm.

"Comrade Mekhova, you have never visited us yet. We all live together in our work; but we don't know how each other lives at home."

Polia shook her long curls, entangling them in a thorny branch. She gave a little shriek, stood still and started to laugh. She took the rough mossy twig in her fingers, looked at it with gay curiosity and smelt it.

"How nice it is here! It's so long since I've been in a wood. It smells of dew and damp earth. And this bitter-sweet odour, it is the buds and the sap of the trees. How long ago since I was here, it seems! As though the last time were in my childhood. Here in these woods we feel not as we are, but as others see us. . . . And for that reason it's just a little sad and painful. When we were working on the mountain it wasn't sad at all; but here these little oaks and this spring-time smell seem to stir me. Probably I shouldn't leave work to go in the country. I'm going to take your husband's arm, Dasha ; he's got enough strength for both of us. After all, we are weak women."

She chattered like a little girl, playing with the branches, laughing nervously, hurrying on excitedly, as though trying to say something grave and important ; perhaps she wanted to weep, perhaps complain, perhaps abandon herself to her own troubled feelings. . . . She ran over to Gleb and took his arm, bending forward and looking across him at Dasha.

"You're not jealous, Dasha ? "

But Dasha, smiling, looked at Polia like a good friend.

"D'you want me to pull your hair, Comrade Mekhova ? If you're so bewitched by this great bear, there's no need to doubt his strength."

"Oh, I know his strength ! His fight with the Cossack on the mountain proved that all right ! "

And Gleb felt Polia's hand press his to her soft full breast. Here was Dasha, and here the curly-headed Polia. Both women passed over his heart like waves which met together in a warm flood. There was Dasha, so fine, so near, difficult to understand and to overcome. And Polia was a weak child, all fire, trembling with emotion and impulse. With his elbows he pressed the arms of both women and began to laugh.

"Well, each one of you sit on one of my arms ! I'm going to carry you both home ! "

Dasha struck him in the ribs, threw up her head and cried loudly :

"Oh, don't boast so, soldier ! "

"There, damn it all—sit down ! Just because you're a couple of militants you think that you're not the same women ? Sit down on my arms ! "

Polia's eyes flashed gaily ; laughter quivered in her face.

"Come on, Dasha, let's make him sweat. He's had a lot to do to-day, his bluff won't carry him very far."

"Come on, you little hares ! You snub-noses ! Sit down now——! "

He stretched out his arms, bending down, and seized the two women below the hips. With cries and laughter they put their arms round his neck, entwining their arms and locking their fingers. Gleb's knees cracked and the blood rushed to his face and neck. Without slackening his pace, he walked firmly on, carrying the two women who were like two little, laughing school-girls.

Dasha sprang down first, gasping with laughter. Polia got down slowly, stealthily pressing against him with her breasts and curls.

" There now ! You see ? So don't accuse me of boasting, you mockers ! "

They were both women, and both had soft full breasts. But Dasha was different—his own ; and Polia was different— a stranger.

Already the sun was sinking, fading beyond the distant mountain ridge ; and the sky above them was a deep thick blue, except in the opal dimness over the sun, where it was stained with fire. The mountains seemed very near, rushing down in streams of black and bronze towards the fissures and terraces of the works. On the right, beyond the slope, along the steep rib, the ropeway cut a sharp yellow strip, like a furrow.

The violet shadows of evening, dim as though strewn with ashes, floated up from the valley along the crater-like gullies. There were still patches and strips on the rocks and slopes which blazed fierily. And here, among the blue cobwebby bushes, in this isolated place with its grass-grown paths, the twilight silence came flooding the land like water. It seemed to flow up out of the earth, out of the wild undergrowth of the forest, and from the ravine where a little brook rustled. The stones in the brook seemed alive like tortoises and the water played there, black, flashing with blue. This valley darkness, charged with the heady fumes of the moist spring earth of the grass, and of unborn leaves in pregnant buds, exhaled the breath of the earthy depths, their tangled roots and airy branches. Through the transparent network of the branches, the tops of the smoke-stacks blazed like orange torches. The Pleasant Colony blinded your eyes with the fiery reflections of its windows. That was up above ; and down below, along the slope, the little houses and the tenements were melting into the creeping twilight.

These two women, Dasha and Polia. One his own, the other a stranger, were equally dear. In two waves they passed through his heart, meeting together in a warm flood. Which wave would recede first from his heart ? Or would they cross each other, leaving him forever in different directions ?

" Yes. What has passed to-day can never be forgotten."

And in Polia's wide-open eyes Gleb read the hidden significance of these words. He understood that there on the mountain peak, on the edge of the precipice, under the shower of bullets, a new and disturbing bond had been forged between him and Polia, without either of them willing it.

Gleb remained silent as though he had not heard what Polia had said. Dasha was walking a little in front, breaking off a black twig here and there.

" What lovely air, Comrades, like honey ! Soon everything will be green and in flower."

Why did Dasha walk on ahead of them ? Was it on purpose ? Had she divined their secret bond ? Perhaps she just wanted to bathe alone in this twilight softness, intoxicated with spring.

" You said well, Dasha ; we're only near each other when we are working ; but as human beings we are apart, strangers to each other. That is one of our painful contradictions. We are only workers in the movement. It we just dare to touch each other, quite simply, like human beings, we become panic-stricken and retire into ourselves. Nothing frightens us so much as our own feelings. If you just look into any one's eyes, they are cold, dead, metallic. We are always under lock and key ; in the daytime we lock up our feelings, and at night our rooms."

" You talk like a sentimental young lady, Comrade Mek-hova. It's true we haven't much time to occupy ourselves with affairs of the soul. People can wait, but your tasks will fly away from you if you're not careful, and you will never catch up with them."

" Yes, many talk like that. But the bulk of them are suffer-ing from loneliness which they are afraid to acknowledge. They're afraid people will make fun of them ; they are afraid of a contemptuous look; they fear that they will be reproached with 'idealogical inconsistency'. But still they suffer—that is certain."

Dasha was walking further ahead of them, snapping off the ends of twigs which broke with a little creaking cry like the cry of a bird. With a clumsy caress Gleb ruffled Polia's curls.

" You sing your serenade in vain, Comrade Mekhova. I've been attacking Dasha from all sides, but she still keeps me in my place."

Dasha gurgled with laughter, and from the distance you could see her teeth flashing.

" Gleb is like you, Comrade Mekhova : he's as tender as you are and always ready to play the bridegroom."

They were going up a path to the roadway. Above the

distant ranges the sun was like blood and the big-toothed black mountains gnawed it as at a fiery pancake. Under the mountain the town stood out with rectangular distinctness : the straight blue streets running from the docks to the slopes, and then leading down into the valley. Between the quays and the breakwater the sea foamed up like mother-of-pearl, throwing up black and red waves. The cubes and towers of the factory were piled up in a profound silence like rectangular eternal ice-bergs.

" I've been asking myself some worrying questions recently, Comrade. The New Economic Policy—we're coming to a period of big contradictions, and we're all pretending not to see them. I'm always worrying and expecting something dreadful to happen."

" What's wrong then, Comrade Mekhova ? You must pull yourself together. Come, I'll give you a nice glass of hot water and saccharine, and then Gleb will see you home."

Polia looked at Dasha with frightened bewildered eyes, and then hurried along the path to a gap in the wall.

Dasha looked after her for a long time, her face smiling with caressing mockery.

" A good girl—and intelligent. But she's broken a spring somewhere. What can it be ? Why don't you see her off, Gleb ? You've made a big hit with her."

" Dasha. . . . Don't let's go into our room. Let's take a walk up the mountain and sit down and breathe for a while."

" Not a bad idea ! Right, let's go to the reservoir."

Gleb was astonished. For the first time, Dasha had taken him by the hand and was walking close to him like a good friend. She was silent and Gleb felt that she was agitated. He felt that she wished to say something, but he could not guess what. Perhaps the kind of word that had been said in the early days of their love, or perhaps one that had never before been said by them. And Gleb was silent, waiting for that word from Dasha.

Past the gardens and little houses they went ; up the slope, over pebbles and gravel, past ledges of rock. The reservoir was high above Pleasant Colony. From here the water was brought down through conduits to the workers' settlement and from there on to the laboratories, workshops, and other factory buildings.

They skirted a pile of fallen rocks and passed a gallery which had been hollowed in the mountain-side, now closed by a padlocked rusty door; and this door, entrance into the depths of the mountain, encumbered with heaps of stones, seemed ominous, like the mystery of an ancient heathen shrine.

They arrived at a wide long concrete platform. It was pleasant and easy for walking, sonorously re-echoing one's footsteps.

At their feet the red roofs of the barracks were piled around their chimneys. Behind these came the buildings and towers of the factory; then still lower down was the purple bay, fringed along its shore with locks of foam. Beyond the breakwaters rose the sea, an immense globe. The horizon dominated the chimneys and the mountain tops; and it was no longer possible to distinguish this distant horizon from the sky.

Workers, solitary or in small groups, walked along the paths between the factory and Pleasant Colony. And far behind the factory walls they could see a girl running, swinging her arms, in the light which was dying under the brown slope of the mountain.

Dasha sat down on the smooth concrete, and about her knees she laced her hands, grained and scarred with work.

" That's Comrade Mekhova taking a walk. She's a strange girl—sometimes as hard as iron, at others shaking like a twig. I'm afraid something may happen to her. Don't you notice how she clings to you? You won't repel her if she takes you to her heart? "

Gleb, dumbfounded, was lying close to Dasha. He saw nothing in her face but a slight smile. What was the matter with her? Was she testing him? Was there a special meaning hidden in her words? He did not know what to answer, whether to be angry or to laugh. She had divined his emotion, had caught in his sudden glances, in his smiles and gestures, the reflection of Polia—the reflection of the ever-dancing sparkle of her eyes and expressive play of her brows. Two waves were meeting and crossed each other in his heart.

" Well, little Dasha. . . . You're looking into all kinds of little corners. You're casting your line wide into deep waters."

Dasha lifted her head and smiled—ah, what a woman's smile it was !—without looking at him.

" Did you think I was talking riddles? I was only speaking straight out. It's entirely your business. You know you've been quite free with regard to women? And, Mekhova and I, haven't we equal rights, as two women? "

" Oh, to the devil with you. You've simply got me ! I don't know how to answer that."

" Oh, Gleb, you're not very sly ! You're not sly but you're a close one. You're weak and not straight enough. Have I thrown any reproaches at you for your affairs with women ? And do you think I'm going to ask your permission for following my own instincts as a woman if I so desire ? "

Her words hurt him to the heart ; she was so irresistible, so fresh and firmly set in her truthfulness, that he was defenceless ; he had no words with which to answer. And then, for the first time (that damned ravine !), he began to feel that he also had changed : that he was not the same Gleb that he was yesterday ; the old blood of him had been burned away ; his mind had completely changed. In almost unbearable pain, his soul rushed out to Dasha in boundless love—not for a woman, but for a human being who stood nearer to him than any other. What would have happened to him had she perished on that day when he was not thinking of her, but lived only for the factory, the engines and the workshop ?

There she was : the woman who had sprung out of the Dasha of yesterday. Well, yes, there had been something of the present Dasha hidden in her old self, but he had been blind to it ; he was just a desirous male in those days.

And how youthful and stormy it had been, that other night ! He had not dragged her to his bed, beating her, twisting her wrist—she had come of her own will, like a little innocent girl, to hold him in that strong embrace. . . .

Under the landing, in the depths, the water was playing, singing like crickets ; surging and humming . . . it seemed that something living and immense was sighing in the void. And it seemed that this great sigh and the twanging of chords were floating in the forest and over the forest, streaming from the purple twilight of the lowlands.

Everything was airy, profound and immeasurable. The mountains were no longer ridges and hollows of stone and rock, but thick sooty smoke ; and the sea in its shoreless flooding was no longer a sea but a blue abyss. And this man and woman seated on the height above the factory and yet with the factory, on a fragment of a planet, flew—above the abyss and yet under the abyss—far away, without knowing it, on a flight into infinity.

Gleb laid his head on Dasha's knees, and saw above her face and the purple sky. Her cheeks covered with a thin, glistening down reflected the hue of the sky. Her eyes expressed wonder and a thought which was formed but still unuttered.

Waves of pain passed through him. She, his Dasha, his wife. And in the midst of this pain one thing only was plain ; he could not kill Dasha ; she had grown stronger than his hand—inaccessible for ever.

" Here on the mountain under the sky it is sweet to lie like this, my head in your lap, Dasha. We have never been such dear friends as in this evening hour. Tell me how you managed to get on while I was away and all the adventures you had."

A flash of lightning suddenly streaked the air and the purple shadows were rent up to the sky.

Gleb raised himself on his elbow. For some time he gazed at the factory buildings ; at the slopes and valleys with their gardens. Lights were twinkling everywhere like stars. Rapture flooded his heart, and emotion caught him by the throat. What was this in his throat : tears or joy ?

" There it is, little Dasha. . . . That is our hands and brains. . . . It's fine to struggle and build up one's destiny. Eh, Dasha ? That's all ours. Ours ! Let it be so. I shall lie in your lap and you can speak to me. There's nothing to dread any more ; and I shall listen to your horrors as to a fairy-tale."

Dasha laid her hands upon her breasts. She was deeply moved and Gleb could hear her heart flooding.

" Well, yes. . . . Now you can stand being beaten with words too. . . . You're not so sensitive now. Oh, what nonsense you talked before, Gleb. How foolish you were ! "

2

THE BIRTH OF STRENGTH

And this is what she told him on that purple evening :

After Gleb had recovered from his wounds, lying in the attic among the spiders and mice, and had gone away one night into the mountains—then, the Greens occupied the thickets and the ravines.

She knew that Gleb had torn himself away from her perhaps for ever ; and she tore herself from him as from one that was dead. She did not accompany him to the threshold, but bade him good-bye in the darkness of the room. She wept without sound, and could not let him go, the dear one, who had taken her soul to himself. When he stealthily disappeared into the night, she lit no fire ; but in the darkness, with her daughter Nurka, tossed in unforgettable anguish till morning peeped in at the windows. And in this tear-drowned agony, she lay in her lonely bed, with Nurka at her heart, and the days and nights went by dimly like wraiths of mist, fading behind the muslin curtains.

And just as suddenly as she had sunk into this semi-existence, without days and nights, so was she shocked out of it.

With clattering and stamping and the muttering and yelling of soldiers with loaded rifles and revolvers, some officers forced their way into her house and a stamping crowd surrounded her crying in chorus :

" Where is your husband ? "

At first she shrank away, because the walls were shaking as was the floor under their feet. And as her heart flooded, Nurka burst out crying and shrank convulsively in her arms.

" Tell us where your husband is ! We know that he's been here ! It's no good looking innocent and pretending to be a fool."

" How do I know where my husband is ? You know better yourselves ! You took my husband away and you haven't told what you did with him. Why do you come to me for him ? "

She did not cry. Her face became blue, and her eyes shone like glass. It was Nurka who cried, and she pressed her close to her heart.

One of the officers—a young one, almost a boy still, bony and malicious—was sitting down, then getting up, smoking and throwing cigarette ends about. He did not take his eyes from her and repeated the same words over and over again :

" Don't be such an impudent liar. You know. You know, young woman ! You know very well ! You won't get away from me."

And suddenly struck the table with his fist.

" You will be arrested at once and shot instead of your husband. Out with it, and don't try to throw dust in our eyes."

She stood motionless as before and replied :

" What do I know ? You can kill me if you like. You dragged him away ; and you can tell where he is ! You can see for yourselves I'm quite alone.—Why do you torture me ? "

The officer was silent and looked fixedly at Dasha. Did

he see suffering in her burning eyes or hear a formless reproach in Nurka's cries ? Suddenly he arose from his chair.

" Search the house carefully. Examine every corner."

They sat her down between two bearded fellows, and they searched the dwelling until morning, rummaging in every corner and crevice, in the closets and among the rags.

" He got away in time, the bastard ! "

Later, in the early dawn, sweaty and tired with their fruitless task, they dragged her and Nurka to a villa. There in a cellar she sat with Nurka among a crowd of strange people, dazed, dishevelled and feverish. There she and Nurka sat until noon. Some of them talked to her, but she did not remember a word they said.

At midday she was taken out of the cellar. The same young bony officer again fixed her with his eyes.

" Well, now, where is your husband, young woman ? Now don't deny anything. Anyway, we shan't let you go until you tell us. If he's safe, what are you worrying about ? Don't be pigheaded, damn it, it's of no use ! "

Tearless, almost fainting with exhaustion, she repeated :

" How do I know, when you yourselves took him away ? It's you who could say how you've tortured him to death ! "

Someone behind her barked like a dog :

" To hell—let her go, Colonel ! Don't you see she's gone mad with fear ? "

But the Colonel's eyes glistened, and he hissed furiously :

" Don't you know, you bitch, that for your obstinacy we shall have to shoot you instead of your husband ? It won't do you any good to play the simple innocent right through to the end."

" All right, shoot ! And then ? And what then ? "

It was not she speaking, it seemed to her, but someone else who vibrated within her like a thin chord.

" You know you've torn him to bits and he's dead. Tear me too. . . . Me and Nurka—! Me and Nurka. . . ."

When her senses returned it was as though the sun had poured balm upon her. She was on the smooth, dusty, burning high-road. In front of her was the factory and there, further up on the slope, the workmen's settlement ; and far away she could see the red roof under which was her room which had been empty since the night.

And now she was again alone. She became friendly with Motia Savchuk and passed whole days with her in her house.

The days and nights were no longer troubled. The days were radiant with the sun and the nights with the stars. And when she sat in her doorway, looking up at the stars and hearing the streams in the valley ringing like little bells, she would think about Gleb. Where was he? Was he alive? Would he come back sometime to her out of the darkness?

One day when the mountains melted in a shimmering mist into the sky, Dasha was sitting as usual on the doorstep, darning some rags. Near her, Nurka was playing with a kitten on the asphalt courtyard. Grasshoppers played music on their combs and over the sea beyond the roof-lines of the works, gulls flashed in the air.

A soldier, his face distinguished by the length of his moustaches, his legs wrapped in ragged puttees, passed by. Soldiers were always passing by nowadays. He came up to the fence and stood there leaning against the posts. This was nothing, there were but few soldiers who did not hungrily accost a woman. But this one spoke to her in an unusual, stern and stealthy voice.

" Dasha, don't jump like a cat. Don't move. News of Gleb. Look! A paper has fallen down. At night-time I'll come to you. Don't be frightened! "

And on he went. She noticed only that his immense moustache and his eyebrows hung like scraps of tow.

She wanted to fly to the fence for the paper, but the soldier turned back once more, frowning with his tufted eyebrows. She understood that she had to wait until he had disappeared. With blood rushing to her heart, her eyes filled with a red whirling, with the last effort of her will, she softly beckoned Nurka.

" Come here to mummie, my darling. Quicker—quicker! Pick up that piece of paper and bring it to mummie. That's right. Come to mummie's arms with the paper. Quicker—quicker! "

Like a baby chicken, Nurka pecked at the piece of paper and picked it up; and like a chicken waddled back to Dasha.

" Here, mummie! Here it is! "

She lay on her mother's lap and began to kick her legs.

A red whirlwind was in Dasha's eyes, her heart was bursting.

These were the words she read on the paper: these were the words written by Gleb. Could anyone except Gleb write like this?

" Dasha, I am alive and well. Take care of yourself and

little Nurka. Burn this at once; and Efim of the Moustache will tell you everything."

Gleb, dear beloved Gleb! If you're still alive and well with courage to face life—then she, Dasha, is also strong and full of courage with which to face life.

At night, the moustachioed Efim came. He smelt of the mountains and the woods, but it seemed to Dasha that he smelt not of the woods but of Gleb. In the darkness of the room, near the window—the sky was flecked with moving stars—Dasha sat side by side with Efim, trembling with joy and love for Gleb. The moustachioed one, with a hoarse whisper, smelling of tobacco and with a revolver in his hand, at once began to speak such words as Dasha could scarcely understand.

"Now the first point, Dasha, you must help us. Firstly, Gleb is dragging his way through the White lines to the Red Army. If he's lucky, he'll get through. If he falls into a trap, good-night! But it isn't about him——"

Dasha, trembling, incoherently, stammered.

"Then, is it—is it possible—. Tell me, Comrade Efim. . . . Could he perish in such a tramping life? Then he's alone? He's alone among these human beasts——"

"Now the talk's not about him in the second place. The second point is a word about yourself, Gleb's word. Take care of yourself and be strong. The times are so uncertain—. You won't lose sight of me. You'll be our Green friend. This comes from me and Gleb, who's hand in glove with me. Follow closely. You're going to do it, not just for Gleb, but for all our brother Greens. For the time being, our band takes the place of your husband. Remember now. I shall be everywhere ready—everywhere at once. You want to organise all the Green widows into a band. You yourself get into the factory co-operative, into the food department. We can settle that at once. Well, that's all! Don't come out, just slip the latch."

"And how about my daughter? What about little Nurka?"

"Put her in the care of a good woman. Nurka won't fly away from you. If you've got another word to say, say it now."

Dasha trembled all over, and however much she tried she could not say the needed word. She only said:

"Perhaps, Comrade Efim, it may be that Gleb is even now walking alone in the night. And death is hovering over him. If it is so for him it should be so for me. I should follow the road that my Gleb has followed."

Efim smiled in the darkness and he tapped her knee softly.

And he went out unheard, as though he had never been there at all, as though he had passed like a dark night-shadow through her dream-thoughts.

There came another time when Dasha shuddered and trembled as she had that night. But that was a long time after, at the end of many long days of obstinate labour.

She confided Nurka to the care of Motia, to whom she gave over a portion of her food ration. Motia was a good woman, a good friend, and she cared well for Nurka.

Dasha began to work for the Co-operative, at the distribution of bread in the bakery. Sometimes unknown men arrived (at such times the blood rushed to her heart) and in return for slips of paper took away sacks of bread "For the workers in the mountain quarries."

There were about half a dozen of the "Green Widows." Half of them were petty speculators, abused and deceived their husbands, carrying on with other men, and soon forgot their old mates altogether. The other three were unemployed, and kept themselves by washing linen for the officers and receiving soldiers and Englishmen at night in order to obtain food. Dasha got them together and gave them tasks to perform : to go to the town and then to the mountains, taking clothes, boots and papers and reports to the Greens, from various important people.

The Green Women included : Fimka, a girl bride whose brother Petro was with the Greens. She had the delicate air of a refined lady. Domasha, a big-built woman with florid complexion, who had three whimpering little children. And Lizaveta, a childless young woman, high-chested and with a brilliant colour, in spite of the famine.

Fimka was submissive, she never refused a man when he desired her, nor did she ever refuse a woman a share of her bread ration.

Domasha was vindictive and ready to gratify her desire for vengeance on every one. Lizaveta was reserved, and during the daytime in front of other people was inaccessible. These were the ones whom Dasha had formed into a group. They were the only people with whom she spent her free time.

Efim, of the long moustaches, used to come to her at night-time and would tap her knees with his revolver while saying :

" You must know, Women-Comrades, the main thing you have to do—keep mum, and die rather than speak. Bite your

tongue out. . . . The tongue's the worst part of human flesh. . . .
If you were ever found out, bite your tongue off and spit it out.
But don't recognise anyone with your eyes. Understand ? The
tongue won't lift a mountain but it can destroy whole ranges."

This was their first teacher, and a sure one.

And thus passed about a year. And this year steeled Dasha
with experience, cunning and strength. How that came to her
she did not know. The other women shared in her strength
and she became their leader.

And it was at the end of this first year that Dasha was again
shocked to the depths. From that time on her eyebrows became knotted, and her eyes cold as crystal.

One morning—it was a fine, bracing morning, clear and
smelling of the autumn—as Dasha stood at the counter with
the bread before the long queue of applicants, some officers
came in, rifle in hand, jostling through the crowd, seizing her
and dragging her out of the shop. The people, terrorised, ran
away towards their houses. She was put on a motor-lorry
among a number of officers and was driven to a villa—the same
in which she and 'Nurka had been locked up before—and
thrown into the same cellar. Just as before, many people were
here, lying or seated on the ground. As before they were all
strangers to her, and each of them wrapped in his individual
misfortunes.

But Dasha was now different from what she had been. She
knew that she was running a great risk and was prepared.
She had thought a great deal as to how she would behave in
such a case—how she would betray no weakness. She could go
through anything : torture and perhaps death. But one
thought lurked in her mind, intolerable : they might try to
force her through Nurka. She could not stand that.

She looked round in the shadows of the moist cement walls
and suddenly saw a great moustache and eyebrows like tufts
of tow. The eyes did not recognise her, they were gleaming
over the others there. She understood : one must not recognise another. Then she saw Fimka, lying on the ground in
disorder shaken with sobs ; near her sat her little brother
Petro, his smooth boyish cheeks covered with down, as though
with dust. He was stroking her hair and shoulders, and caressingly whispering to her ; his face was that of a man recovering
from a drinking bout.

Here for the first time she realised the horror of human
suffering.

The moustachioed man was dragged out first, and she after him. They brought her into a room, but Efim was not there then. The same vindictive young Colonel was there and he recognised her at once.

" You've come to visit us again ? Well, this time you won't get away from here. Well, how have you fed the Greens ? Why did you lie when you told us you didn't know where your husband was ? "

Dasha put on an imbecile look and staring at the Colonel answered :

" How do I know where my husband is ? You've taken him away from me and now you turn round and ask me about the Greens ! "

" We'll verify this. Take her into the kitchen and feed her well."

She was dragged to another smaller cellar. The floor was covered under an offensive congealed mat which stank of decaying human flesh. In the filthy slime were clots of congealed blood. A naked man lay on the floor, abominably dirty ; he turned his head from side to side in the viscous slime, bathed in his own blood. Two big Cossacks were whipping him, their hoarse panting mingling with the whistle of the swishing leather whips.

Someone, she could not remember who, burnt her back and shoulders with fire, but it was really a blow from a whip. She screamed savagely.

" One ! Two ! Now you've got it, bitch ! See, you'll be down there in a minute like him ! Show this beautiful creature that carrion over there. Do you recognise this swine ? "

She felt nothing but her nauseated heart. She gathered together all the strength of her soul so as not to fall down.

" Why are you torturing me ? What for ? How should I know this man ? "

" Give that fellow his second course ! "

And again they fell upon Efim with their whips, and he turned his head first to one side and then to the other and was silent. And Dasha felt the great sacrifice and the terror which lay in the silence of the moustachioed one. And she realised that only one thing was necessary : to be silent, even until her ribs cracked ; to be silent even if it suffocated her heart.

" Well, speak, woman of the devil ! What kind of goings on have you had with this rascal ? If you tell us we won't bother him any more and we'll let you go home."

"I don't know about any goings on——. I've been left without my husband with my little daughter. . . . Why do you torture me so?"

Again an unbearable fire burned through her. Her heart seemed to burst, she cried out shrilly:

"What have I done to you? Why do you beat me so?"

"Speak! Just one word and we'll let you free."

As soon as Dasha heard these last words she realised that they knew nothing about her business. They had arrested her only because they had done so on the previous occasion. They had not taken any of the other women. Ah, but Fimka? Fimka was different: it was because of her brother. Probably they had taken her by accident in her home. Dasha understood this now, and her blood flowed again in her veins.

"Stop torturing me. I work and don't interfere with any one."

"Give that fellow another ration! Let him have it! Harder! Make him grunt!"

Efim's body lay in the mud already shuddering in the preliminary convulsions of death. The Cossacks, tired out, covered with sweat, continued to flagellate the bloody flesh. Their whips scattered drops of blood and minute morsels of raw flesh.

The body of Fimka's little brother Petro fell with a moan of terror into the gory filth, beside Dasha. Covered with mud, with animal terror in his eyes, he jumped to his feet, slipped and fell again; again he bounded up and began to run with naked feet in the mire. The Cossacks leapt after him, their whips raised. Petro howled with his whole body. He escaped them once more, and ran, blind and lost, in the other direction. But a Cossack, jumping in his path, whooped and gave him a blow with all his might on the knees. Petro howled like a dog and fell down heavily on his belly in the slime.

With dead eyes, Dasha looked at the torturing of her comrades. Dumb, with bursting brain, she could not turn her gaze from them. She saw only blood which boiled and bubbled like the moving sea. In the air was blood, and blood was in her brain; behind the dusty window-holes was blood.

She recovered consciousness in that bright room where the Colonel was sitting, frowning, smoking and vindictive.

"Well, young woman, how do you like our kitchen? Now tell us what you know."

"But I know nothing——. Nothing at all."

" Didn't you recognise that lad or that girl ? "

" I know Fimka and Petro. I've known them ever since they were children."

Two officers, as young as he, whispered something in the Colonel's ear. At first he frowned, and then sucked in his cheeks.

" Give her to us, Colonel ; we'll disinfect her a bit."

Straight into her face, grimacing, they breathed horrible words, more painful than the whip.

She threw herself in the corner of the room, her hands extended.

" No ! No ! I would rather die ! Don't ! "

The Colonel raised his hand, smiling.

" All right, it won't happen if you will only tell the truth. Come here and tell us."

" What shall I tell, when I know nothing ? What do you want from me ? Aren't you ashamed? You are still young——."

The Colonel leaned against the back of his chair and screwed up his eyes spitefully.

The two officers seized her under the arms and dragged her into another room. They flung her on the floor, dragged the clothes from her shamelessly and violated her.

Till midnight she lay, half-naked and half-dead, in the cellar. As they had thrown her so they left her. Fimka crawled up to her, moaning, then without speaking laid her head for a moment on Dasha's breast, and then crawled away. Twice she seemed to see Nurka : the child was stamping with her little feet, dancing the wild Hopak dance, tipsily. Dasha stretched her hand towards her and shouted in terror and disgust :

" No, don't ! Don't, little Nurka ! "

She was crawling towards her, like Fimka, imploring in despair for she knew not what. Then Nurka came no more into her mind. She saw no more of her as though Nurka were the extinguished image of a dream.

After midnight—she remembered it as though in a dream— she was brought to herself by the noise of a motor-lorry. She lay upon its wooden floor among others who crouched and lay there. Bit by bit she recognised Fimka, her little brother Petro and Efim, the moustachioed one. Around them stood officers and Cossacks with rifles in their hands. All were silent, benumbed like corpses.

Only one thing remained vivid in her memory : the many-coloured stars which seemed to be so near, within arms' reach.

She had no fear. She knew she was going to her death. The lorry would stop and they would be thrown out, and they would be led to the seashore—then she would be no more. She knew this—but she had no heart, only a block of ice. There was no terror, only this unbearable coldness in the heart. It was all so simple as though it had no existence in reality ; and yet quite ordinary, the tedious progress of a dream which one does not credit while dreaming, knowing that these images will soon pass. Nurka was forgotten, as though she had never existed ; then suddenly her image flew past her, with little hand outstretched and one short outcry : " Oh ! " This shook her like a blow of the whip in the cellar. Then Nurka disappeared again and was forgotten like a dream long past.

The comrades lying on the floor of the lorry were shaken about like corpses : it was Efim (he had been thrown into the lorry like a corpse) and Fimka and Petro. Dasha had no pity for anyone ; her heart was no more than a lump of ice that could never melt.

When the car stopped, Dasha was no longer alive ; it seemed that her life had ended with the motor's movement. When she was pulled off the lorry to the ground she stood as motionless as she had lain. Close to her stood Fimka, shivering with the cold, catching hold of Dasha's dress, and pressing herself close to her like a child. The long-moustached Efim lay at their feet like a corpse. But Petro was stamping crazily in one place, disfigured by the whipping and turning his head—his face was black with blood—howling, spitting, grunting.

And then Dasha (but it seemed to Dasha it was not she, but some other person) whispered hurriedly and sternly into Fimka's ear :

" Be silent and silent and silent. Silent and silent. Blind, dumb . . . silent ! "

It seemed as though a great crowd flung itself upon her, throwing her to one side.

It was the four Cossacks who were pushing Fimka and Petro with their rifles. Submissively and silently, taking short steps, and without turning back, they went. But when they were a little distance away, Fimka cried out and flapped her arms like a bird fluttering. She tried to run back, began to wave her arms madly.

" Dasha ! Dasha, dear ! What are they doing with me, Dasha ? "

They pushed her on, swearing at her; she shrieked, stumbled, then fell on the sand. They seized her arms and dragged her to her feet. She walked a few steps in silence, then stopped and shouted concernedly to Dasha :

" Dasha, what have I done ? I have left my shawl in the automobile ! "

Again a storm of oaths drowned her words, and she was violently shoved forward.

There in front of them on a sandy headland which melted into the sea like a dull red mass, where the sea, without reflecting any lights, receded into a singing darkness—there Dasha saw dim shadows that seemed to be dancing, drunken.

Again Fimka's shrill shriek.

" I don't want to ! I can't ! To die young—I want to see it with my own eyes ! "

Right up to the volley she did not stop crying out.

" Go away ! Go away ! With my own eyes, I want——! "

And when they fired, it seemed to Dasha that the sea clamoured and sang with Fimka's cries.

A shadow came close to Dasha.

" For the last time : show us who is working with the Greens. I give you my word of honour to let you go home at once then. Or—do you see ? In a minute you will be over there ! "

And Dasha replied as before, putting on that foolish air.

" I'm only a woman ; I can't tell who is Green and who is not Green. I've my little daughter Nurka, and I work. . . . For one must live."

And she began to cry. She was really crying, but it was not she who cried, but Nurka, her little daughter, within her heart, fluttering like a little bird.

" All right then ! Get hold of this fool, now. Carry him over there by his hands and feet."

And they dragged away Efim. And this time, Dasha heard only one report instead of a volley.

Again the shadow of the officer approached her.

" I give you half a minute's time."

" But what can I say ? Well—shoot ! Shoot, then ! "

She felt that only a moment would pass, and then she would fall on the sand convulsed like Fimka, and she would cry out loudly. Her heart was melting and breaking up.

Suddenly she seemed to be flung through the air, and her head banged against some iron.

Again the lorry was shaking and rattling; again the stars scintillated like golden gems within arms' reach, and over the mountain the sky burned like a fiery mist.

This time they did not throw her into the cellar, but led her into the other room, where the officers had spoken with her. The young Colonel, without looking at her, said carelessly and distinctly:

" Engineer Kleist has made himself responsible for you. We have no confidence in you, but we have in him."

. . . Motia's a good woman and a good friend . . . and at this very time her children were dying from the plague. . . .

" You can go," the vindictive Colonel was saying. " But remember, if you get caught again you'll never return home any more. And remember another thing: nothing has happened to you here and your eyes have seen nothing. And if ever you blab the same will happen to you as did to those dogs. Clear out of here! March! "

After this Dasha never shuddered again; and always her eyebrows were knit in a deep frown, from that time on.

She said nothing to anyone; yet learned to speak in season and to the purpose. She never got home until midnight, and her room became stained with damp, and full of cobwebs; and dust settled in the corners. The flowers at the windows faded and dried up. Her face grew paler and her eyes cold and transparent. She passed many hours at Motia's home, with that good friend and housewife. She became friendly with Savchuk and Gromada and would sit a long time in the yard of the factory with the hunch-back, Loshak. They were secretly preparing to welcome the Red Army. She acquainted Loshak, Gromada and Savchuk with her secret work. Once they used to sleep at night-time and look at the mountains by day. And now their eyes were sleepless in the nights, and in the daytime they seemed blind.

Soldiers came, with a dumb questioning in their eyes. They pretended they had come to play the fool, to amuse themselves with the young widows. They came once or twice, then disappeared; then in their places came others. And where the first ones had gone to no one could tell from Dasha's expressionless face.

Thus it was, for the first time, of her own free will, without being untrue to Gleb in her own soul, Dasha had relations with other men; and when she recalled it she had no regret. It was as if this had become part of her perilous work under the eyes of the counter-espionage. Some dull-eyed soldier would come to her and would not go away into the mountains ; and would say from his heart :

" I can't go like this without you, Dasha. I can't be like a wild beast in the woods. Embrace me for the last time. There will be no terror for me afterwards."

It is true there were moments when she also lost her head, but this was her sacrifice. Why was this sacrifice more than her life ? Yet this moment filled the man with strength and courage.

In the harbour, British ships lay at anchor, taking on board crowds of rich and highly born people who had fled from the north.

And somewhere behind the mountains, the earth shook with a dull subterranean thunder, and at night shells flashed in the sky like shooting-stars.

On one hot spring morning, rayed with the sun, when one could not distinguish the sky from the sea and the quivering air from the trees in bloom, Dasha, her red kerchief round her head, strode through the rubble and the corpses of men and horses, through the stench which came from the panic-stricken death of the White hordes—into the town to look for Communists. She went quite alone, while the citizens and workers, still terrorised, did not dare to come out of their holes.

She went on ; her eyes and her head-band burned among the sunny beams and in the blue of the sky and the sea. Her eyes burned with an amber lustre, and the band, scarlet like fresh blood.

She met some Red soldiers on horseback, with red arm-bands on their uniform sleeves, and these arm-bands glowed like flaming poppies. She looked at them and laughed, and they beckoned her, laughing also and shouted.

" Hurrah for the Red kerchief ! Hurrah for the Red woman ! Hurrah ! "

Crushed, Gleb lay for a long time without moving, his head in Dasha's lap, without being able to speak. Here she was—his Dasha. She sat near him like his own wife ; the same voice, the same face and hands, and the heart beating as before. But this was not the Dasha of three years ago ; that Dasha had gone from him forever.

An inexpressible tenderness shook him painfully. He embraced her with trembling hands, and, choking, fighting back tears, he moaned with anger, helplessness and fondness.

" Dasha, my dove ! Ah, if I'd been here in those days when you were suffering alone. . . . If I had only known ! And now my heart is bursting, Dasha. You were sleeping with strangers. . . . Dasha ! I could strike you and torture you. . . . Oh, why did you tell me this, Dasha ? But I cannot lift my hand to you. . . . My hand has withered—curse it ! But you . . . you—alone with the soldiers. . . . Can I understand it ? Dasha ! Well, so be it. I can't make laws for you. . . . But I've nobody dearer than you. . . . You are alive. You went alone, and you found your own ways of fighting. Dasha, my dove, my darling ! "

" Gleb, you're a good man. You're stupid, Gleb, but you're good ! "

And so they stayed until night fell, sitting closely embraced ; as they had not sat since the first days of their marriage.

Chapter XI

IN THE VICE

I

THE MASTERS' HANDS

UNTIL sunrise Gleb was visiting one dwelling after another, personally directing the work of the detachment.

Their rifles slung on their backs, the vigilant silent figures of the workmen stood in the streets. In the streets, which were half-vanished in the darkness, the tramp of heavy boots filled the night with terror. Already the air shimmered with the blue dawn, and the stars, paling, seemed near and spring-like.

Shuk was on guard. This was not the same Shuk, the loafing, suspicious buffoon and slouching disturber, who now stood before Gleb, but a strong, menacing soldier. As Gleb approached him he did not break into his usual flood of exclamations ; he kept his rifle firmly grounded. From the open doors of a detached villa with big bay windows, the mewing hysterical cries of women were issuing.

" Who's working here, Shuk ? "

"They're searching here, friend. Can you hear how the woman's shrieking ! Savchuk ! Savchuk, your wife, Serge and the two Chekists. Go and have a look at them stripping the bourgeoisie ! "

" Well, and how's your work in the Economic Council getting on, Shuk ? Have you caught many fleas ? "

" Ho, ho, friend. . . . Just pay a visit to Shibis ! I felt like standing them all up against a wall to-day. You can't imagine what scoundrels they are. And as for Shramm, I'd stand him up first, or I don't know my own mind ! Imagine, they've been starving all the men who are felling timber in the forest, and themselves getting as fat as rats in a granary. How I hate to see the working-class cheated like that ! Just wait a bit, friend : we'll give them such a smashing, they won't know where they are."

A Red soldier, with his rifle, stood in the half-light of the corridor with its great windows. Through the open door, among the shadows, one could see a dishevelled woman, stretched on a sofa, sobbing and wringing her hands.

A hard, hurried job was being carried out there : the furniture was groaning as it was shoved about : voluminous bundles fell softly to the floor ; heavy boots tramped and slid.

Gleb entered, brusque and military, boldly trampling this cultured intimacy. He had no eyes for the woman on the sofa who, half-clothed, with tearful swollen face, looked with terror at these men with rifles who stood guard, and at those who were emptying the drawers, wardrobes and chests. Most likely she didn't notice beside her a little bare-kneed girl, who looked inquisitively at these unknown people who had so suddenly and noiselessly descended upon them in the night.

A man in slippers, braces and shirt-sleeves, with gold pince-nez and a long pointed beard, stood bewildered by a large writing-table. Lonely and proud, he shrugged his shoulders and smiled convulsively.

With the skilled hands of a good housewife, Dasha was carefully putting aside all that she could find that was plain and most useful among the linen, clothes and household utensils. She was placing them on sheets which were spread out on the ground, or into travelling baskets.

" This is for the Children's Homes . . . for the little ones. This for the Maternity Homes. Ah, this is good stuff ! They've got a lot piled up here ! This means clothes for such a lot of children ! "

Savchuk, clumsy as a bull, was turning out cupboards and chests of drawers. His soiled feet were white from the strain and his face empurpled.

" Oh, the devils—what stuff they've hoarded up here for themselves ! While our swineherds were making pipe-lighters and carrying sacks around the country, these vile people were getting fat as pigs in their hidden corners. Ha, ha, here's some music—no balalaika, but a regular barge ! " He was drumming the piano now. " You'd have to be big as bulls to play on this ! "

Serge stood there, his rifle in hand, and did not know what to do. In his youth he had visited this house. Chirsky, a well-known lawyer, in years gone by was friendly with his father. He was a socialist, a member of all the Imperialist Dumas, a member of the Constituent Assembly, elected on list No. 7.

Serge did not look at him and was fighting down his own agitation. He was afraid Chirsky would come up to him and offer his hand and begin to speak to him like an old acquaintance. He pretended not to recognise him and clenched his teeth until it hurt. He wished to be firm with his comrades, but he felt his legs tremble at the prospect of some scandalous incident happening.

And that which he had looked forward to as frightful and irreparable happened quite simply and unnoticed. Chirsky was staring at him and smiling fastidiously, waiting the moment to pass him a word.

" So, Serge Ivanovitch, you also are engaged in such unbecoming affairs as this attack ? In your language and mine we would call this robbery. You will most likely go on from here to your father, Ivan Arsenitch, and perform the same operation. Probably you will leave your father just a little more for himself than you have left us here. Here you are taking our last suit of underwear. Aren't you preserving for yourself the inviolability of inheritance ? Perhaps here too, for the sake of old friendship, you will make some allowance ? "

The woman stopped crying and stretched out her arms to him. Tears trickled down her cheeks and trembled on the sagging pouches of her double chin.

" Serge Ivanovitch ! My little dove. . . . There was a time when you were a dear friend of ours ! What are you doing here ?, Can it possibly be you, Serge Ivanovitch ? "

Forcing himself to be immovable and stern, Serge gripped his rifle till his finger joints cracked ; there was a singing in his head. Without looking at Chirsky, he said sharply :

" Yes, my father will have the same treatment as you. Like you he will be turned out of his house and will not return to it."

When he had said these words he felt suddenly relieved. The man standing by the table seemed comical in his faded dignity and presumption.

" So, so. . . . You've learned to be fierce enough I see. Congratulations ! "

Dasha had found a big doll, a fat one with big eyes and yellow wool on its head. She smiled and stepped up to the little girl.

" What a wonderful doll ! Take it, little one ; she's been lonely without you—she thought she'd been lost. How nice you look together, you and the doll ! "

The girl jumped off the sofa and took the doll with both hands. Dasha smiled and patted her on the head.

Horrified, the woman rushed over to the little girl and seized her hand.

" Nina, don't you dare ! I forbid it ! Come here—! Don't you see, they're not ashamed to take your last little chemise from you ? Throw the doll away ? Come here at once ! "

The girl pressed the doll to her breast and threw herself on the sofa, covering it with her body.

" It's my doll—mine ! Mummie, dear ! "

The knot of Dasha's eyebrows contracted.

" Aren't you ashamed of yourself, madam ? "

Savchuk sniffed and grumbled. He was carrying the bedding from the bedrooms, great heaps of clothes which he threw on to the floor. He wiped the sweat from his forehead and glared like a wolf at the people and the goods.

" There ! These heathen—what a lot of stuff they've stored up ! This job is worse than the coopers' shop ! Damn it, I'd rather work on the ropeway ! "

Dasha came up to Gleb and reported briskly :

" An inventory has been made of everything, Gleb. Everything needed has been taken. We've left them one change of linen and clothing. I have decided to expropriate the pictures and other rare things like clocks, china, toys and books. Whew, there's all the books in the world here ! To-morrow we'll put the seals of the People's Commissariat for Education on the books. Everything else and this piano will go to the Children's Homes and the Clubs."

Gleb was cold and reserved as one who commands.

" All right. Leave everything except the linen in its place. A guard of two men must stay here. Finish up here ! "

" Good, that's what I thought. We're waiting for the carts."

She walked away stern and preoccupied.

Gleb went up to Serge and took him on one side.

" Where's your old man's house ? I'm going to pay him a visit."

Serge could not tell whether there was irony in Gleb's words or just a friendly joke. He choked down his anxiety and shouldered his rifle.

" I can go with you, Comrade Chumalov ; it's not far from here."

" No, that would be a mistake. It would be too painful for

the old man. We're not doing this to torture people, but to execute our business."

Serge pressed Gleb's hand tightly and turned away.

In the starlit dawn the houses appeared blue. Mist was drifting down from the mountains and purple shadows floated over the bay. The morning song of the birds resounded. Mysterious torches—now near, now far—lit up and vanished again in the steel-like opacity of the mountains.

Gleb's path was barred at the cross street by a compact mass in military array with bayonets bristling. With rhythmic step the Red soldiers were marching. Most likely there were many columns of them which were not visible, but the stir of their movement was everywhere over the town. In the alleys and along the paved ways. The clanging carts rolled on. The Red Army, a campaign, field-work. . . . It was such a short time ago ! How he loved them ! Gleb's helmet had not yet cooled down after fire and forced marches. They were marching, and their bayonets wove a harmonious movement. They were marching and he was here. Why should he be here instead of taking his place in those ranks ? He, the War Commissar of the regiment. His helmet burned his head with the unquenched fire of action.

Sobbing, with long strides, he hurried towards the long rows of bayonets, for a moment to mingle with the elastic rhythmic ranks and render them the greeting of a Red soldier. But the column wheeled abruptly, disappearing round the corner, and he saw only two Red soldiers, one behind the other, silently hitching up their knapsacks and swinging their rifles, hurrying to catch up with their comrades.

2

SENT OUT TO PASTURE

Gleb came through the garden gate and saw something different from what he had seen at other houses. Mekhova stood before a pile of clothes and rags and laughed. Gromada and Loshak were passing in and out of the house, carrying armfuls of books and other objects. At the open door stood a merry old man, laughing and shouting.

" Everything, everything ! Take this, and this too. All this rubbish was acquired by a man in order to concentrate his life upon one spot. Generally the concentration of life upon one spot continues, my friends, until the moment of death—that is to say, a state which negates the three dimensions. That is the ideal, measured by the absolute norm : nothingness. Isn't that so, friends ? Isn't it curious, interesting and amusing ? "

Mekhova was looking at Gleb from where she stood, her eyes wide open, and in her smile and her eyes he saw wonder, mingled with an intoxication.

" Gleb, look at this wonderful strange fellow. He's Serge's father. He's a man who can say much more than ordinary people. If you had only seen with what enthusiasm he met us, and with what joy he's breaking up his home ! "

She was shivering in the chilliness, and caressing him with her eyes.

A man with only one arm, a nose like an eagle, and an un-usually short upper lip, passed near Gleb with military step. As he went by he glanced sharply at Gleb and with a springy step walked towards the gate.

A burning shock passed through Gleb.

" Citizen, I ask you to return ! "

The one-armed man turned quickly about and still stepping elastically and with the same sharp look came up to Gleb.

" Who are you ? Your social position ? "

Without changing his expression the one-armed man stood at attention before Gleb.

" Dimitri Ivagin, formerly Colonel and now a citizen of the Soviet Republic. The eldest son of this merry old man and the only brother of the member of the Communist Party, Serge Ivagin. Do you want my papers ? "

" Keep your papers. Your room will be searched. Please remain here."

" My corner is in my father's dwelling. Everything down to the last scrap has been already carried out. Only my pockets have not been searched. Do you wish to see them ? "

An indefinable mockery played in the cold gleam of his eyes. Gleb's unquiet gaze returned Dimitri Ivagin's sharp look ; he clenched his teeth.

" I don't want to see your pockets. You may go."

Ivagin clicked his heels together and turned away.

In the room the old man, whose beard stood out at right angles to his chin, tripped hither and thither, bustling and burning with enthusiasm, uttering little impulsive cries.

" Real freedom, my friends, lies in the complete negation of geometrical designs and their material realisation. The Communists are strong and wise because they have turned Euclid's geometry upside down. I recognise them and love them because of their amusing revolution against permanency and all such fetish forms. Don't leave anything here, my friends ; that would be inconsistent of you and disagreeable to me. To be tied, even by one little rotten thread, to the sides of a cube, prism or triangle, is more fearful than to be buried under mountains of rubbish."

Loshak rolled his eyes—only hunchbacks can frighten people by rolling their eyes this way—in his smoke-stained face and continued his work. He gathered an armful of clothes into a heap, gazed at the old man, reflected for a moment, and then burst out in his deep voice :

" Get out into the open, father. We're going to send you out to the grazing grounds. Get busy and look for a place for yourself out there. Don't grouse at poverty, and don't call up the shadows. . . ."

The old man was laughing and waving his arms in rapture.

" Yes, that's right. . . . Your strictness comes merely from your unconscious humanity. To send a man to the grazing grounds—what could be more ideal than that condition ? The earth, the sky, infinity. . . . Yes, yes, friends ! But why didn't my son Serge come with you ? I would have liked to have seen him in the rôle of a triumphant lictor."

Gromada, shaking his head, was gathering up books, clothing, rugs in the cupboards, chests and corners. He was becoming bored with the old man's chatter.

" Don't talk through your hat, daddy. I propose that you make yourself useful on the labour front. . . . Er, it's very choked up just now, you know, with all kinds of rubbish . . . but Loshak and I are trying to clear it up. . . ."

Gromada was always the same : a little man with a big name and a user of big words.

Gleb went up to the old man and held out his hand to him.

" Well now, have you been well cleaned out, my dear old fellow ? Your son Serge has also been working hard to-night at the searching."

" Good, very good. It's a pity that he didn't come here— a great pity, I'd have liked to have had a look at him——"

" You can remain here if you wish : this room is yours. You needn't trouble. You're one of our cultural workers. Anything you wish to keep will be left with you."

The old man looked at Gleb in terror. He nervously plucked at his beard.

" No, no ! Take everything, everything ! This has been so good, magnificent ! "

Gleb shook his head and looked with disdainful compassion at this bustling, enthusiastic old sage.

" His head's like a windmill, Comrade Chumalov, with his damned ideology."

Loshak was rolling his eyes and bellowing confusedly in his bass voice.

Gleb looked at the old man, shaking with inward laughter.

" Well, dad, you can live as you like. I didn't know that Serge had such an interesting old man."

He again shook his hand and hurriedly went out.

3

THE GRAZING GROUNDS

On the other side of the bay, beyond the factory, the mountains were brown and pitted with black hollows. The sky at the zenith was blue and deep, and fiery over the hills. The peaks of the ridge were sharply defined in a dazzling line like molten metal. But from the mountain passes, dense clouds of wreathing mist, lit by an internal fire, poured down in snowy cataracts.

The factory across the bay towered like the far-away castles of fairy tales. The supple smoke-stacks were blue, and lithe and straight they flew upwards to meet the crawling snow-drifts of cloud. The sea under the mountains was blue as the sky with light and black scales were upon its surface.

On the other side, behind the town, the crests of the mountains glittered in lilac heat, while lower down they were misty with the shadows of morning. The town—its stone piles garlanded with the blue haze of gardens—crept like a giant along the slopes right down to the sea, where it was mirrored in innumerable tossing fragments.

In the main street was a great crowd, tumultuous as at a fair. Women's shrieks and hysterical weeping cleft the stony length of the street. The noise and the shouting was converting the crowd into a panic-stricken herd and convulsing it by innumerable gusty brawls. In the centre were terror and despair. The men stood submissively—dull, blinking in pale-faced confusion. The women, with bundles and boxes and with children in their arms or holding their hand, were sitting on their burdens of household goods, shrieking wordlessly, weeping, or standing silently, or lying down quietly with mad eyes. In some places the weaker ones were the victims of a seizure, and around them noisy and despairing people were standing, not knowing what to do.

Chirsky stood a little apart from the crowd; he was still in shirt-sleeves, braces and slippers, and was bare-headed. A dead smile was on his face. He was looking distractedly at the surrounding houses as though he had noticed them for the first time; then he would look at this crowd, which he could not endure. His wife sat on a bundle, dishevelled, half undressed, and gazed at a fixed point. Her florid, fleshy face was swollen. The little girl was dancing to and fro between her father and mother, crying rhythmically, and clutching her big doll with both arms.

The carts, loaded with large white bundles, were crawling on in single file. At the rise of the street they could be seen emerging from the hollow—the white bundles and the heads of the horses.

On the second cart stood a Young Communist with bare chest and curly head. He was kicking his legs and playing a polka on his guitar. Somewhere in the distance an asthmatical concertina was hoarsely wheezing and moaning.

The Special Communist Detachment lined the road on either side, each man seven paces from the next, with grounded rifles. The rest of the Communists, haggard and morose from sleepless nights, were looking at the crowd without seeming to see it. In the side streets trampled and shouted another crowd: small traders and other petty bourgeois, who had come out to see this unusual sight.

The petty bourgeois women do not look abroad for laughter. They are soft-hearted—they are fond of burials and tears; and at a wedding it is not the dancing, but the sorrow and tears of the bride that attracts them.

Such is the life of the petty bourgeois woman; she will welcome a stranger in tears rather than one who comes with laughter.

So here in their hearts, the lower middle-class women felt the call of abundant tears; and they were running in from various parts of the town, from their own little houses or from nationalised flats, to revel in the moans and sobs of these

oppressed, honourable and respected families. Greedily and
sadly they gazed at the sobbing women, and their puffy faces
were watered with greasy tears.

Somewhere in the distance an order was given. Other
voices passed it down the length of the line. The convoy
shouldered arms, the crowd shuddered, a deep sigh rose; it
became agitated, rushing hither and thither as on a market
day. Sobs, hysterical cries, exclamations and shouts of these
fear-maddened people threw them together into close groups,
dominated by disorderly panic. There was no air, no streets,
no houses—there was only an orgy of death and a mad despair.

The first carts of the caravan began to rumble on and the
crowd, with a storm of sobbing, surged in a broad wave along
the street.

Serge was walking behind Dasha and behind him came Shuk.
On the other side of the street—one could see them through
the crowd—were walking little Gromada, the hump-backed
Loshak, and Mekhova.

A vague anguish filled Serge's breast. What they were
doing was ugly, revolting. Surely the Party could not author-
ise it. Why this crowd? These women convulsively sobbing?
These children in their mothers' arms? The Party could not
approve of this, he thought; for Serge it was too heavy, more
than he could bear.

Over there was the little girl with the doll; she was holding
her mother's hand and in her other hand she grasped the doll's
arm.

Chirsky walked on calmly, his head high, with sacrificial
dignity; his braces slid up and down on his shoulders, and
his hands were in his trouser pockets.

A very old woman in bonnet and shawl, stooping, leaning
on a stick, walked as though in a religious procession with
cross and banners; a white-clad young girl supported her
by the arm. They were not crying and had faces like nuns.

Serge saw his father a little way in front. He was walking
alone, sometimes surveying the crowd, his eyebrows raised
in a smile. He was bare-footed and his breeches were ragged.
He walked strangely: at one moment quickly with little
steps, overtaking the others; then he would stop. And then he
would ramble on slowly, deep in thought.

Suddenly he caught sight of Serge and began joyfully to
tug at his beard. He raised his hand in greeting and waited
till Serge came up to him.

" You are my guard, Serge, and I the wise man going into banishment. Isn't that curious ? It's really not becoming for you to have contact with me as long as I'm your prisoner. I only want to tell you that the weapons with which you guard the citadel of your revolutionary dictatorship are laughable and senseless. Your rifle looks more like a flute on the shoulders of such a fierce Bolshevik as you. But you can envy me : just now I feel the world limitless as Spinoza never felt it, although Marcus Aurelius dreamed of it in his long nights."

Since Serge had seen him last his father had aged greatly ; the death of the mother had been the final blow. His rags were like a beggar's. He was dirty and unkempt and his feet were wounded and suppurating. A sickening compassion, amounting to physical pain, burned in Serge's heart.

" Have you nowhere to go, father ? Why don't you settle down with me in my room—we can live together. You mustn't go, father ! Where are you going ? You'll perish, daddy ! "

The old man raised his brows in amazement and laughed like a child.

" Oh, no, my son ! I know too well the price of my liberty. I am a man, and a man has no place because there's not a hole that can enclose the brain of a man. Events are the best teachers : see how liberty vanquishes the slave and what a curse are wings to a hen."

Noiselessly Verochka joined Serge. Most likely she had been walking along with the sightseers. With her usual surprised look, trembling all over, she began whispering indistinctly into Serge's ear. And all that Serge could seize was that this was a tearful appeal.

His father laughed and waved his hands ; joy glittered in his vacant eyes.

" Ah, Verochka ! Unlimited source of love. . . . How does my Golgotha affect you, little girl ? Now, come here, come here ! "

" Ivan Arsenitch ! Ivan Arsenitch ! How happy I am ! Serge Ivanovitch ! I am so very happy ! "

She flew over to the old man and took him by the arm. She walked on with him like a daughter, her face shining with tears.

" Father ! "

Serge wanted to tell his father something, but he had forgotten what. He stretched out his hand to him. But no one took his hand and it dropped. His father with Verochka was walking away from him into the crowd. But once more the old man turned to look at Serge, like a stranger—with a deep furrow in his brow.

" Look, little Serge, how history is never new : I am a certain blind old man, Œdipus, and this is my daughter Antigone."

He laughed, a stranger, remote, who had gone away into a world which Serge could not understand. Serge readjusted his rifle on his shoulder, clenching his teeth painfully. Within him the last bond broke.

The crowd halted in an empty stretch of waste land, with high grey grass, not far from the docks. The crowd sat down on their bundles among the grass tufts. The carts had taken their loads to the warehouses of the Soviet.

On the quays was a long, coloured line of moving people. It was the petty bourgeois women from the town who had followed the crowd.

One heard no more hysterical crying, sobbing and clamour. Some were lying down, others sitting, others wearily stamping on one spot—they seemed like sick folk. Did it matter what might happen afterwards ? The children cried, jumped and tried to play ; it was so nice to run on the grass, with the sun coming out from behind the mountains and burning amidst the morning mist ; and the sea which was so near seemed blue and gold right up to the horizon. Only they were hungry . . . hungry ! The children played and cried : hungry, hungry !

Near them were the landing-stages, but there were no ships, and they were overgrown with grass. The torment of an exhausted crowd resembles hope : the smoke would rise in a minute from the funnels of ships on the glittering swell ; the sirens would shriek ; and the people would run jostling along the quay, intoxicated with the joy of departure.

Gleb looked mournfully at the sea and then in the direction from which Lukhava's detachment was to come, with the carts piled with goods and chattels and the families of the working people.

At night, within the garland of the mountains, rising in stony darkness, fires were flashing like burning birds hurling themselves into the depths from their secret eyries, dropping burning feathers from their wings and croaking words of evil augury. The depths of the night were shattered by a regiment of Red soldiers in battle array. With stony steps and stony faces they went through the menacing shadows at the ominous call of the fiery birds.

This crowd, ravaged by the night, after their convulsions of despair, were weak and obedient as sheep. A useless, foolish flock. Night of sleeplessness, and this seething stagnant mass. . . . Was it worth while to waste energy on this rabble, to terrify it once more before casting it out as one throws filth into the backyard ? Why this unnecessary crying of children, and all this mad panic of living corpses ? This crowd, stinking of intimate household sweat, terrified like sheep driven to the slaughter, groaning with misery and madness—from them arose a nausea which wrenched his entrails. One would have to destroy these nests in some other fashion. These children would carry their fear and terror with them into the future ; because children never forget fear and terror.

The Red regiment, in battle array, soothed Gleb's trouble. But this night of turmoil, reeking of underclothing and stinking of bedroom linen, stirred his soul with outrage and anger.

The principal thing was not this, however ; it was something else. The factory with its thundering roar . . . the docks and the ships which would grow out of the sea. Thousands of workers amidst the thunder of machinery. The earth flaming with golden wheat. This was not here. . . . There in the mountains and beyond them was artillery, and the Red soldiers were loading their rifles in the trenches. And in the fields was desolation ; bands of brigands roamed the land, while famished, naked, barbarised people lay dying on the neglected soil.

To drive away this blind crowd of loafers, whistling and stamping with one's foot ; to prepare one's self for nights in the mountains, winged with fiery ominous signs.

Mekhova, with a rifle across her shoulders, came up to Serge. She had not slept all night, but her eyes burned with the lustre of morning.

" What a long time it is since I've lived through such exciting moments, Serge ! It's just as though I was going through the war and in the October days. It's good, wonderfully good ! Well, and you ? Why are you so dull, Serge, eh ? "

Her words resounding with joyful emotion seemed to come from far away. He heard her and heard her not, and it seemed somehow as if she had been crying out like this for a long time past. He answered inarticulately as in his sleep—not answering her, but that distant voice ; and it seemed as though someone answered her and not he.

" I have a headache."

" What's the matter with you ? How can you think about your head when one's blood is boiling as it used to in those days ? There can be no headaches now—! The New Economic Policy—to the devil with it ? Where is it ? Nowhere ! We shall turn these people over on to forced labour to-morrow. Do you hear, Serge ? "

" I don't know. . . ."

" What do you mean—you don't know ? What are you talking about ? "

" I don't know."

He was standing, quietly looking at the crowd, his rifle in his hand ; strange and reserved. Mekhova walked away from him through the high grass, hurrying and stumbling, but where she was going he did not know. Had the incident happened or not ? Was it Mekhova or someone else ? Perhaps it had been just an illusion.

Along the cobbled high road came a train of carts. They were loaded with household goods upon which children were seated, and beside them were walking working men and women. Lukhava was clearing his way through the long grass with lengthy strides ; his brisk pace made his hair flutter like black flames.

With flaming face Polia ran up to Gleb.

He stuck out his chest and waved his hand.

" Comrades, get into line ! "

The Communists came running along, breaking through the crowd, coming up to Gleb.

" Now then, Citizens, take your things. . . . Get ready to march to your new shelters. You've been living in palaces, now try huts for a while. There, in the suburb, you'll be shown open doors. There're enough rooms and drawing-rooms for you—you'll be richly provided ! You'll sleep on spring mattresses and rest on sofas. March ! "

Worn out and exhausted the people were sitting on the grass or on their bundles ; they remained flabby, blinded and deafened. Ivan Arsenitch separated himself from the crowd and left first, walking across the grass with Verochka. They walked slowly, tenderly embraced, as though they had come out for a customary morning walk. The old man was smiling and gesticulating, speaking to her with enthusiastic animation.

Then some others got up and walked with their bundles and baskets, following them; and then more and more. Then suddenly the whole crowd began to hurry, crawl, turn round and round and run. It began to disperse in various directions, along the high road, over the grass or back into the town.

Lukhava ran up to Gleb; overcome with fatigue, he caught hold of his tunic.

" Come to the Party Committee at once with the detachment. From to-night on we shall be on a war footing. A battle is going on beyond the mountains. The Whites and Greens have joined forces. The town is threatened. The ropeway has been damaged. All the workers have run away from the wood-felling. The Red forces guarding the ropeway have had losses."

" What are you jabbering about, you damned fool? The ropeway? Ours? What are you talking about? "

" Yes, our ropeway. Hurry up! There's a meeting at the Party Committee's rooms."

Clenching his jaws, Gleb smothered the roar of a wild beast within himself.

Chapter XII

THE SIGNAL FIRES

ON GUARD

GLEB'S detachment was posted at the foot of the mountain, behind the town; here were the vineyards and market-gardens of the suburbs.

In the daytime, during the drilling at the barracks, one could hear the guns back of the mountain, roaring like thunder; behind the misty ridges a battle was going on. The Special Detachment was getting ready to reinforce the Red troops. During the night, in full strength, it was guarding the town.

During the daytime the town with its empty streets sank into quietness and fear, and at night-time it died in the darkness. The electric lights no longer shone in the factory; and the windows of dwellings were well-covered with shutters and curtains.

Only in the offices amidst jostling and tobacco smoke was activity evident. And in the streets, citizens and strayed members of the Trade Unions raised their eyebrows significantly when they met. Whispering and murmurings flew over the town with the whirlwinds of dust, and the mountain breeze carried them into all the crannies of the town and into the mountains and quarries where under every bush and stone an unseen foe was hiding.

A part of the Women's Section, with Dasha at their head, went with the Ambulance Corps to the fighting zone; the other part, under Polia's command, were working with the Communist detachment in the barracks, and were hurriedly preparing for the removal of workers' families in the event of evacuation.

Gleb met Polia several times a day; tireless, she ran to the Trade Unions, workshops, Trade Union Council, Party Committee and Soviet Headquarters, placing her women at all points and in all organisations in order to maintain the activity and also, in the event of the order being given, in order to be able to evacuate in a few hours several thousand women and children.

Trains, with steam up, stood by the factory, on the quays and in the suburbs, all ready for their passengers and freight ; and the panting of the locomotives mingled with the distant breath of the guns. Polia had not slept for forty-eight hours. Her eyes were rather feverish and her face had a hectic colour.

During that day she had found herself free for a moment to run to Gleb at the barracks ; her dry lips had parted in a smile. She did not notice how her cracked lips bled, dyeing her teeth and mixing with the saliva.

" Here's where the real work is, Gleb. We've lived through a lot, learning by heart theses about the Trade Union movement and the New Economic Policy. We were turning round and round on the same spot, every day in our routine. We were becoming deaf and blind . . . we were developing bureaucratism. We were killing our living force in order to become professional officials. . . . The New Economic Policy—. Once I heard a waterman—a diver he was—say : ' This New Economic Policy is a great invention : restaurants, wine and beer, on draught or in bottle. I'm going to vote for this with both hands ! ' No, Gleb, it won't be like that. The Tenth Party Congress will not enter on that path."

Gleb grounded his rifle and laughed.

" Don't go hopping like a hare, Comrade Mekhova. We'll kick these bandits out now and that will be the end of your ' real work.' The Party Congress will take place and then we'll bring about this wonderful New Economic Policy. And as for your diver, we'll put him in the communal administration and let him start all kinds of restaurants and make lots of money for us."

Polia, shocked, trembled, and her eyebrows quivered with anger.

" That will never happen. The Party simply cannot handle the question in that way, as you want it to. We can't betray the revolution ; it would be worse than death. It's impossible ! We've defeated the intervention, and the blockade is a stupid adventure. Our revolution has set fire to all the world. The proletariat of all countries is with us. Reaction is powerless. And isn't the New Economic Policy reaction ? Isn't it the restoration of capitalism ? No, it's nonsense, Comrade Gleb ! "

" What are you talking about ! How can it be reaction when it's a matter of getting the peasant in line with production ? "

" What ? Does it mean there would be markets again ? Again the bourgeoisie ? Do you want our factory to be given as a concession to the capitalists ? They talked about it to-day at the Soviet Executive. It seems that Shramm has sent a report to the Head Office of the Cement Trust. I suppose you'd be glad to see that—yes ? Such reaction would please your soul ? "

Red patches showed on the cheek-bones of her pale face ; beads of perspiration shone on her brow and lips.

Gleb's face became grey ; astounded he bent down to Polia.

" What, what, Comrade Mekhova ? Concession ? What are you stuffing me up with now ? That the workmen would give up their factory to the bourgeoise ? What the hell ! I'll show the bastards concession ! "

" Aha, that's touched you, hasn't it ? Yes, and that's your lovely New Economic Policy. . . . You try to start it ! Concessions, restaurants, markets. . . . Kulaks, schemers, speculators. . . . I suppose you'll tell me something consoling about the Workers' Co-operatives ? The Food Tax. . . . The Co-operatives. . . . Perhaps that is necessary. But not retreat, Gleb, not that ! Anything but that ! Heroic exploits for the immortal revolution ! That's what we want ! To deepen, to light a universal fire ; not to abandon conquered positions, but to seize new ones. That's it ! "

And away she ran, red spots on her cheeks like danger signals —leaving Gleb standing there, startled and meditating upon what she had said.

That night Gleb found himself in the valley behind the town, at the head of his detachment, guarding the high road near the outskirts. His men were spaced out along a curved line rising from the high road to the slopes of the mountain. A patrol of three comrades was going through the suburb, disturbing the timid dogs, by whose barking it was possible to follow the routes of the patrol. Gleb and Serge were standing at the fringe of the wood, watching the fiery torches in the mountains.

A flame flashed like a red bird in the obscurity and flew upwards. It flew up like a rocket and cleft the darkness. For a moment in its light one could glimpse an outstretched hand, then a man's shoulder.

Very far away in the valley a similar flying torch flamed high and then flew through the darkness like a falling star. Higher up another one trembled and spun round—and then more and more. The torches flashed, went out, beckoned and twisted in serpentine convulsions.

Behind the two men lay the forest. One could not look into it. Only the trees close to the high road waved their shadowy cloaks. Their winged branches were spread out, between them lay heavy shadows shrouding the snake-like boughs. This night, as on the day before, the townsmen were paralysed with fear before the death which was approaching from the mountains: A terror-haunted stillness pulsated through the town. At night, the town feared its own whispering and hid underground. In the wood also there was silence. It was drifting up from the depths, odorous with moisture and soil. New-born leaves fluttered like butterflies, everywhere a distant fantastic music was diffused, a fairy-like mysterious buzzing.

Everything seemed fantastic to Serge, changeable, limitless. The primeval darkness bred terror in one's mind at its hidden secrets.

As a scholar, he was accustomed to have his nights lit by electricity; now the mountains and the starry sky seemed as near and comprehensible as stone houses, the boulevardes or the squares. In the daytime, his rifle did not feel heavy; now it had grown into the earth.

A fiery bird fell and began to flutter in the bushes; sparks flew from it fan-like and expired. Then the darkness grew thick again, quivering, uniting itself where the fire had been. In the mountains and valleys, far and near, the red stars and the flaming birds still flashed.

Gleb laid his hand on Serge's shoulder.

" He must be caught, damn him ! He's asking to be shot ! "

" Yes, he's quite near. It's he who is burning English powder. You see ? Without doubt he knows that we are here, and he's not afraid of being shot. But we're too late, Comrade Chumalov, he's done his work. See ? It's gone out. He's not taking any more risks than he has to."

Gleb calmly lit his pipe and gazed at the wandering lights in the mountains.

" If he didn't think that you and I were fools and cowards he wouldn't come dancing under our nose. He'll play around here a good while yet. You'll see."

Serge looked along the high road. Dust arose from it and was lost in the darkness. There, where one could no longer see the road, stood an immense tree, tufted and rugged, rearing itself like a black mass. It seemed to Serge that in its branches a match was spluttering but could not light.

" Foes everywhere, Gleb. It's not surprising if they're close to us."

Beyond the wood was the railway station, but there too it was quiet ; the night alone sighed like a sleeping beast.

Not far away on the high road a cart was creaking and rumbling.

All this was nonsense. The most important thing was this : in the storm all the work which had begun with such enthusiasm had been carried away. The ropeway had been destroyed and the trucks again were lying among the stones and bushes as in the days when Gleb was walking among the rusty junk with anguish in his soul. The Diesels were still again and the workshops empty. Again, idleness and shadows. The evacuation of the refugees, hunger, privation, a state of war. Once again, the rifle in hand. Again perhaps trenches, marching, soot and dirt and smoke of the guns—not the soot and dirt of toil.

Had he sufficient strength to organise all the forces in order to fight on the industrial front, when everything from engines to nails had been destroyed, plundered, covered with rust. When there was no fuel, no bread, no transport ; when the trucks were piled up on the railway track, when no ships ever lay at the quays. Hadn't the Chairman of the Soviet Executive, Badin, been right, when he had looked on him as a fool who didn't realise what he was undertaking ? An upstart, a bully, a boaster, unable firmly to hold the little they already had, while the enemy was threatening the very existence of the workers' power. How then was it possible to make plans for the revival of the factory ? How could one think of that now, when people were condemned to famine rations and some were so weak they could not stand the strain of a working day ? What was the good of production, when the economic life of the republic had been paralysed for years to come, and the country was dying from hunger and lapsing into barbarism ?

Again a torch flamed, but it was now further off and higher. Bushes and rocks glowed red and seemed to be living, moving. Fiery bats were flying in the mountains. Behind the town, shells were exploding like dazzling flashes of sheet-lightning in the misty sky.

" I told you, Serge—! Look there ! The swine have started spitting again ! "

" That's all right. I've never seen any illuminations like this before. It looks as though we were surrounded."

" As though we were in a sack, curse it ! The only way to get out is to jump up into the sky."

" In these hours of the night, Comrade Chumalov, I'm thinking about the future. Our children will imagine us great heroes, and will create legends about us. And even our ordinary daily existence and our hunger, the forced idleness in production, even the watch you and I are keeping to-night— all will be raised to a higher power, as they say in mathematics. It will all be reflected in their imagination as an epoch of heroic exploits and titanic achievements. And we—you and I—little grains of dust in an immense mass, we shall seem to them as giants. The past is always generalised and exaggerated. They won't remember our mistakes, cruelties, failures, weaknesses, our simple human sufferings and our damnable problems. They will say : ' These were the people who were destined to conquer the whole world.' And they will visit our graves as if we were inextinguishable beacons. When I think about this I feel a little bit ashamed, and at the same time I feel happy for the responsibility which we are carrying for the whole of humanity. The future oppresses me, Chumalov ; our immortality is too heavy a burden."

" Well, that isn't so important. What will be, will be. History goes its way. What's important to me, damn it all, is how we're going to get a move on with the work. We've set up a ropeway and these swine have broken it down again. We'll have to start everything from the beginning again. We'll get the factory working, I thought, and then this band of robbers got going. It's interfering with our work, that's what's so disgusting."

" You think too simply, Chumalov. Your brain's been put together with bricks, clean cut, in an economic way. The cells in my brain are like birds in a cage."

" What a head you must have then, Serge ! It's not good to keep such creatures in your brain ; they cry out—. And you can't let them out, it only makes a lot of noise for nothing."

The night yawned from its limitless depths, and the ominous fires continued to wound the darkness. The flames flew restlessly like owls, and the electric floods in the far clouds inspired one with a mysterious dread. The great hour was approaching. There, beyond the mountains, among the red-hot torches, in the narrow valleys, there lay the beast which they had not yet slain. He was moving unseen from the Cossack villages. The bearded Cossacks were coming in a horde, grinning like man-eaters, with whoop and yell and swords empurpled with blood. The Cossack villages would release their thousands to come on across the land like a swarm of locusts, covering with smoke and blood the fields, the mountains and the feathery grass of the steppes.

The mountains and woods swarmed with human beasts. In the daytime they hid in the thickets and caves or walked in the town, masquerading as friends of the revolution. They were everywhere : in the ranks of the Red soldiers, in the offices of the Soviets and in the houses of the peaceful, harmless, petty bourgeois. Who could point them out, name them, crush them as one would adders ? And when the night came they crawled out, concealed by the darkness, to do their treacherous work. Now they were lighting their signal fires, and the fires were burning bright and flying about the fields, beckoning, searching and laughing, with the sinister laughter of birds of prey.

The metallic clatter of a wagon was heard over the high road. The hoof-beats of a tired horse were plainly audible. Sleepily, hoarsely, voices were muttering indistinctly.

Their rifles under their arms, Gleb and Serge went along the road which disappeared into the profound obscurity. Everything, the earth and the woods, was sinking in this darkness ; as there was nothing upon which to rest the eye everything appeared to Serge unreal, immaterial. At each step one's heart beat faster, as though one would put one's foot down here and instead of a hard road find a swamp or black precipice.

They could clearly see the horse. Its head was dimly lit by the far-off flashes and the fires on the mountains. There were black shadows on the cart. There were many of them, the wagon appeared very high and big.

" Halt ! Who goes there ? "

Gleb, in the middle of the road, stood before the horse with his rifle advanced.

" Wounded ! "

" The pass-word ? "

" What the devil's the matter with you—pass-word ! Can't you see our bandaged heads ? "

" How are things up there ? "

" Go and have a look : take your part in the game—then you'll learn. The rats have crawled into their holes and we're firing. . . . They've been dosing us with shrapnel. . . . It doesn't matter. We're arranging some good traps for the sons of bitches. They're squeaking and jumping like pigs. We caught about fifty officers and flogged them to bits. They were rolling their eyes like toads. Two little sisters have been amusing the chaps to-day—they nearly laughed their guts out. We stood them up on the edge of a rock within aim. One of them screeched : ' Beasts, dirty fellows ! ' And then—head over heels, over she went ! Then the other : ' Loafers, bare-footed rascals ! '—and then, over she went. It was a performance, I tell you ! "

" What about the reinforcements—do you expect any ? "

" What the devil for ? We won't be long finishing them off. Casualties—not many dead. And wounded—here's the first lot. The rest are in the trenches. Our chaps are all round them up there, they're trapped. They can't move, advance or retreat. We've got the bastards ! "

" That's brave fellows !—Forward ! "

2

THE PRISONER WITH THE EMPTY SLEEVE

The mountains bloomed like gardens of flame. The sheet-lightning from the guns was shimmering over the sea in the mist.

Serge and Gleb, rifle in hand, like silent shadows, were ascending the slope among the bushes. Fire burst out in flashes before them, leaping over the ragged clumps of bushes, scatter-ing sparks, dying out and then rising like a flaming bird.

They passed by the slaughter-house. The fence was gone—it had been destroyed. There were gaps in the doors and win-dows. Perhaps there were enemies there also ready to shoot.

" Soft as a cat, Serge ; don't touch the bushes. Hold your rifle more firmly. We're going to catch him alive."

Gleb went stealing along, his body stretched like a dog. Serge was full of a vague joyousness. He was unconsciously smiling, his eyes fixed on the fire. His hands and feet shook, as though he were flying, dizzy-winged, down the heights. Broken cobwebs were sticking to his face. His eyelashes were wet and glistening. Warm fermented airs arose among the bushes; it was the cooling stones breathing. And the spring leaves of the elms and birches were breathing into the air.

The night was deceptive : objects seeming sometimes near and then far away. But the man there was clearly seen, illuminated by the torch. He was running up the mountain in a zigzag course, turning every now and again and raising his right arm above his head ; his silhouette was lopsided. His military shirt and cap were fiery at their outlines. The right sleeve dangled like a rag. Gleb and Serge crouched down, they looked at each other closely, and they understood each other.

" He must be taken alive, Chumalov, absolutely ! Don't you see ? "

" All right, don't muddle it, and we'll catch him. Now, watch him—. With all your eyes ! "

The blood was thumping in Serge's temples. There were so many men with only one arm. There were so many of them now. They always caused him a certain disquiet, and in their empty sleeve he felt a threat and a blow. His brother too had an empty sleeve. He also wandered about like a mysterious phantom.

The armless man stopped and attentively listened about him. He stood with his back turned to them and they caught his profile for a moment when he turned his head. And in this illuminated instant Serge seemed to recognise the familiar cruel beak.

A flame leapt up like a fiery serpent and dashed into the bushes like a rocket. The darkness became thick. A few steps were heard on the stones, and the bushes began to murmur as though from a light gust of wind.

" God damn it ! He's slipped off ! After him, Serge ! We must corner him ! "

Gleb dashed into the bushes, kicking the stones with his heels and disappeared into the darkness. Pebbles and rubbish were cracking under his feet and flying aside like fragments of glass. Serge leapt after him and again he felt that he was growing light as air, winged like a bird, and was flying towards the shimmering glare in the sky and the mountain fires.

" Halt, you bastard, or I'll shoot ! Halt ! "

In front Gleb was roaring like a bull, and Serge heard neither the sound of his steps, nor cries, nor shots, in that infernal darkness. He was flying lightly, not feeling the earth under his feet, nor hearing the whistling of the wind in his ears, nor feeling pain from the thorns of the bushes which struck at his face and were tearing his skin. He was choking and shouting, but he did not hear what he was shouting.

Out of the darkness came a frenzied horse, galloping madly. He snorted before Serge, reared high, stumbled against the rocks, kicked wildly in the air, his tail flying, snorted once more and vanished. And where the horse had stood was a black gulf.

Serge stopped and listened. Far away the hooves were smashing the stones, and Gleb's cries were heard no longer. A wild alarm shuddered in the air, in the glare of the guns ; and the mist was phosphorescent. It was impossible to distinguish where the sea ended and where the sky began. The town below lay spread out like a cemetery : great dark walled blocks like giant tombs. Serge looked behind him : the torches flashed still in the mountains. On the other side the mountains were yet higher, in battlements, and all over their crests were swarming stars. They lit up, then died, flew about like fiery snakes, flared up like bonfires and rushed in flaming torrents from the tops down the valley and slopes.

Down below in the valley men were sighing and murmuring, and perhaps the gods were fighting over carrion. The stones were clattering like potsherds. Somewhere near was Gleb and the one-armed man : one of the two had to conquer. There were so many one-armed men. So why should this particular one, who had just disappeared into the darkness, trouble Serge so much.

Serge began to climb down the slope. The soil broke under his feet, turning to dust.

Among the boulders Gleb was bending down over something and growling, his whole body torn with effort. Serge saw that his knee was planted on the chest of a prostrate man, and he was gripping his throat with both hands.

" No, you yelping swine, you won't get away ! You're finished, you bastard ! I've got you now ! Here, Serge, give us a hand. Search him ! "

Feverishly, with trembling hands, Serge ransacked the pockets of the man's tunic and breeches. He found only a packet of tobacco, matches and a crust of bread. But when his hand touched the stump of the missing arm he was suddenly pierced by a cry which froze him.

" I knew it, Gleb. This is my brother ! My brother, Gleb ! I'm going to kill him, Gleb ! I shall shoot him——! "

" All right, but pick up his rifle from under my feet. Now, friend, get up. Get up, Serge, and stand by him with your rifle pointed. Or as he's your brother, shall I leave him to your mercy ? Well ? What have you to say in his defence ? "

In this raillery Serge sensed a certain hostility. It seemed to him that Gleb's eyes were like burning coals.

" Stop joking, Chumalov. Lead him away or I shall kill him on the spot. You have no right to speak to me in that tone."

" All right, don't get sore and take offence——."

Serge's hands and knees trembled.

Dimitri got up. He wished to shake the dust from his clothes, but his hand was tightly held by Gleb. He was choking and coughing.

" Another unusual meeting, Serge," he said. " Anyway, you're not worth the little finger of this wild fellow, War Commissar Gleb Chumalov. We had the honour of meeting each other in my gay father's house, when you were robbing him. I regret that my brother Serge was not there then ; I should have shot him through the head. My one hand can still perform wonders."

Gleb bent over, looking closely into the one-armed man's face, but did not release his hand.

" Aha, an unexpected meeting, my heroic Colonel ! In the old man's garden I properly played the fool. I should have hooked you then. Well, let's get on, boys ! We'll go to see Comrade Shibis ; he will welcome this guest ! "

Dimitri wished to speak, but laughter obstructed his words. He was choking in his effort to suppress his hilarity.

" I'm very flattered to walk with you, my friends. Especially with you, my brave Commissar. But won't you let go my hand ? I'm neither a child nor a young lady that such tender care should be shown me. The vanquished enemy will walk with you just as proudly as will the victors. Only please remove my brother a little way from me. I'm not sure that he isn't suffering from feminine hysteria in its gravest form. Calm yourself, little Serge, you are really much too excited, my friend."

Serge's teeth were chattering, and he could not overcome a deadly nausea rising in his chest. He made a tremendous effort not to shout and fling himself on his brother in a fit of wild anger.

Dimitri was laughing like a real merry fellow.

" It's true, isn't it, Serge, that you and I never walked together before with such pleasure as on this occasion. Such moments must be cherished—especially when they are the last we shall live. But you'll kill me with your ferocious looks, you fierce person. Take it more easily, can't you? You're even too pitiable a slave of your Party to be able to control yourself in the foolish hour of your success."

They came up out of the ravine and followed the mountain path.

On the mountains and in the troubled sky the glare of the guns flashed intermittently.

"All the same, your work is no damn good—you cheap rabble. To-morrow your brains will be fouling the cobbles. It's a pity I shan't see it with my own eyes. And as for you, Serge, I would have had great pleasure in hanging you publicly at the gate of our house."

Serge began to laugh, and was astonished that he was able to laugh at that moment.

"Could one ever expect, brother, that I should lead you to your death? But it is so, you see? I shan't watch you being shot. But the fact that you have been caught, and that I had a hand in catching you, gives me great satisfaction."

Dimitri laughed amicably, with open-hearted gaiety.

"You'll make me ill laughing, little Serge! You are really an incomparable comedian."

Gleb released Dimitri's hand and shouldered his rifle.

"Well, Colonel? But this is a jolly walk on such a rotten night! If the respectable citizens could see us now, they'd say: 'There're some gay pals having a merry time!'"

Dimitri continued to laugh, but now there was a sharp point in his laughter. It seemed now to Serge that he was really laughing no longer, that sorrow had overcome him, and the desire to say something which human words could not express.

"Yes, yes, very gay indeed! I do regret, Serge, that you're not going to take part in this merry game called an execution. I should like it very much: it would have recalled our childhood. Do you remember our childish days well? I would like to see your rifle pointed at my breast. Won't you do it now? Your dungeons are worse than those graveyard nights which frightened me in my boyhood. I don't want my soul devastated there. Accompany me, Serge, right to the end; that would be very beautiful—a heroic theme. Two brothers in the grip of an implacable antagonism, uniting two drops of blood into one. It's tempting, eh? Romantic?"

A town patrol with rifles at the ready came towards them.

Chapter XIII

SLACKENING PACE

I

AT THE TURNING POINT

AGAIN came the quiet strenuous days of economic activity. Again the daily, imperceptible work in the departments, in the organisations and in the factory.

These days were just the same as before the uprising of the White-Greens and of the Cossacks. Documents once more rustled in the offices and again sessions were held of the Soviet Executive, the Trade Union Council and the Economic Council, amid suffocating tobacco fumes, floors covered with cigarette ends, endless discussions, resolutions and plans. But no longer did one see by night the shifting torches in the mountains. Saturday was the market-day for country produce —potatoes, flour, vegetables, eggs, poultry and game—which were piled up on the market-place to overflowing ; and the air smelt strongly of horse-sweat and manure. In the valleys, where once hardly a rider or pedestrian could pass safely, the paths through the woods were now peaceful and crowded with numbers of people, walking, with creaking carts, and with the slow songs of the peasants.

Once more the people of the town, tradespeople and busy persons in military tunics and leather coats, with and without portfolios, came out from their tightly closed dwellings and basements into the streets. No one thought now of the evacuation scenes and the thunder of guns and the nights of terror through which they had all passed.

Within its mountainous shores, the bay was as blue as the sky ; and along the quays rolled carts and motor-lorries. On the roadstead beyond the moles, as far as the horizon itself, twinkled the white sails, sharply outlined, of the fishermen's smacks. Early in the morning appeared—they knew not from where—Turkish feluccas, dancing on the waves, scraping against the concrete quays, their masts designing arabesques against the sky. Unoccupied persons no longer dolefully raised their eyebrows when meeting, and whispered in corners at cross-roads and on footpaths ; but they now spoke right out in business-like tones about the New Economic Policy, the rate of exchange, the Turkish feluccas and contraband.

In the principal street, in front of the shops which were previously used as storehouses for various economic organisations, drays and lorries rumbled. The horses stamped and neighed and the draymen all day long were yelling and swearing under the weight of bales, boxes and bags. The main street burning in the sun, scented with spring, was being cleaned up and tidied in the expectation of new developments. There had once been a time when it had been gay with smart shop windows, smelling of perfumery, rustling with the silken promenading of fashionable ladies, and at night time bathed in the glare of illuminated signs. The street was dreaming of a to-morrow, smiling and well-fed, like the bygone days ; a to-morrow without the Cheka, without bread rations, without obligatory housing control, without registration and re-registration, without compulsions or forced labour.

Women and young girls, skirts pinned up above their knees, stood on window-sills and step-ladders, washing the big panes of plate-glass, and the long-accumulated dirt was running down in brown streams on to the pavement. From the dim interiors of the shops came a mouldy smell and the damp coolness of a cellar. The songs of the girls echoed in the emptiness of the shops, broken occasionally by a squeaking laugh and by orders passed from one to the other. In front of the open doors and windows people wandered, here and there, forming groups, looking long with anxious curiosity into the shops, at the wet window panes and the women's bare calves. Square and oblong white notices, written in large black capitals, showed up brightly on the clean plate-glass windows, behind which were the black interiors where hammers banged and saws hummed.

A Co-Operative Store will Shortly be Opened Here.
A Cafe will be Opened Here in a Few Days.
Retail Co-Operative Department Store.
Commercial Manufacturing Company.

On the smooth, grey walls of the Town Hall—now the Communal Administration Centre—appeared in enormous letters :

HE WHO DOES NOT WORK SHALL NOT EAT.
ON THE RUINS OF THE CAPITALIST WORLD WE SHALL BUILD
THE GREAT EDIFICE OF COMMUNISM.
WE HAVE LOST NOTHING BUT OUR CHAINS AND SHALL
GAIN THE WHOLE WORLD.

On the market-place new stalls and tents were erected. There axes were swinging, golden shavings falling ; and in the streets of the town there was the smell of pine-resin and paint.

Outside the Department of People's Education, from morning until four in the afternoon, school teachers with blue, drawn faces were crowding. They were standing or sitting on the pavement in groups, or stood along the wall in a queue, resigned and obedient, like blind persons. They had been gathering like this every day outside this building, all through the winter and the month of March. The school buildings were occupied by the officers of various departments. The libraries and class-rooms had been pillaged, and the desks broken up for fire-wood. And there was a lack of paper-money in the Educational Department. Why then did they come and wait there so humbly for the wages that had not been paid since Autumn ?

When Serge came out from the sessions of the Collegium on to the street, he would immediately get jostled and breathless in the compact jam and tumult of the teachers. He could see neither street nor pavements, and the air was heavy and suffocating from the effluvia of unclean bodies and clothes, and compact of blue faces, dull, distressed eyes, whining entreaty and humility. The herd formed round him into a spongy, impenetrable mass, wailing and supplicating like beggars ; dry teeth between earth-coloured lips like those of a corpse. And it was always the same words he heard, groaned and whispered, singly or in chorus.

" Serge Ivanovitch ! Serge Ivanovitch ! Dear Serge Ivanovitch ! You were a teacher yourself—. You know what it means. . . . What, then, Serge Ivanovitch, can be done ? "

Serge squeezed through the begging crowd, seeing no one, looking past everyone and smiling confusedly. He was worried by a vague sense of guilt in the presence of these half-dead creatures.

" I can't do anything, Comrades. I have made a request, I've claimed and demanded, but what can I do ? I know all about it, Comrades, but I can't do anything now. As soon as there's an opportunity. . . . I don't know——."

And he hastened on, but without getting away from the crowd, without escaping from these submissive dog-like eyes and corpse-like cheeks.

Again they had a Sunday's voluntary mass work. Again thousands of workers clustered ant-like about the cable-way, thundering with hammers, pickaxes and spades. Gravely leaning on his stick, Engineer Kleist was personally supervising the work. By evening the ropeway again began to sing flute-like with its pulleys; and the wheels again began to swing their spokes in all directions and at all angles.

The workmen of the Forestry Department filled the street in front of the Economic Council. In rags, unshorn, their faces ingrained with dirt as though they had just come from work, their axes at their belts, they were pushing on the front door; eyes bulging, they were bellowing and yelling as at a meeting, and some sighed deeply without words.

The doors of the Economic Council were locked; and the crowd were trampling on the cobbles and on the side-walks, crushed against the walls and doors. In front, against the door, the first-comers were shouting in hoarse cracked voices.

" Bring the Economic Council here! The rascals of the Forestry Department! Hand over those thieves and robbers, bandits! What's the Cheka doing? It should look out of its eyes and not out of its backside! Let's see the Communists! What are they doing there behind the doors? "

Other workers were seated on the pavement or leaning in compact rows with their backs against the walls, chewing their bread rations. They sat in the sun, stupefied by the heat, the smell of asphalt and the fiery dust. Half-dozing, they were looking lazily through their eyelashes at their comrades in the crowd who had gone crazy; or perhaps they looked at nothing but just spoke quietly and idly, amusing themselves by spitting on the pavement, or went in groups round the corner to the gate of the courtyard to urinate, jostling elbows and shoulders.

All at once Shuk jumped up on the steps of the porch and waved his arms; a hush descended upon the crowd.

" Comrades, listen! "

And Shuk raised his hands again above his head. Then he took off his cap and holding it up in the air, gazed at the crowd in a threatening, bovine way. Even from the edge of the crowd one could see the drunken moisture in his eyes.

" Comrades, I know this bunch of loafers all right. Look, Comrades, I've tied them up with a good rope."

Grinning broadly, Shuk made a gesture as though he were twisting someone's neck and continued :

" I unmasked them all ; I've stood them up against a wall ! They're eaten up with bureaucracy, the loafers ! We of the working-class, we know how to tackle them ! You haven't seen them, but I have. They wear braces and wipe their noses with handkerchiefs. Have we got braces ? Have we got this impossible stupidity of handkerchiefs and expensive false teeth ? They've put all the gold into their false teeth. But I uncovered them, Comrades ! "

Only those in the front row could see how Shuk suddenly stumbled down the steps of the porch and, astounded, came flat up against the wall on the pavement. In his place there stood Badin, Chairman of the Soviet Executive. His face was immovable, his eyes lustreless. This was no man, but a bronze idol.

He commenced speaking quietly and calmly, as if he were in his office ; but his voice was distinct and resonant.

" Comrades, in our town there are twenty thousand organised proletarians. Of these twenty thousand, you, just a small group, come here yelling as though at a country fair ; with your squabbling you're shamefully disorganising the orderly ranks of the revolutionary workers. It's disgraceful and criminal, Comrades ! What's it all about ? What do you want ? Haven't you a Trade Union ? Is there no working-class machinery through which, without wasting time, you could have put forward all the questions which are exciting you now, and through which they could have been decided as urgent matters ? "

The crowd swayed and exploded in an uproar of voices mingled with the stamping of feet.

" Bring the robbers here ! Bring the thieves of the Forestry Department ! We shan't return to work ! We want clothes— food ! We're not convicts ! Robbers, sons of bitches ! "

Badin raised his hand. His expression did not change ; it was as before, immovable and metallic, hard as bronze.

" I didn't come here to argue and quarrel with you, Comrades. All your demands, which will be presented by your delegates, through your Soviet organs and the Trade Union

Council, will be satisfied. Go back to your places in a quiet and orderly manner. And remember that, in these difficult days for the Republic, every hour of idleness brings irreparable damage on the economic front, and the blame will fall only on you. You won't be able to wash out the shameful stain you are putting on our proletariat. It has performed too many heroic deeds to submit to this disgrace. It's not all of you who have engineered this humiliating move ; it's just a few individual instigators. I know who they are, these intriguers and disruptors ! Here's one now who spoke just before me—Shuk. I've known him for a long while. I shall make an order for his arrest at once."

Hardly had Badin finished, when Shuk, all disordered, pale, with eyes starting from their sockets, began to jump up and down in front of Badin, howling piercingly like a dog.

" It's not true ! Not true ! Comrades, it's a lie—! Comrades, I can't stand this———."

In the front rows of the crowd, near the Executive Chairman, hands and bodies were moving and tangling, and an enraged, deafening uproar drowned Shuk's voice. The crowd began to sway and stagger, all arms upraised, and it seemed that the next second some mad act of violence would break out, here by the wall and entrance.

" Hit them, smash them ! Beat the Red-tape bastards ! The swine ! Our Shuk ! Put him up on our shoulders ! Good old Shuk ! Shuk ! "

As before, the Executive Chairman was standing on the top steps of the porch, dressed all in black leather, motionless, with face of bronze, gazing at the howling crowd ; and his eyes were as empty as black holes.

He gazed steadily without blinking, waiting for a few moments to pass by, when the crowd would fall back on itself and again become sheep-like and subdued.

But that moment did not come. Lukhava suddenly interposed. His black hair flew as did his winged hands. In a piercing, bird-like, alarmed voice, with the usual enthusiastic stress, abundantly salivated, he cut short the enraged animal uproar.

" Comrades, a word ! Keep still and listen ! "

The crowd stirred and flowed backwards for a moment and out sideways along the street. Then again it pressed massively towards the porch.

" Lukhava ! Let's have it, Lukhava ! Comrades, Lukhava's going to skin them ! Give it to them hot, Comrade ! "

Lukhava's hair was flying; his face was all sharp angles—cheek-bones, nose and chin. It seemed that his eyes were breathing: one moment flaming round and deep; then quivering under the eyelashes like two tiny fiery points.

"What the hell are you playing this silly game for here, Comrades? Stick your axes in your belts, your knapsacks on your shoulders, and march! Clothes and boots are growing on the trees in the forest! Comrades, that's a joke, if you like; but this is how it is: in an hour we'll be starting off. The meeting-place is at the Trade Union Council house. The supplies will be loaded on lorries. The Party Committee has appointed Comrade Shuk in charge of supplies. Each one will be given a suit of overalls. The staff of the Forestry Department will be dealt with. Get into line and we'll get moving."

Murmuring and yelling, the crowd was heaving around the porch; his arms and legs flying, Lukhava was tossed high in the air.

Then the crowd marched down the street, wheeling round the corner in the direction of the docks.

Badin and Lukhava, standing by the wall of the building, were glaring at each other. Then Badin spoke:

"I have already reported to the proper authorities the way in which you rushed the eviction and the squeezing of the bourgeoisie. A limit has to be set to this tomfoolery, dear Comrade. What power had you to destroy the Forestry Department without a decision from the Soviet Executive? I shall report this to the Regional Soviet, and then you'll all be put in your right places."

Lukhava smiled, screwing up his eyes, which were gleaming behind the lashes with laughing sparks.

"Bu-reau-crat!"

Again they glared at each other and then walked off in different directions.

2

WITH PERSISTENT STEP

From the windows of the factory management, straight in front on the slope could be seen the club "Comintern." In the daytime only bare-armed, barefooted young Communist Leaguers were there, in shorts, practising physical culture.

Farther away, in the airy distance, from the bottom to the

summit of the mountain—a height of 2,500 feet—the ropeway lines stretched like cords. Above and below, meeting, passing, approaching and parting, the trucks were crawling. In the distance they looked small, like tortoises, and were gliding slowly and gracefully : five minutes to go up, five minutes to come down ; and meeting every quarter of an hour. They went up empty and came down loaded with logs packed in square masses. One could see the wheels of the transmission tower swinging in various directions and angles. From the top of the mountain, down past the ropeway, down the slope, lorries and carts were driving along the road which had been newly built up. Over there and in the wood, were working the men of the Forestry Department, and the factory workmen were directing the ropeway.

Gleb, as representative of the workers, spent whole days in the management offices of the factory. There were specialists sent by the Economic Council, who did not themselves understand the work of the factory. They had been there for a year already and were still studying the complex system of the works. Their hair was combed smooth, they were absolutely pale from much washing, and they wore neck-ties. They were all smooth-shaven like Englishmen, blond, and could hardly be distinguished one from the other. It was difficult to tell what they were doing at their oak desks, why they were speaking in undertones, in confidential murmurs. Their faces were cold and official and they looked at Gleb with vague interrogation in their eyes (at the Economic Council they looked at him like this too), and they always answered his questions at first with dumb astonishment, and then in singular terms in an undertone, through the smoke of a cigarette, and with pensive idleness. And Gleb did not understand the terms which they used except one which he had long ago learned to hate :

" Bureau of Industry !"

In view of Gleb's report, the Communist Group decided to demand a detailed report on the Factory Management at the General Meeting of the workers. It was decided that everything should be revealed with regard to the situation, and then to demand the intervention of the Workers' and Peasants' Inspection. Gleb had studied the situation until he was exhausted, not believing anything by hearsay. He voluntarily saddled himself with the difficult task of analysing figures, reports, account books, documents, orders and specifications. The first days, his heavy hands hardly obeyed him, and his tongue positively hurt, so many times did he moisten his rough-skinned fingers to turn over pages and papers. The first days his head swum and he understood nothing in this great pile of figures and tables. The blond, close-shaven specialists answered his questions with unctuous courtesy, gazing at him with an amazed interrogation; and behind their gaze was a well-hidden mockery and contempt. Gleb was polite to these specialists, so careful of their toilet; he also spoke in undertones, asking silly questions which provoked a smile from them. But there were other questions, over which he had been thinking during the night, which disquieted them and cornered them; and then they answered with but one word:

"Bureau of Industry. . . . Economic Council. . . . Cement Trust. . . . Council of Labour and Defence. . . ."

Gleb gazed out of the window at the work of the ropeway, studied the affairs of the factory which were supposed to be known only to the specialists, and calculated how much wood could be delivered from the Forestry Department before the New Year.

One cubic sashin in half an hour; in a day, working two shifts, 24. In a month 600; and up to the end of the year, 4,800. It's not much—not enough to prevent a crisis. The ropeway would have to work through the winter.

From the bottom of the mountain, the wood was brought away by another ropeway. The trucks like tortoises were crawling from the factory to the foot of the mountain, and thence back to the factory, passing each other; going up empty and coming down loaded. Below, the trucks were detached from the steel cable, pushed on to the lift on the top of the tower, and then descending, creaking, into the depths of the factory, down with wood, up empty. At the bottom of the shaft, whence rails ran through tunnels and along twining paths, they were again seized by cables and dragged into darkness; from there they crawled back empty, and, entering the lift-shaft, flew up to where a light was shimmering high above in the blue.

Gleb often came here, and when he passed he would be intoxicated with the electric whirr of the wheels, with the clashing and creaking of the trucks, with the furious energy of the toil-drunken workers. Then he would throw aside statistics and tables and would plunge into the work of the

gangs. He noted that the workers now had different faces—
no longer typhoid-blue, but sweaty and sunburnt, with tension
in their eyes and their bare chests heaving with effort. Good!
The resurrection of toil. Blood flowing warm, which could
never grow cold again.

At night he no longer waited for Dasha as formerly, he
did not lock the door and went to bed early. He didn't know
at what time Dasha came home. And if he awakened for a
moment to her presence, he would see Dasha sitting at the
table, her head on her hand, her lips moving soundlessly,
reading. In the morning, when he went to work, Dasha would
smile at him with a richly blooming joy.

And during the nights now—and sometimes during the
day—Polia came to him, behind Dasha or through Dasha, and
touched him with her curls. She came looking at him
attentively, ready for a caress, with such large appealing
eyes. . . .

3

ALARM

He would have to find out for himself what the Industrial
Bureau was, this impassable bulwark of the Economic Council
and the factory administration. This massive rock stood in his
path all the time, and his questions rebounded from it
unanswered. He decided to go and learn on the spot. If
necessary he wouldn't come back, but would go straight on to
Moscow, to Lenin, to the supreme Economic Council, to
the Council for Work and Defence—to relate everything,
unmask everything, break heads, make a scandal, rouse up
everyone, but get what was needed: at all costs to get the
factory in real working order.

In the administration of the factory there was nothing but
waste, inactivity, sabotage. In the Economic Council, sabotage,
bureaucracy, and some invisible internal activity which one
could not fathom. The people there were all importantly
businesslike, with fat portfolios, clean-shaven, like Communists.
The three-storeyed house shook with the bustling crowds,
rushing from door to door, and every day from ten till four,
you could see the side-walks near the building blocked with
crowds of extraordinarily talkative people—persons who
in bygone days used to hang around the cafés and the stock-
exchange. You only saw this crowd around the Economic

Council. There was nothing like it at the Department of Public Health, nor at the Department of Education, or of Social Insurance. But there were quite a lot of people also at the Department of Agriculture, at the Communal Administration and at the Department of Foreign Trade.

Before he left Gleb went round to the Soviet Executive, to the Economic Council and to the Party Committee, collecting materials, specifications, plans and decisions. Badin gave him a letter of introduction to an intimate friend and comrade, a member of the Regional Bureau of the Central Committee of the Russian Communist Party; he also bore a letter from Shidky to a member of the Regional Control Committee.

He was hurrying along the street on his way home. From the factory to his home was four versts around the curve of the bay. As he walked along it seemed as though he saw the street for the first time. It wasn't the street of a month ago. Then the shops with their big plate-glass windows had been empty or were used as warehouses by various departments, and the windows were dusty and plastered with mud. But now—they were still empty, but one saw:

A DELICATESSEN SHOP WILL SHORTLY OPEN HERE.
CAFÉ. ORCHESTRAL MUSIC DAILY.
TRADING COMPANY.
COMRADES, STRENGTHEN THE ALLIANCE BETWEEN THE TOWN
AND THE VILLAGE!
OPENING SOON.
HE WHO DOES NOT WORK SHALL NOT EAT.

An ironical hand had obliterated the first " not " in the last of these sentences, which was on the wall of the Town Hall, and passers-by, unaccustomed to this new combination of words, stopped, laughing, to read:

HE WHO DOES WORK SHALL NOT EAT.

Workers' rations. . . . Pipe-lighters and smuggling. . . . Trading Company. . . . Savchuk barefooted and ragged. . . . Starving children in the Children's Homes. . . . Ruin and the lapse into barbarism. . . . A café with a string orchestra. . . . The first shop-windows commencing to bloom. . . .

Gleb stopped suddenly, disquieted, incapable of formulating the great question which was confusedly arising in his mind.

Yes, the New Economic Policy. . . . Regulation and Control. . . . Markets. . . . Food Tax. . . . Co-operatives. . . .

Yes, café and string orchestra . . . but half a pound of rationed bread ? And the Trade Union card entitling you to a share of certain necessities : a yard of chiffon, a moustache-binder, or ladies' suspenders ? Why are the shop-windows filling so quickly ? Why was there such a constraint and alarm in his soul ?

On the other side of the street he saw Polia outside a café. She was looking in through the window and couldn't tear herself away. A man in a new tunic came rushing past her with a portfolio—who does not carry a portfolio now ? He jostled her with his shoulder, pushing her away from the window. Without taking any notice she took up her former position.

Gleb crossed the street and stood shoulder to shoulder with Polia. In a minute she would notice him and would start. But she did not notice even him ; she was staring into the depths of the window. There in the twilight depths shades rose from the past—seated in pairs and groups at little tables.

Café. . . . In a short time. . . . Hot pasties with all kinds of filling. . . .

Out of the darkness beyond the window came the thin sound of phantom violins.

Behind, on the pavement, a nasal voice spoke volubly of business :

" With a stabilised currency, only with a stabilised currency. . . . A journey to Sukhum. . . . The goods have just been delivered from abroad, freightage prepaid. . . . Feluccas. . . . The percentage of net profit ! "

Gleb looked round and saw the lawyer Chirsky. With him was a former large wine-grower on the coast. He used to meet him in the Economic Council. He met Chirsky there too. What sort of business had they at the Economic Council ?

To hell with them ! In the factory there was still the atmosphere of October, and one's head had not yet recovered from the Civil War. But when one came to town it seemed as though a strange change had taken place and that the world had altered.

Gleb playfully pulled the portfolio from under Polia's arm. She started and gazed at Gleb in fright. He saw a suppressed shriek in her eyes.

" Not worth looking at those wasters, Comrade Mekhova. Don't be envious ; if you are you'd better drop in and have a bite. Come, let's go to the Women's Section."

" Tell me, Gleb ; do you understand it ? I was walking

along the street and staring at the windows like a fool. What has happened to me? I can't understand it, Gleb."

"Go to the Women's Section. Let the real fools and scamps do the staring."

He took her arm and led her along the street. Polia threw frightened glances at the windows and doors of the shops, and her eyes quivered like dew-drops in the wind.

"I shan't go to the Women's Section to-day. Dasha's there. She's a woman in a thousand, Gleb. She'll go far, you'll see. Besides, what can one say about the others, when one doesn't even know about one's self? Yesterday I was one thing and to-day I'm another."

"It's shameful, Comrade, for a leader of the Women's Section to be in a panic. You must hit out and not cry and hop around. If you feel bad, don't show it. It'll pass off in a while if you just keep hold of yourself."

He spoke roughly, but he pressed her hand affectionately.

"What's the matter with me, Comrade Gleb? Perhaps you've the strength to stand up in all this muddle. It's as though I were infected with the plague. I feel the earth trembling underneath my feet. You know I've been at the front and have seen really terrible things. Twice I've been threatened with certain death. I took an active part in the Moscow street-fighting. But now I'm going through something that has never happened to me before. It's as though a vile crowd were jeering at me and I'm ashamed because I cannot protect myself. Perhaps this must be so? Perhaps it's inevitable? It's the unavoidable result of our struggle and sacrifice? Is it really so, Gleb? Perhaps you're as crazy as I am? Do tell me frankly. Perhaps, Gleb, you only appear strong, by habit?"

They arrived at the House of the Soviets. Polia stopped but could not leave Gleb; it was evident that she feared to be alone and also to be in public. Gleb was troubled. What was agitating him: was it Polia's words, or was it that she was attracting him to herself?

To give the factory as a concession. Gleb grew alarmed at this dreadful word.

Nobody knew who had cast this word upon the winds, and he could obtain no explanation. It was but a furtive stammering rumour, which dissolved mistily when one sought to grasp it. But the street screamed the thing, with its staring shop-windows and the busy shuffling of speculators and tradesmen. That was another matter. The hoops of the barrel had burst, and through the chinks the stinking slops had run out; out of dark corners and crevices wood lice and worms were crawling. One could not kill this new devilry with a stroke, one must have a sensitive nose and go calmly about cleaning it up.

Polia. Here she was, near to him, and in her words there was such intimate friendship. She required his strength now. He felt that she was greatly troubled, but he could not gently and cautiously set about gaining her confidence; perhaps he did not know how, perhaps he had not the habit of it. He wanted to say a cheering word to her; to cover her, as with a cloak, from the cold, and in a soft whisper to pour out his heart to her.

" I'm not going to the Women's Section. Come to my house, you can sit down for a while. I shan't feel so wretched with you there. You can leave soon, but I shan't have the feeling of being alone then. You may be able to say just the word which will soothe me and will help me to see things with different eyes."

She pushed him gently to the glass doors of the porch.

And all the way to her room—up the marble staircase and along the narrow corridor, she did not let go his hand, repeating all the time, over and over :

" Must it be so ? Yes, must it be so ? "

Her room was bright and sparsely furnished. There was an iron bed, covered with a grey blanket, and a white pillow. Over the bed, Lenin's portrait. A little table stood near the window on which lay a pile of books and papers. But Gleb only felt one thing : the room breathed of Polia. If he had not known that she lived here, all the same he would have discovered it by the aroma.

She threw her portfolio on the table and stood leaning against the wall near to it. Nor did Gleb sit down, but walked up and down. He stopped near the door in the left-hand wall.

" Who lives behind this door ? "

" That's Serge's room."

He knocked at the door. An empty echo resounded. He approached the door in the right-hand wall near to Polia.

" And in here ? "

" I'm afraid of that door. The Chairman of the Soviet Executive lives there. I don't like him. There's something so heavy about him, and I've always a presentiment that the

door will open and that. . . . Something will happen. . . .
I don't know what : something dreadful."

"He's a great one for the women, is our Chairman."

"Why ? How do you know that ? "

Polia began to laugh, but her laugh soon vanished. Her
eyes were thoughtful ; she was brooding over her own pain.

"He runs after women. I shall have to settle his account
sometime."

"What a slave you are still, Gleb! After all, finally we shall
have to have a revolution within ourselves as well. Yes, there
must be a ruthless civil war within ourselves. Nothing is
more fixed and tougher than our habits, feelings and preju-
dices. I know that jealousy is seething in you. Jealousy is
worse than despotism. It is an exploitation of one human
being by another that can only be compared with cannibalism.
That's what I have to tell you, Gleb : you'll never get nearer
to Dasha in that spirit—you'll be beaten."

"I'm already beaten, damn it ! "

"There you are ! And you deserve it. It serves you right ! "

"That's true. There's a certain snag in these things, in
love. It's something one ought to try to comprehend."

Polia looked around, startled and perplexed. She put her
hand to her curly hair, and grimaced as though she had a
headache.

"Yes, it's a hard nut, Gleb ; but it has to be cracked. And I
believe the kernel is very bitter and poisonous. It must be so.
Well, if it is so, devil take it, it must be ! When one's blood
was poisoned, one found also in blood the antidote. What is
the antidote for the dull routine which returns from the
accursed past ? That's where the terror is. It's always more
difficult to fight with one's self, because in the daily routine
one is sentenced to loneliness."

She stood before Gleb, so simple, frank, so lost in her
bewilderment, so trustful and so near, as though he had known
her for a very long time, as though she had always been like
this : disconcerted and rebellious. He had only to embrace
her, to take her into his arms, and she would snuggle up
to him like a child and become so close to him ; and his caress
would appease her, and she would laugh once more as she had
not long ago.

In a surging of silent tenderness he pressed her breast to his
and stroked her locks with his cheek. At first she was frightened and shrank from his hands. Then she trembled, put her

arms round his neck and looked at him through her tears.

" Gleb, my dear ! If you only knew how I needed your courage and strength ! I feel terribly depressed, Gleb. Do understand me, Gleb, and don't despise me. You're nearer to me than anyone else, and I love you very much."

Gleb was silent, still pressing his cheek to her hair. But when he had carried her over towards the bed—she yielding herself to his will—a knock sounded on the door.

" Comrade Mekhova, may I come in ? Are you there ? "

The door creaked. It was Dasha. Her red headscarf flashed and the face was the same : serene, with courageous eyes, her young smile, and her face still uncooled from the sun.

" Well, well, is that Gleb ? You restless fellow, have you even intruded here ? What a fellow ! "

She burst into a gay laugh, but just for an instant Gleb saw fright flash in her eyes, and a sudden pallor pass over her face. But perhaps this was only imaginary, because Gleb himself grew afraid and could not immediately control himself. Mekhova moved away from him and began to laugh : Dasha is no fool, and her eyes can note lesser trifles than this.

" You're not jealous, Dasha ? I wanted to borrow some strength from your Gleb. He is so solid, nothing seems to worry him."

" Why do you say ' my Gleb ' ? Now, of course, he'll imagine that he's the strongest man in the world ! But there are many things, you know, that Gleb still doesn't understand. It's true he's a wonderful man ; but how stupid he is still, Comrade Mekhova ! Oh, how foolish ! "

Gleb stood between them ; he put his hand on Dasha's shoulder and then on Polia's.

" Damn it all ! I've got to understand this business even if I break my head. It seems clear enough to Dasha, and so she isn't troubled any more."

Dasha laughed and approached the table.

" I come from the Women's Section, Comrade Mekhova. The Women's Conference will shortly take place. Had you forgotten it ? To-day at five o'clock there's a meeting at the Trade Union Council and you have to make a report there."

" Yes, I remember it, Dasha. But it would be better if you made the report. I just can't collect my thoughts to-day. Please, Dasha, make the report and I shall rest until to-morrow and pull myself together a bit."

" All right, Comrade Mekhova. I'll do it."

She put her arm round Polia and looked at her sternly and frowningly.

" Comrade Mekhova. . . . I understand. . . . Don't fret, my dear. We must always be prepared : our head on our shoulders and holding our heart tight with both hands. Get a tight hold of your feelings, Comrade Mekhova, and take care of your health. And as for you, Gleb, my dear Comrade, you need not listen to this. But why are you running away ? Stay here. You weren't here in secret, were you ? Oh, and I knew nothing about it ! "

Dasha's eyes were moist. Polia was looking through the window and she laughed like a sick person.

" God damn the women ! Pretty hard to understand, damn it ! "

And Gleb left the room, red with shame and stupefaction.

In the corridor he met Shibis. As usual, Shibis neither greeted him nor shook hands. He was walking jauntily, but heavily, and looked at him without blinking, as at a stranger.

" Oh, there you are. Listen, the Forestry Department has got into a hell of a hole. There's been such a dust kicked up that the whole Department's covered with it, and the place is like a madhouse now. Shuk has proved himself to be a damn fool. I haven't slept to-day. I don't sleep at nights ; I usually take a sleep in the morning and after dinner. I'm going to lie down for half an hour. And, you know, your one-armed man was a marvellous specimen of humanity. They shot him down in the cellar. I spent several nights chatting with him with great pleasure. The bourgeoisie knew how to give that youth a high culture, and we have much, very much, to learn. In order to master culture one must know how to use it, and that is not so simple. Bear that in mind."

" Stop, stop, Comrade Shibis ! That's clever ! So you walked round and round them, round and round them, and then suddenly got the whole lot. Why, even Shuk gave up loitering and chattering at that time."

" Ah, that's because he happens to be in good hands. Out of the twenty we're sure to shoot a good half. With these entertainers we'll fix up a public performance in the State Theatre : I'm passing the affair on to the Revolutionary Tribunal. But we're going to get it in the neck for the expropriations. Tomfoolery—it was done during the Party Congress. Someone is going to get it ; who will it be, do you think ? "

"I think, Comrade Shibis, that it's impossible to get the better of Badin without a struggle, and you can only send him up in the air with dynamite."

"Yes, but we've already laid the train. Don't forget that the reversion to daily routine means dissensions, and dissensions mean—heroism turned petty bourgeois. I always sleep with open windows and doors. Sleep is very healthy and fresh in the daytime, because it's saturated with people and the sun. My merriest time is at night. Come and see me sometime and we'll pass some pleasant hours together. At night time, one always sees more than in the day."

"Doesn't Comrade Lenin sleep at night, Comrade Shibis ? I've heard that he's as sleepless as you are, and loves artificial light."

"I don't know. I also think he loves the light."

"Well, what does it mean, Comrade Shibis : on the street they announce that a café will open, with an orchestra. Is all the old devilry going to start ?"

"Well, has that frightened you ? I shan't be here much longer. I have to leave for the army. And as for you, train yourself a bit more and learn the ABC of politics. I'm not worried at all with all this. One must understand to look at the sun and at blood in the same way, without blinking. Not be afraid that the sun will burn one's eyes, or that blood will poison one's soul. So that the sun and the blood have to be mixed together in a trough."

He raised his eyebrows and laughed and again Gleb saw in his eyes that childlike clarity, and in the pupil that fiery point which moved unceasingly.

Shibis went along the corridor with his jaunty but heavy step ; and for the first time Gleb felt that Shibis was mortally tired and carrying an unbearable burden.

Chapter XIV

THE RETURN OF THE PENITENTS

I

THROUGH GOLGOTHA TO CANOSSA

SHIBIS, Shidky, Gleb, Serge and Polia took their place in the boat.

Shibis raised his hand, looked at each one of them, and showed his teeth in a childlike grin.

" Ready, Brothers ! Hold tight ! Let her go, sailor ! "

And he gave a mighty slap on the back to the sailor, who had a soiled and scarred face, like a kicked-about bucket, and enormous veined hands.

Far away in the roadstead through the hot shimmering air could be seen a steamer, lying like an enormous rock arising from the water. This was the first transport of the penitents.

The reflections of the quays lay broken on the green swell, they also flew in the blue depths, and were flecked with fat, multi-coloured blots and floods of oil. At the prow, the green surf broke with the sound of glass and was scattered to both sides. Astern, behind Gleb and higher than his head, was a snowy swelling mass of water.

Near the mole two dolphins were rolling over and over like wheels of bronze. Sparks shot from their round backs, pricking one's eyes painfully.

On the quays—a great mass of people. In their movements was a kaleidoscopic play of colour. Also in the water were reflected the colours of the crowd, shifting like flower-petals, flashing in the waves.

It was so long since they had seen a steamer. All the steamers had gone away with the Whites when they had fled. It was dull for everybody without steamers in the port, so that when one arrived it was a fête.

On the deck of the vessel, from prow to stern, clustered a mass of people. From the distance it looked like a mass of little winged creatures, like a lot of cormorants in repose, drying their wings in the sun.

Serge looked at the huge black steamer, biting the nail on his little finger. Gleb struck him on the hand, but could not make him stop.

" From Golgotha to Canossa. . . . Such is the way of counter-revolutions."

Shidky squinted at Serge, his nostrils were white.

" Stop it, Serge ! That's the raving of an intellectual. Only the Smenoveshovsi[1] speak in that way now."

But Serge went on speaking to himself, or perhaps to everybody at once :

" There were three hundred men on this ship and fourteen officers. When they wouldn't let them put in at Tuapse, they said : ' The steamer will not return. Take us to such and such a place. Let's land and be shot.' That was magnificent. They represented an enormous amount of energy, such as we must transform and use."

Shidky snapped his teeth.

" How much energy did they take from us ? How much of our blood and strength have they swallowed up ? Did you reckon that up ? It's enough to make your head swim ? "

" Well, and what about it ? Suffering and blood are inevitable. Blood is turned into suffering, suffering is transformed into great exploits and through the masses into world-wide struggle."

Polia looked at Serge and began to laugh. She was once more blooming with spring-time joy, and the sun once more scintillated beneath her brows.

" Ah, little Serge, you're a fine hysterical one ! How our hefty delegates would have dropped on you if they could have heard your wisdom ! "

Gleb looked at the dolphins. The two paddlers, one after the other, were turning round and diving under. With graceful upward swings they were cutting the thick milky foam with the sharp swords on their backs. When they disappeared below the surface, the water came together above them dense, waveless and without a splash.

With the same power the wheels of the Diesel engines in the factory were flashing and charging the soul with their electric floods. Once upon a time many of those wheels re-

[1] Literally: changers of milestones. Those who change their political orientation easily.

volved, but now only two. Their life was transfused into the
mountain gully, where the tortoises—the two trucks—crawled
up and down, along the ropeway, approaching and crossing
each other. And nearer, below the slope, a long file of such
trucks, passing each other. But these two dolphin-wheels,
charged with vital animal blood, were carrying into the sea's
bosom the lavish precious energy of the sun.

Already the quays were far away. The mountains glimmered
with a copper tint in their clefts ; they rocked and swam in the
sea, covered with a violet mist. The boat played in the swell,
and the ship rose and fell, blocking out half the horizon, piled
up like a sky-scraper. Shibis, Shidky and Polia all seemed tiny
and clear-cut as in a convex mirror. Gleb felt small also, but
his heart was big, bigger than himself.

Serge could not take his eyes off the steamer ; he was still
biting the nail of his little finger.

In the womb of the ship, iron chains clashed and rattled ;
a thunderous reverberation was in the air.

" To the gangway ! "

Above, the deck was lined with a garland of dusty faces.
They gazed down with bleared, unblinking eyes. Thousands
of hands fluttered out frantically. There was a stormy bellowing uproar. High up above the rigging a blue smoke was
whirling. Down below in the oily swell, splashing and rattling
like a machine-gun, was a little motor-boat with a piece of red
cloth at the stern. A little, menacing, fiery atom of dust of the
R.S.F.S.R.

An Englishman in a gold-laced uniform—doubtless the
captain—motionless at the rail of the bridge, impassively
gazed down at the motor-boat below.

On the distant docks a field of poppies bloomed and undu-
lated ; and in the bosom of the ship iron rumbled and clashed
with a dull shaking thunder.

2

TOOTHLESS WOLVES

Thus it happened that the Bolsheviks clattered with their
heavy boots upon the deck. It was all the same to them :
whether they were at the Party Committee's rooms or on the
deck of an English ship. But these people were not like those
who, in the past, had trod that deck. They were of the past and

were forgotten : but these it would not be possible to forget. Never could one forget these dreadful people out of a dreadful land.

A great crowd was jammed together, stinking and sweating. Corpses risen from the tomb. Mildewed typhoids. Blue, swollen faces and mad eyes. Ragged spawn of the barracks. It was impossible to distinguish who were officers and who were soldiers, in this grey herd. Heavy and silent stood this crowd of condemned beings.

Shidky, who looked like an Englishman himself, was speaking to the gold-laced Englishman.

Shibis, in fawn leather, looking like a bronze figure, was speaking clearly and impassively :

" Officers to the front ! Let the others stand back ! "

The crowd shuffled noisily, clearing a space on the deck. It looked like the scene of an execution.

Ragged creatures, still preserving a martial bearing, pushed their way through the crowd. Their once well-cared-for faces were now swollen with hunger and ingrained with dirt. It was impossible to tell with what frenzy they were possessed—were they drunk with despair or with the joy, or in the fury of self-immolation before their fate ?

Polia smiled insolently. And whilst Shibis was speaking she talked to Gleb.

" Look, Gleb ! These people look as though they had already been hanged. They used to kiss the hands of the ladies. . . . Now they're like dung-beetles."

Shibis' voice was even and gloomy, like the mask of his face.

" You are our foes ! You hate us ! You have destroyed us by the thousand, the workmen and the peasants. You have come here hoping to find not death but life. Why have you come to Soviet Russia ? "

An old man with a silver-grey beard stepped forward. But perhaps he wasn't an old man ; perhaps his face was just mouldy ?

" We are not afraid to answer you. Oh, no. . . . We are only people who are deadly tired. A defeated enemy is no longer an enemy. Have we suffered less than you ? We have only our homeland ; and nothing outside of it. We cannot exist outside of it. We are accursed, but in this accursedness is our expiation. Let our country even demand torture and death from us. We are ready ; we submit. You will not refuse us this joy ? "

While speaking he had not looked at Shibis but proudly raised his head to the sun.

Shibis watched him silently and attentively through the net of his eyelashes.

They were all silent. The silence exhaled a unanimous sigh. Everyone was waiting for the moment when the tension would give way, and then there would be an outburst of cries.

A very young little officer suddenly began to shout hysterically :

" I've been deceived ! I was blind ! Yes, I am a murderer. Let me justify my life. Even if I die let me vindicate myself."

A sigh of repressed agitation passed over the crowd. Shibis carelessly waved down the cries of the little officer.

" Very good. But how will you prove to us your sincerity ? How will you prove that you are speaking the truth ? "

The little officer ran up to Shibis, tearing open the breast of his tunic.

" Shoot me now ! Shoot ! "

Shibis calmly waved him back.

" Return to your place. If you wish, you need not come on shore but may return to where you came from. Are you certain that we are not going to shoot you ? "

The officer raised his hands. His sleeves fell down his skinny arms almost to the shoulder. The red fists at the extremity of those dead white arms did not seem to belong to him.

" You can't kill me—you can't ! I want to live . . . to live ! "

They took him by the arms and walked him away. He went on screaming :

" To live ! To live ! "

Polia frowned and smiled ; her eyes were big and round with joy.

" What weak nerves these slugs have ! Why the devil did they surrender to us, Gleb ? Ask them, Serge. They won't understand me."

Serge pressed hard on Shibis' shoulder. His voice was broken with excitement.

" Comrade Shibis, have the courage to speak to them in other words, more worthy of us. It's always easy to jeer at people. You should assume a more difficult rôle : speak to foes as to human beings."

Shibis looked at him distractedly, like a blind man ; and said through clenched teeth :

" I shall send you ashore at once, Comrade Ivagin. What's the matter ? "

The crowd was stamping and shifting, and coldly and silently gathered round them. Dirty scare-crows were climbing upon the ventilator shafts and upon each other's shoulders, crawling up the rigging like snails ; they were looking in stupid bewilderment at these people and trying to guess whether they were cruel and dangerous or only ironically jesting. They were all expecting something terrible, that the taut gloom would suddenly explode like a distended bladder ; some sudden, crushing catastrophe would arise with uproar, and then everything would sink to ashes. But then everything would at least become simple and clear and their doubt would be gone.

Gleb was gazing at the stinking human mass, at the moist faces ; he did not pity anyone—it was just curious and laughable.

Wolves. . . . Yes, there they were, the wolves . . . with bloodshot eyes they had been over-running the vast spaces of the Republic. Three flaming years of suffering. In the fight against them, Gleb had learned to hate them, because death had always been over him, in gale and tempest ; the nights had been red with fire, and the days poisoned with blood and smoke. And now there they were, these wolves. Their eyes had dimmed and their jaws were toothless.

Gleb listened to Shibis, smilingly. Well-spoken—but not enough. It should be more vigorous. He was grinding his teeth. He felt an intense desire to burst out laughing and cursing.

A man stepped out from the group of officers. He looked as though he had been put together from a pile of assorted fragments. He had high, heavy cheek-bones. He came close to Shibis, almost touching him with his shoulder.

" You, with your talk of scorn and cruelty. You think that you have hit us hard, eh ? "—and here he raised his head high. " You think you have astounded us ? You—you are only children. . . . And babies don't know what nightmares are. Well, this is poison to us, eh ? But—you know—we were poisoned long ago. . . . So much that now we cannot feel it. Your blows do not hurt us. . . . If you succeed in hurting us, you will have learned more than now . . . eh ? I have finished——! "

Drearily he turned round. Shibis smiled through his mask.

" You're right. But it's in vain that you affect this boldness.

You know well enough what kind of hurt we can inflict upon you. Isn't it so ? We cannot be accused of being frivolous or unjust."

The man walked off without looking back.

The boyish young officer ran up again. He had recovered somewhat from his attack.

" We can only take revenge now. Revenge ourselves more pitilessly than you. Revenge ourselves on everyone—on the whole of Europe. On the whole world. I shall know how to vindicate myself ! "

Shibis narrowed his eyes and his face became small and sharp.

" We don't seek vengeance—bear that in mind. We're fighting for the great ideals of humanity—for Communism. Those who want revenge we destroy as criminals. We have a good mill and we grind small ; you'll see it."

The officers were silent. Their faces were grey.

Shibis looked at the sun, which lit innumerable points in his eyes ; and suddenly the mask dropped from his face.

" We open the doors. . . . In the name of the toilers, we forgive. You will contribute your strength to the Republic of the Soviets."

One could not hear another word. Thronging, surging, jostling each other. . . . A witches' dance ! With open mouths and staring eyes they rushed round Shibis. Shibis was shouting, Mekhova was shouting, Serge was shouting. Gleb, also, was shouting at the top of his voice ; a moment after, he could not remember one of the words he had said. A ragged soldier, his naked shoulder showing through his torn shirt, lay on his belly, crying and sobbing. Someone was swearing amazingly in a joyous, choking voice.

Serge's hands and legs trembled. He moved aside a little in order to calm himself.

The masts were swinging like branches in the air. The antennæ stretched from mast to mast hummed like a zither-string. The sea and air seemed full of fiery floods. Serge believed that life was immortal, and that the birds with their shimmering, explosive flight would bring to the air some strange and coloured blooming.

Shidky was speaking to the gold-laced Englishman. The pipe in the corner of the captain's mouth trembled alarmingly ; and his eyes bulged, uneasy and green, like those of a screech-owl. By sheer will-power he was keeping a grave, proud

countenance. Suddenly, he stiffly raised his hand to the peak
of his cap and began to walk with a heavy camel's stride to the
deckhouse, his fat posterior waggling from side to side.
Shidky looked after him laughing and, meeting Serge's eye,
winked, his Asiatic nostrils distended in a broad grin.

3

THE RED FLAG

The crowd absorbed Gleb. There was the crowd only and
no Gleb.

A Cossack in a torn Tartar vest, bare-footed, and with
tufted beard, stood facing Gleb. Between his hands he held a
strip of red cloth. The Cossacks and soldiers were intermingled
—all dressed in coarsely woven shirts. One wore a Turkish
fez under which one could hardly see his face.

" This flag is red. Although it looks like a rag, Comrade,
to you whose eyes are accustomed to red skies. Look, lad,
not with the eyes of everyday, but from the heart. I'm speaking
from my soul, Comrades : this is our fate, our blood—this
flag. I'm a Cossack, a sharp-shooter, I give you my word !
And we're all Cossacks : warriors of the Kuban and of the
Don. But we have all travelled the same road of suffering.
Isn't that so, my lads ? Am I saying the truth, friends ? "

A deep sigh shook the crowd.

" True, Cossack ! Well said ! "

The Cossack crumpled the red rag and then again spread it
before Gleb. In the sun it seemed ragged and creased. Spots
of oil showed on it.

Gleb took the rag and held it tightly grasped in his fist.

" Oh, so it was a shirt ? Is it from a man who was killed ?
Is that why it is stained with blood ? "

" Sure—blood from his guts. With his blood we are going
home."

Again a heavy sigh arose from the crowd. There was
moisture in the Cossack's eyes. Why was his face so red ?

" In Gallipoli we said : ' Devil take it all, boys ; let's go
home.' We rioted, the whole lot of us. And he was at our
head ; he, the Cossack Gubati. They caught us——. Him too.
We were driven like cattle to the slaughter, and they beat us
with sticks. Beat us all, me and all of them. . . . Beat us till
the blood came, and, as for Gubati, they beat him until his

bones showed. We got out of it, but he was dying. ' Here,' said Gubati, ' I'm dying. Take the flag of my blood. This shirt will be your flag, the road to your freedom, the road to our brothers, the Bolsheviks.' That's what our father, the Cossack Gubati, said. And this shirt is our flag until death. I have carried it buried in my breast, in my soul, secret from all eyes—. And look, Comrade dear, how it flutters and flames, so joyfully it almost hurts."

The words of the Cossack were tumbling out hurriedly ; he was waving his arms and the red cloth fluttered like a red bird over the people's heads.

Gleb took off his helmet and stood bareheaded like the rest.

" A wonderful flag, truly. A precious flag. Look here, I've been a regimental commissar, but now I'm a workman. You haven't forgotten those hellish days ? Look over there at the factory's smoke-stacks tearing the clouds. I'm over there as a mechanic and the workers' representative. We've thrashed Denikin and Wrangel—ourselves, with our own hands. With our blood we have smashed the enemy. What flag have we ? There, look at the factory. It's still cold. We've moved it a bit away from the dead point, but it's not moving yet. The factory is still dark ; who'll light it up with his blood ? No one can beat us. The factory's just starting to kick, by God ! Our hands and our blood did it ! Over there—you see ?—the work on the mountains. The trucks. When night comes, you'll see electric light everywhere. A hell of a lot of stars, made by us ! "

" Yes, yes—we're all ready for work. But over there in the foreign countries, working-man's blood is poison. . . . That's how it is."

Near by, five of the ship's seamen were standing in a little group, their pipes between their teeth. They were blinking, calf-like, and listened as though they understood. Gleb looked at them while he was speaking. Helmet in hand he waved to them to come nearer and nodded to them.

" Hullo, Englishmen ! Come over here and let's have a little chat. Come on ! "

The sailors looked about them. Were they being watched ?

They walked nearer and saluted, their fingers to their caps.

" Now, try and understand us, Brothers, not by words, but by my face. Look ! I'm a Bolshevik "—he pointed to himself with his helmet. " Those are Bolsheviks over there." He pointed towards the town. " And where are your Bolsheviks?"

The sailors shifted their pipes.

" Bolsheviks—! Hurray—! Proletarians. . . ."

" Have you heard ? The workers smell the same in every land. Isn't that so, Englishmen ? What's your most important word, you English ? Your best, most important word, that everyone can understand ? Important words, important deeds. That's how you've got to put the question, dear Comrades ! "

One of the sailors walked up close to Gleb. He had a red face, red hands and red hair. Taking his pipe from his mouth, he raised his hand above his head and said sternly and earnestly :

" Com-in-tern ! "

And after him the other sailors, like a chorus :

" Com-in-tern ! All right ! "

Gleb stamped on the deck, enraptured.

" Ah, the rascals, they understand us, eh ? You see it's quite easy to understand each other, without any trouble ! Just one word, and it went to the guts of them ! "

He grasped the sailor's hand and shook it heartily, laughing.

The Cossack with the flag stepped forward.

" Here, I know how to speak to them, Comrades. Let me give them some good stuff ! Listen, Englishmen. . . . Join with us—and you—and you ! Join the Bolsheviks ! Send your officers to the devil, like we did. Hang the officers to the mast, and we'll make the ship over to working-class Russia ! "

The sailors laughed and exchanged a few words with each other.

One must drive it into them, until it hurt, what we have gone through. Let them feel the pain which has been given us.

Putting his hands on their shoulders, Gleb spoke to the seamen, sternly and directly.

" You Englishmen—fools !—Comrades ! What worthless scamps are you English ! Look at that factory over there—how powerful it was ! The mountains trembled with her power and almost burst ! Now, there's just a whisp of smoke. . . . It's almost dead. It hurts one to see it, Comrades, Englishmen. Coal is needed, machines, transport, material, building material. And then you—you come with your intervention, swine, scoundrels ! And when one asks you for something, you're as coy as girls : ' I'd like to—. I really want to—. But the capitalists won't let me.' And then, the Comintern, you hardly dare speak of that. Although we're beggars and are starving, all the same we have Lenin—. Yes, we have a Lenin, you Englishmen ! And what about Lenin in your country ? "

The sailors gesticulated now, all talking together. Puffed out their cheeks, banged their fists upon their palms.

" Lenin's all right—. Lenin. . . . Lenin. . . ."

Gleb didn't laugh at them ; but the sweaty compact crowd did with all their might.

" Aha, you Englishmen ! Who can call us slaves ? And we call out to the whole world : Comintern ! Soviet Russia ! English brothers ! Proletariat ! "

Shidky came up, working his way through the crowd, and went straight up to the sailors. He began to speak with them in English, and at once they became engrossed and serious.

Gleb could hardly recognise Polia : she was so different, excited, full of energy, feverish ; she couldn't keep still and her eyes could not contain her joy.

" All right, Comrades. I want to see your sailors ! Lead me to them ! I know that they've been shutting them away from the Bolshevik infection. That doesn't matter, we'll get hold of them. Let's see them ! Ask them about it, Shidky ; go on, talk to them, that's the thing to do ! "

The sailors were grinning broadly and blinking eagerly.

One of them, a lanky fellow, pressed his palm against his round cheek. The muscles of his face played like violin-strings. Polia, astonished, raised her eyebrows and said roughly :

" Blockhead ! "

The crowd burst into a hoarse laugh. Two soldiers came crawling on all fours along the deck, screeching convulsively :

" Oh, I'm dying—! Oh, you sons of bitches—! I'm dying ! Oh ! "

Polia took the lanky sailor and Shidky by the arms and dragged them along towards the stern. The crowd surged after them irresistibly.

4

THE GIRL ON THE STEAMER

A girl stood on the deck of the steamer, gazing at the town. Seen from behind she looked quite young. Her hair was black and lustrous.

Serge seemed to remember having seen her in the crowd—or, rather, he had not seen her, but only her eyes. But by her eyes he recognised her. Fever burned in them, and tears that had never dried. Then she had disappeared; her eyes had been lost in the crowd. Unconsciously, he had been looking for her for some time, through his sorrow and fatigue.

When he again saw her on the deck, standing near the railing, he silently approached her and stood by her side, also looking out towards the town. In such a silence there are sometimes unforgettable moments of unspoken communion.

The poppy-field of people upon the docks was fading. They could not face the wind. The wind played like a cat with the petals, which shrank coyly. Painlessly they were detached, and laughed with the wind as they went. The quay was fading and emptying. The town was exhaling towards the sea the heat of its stones. And the grey-blue streets, framed in waves of transparent green, were aspiring towards the mountains with the factory smoke-stacks.

The green sea, full of fecund life, seemed to be swallowing up the blue sky and fiery clouds. The fading buildings and mountains seemed to be streaming into the far abyss, like thick torrents of lava. And the mountains, the town and the sea were shimmering and heaving like a mirage in the opal mists, in the smoke of the burning dross of the day.

This young girl at the railings, could she feel all this?

Serge felt that she did and he looked at her questioningly. Where had he seen this girl before? Nowhere. Only perhaps in his dreams.

She gave him a rapid but attentive glance. An anxious question welled up in her eyes. Was it so or not? Serge saw that she smiled.

Without looking at him she said, as though speaking to herself:

"Yes, I have been waiting for this. . . . Like all the rest. . . . I came here and have been waiting. And now. . . . I have been through it all. How well you understand how to torture! To torture and to overwhelm one with joy—both at once. With one single blow. You Communists are frightful people. Do you come from a nightmare or have we only lived in dreams?"

Serge moved just one step towards her. He stretched out his hand along the rail.

"Why a nightmare? It's a much simpler and deeper

matter. We are people of merciless action, and our thoughts and our feelings belong to that which one calls necessity : the inevitable and incontrovertible truth of history. We're just too simple and too sincere—that's all. And that's why you hate us."

The girl cast terrified eyes on him.

" Oh, no ! Here is a horrible beast and the grandeur of creation, both in one. Why ? There are so many heroes among you, but also so many villains and cannibals."

" Perhaps so ; but our names will last through the centuries. We shall be forgotten as villains, but known as creators and heroes. Suffering and bloodshed are the price of immortality."

They were silent for a while. The girl was looking at the waves. Then she said quietly :

" I have suffered too much. You know it. I have learned to forgive, even to the point of justifying."

" We also forgive. You have experienced it yourselves. We're as merciless in our forgiveness as we are in our fighting."

Confusion, fear and admiration struggled in the depths of her eyes. She stretched out her hand to Serge. It was small and it trembled.

" Help me to understand you all and to love you. Would you allow me to write to you, it would help me ? "

Serge turned away from her, suddenly cold and distant.

" I can't help you at all. Only stern work can help you. One has to commit oneself to new streams of life. One must stand in a new relation to the world. You are going ashore and will perhaps be born into a new life."

She bent over the railing, crushed by his words.

" Ah, to be born again is as terrible as to die."

He did not answer her, but turned away and walked towards the crowd.

5

CAPTURE OF HIS MAJESTY'S STEAMER

Beaming with enthusiasm, Polia was walking at the head of the crowd. Behind her, in a group, came the sailors and then the Cossacks and soldiers, stamping and uproarious.

Warm steam like a sweat-bath. Stuffiness and dizziness. The deck blazed with the heat, and it seemed that it could at any moment rise in fire and smoke. A wild uproar. Shidky and Gleb were being tossed high in the air by the crowd and falling back on scores of out-stretched arms. And as they flew up, a great cry arose, accompanied by a thunder below in the engine-room.

" Hurrah ! Hurrah ! Hurrah ! "

The gold-laced Englishman was gabbling in front of Shibis. The pipe in his hand was dancing, and it seemed it would break at any moment. Shibis, in tan leather, stood motionless, gazing at him through the mask upon his face. Then he tore off his leather cap and waved it before the captain. But still he stood immobile, only his lips were moving. The captain shivered, cold as a corpse.

The Bolsheviks were masters on His Britannic Majesty's ship. This herd of vagabonds, eaten up by lice and hunger, had a formidable power, which in one instant could capture his ship and overpower his will and iron discipline. He was a prisoner : a pitiable little grain of dust swept on by this mad and burning whirlwind.

Polia jumped up on a box. She tore off her red headscarf, and her hair shimmered like gold in the wind. She stretched out her arms like wings. Her face was the face of one possessed.

" Long live the Proletarian World-Revolution ! Down with Capitalist England ! "

" Hurrah ! Hurrah ! "

The little boyish officer was shouting at the top of his voice and clapping his hands.

The captain was shaking as in a cold wind and sucking the air through his extinguished pipe.

Shibis waved his cap and went towards the railings.

" Comrades, to the gangway ! "

And the crowd became suddenly silent, sinking back troubled.

Only the red rag with its dark bloodstains still fluttered overhead.

The girl was looking at Serge and smiling through her tears.

Gleb waved his helmet to the crowd and to the sailors and Polia was waving her red headscarf.

Iron thunder filled the entrails of the vessel, and it seemed that the decks were glowing with heat.

Chapter XV

SCUM

I

THE DAILY ROUND

ALL that summer there had been no rain; the sky looked bronze over the bay and the sea beyond the breakwaters was like a mirror. And in the mirror the sailing boats, the feluccas and the distant sandbanks were blazing in the whirling waves of heat. Near the shore the sea was transparent and green, with blue shadows, and with mother-of-pearl oil-stains; jelly-fish and seaweed floated in this blaze like blood-gorged flowers. Soft breezes passed through the town, smelling of sulphur or of the sea. There was no more horizon and the sea and sky were fused into one aerial ocean. The heat rose like steam above the mountains, and in the valleys the lush vegetation crowded luxuriantly. The slopes and ribs of the mountain glimmered with iron and sulphur through the mauve mists and were no longer reflected in the sea. All day long, on the beach around the bay, dense crowds sprawled on the sands or bathed in the water, walked among the boulders on the shore, and along the cliffs.

The stone and iron, and the cobbled streets in the town, blazed unbearably. The people were suffocating under this sun and among these burning stones; and were blinded by the glitter of the pavements and the burning air. On the boulevards in the shade, one's mouth was dry, and a dry warm wind burned one's face. The acacia leaves smelt as though they were burning. The streets were deserted and shimmered glassily. It seemed that people were fleeing from this infernal furnace and that all active life had stopped; and there was only emptiness and indolence. One only saw here and there half-naked shadows carrying heavy portfolios crammed with papers; staggering, with turbid eyes and sweat-stained faces, they seemed to struggle under the load of their own weight.

The shop windows made an elegant display ; and from the gaping doors of the cafés, the dull hum of many voices resounded ; also the clattering of dice, and the soft mysterious melody of violins and the sighs of the piano.

For the first time, in the communal dining-room of the House of the Soviets, there was the smell of soup with meat in it, tomato sauce and vegetables. But the old rancid smell of beans—shrapnel, they used to call it—still lingered among the tables, the walls and the utensils, poisoning the aroma of the meat and of the potatoes fried with onions.

At the dinner hour, all the responsible workers, all the leaders of the town's administration, would meet in the dining-room of the House of the Soviets. They would sit at table in groups or pairs and in the whole room there would altogether be about a hundred of them. And there would be a din of conversation in the room, amid the exhalations of the food, mingling with the clatter of the plates and knives. Through the open windows the sun streamed from the blazing streets, and the air was blue and heavy with dust and tobacco smoke.

Badin always dined at the same table as Shramm and the superintendent of the Public Health Department, a stout doctor named Suskin, always taciturn, shy and timid, sweating, deaf and absent-minded. Obese, never shaven, his scalp covered with stiff horse-bristles, he would look perplexedly at Badin and never understood what the Chairman or his companions were saying. Therefore he obligingly approved of what everyone said, repeating over and over again, not from the throat but from the belly, long-drawn out :

" Ye-e-e-es, ye-e-e-es."

It was difficult for him to speak, as he had an unusually large tongue ; there was too little room for it in his mouth, and in conversation it peeped out like a slug. Suskin could not get his words out ; they stuck in his mouth and splashed about in the saliva with his tongue, suffering from their inability to escape.

The Commissar of the local Food Department, Khapko, often sat with them. He was like a little Kulak, round, quick and attentive like a sparrow. He used to sit a long time eating —longer than all of them, and was always looking round on all sides, sternly and suspiciously, watching everyone, who they were and what they were eating. He would often jump up and rush into the kitchen and scullery ; or would run over to fellow-diners who left their tables dirty ; or to the Soviet

young ladies who were throwing bread-crumbs at their
cavaliers.

There was a little recurrent break in his voice and he
squeaked like a knife on a grindstone.

For instance, he would come rushing into the kitchen :

" Here, you—! Who's in charge here ? Bring the superintendent of the kitchen ! Now, why are the portions so small ?
You're stealing, you scoundrels ! You watch—I'll show you !
To-morrow I shall have the Workers' and Peasants' Inspection
here to go over everything."

Or in the dining-hall at the tables :

" Now, Comrades ! It seems you think that the Food Commissariat exists just for you to scatter bread all over the floor,
free of charge ? Look out, we'll teach you ! Now, you little
ladies, pay attention : this is not a café chantant and there are
no private rooms here ! Get down on your knees and pick
up those little bullets of bread which you've been throwing
at these idiots during your flirtation ! Come on now, pick them
up ! Where are you from, anyway ? What office do you work
in ? Well, I shall request that you be dismissed. These intellectuals' tricks, Comrades—they won't go down with the
dictatorship of the proletariat ! "

Loud quarrels and altercations would break out in the
dining-room whenever he appeared there.

These three men didn't take their supper in the hall, but met
in Shramm's room for this meal. Shramm's room had fine
upholstered furniture, fur rugs and carpets. Sometimes they
sat there until dawn, and what they did there—no one knew.
Only in the morning the chambermaid at the House of the
Soviets would find bottles under the table, and would sweep
up sausage skins and empty tins ; and the air smelt of cigarette-
ends and stale drink.

And once, for several consecutive evenings, they noticed
a man of Asiatic appearance, with blood-shot eyes and a great
hooked nose, on watch at the door of Shramm's room. This
was Tskheladze. He had once been in the Greens, and for two
years was a fine partisan ; he then became an employee of the
Food Commissariat. Barefoot, dressed in an old military
blouse dating from his guerrilla campaigns, he patiently and
silently stood at the door, his ferocious eyes staring for hours
at the door-posts, and listening for hours to the hidden voices
within. When a footstep sounded behind the door, Tskheladze would move aside. When the door opened and one of

the four men came out to go to the lavatory, Tskheladze, bleary-eyed, would glance through the open door at the interior of the room, devouring with his hungry eyes the secrets of Shramm's cosy little nest. They took no notice of him when they came out, just passing him by ; and did not guess why evening after evening this stooped broad-shouldered Georgian was standing there. There were always so many people standing about in the corridors of the House of the Soviets. And Tskheladze differed in no way from the rest of the loiterers there.

It was Khapko, the Food Commissar, who first caught him listening at the door. Tskheladze had no time to step aside— Khapko had a quick bird-like step. So he stood face to face with Khapko.

" Hullo, you ! "

Khapko eyed the Georgian from head to foot.

" What's all this ? What are you doing here, dog-face ? Are you spying ? Give me your Party card ! Quick ! "

Tskheladze flushed deeply. His eyes became round and bulging, malicious. He stooped still more and bared his teeth.

" What do you mean—' Hullo, you ? ' Who are you questioning ? What are you doing here, anyway ? What game are you up to ? Tell me, please."

Khapko, looking just like a fighting-cock getting into action, seized him by his blouse and promptly set to work on him with his hands. Tskheladze, hampered by his wide pantaloons, made a sudden half-turn and bumped up against the wall with his chest and head.

" To hell with it ! We're not living under the Tsar, you filthy scoundrel. For these tricks, you bastard, I'll have you thrown out of the Party. I'll not allow you to carry out counter-revolutionary activities under the rule of the proletariat. No ! "

Pinned to the wall, with arms stretched out, deafened, Tskheladze, infuriated and bewildered, gazed at Khapko ; he was breathing heavily and his bloodshot eyes would not stop rolling ; it seemed they would jump out of their sockets into the air like balloons.

Badin came out of the room, stepping heavily, with his hands in his pockets. He came and stood very close to Tskheladze.

" What's up ? "

" Just a son of a bitch of a spy. Ah, you're not in Menshevik

Georgia now ! · Arrest him on the spot and send him to the
Cheka. Do you think, you swine, that the Soviet Government
exists for you to spy upon responsible Soviet workers, who
work all hours and don't sleep at nights ? Comrade Chairman,
take his Party card away from him and give him one in the
jaw ! "

Badin looked closely at Tskheladze with eyes black as night.

" I know you well enough, Tskheladze. Khapko is lying.
He has drunk too much spirits and has made a fool of himself."

Khapko, astounded, squeaked like a bird, choked and beat
his head with his open hand.

" What—! Chairman ! The hell——! "

" Speak, Tskheladze. I know beforehand what you will say.
Speak out straight, honestly and firmly."

Tskheladze's lips trembled and his face was covered with
sweat from the strain and the suffering.

" Yes, I went—went and listened, yes ! I went and watched,
to see you building up working-class policy. . . . What were
you doing ? Why are you always with scoundrels ? What were
you doing for the worker ? What do you know ? D'you know
hunger ? Do you know bloodshed ? Do you know misery ?
Have you no shame ? Oh, my Comrade ! "

Badin stood like an image before Tskheladze, attentive and
grave. Khapko was laughing drunkenly, with a squeaking
whistle. Badin placed his hand on Tskheladze's shoulder and
spoke—his voice came from his whole body.

" Comrade Tskheladze, go home. To-morrow you will
receive an order to go to a rest-home. You must get a bit
stronger. You see, I make no secrets of my actions, and you
have no need to keep a watch on your Comrades. In this
respect we have our work very well organised and we do not
need your amateur assistance. Go ! "

He turned his back on him and returned to Shramm's room.
Khapko surveyed Tskheladze again severely from head to foot,
imitating Badin ; then he put his hands in the pockets of his
jacket, growing still shorter and rounder.

" All right, then ! Well, Brother, I shall get you ! Damn it
all ! "

Stooping, confounded, Tskheladze went along the corridor,
staggering as though he were ill, his shoulders rubbing against
the plaster. At Shidky's door he stopped. He did not know
whether he himself had opened the door, or if it were already
open ; he only felt a hand seize him by the arm and draw him

into the room. At the threshold he stopped and saw the little
lamp over the table, behind the dim shadow, suddenly go out.
Silently the shadow walked by him, and the little lamp flashed
again, lighting up the sordid bareness of a small hotel room,
whose walls were covered with spots of mouldy dampness.

" Well, come in and sit down for a while. Tell me what has
happened there. What the devil are you doing round here at
midnight, anyway ? "

Shidky again took the Georgian by the arm and led him
to the table. He seated him on a stool but himself remained
standing before him, slightly astonished, his nostrils pale, his
eyebrows lifted with a faint derisive smile. Tskheladze threw
him a glance full of anger and appeal. He sighed and his eyes
filled with tears. In the weak electric light his hollow cheeks
under the projecting cheek-bones seemed to be deeper than
ever. He brought his fist down furiously on his knee. He
jumped up and through his tears looked fixedly at Shidky ;
then he sat down again, contorted with despair and fury.

" Comrade Shidky, they must be shot. We must shoot—
you have to shoot—. What is happening ? How shall we look
after the workers' welfare ? I shed blood—I have ten wounds.
Where's my blood ? And hunger ? And ruin ? Where's the
Party, Comrade Shidky? But what are they doing?—They are
making a scandal, shameful ! Oh, shoot me, Comrade Shidky
—I cannot live among this filth and meanness. I can't bear it ! "

Shidky walked past Tskheladze silently, pacing up and down.
He was troubled and his eyes tired with thought. Constantly
he put his hand to his head, rumpling his hair nervously at the
back. He came up close to Tskheladze, placing his hand on
his shoulder. He would have liked to have soothed him,
affectionately, without words, but did not know how. And
this unaccustomed tenderness brought a shy smile to his lips.

" You're a funny chap, Tskheladze ! Why do you cry about
trifles ? To hell with them ! Go on with your work and know
that you're more valuable to the Republic than all of them put
together. Spit on them, if you can't knock 'em down ; or go
for them along Party lines."

Tskheladze again looked despairingly and entreatingly at
Shidky ; he made a vague gesture and dropped his head on to
his hands.

Shidky began to walk up and down the room, not looking at
Tskheladze. He was thinking and biting his nails, first on one
hand and then the other.

" And here's another thing, Tskheladze, not your case. Your case is too petty. There's a terrible whirlpool, and we're all in it. We're going to be subjected to a dreadful trial, worse than civil war, ruin, famine and blockade. We're in the presence of a hidden foe who is not going to shoot us, but will spread before us all the charms and temptations of capitalist business. We control the whole of the economic system. That's certain enough. But the petty trader is crawling out of his hole. He's beginning to get fat and re-incarnates in various forms. For instance, he's trying to instal himself in our own ranks, behind a solid barricade of revolutionary phrases, with all the attributes of Bolshevik valour. Markets, cafés, shop windows, delicacies, home comforts and alcohol. After the war atmosphere people begin to throw off the fetters. That's something we should be afraid of. There is panic, lassitude, revolt. . . . It's not from tiredness—no : it's a healthy revolutionary protest, coming from an over-developed class instinct, from the romanticism of the war period. Here we have the old methods of struggle—but precisely these old methods are no longer of use. The foe is mean, cunning and difficult to catch. We must forge a new strategy. It's impossible to win just by indignation and revolt ; that would merely mean reaction and hysteria. In this case we have radically to change ourselves, harden ourselves, fortify the Bolshevik in ourselves for a long, lingering siege. The romance of the tumultuous battle-fronts is finished. We want no romance now. What we need now is quiet, cold and resourceful administrators and hard-headed labourers with strong teeth, the muscles of a bull and healthy nerves. One must be a Bolshevik all the way through, Tskheladze. Calm yourself, Comrade, and let us think together over these various questions, which demand a good deal of brain-work. . . ."

Tskheladze looked at him with staring eyes and strained attention ; his narrow brow was contracted in deep moist furrows beneath his bristly hair. He was trying to understand and absorb Shidky's words.

But in despair he pulled at his damp hair and shook his head.

" Can't understand at all. . . . What rot are you talking ? I'm a simple soul and my words are simple. Tell me why are you turning my head ? What kind of an answer is this ? Have I suffered ? Yes ! Was I a fighting Green partisan ? Yes ! Didn't I fight the White Guards ? Yes ! Have I the word and the blood of a worker ? Yes ! But where is my class now ? The dogs are eating it—. You'll say : ' No,' won't you ? Into what villainy men have grown. . . . Do you understand ? There's nothing left—. It's the finish ! "

He got up and walked rapidly from the room, and Shidky could hear the tears choking in his throat.

For some moments Shidky listened to the retreating footsteps of the Georgian, then began to walk up and down the room again, without stopping, biting his nails, first on one hand and then on the other.

He could not get over what had just happened. By all appearances this sort of thing had been going on before to-night. In the past, members of the Regional Bureau of the Central Committee of the Party used to descend suddenly and unexpectedly upon them, in order to see that discipline was maintained; and also in the past, there used to be the strictest kind of criticism through the Party Committee. This was natural and necessary. Just as before, the responsible workers maintained their tense silence and respectful vigilance with regard to the cold and official Comrade from the Regional Centre. And as always the ritual of the sitting began in the same soulless manner :

" Dear Comrades. . . ."

But what had quite recently happened, a short time ago, under the conventional form of a business meeting, had been so unexpected and painful.

The side-tracked affair of the expropriations. . . . It was hardly mentioned. . . . At every sitting held in the presence of the blond intellectual from the Regional Centre, there had been disputes between him, Lukhava and Badin. There would be crushing criticism from the blond Comrade on the work of the Party Committee. . . . He spoke of the Control Commission. . . . Hints about the transfer of certain militants to lower grade duties.

Was this just intrigue and quarrelling between man and man, or a struggle between two different powers ? The Comrade from the Regional Centre, like everyone else, referred to it as a mere quarrel. This was so simple. And each sat in his corner watching the issue of this struggle. Stories and rumours were carried around. They were dividing up into hostile camps.

To leave this struggle, beaten, when one knew one was in the right—that was too difficult. It couldn't even be thought of because it would mean the end. Once one fell one would be crushed. It was a fight to a finish: constant, persevering, assiduous, where every weapon must be used, and all the mistakes and weaknesses of the enemy utilised. Badin fought skilfully. He knew to perfection how to profit by the bureaucratic apparatus, his administrative experience and his own instinct. He must be attacked from another side. One is not always a strong man when one seeks the support of the broad masses. The masses are like a stick with two ends : one can be their leader, but also one can be their victim, their slave and demagogue. Shidky stood near to the masses, while Badin stood above them, detached. But the Comrade from the Regional Bureau always cited Badin as an example to Shidky. Shidky would never forget his words :

" You are still a comparatively young member of the Party. You haven't yet the necessary strong self-control, the right appreciation of the given moment ; you do not thoroughly plan out your work and therefore you fall into wild mistakes. Comrade Badin has been through a tremendous amount of training in Party work and Soviet work, and you can learn a great deal from him. Why didn't you two co-ordinate your actions and together come to a correct analysis of the objective situation, thus forcing events to assume different courses and forms ? I'm telling you this because the Bureau of the Central Committee appreciates you nevertheless as a clever worker and realises your devotion to the Party."

" Nevertheless ! " . . . This blond intellectual had taken upon himself too responsible a rôle : to be his mentor in the name of the Party. All these eagles of passage were not really so very dreadful and important as they seemed in the provinces.

One thing was clear : there was no more romance. Romanticism was dead. It belonged to the past. The triumphant heroism of revolutionary action had passed into history and the crashing hymns would be heard no more. No more heroic deeds—but action. One had to absorb new energies, to know how to transform the least facts into certain and obedient weapons in the everyday struggle.

Shidky knew what was going on in Shramm's room. He knew why it was so comfortably carpeted and furnished. He knew that Shramm had not noticed the defalcations in the Forestry Department. Shidky knew all this, but he did not sound the alarm, so as not to disorganise the Party work. He was waiting for a favourable situation, to deal a quick well-aimed blow. There was no romance any more—that belonged to yesterday. To-day, cold calculation.

Why not stir up to-day the dirt of the daily routine of these petty existences hiding behind the door of Shramm's room? Why shouldn't he unearth the written orders in the Department of Health from them for sausages, ham, preserves and alcohol?

He went out into the corridor, biting his nails, and went out into the darkness of the night to the place where a pale reflection upon the wall told him that this was the open door of Shibis' quiet room.

2

A DIFFICULT TRANSITION

Gleb obtained the inclusion in the agenda of the Economic Conference of a report on the necessity for the partial resumption of work in the factory.

The storehouses were empty, the report said. There were enough staves for making a hundred thousand barrels. One could commence at once to start the cement mill and burning cement in one of the furnaces. The chalk was all lying ready in thousands of cubic feet, at the quarries. It was only necessary to bring a second ropeway line into action in order to convey it; the first one would continue to serve for the transportation of wood.

Gleb presented the report himself, with Engineer Kleist present in his capacity as an expert. Shramm argued coldly and dully against the project; he again talked about ' a sound productive plan,' about ' thoroughly co-ordinated organisation,' about the Bureau of Industry and the Cement Trust. Badin, dressed in black leather, was sitting in his usual attitude, leaning on the table; he was silent; looking from under his brows at Gleb, Shramm and Engineer Kleist. One could not gather what his attitude was on this question, whether he was on Gleb's side or Shramm's. Shidky and Lukhava spoke briefly and decisively in favour of the acceptance of the report and moved a resolution: " To begin without delay preparations for the restoration of production."

Badin leaned back in his chair and for the first time smiled at Gleb in a friendly manner.

" There are no other motions. There is no need to take a

vote on Comrade Lukhava's motion as no one has spoken against it."

Shramm unnaturally constrained, like a wax figure, cried suddenly, like a ventriloquist :

" I object categorically and finally."

" The resolution has been accepted ; Comrade Shramm has offered no objection from the point of view of principle."

" Yes, I have ! "

Badin did not look at Shramm, but his eyes smiled at Gleb.

" Comrade Shramm has no objection. Under the conditions of the New Economic Policy the necessity of reviving the productive strength of our republic speaks for itself. The question of starting the work of the factory is an immediate one. We are entering a phase of strenuous economic reconstruction. Even at the present low rate of productivity of labour, it would be possible for the factory to produce enough to satisfy the building needs of large towns and industrial districts. The question is decided. It requires now only detailed examination and treatment. But our Comrade Shibis has something to say."

Through his half-closed eyes, Shibis was looking at Shramm from his dark corner behind the table ; he seemed drowsy and bored.

" Yes, I also say that Shramm has made no objection. Shramm cannot object, and even if it appears that he does—do not believe your ears. Shramm no longer exists : Shramm is an anachronism."

And Shibis relapsed into his boredom and blind fatigue.

Gleb noticed how Shramm's effeminate face quivered convulsively and became very old ; and his eyes suddenly became filled with darkness and terror.

The Food Commissar, Khapko, surveyed them all with the stern eye of a master, banging his hand upon the table.

" Right . . . ! Take care, you people ! Now they're going to take your last pair of breeches. And in another month we'll be going stick in hand to make the alliance between town and country. Come on with the Food Tax, we'll say ! This isn't the year 1918 for you ! This is the alliance of town and village ! Oh, hell ! "

No one listened to him ; they were accustomed not to listen to his jokes, which he would utter sternly for the benefit of everyone. But he was the only person to listen to them or think about them.

Lukhava nervously walked to the table and made the following proposal :

" That we send Comrade Chumalov to the Bureau of Industry in order to obtain the prompt fulfilment of the decisions of this Economic Council, and to secure the further supplies needed for the factory."

Again nervously and quickly he walked back to his place by the wall. He sat with his feet back under his chair and his chin on his hands.

Gleb went up to Engineer Kleist, took him by the arm and laughed.

" Well, I'm going, as sure as twice two make four. Eh ! I'll stir up a stink at the Bureau of Industry ! What do you say, Comrade Technologist ? And, you know, Comrades, this man is not just a technologist, but he's pure gold—a famous specialist of the Socialist Soviet Republic. The real thing ! "

The next day Gleb left to go to the Bureau of Industry, promising to return in a week's time. At the factory the work was proceeding : they were repairing the buildings, the railway lines, the engines and the machinery within various departments. From morning till four o'clock in the afternoon, without a stop, the burning air between the mountain and the factory, the air which quivered with dust and foliage, resounded with the clash of metal, the rattling of trucks—to all of which the power-house played a monotonous humming accompaniment.

The ropeway for the delivery of wood was in continual operation ; the trucks rumbled and the steel cables hummed. Trucks rattled along the quays, cuckoos were calling, and the wood was falling thunderously into the empty wagons.

In the blue and glittering bay, lonely ships rode in incomprehensible sad expectation.

Dasha was frequently away from the Women's Section, at conferences and on official journeys. Every week Lizaveta assembled the women in the hall of the club ; and, until midnight, through the open windows, came a wild uproar to disturb the pensive quietude of mountain, woods and valleys.

And when they started for home in the darkness, they continued their shouting ; and their shrieks reminded one of their former quarrels about hens, eggs, and other housewifery interests. But, listening attentively, you would notice that, with all their shouting, they weren't quarrelling ; it was only the excitement of the discussions at their club, which they had brought with them into the street, into the night silence.

" Lizaveta is wrong. I tell you she is not right ! "

" Don't talk rot, Malashka. She's right ! We women are all a lot of fools ! "

" Well, if you are, I don't want to be one. I'm going to cut my hair—. Plaits, my Comrades, are a hangman's noose for the women. They're for a man to hang on to—a misfortune for the woman——! "

" Nothing of the kind ! Damn it, I'm not going to be led about by a loose woman. I shan't take my ikon down and shall go to church in spite of her. Lizaveta's home is a strange bed and the Communist gang is her church."

" Yes, and look what's coming to the girls and boys. The Komsomols ! [1] There used to be the fear of sin and they used to respect people, but now—Komsomol ! "

" It's you who are fools, you other ones. Don't your men beat you enough ? "

" You're a fool yourself ! And you'll be a worse fool if you quit your children, husband and home ! "

" Yes, because they don't take enough care of the working people. They put up all kinds of shops and cafés and have let the women go to hell. Starve, if you like. . . ."

It was like this every week ; whether Lizaveta and Domasha were in charge of the meeting or whether Dasha was there to help them.

Through the help of the Communist Group and of the Club, they had organised two groups for the " liquidation of illiteracy"; and when they started their first lessons, there were only women at the desks. Dasha's speech that night went straight to the hearts of the women :

" You must realise, women, that to-night by attending here so well you have beaten the men, and have given good proof of your proletarian class-consciousness. . . ."

And the women shouted and clapped their hands ; and their fresh gaiety resembled that of festive birds.

Every morning and evening Dasha called at the Children's Home, called the Krupskaya Home, to kiss Nurka ; and she saw that Nurka was flickering out from day to day like a candle. The child had become all bones, and the skin on her face was yellow and rumpled like an old woman's. Nurka would look

[1] A current abbreviation for Communist League of Youth.—Tr.

at her mother with her dark, sad, sunken eyes, and Dasha felt
that these eyes had witnessed something great and indefinable,
and that therefore the sun and the sky had grown for her small
and distant. Nurka was usually silent and pensive, these days ;
and seemed quite indifferent when Dasha parted from her.

And, that year, for the first time, Dasha suffered intolerable
anguish, but she hid it deep within herself. No one seemed
to notice this pain in her, only Comrade Mekhova glanced at
her once from her place at the table and then, suddenly, in
alarm, her gaze fixed itself attentively, disquieted.

" What's the matter with you, Dasha ? I believe you have
some trouble. . . ."

" Oh, have I ? Where did you get this fancy, Comrade
Mekhova ? "

Polia remained silent for a moment, examining Dasha
attentively with her tired eyes. And something in her eyes
reminded Dasha of Nurka's sad gaze.

" Dasha, I did not know that you could lie or deceive."

" Well, all right : I have some trouble, Comrade Mekhova.
Why do you want to know what trouble it is ? It doesn't concern anyone."

" Yes, that's just it, Dasha ! We're strongly organised,
strongly bound together. But we're terribly apart, one from
another, in our private lives ; and none cares how the other
lives and breathes. Yes, that's just it—that's the terrible part
of it. By the way, you always seem to dislike it when people
talk about this."

They both grew silent, apart and shut up in themselves.

Nurka was melting away like a burning candle—Nurka,
the only, only Nurka. And no one could say why she was
wasting away. What was the good of doctors if they couldn't
give you a single plain word and had no power to cure the
illness which was consuming the child. This little one, after
all, needed such little help from the adults. Yes, it was true :
the doctors could not help in this affair. Dasha knew better
than all the doctors in the world why Nurka was fading out like
a little star at dawn. It is not only the mother's milk which
a child needs ; it is nourished also by the heart and the tenderness of its mother. The child fades and withers if the mother
does not breathe upon its little head, if she does not warm it
with her blood, and does not surround its sleep with her care
and presence. A child is like spring apple blossom ; Nurka was
a blossom torn from the branch and thrown upon the highway.

The fault lay only in her, Dasha, and she would never be able to throw it off. It was not the fault of her own volition, it had come from somewhere outside, from life, from that strength in whose power she was herself, to which she could not give the appropriate name. The words—revolution, struggle, work, Party—resounded like empty barrels. But the essential content of these words was something immeasurable, unavoidable, which she carried within herself; that was all: there, there was no death, and she herself was an unseen grain of dust.

But Nurka was wasting, Nurka was going out like a spark. Nurka was there now—and then there would be no Nurka. Once, she had kicked joyously in her arms, pressed to her breast; then she had begun to crawl, learning to walk and to lisp her first words. Then she ran about and played. She grew. And even when death was grinning in Dasha's face, Dasha could not forget her child. Then Nurka disappeared, dissolved into her blood with the rest of the past; and when one day Dasha was being marched up to the noose of death, it was without thinking of Nurka, who appeared at the last moment only like a far-away ghost.

Now she saw Nurka alive, with the face of an old woman and with sunken eyes made sad by death; and once again, as long before, she felt not strong enough to step over her body. And she saw: Nurka was her life's sacrifice; and this sacrifice was unbearable for her.

And this was a conversation which took place between Dasha and Nurka one morning:

" Nurka, do you feel any pain, little daughter—yes ? "

Nurka shook her head. " No."

" What do you want ? Tell me ! "

" I don't want anything."

" Perhaps you'd like to see daddy ? "

" I would like some grapes, mummie ! "

" It's still too early, my dove ; the grapes aren't ripe yet."

" I want to stay with you, so that you'd never go away—and always be near. . . . And some grapes . . . near you, and grapes. . . ."

She was sitting on Dasha's knees, the warmth of her body melting into Dasha's warmth.

And when Dasha put her to bed, Nurka lay looking at her for some time with her deep eyes ; she was withdrawn into herself. Then, responding to Dasha's silent tearful look, she said :

" Dear mummie ! mummie ! "

" What, my sweet ? "

" Nothing, mummie. Mummie, darling. . . ."

Dasha left the Children's Home. She did not go as usual down the high road to the Women's Section, but walked into a thicket where she flung herself down on the grass. And here, in this lonely and unobserved corner, smelling of earth and vegetation, while the sun showered tiny flecks of light through the foliage, she lay crying for a long time, digging with her fingers into the mould.

One night, during Gleb's absence, Badin drove up to her house in an automobile. She heard the car panting outside the window and walked out of her room. On the shadowy porch they collided, breast against breast. Badin wanted to embrace her, there, at once, but she sternly pushed him away.

" Comrade Badin, that will never happen again."

Badin let his arms fall, and became heavy and motionless.

" Dasha—I want to be alone with you. . . . I hoped you'd receive me a little more warmly."

" Comrade Badin, go away at once, please, and don't chatter here in vain."

He went away. She went in, closed the door firmly and shot the bolt.

3

NIGHTMARE

In the morning, when Polia went to the Women's Section, or when she returned home after four o'clock, she ran along the streets as though blown by the wind. With long strides she hurried over the pavement, the cobbled streets, the quays, neither looking round nor distinctly seeing the people before her.

People walked by her side, met her, followed her, passed her, were reflected in her eyes as faded shadows. But she saw no faces ; she saw only feet : feet in boots, bare feet, or feet in ragged wrappings ; trousers, skirts, and women's socks, fallen down about the ankles. Just a lot of dusty feet unweariedly moving backwards and forwards. She did not look around her; she saw only the feet, her own and those of strangers. She could not raise her head to look calmly and steadily at the shop windows or through the open doors or at the people who appeared so different from what they used to be. She did not look, yet, somehow, knew that the women were not the same as they had been, a short time ago, in the spring : their clothes were smarter, flower-trimmed hats, transparent muslin, fashionable French heels. The men also had changed : cuffs and ties and patent leather boots. Again there was a smell of perfume ; voices sounded loud and joyful like those of birds. Through the open doors, in the cafés, one saw phantoms crowded in and out of the blue tobacco smoke, amidst the dull uproar of conversation ; china was rattling, dice clattering in some game of chance, and from the depths of the tobacco-filled den issued the tones of stringed instruments.

Where did all this come from ? And why did it come so quickly, so impudently and abundantly ? And why did this all pass over her, Polia, oppressing her and filling her mind with trouble and melancholy ?

It was as though she had strayed into a strange land, where she was lost ; as though something had disappeared which was precious and irreplaceable, something without which she could not live. And also she felt shame, dishonour and an indefinable anxiety. She was afraid that some workman, or one of those ragged creatures, eaten up with hunger, with bleared eyes, would come up to her suddenly and ask :

" Well ? Is this what you've come to ? Is this then what you wanted ? Strike them down, these rascals and hypocrites ! "

And this constant fear filled her with hallucinations.

One day, in the beginning of August, she saw on the quay, on the car-lines, in the coal-dust of the wharves, she saw a great crowd of ragged, hairy, wild-looking people. They lay in heaps or sat, or moved about jostling each other. Men, women, children. Babies cried, choked and sobbed. Someone was groaning dully. The women were picking lice out of each other's hair. The men were searching for vermin in their shirts and the seams of their trousers. The faces of all of them were bloated.

Busy passers-by would stop, curious, and would sniff the air, astonished.

" What's this ? Starving ? Famine ? "

And from the dirty, stinking, ragged mass, hoarse voices would cry :

" Starving ! God has brought us here to punish us . . . . Perhaps we can get better. . . . We come from the Volga— from the famine country. . . . Starving ! "

In pain and terror, Polia went to the Party Committee, all the time pursued by this trembling hoarse voice, amidst the groans and the stinking bodies and the pitiable squeals of the babies.

" Hunger ! Hunger ! "

And afterwards, every day, one saw these famished peasants, whole families or individuals, with sheep-like faces, coarse clothes and bast shoes, leading or carrying children, and groaning in their weak stammering voices through the streets :

" Help the starving. . . . Brothers ! Help us ! Hunger ! "

At night Polia was tormented by nightmare and could not sleep for hours. And at these times she heard that which she also heard during the day, distinctly, irritatingly, tormentingly : the string orchestra playing, distant and appealing ; the dice rattling ; and under the window in the street, dull voices complaining, crying :

" Help. . . . Brothers. . . . Starving. . . ."

She would spring from her bed and rush barefooted and with beating heart to the window and look out into the night. Silence, darkness, solitude. She listened and then again returned to the warm closeness of her bed. She would fall asleep. Then wake again from some strange disquieting shock. Again the distant violins, the rattling of the dice, laughter—and the heart-breaking entreaty and the crying of babies.

On one of those sultry sleepless nights there happened that which she had long been expecting as inevitable.

Somewhere in the corridor a door opened, releasing a din of voices and laughter. The voices resounded down the corridor, mingling with indistinct shouts.

Again the door opened suddenly and the uproar arose ; then the voices and steps passed out into the quietness of the night. Far away there was a melodious tinkling and phantom violins played softly in the night. She understood : it was only the sad vibration of the telephone wires outside her window.

" Brothers. . . . Have pity. . . . Help. . . . Hunger ! "

She could not sleep.

The songs of the working masses. Masses passing in whirlpool and torrent, red faces, red flags, the Red Guard in a glittering rain of bayonets. . . . Comrade Lenin on the Red Square in Moscow. . . . From far one could see his teeth glisten, his chin protruded, and he flung out his arms—calling on the people—with the fingers apart ; how under his cap his face was set. It seemed he was laughing. Nothing remained in the memory except these beckoning hands, the white glimmer of his teeth and his lined cheeks. How long ago ! Like a dream, like vague images of early childhood. The northeast wind was sweeping the dust along the streets. . . . Dust and ashes. . . . Why was there no dust before, why are the burning days and nights now choked with ashes ?

In Serge's room there was also silence, hardly stirred by the rustling of paper. From time to time there were steps as of one who paced his room in thought. Good Serge ; he too was not sleeping. He measured his sleeplessness by the number of pages read.

Someone knocked at the door gently—she did not know who.

" Who is there ? "

Badin's voice ; and by its sound it seemed that he was smiling.

" Polia, little Polia, are you asleep ? Dress and come out for a moment—we have some work to do."

" I can't, Badin. Wait till to-morrow."

" Impossible, Polia. Get up and come out."

His voice became obstinately insistent. The latch clicked and the door opened. A dim light shone in from the empty corridor. What was this ? How did it happen that she had forgotten to lock the door that night ? Then she saw Badin. He looked unusual : half of him was white, half black.

" Well, it's better like this. You are a little bit difficult."

He shut the door and turned the key. Again the walls disappeared in the darkness which had become limitless. And in this dense unbearable shadow, he moved towards her— inescapable, inevitable.

She held out her hands in terror, breathless, and whispered uncomprehendingly.

" What do you want, Badin ? What do you want ? "

She had not time even to lower her hands. With his frightful weight he fell on to the bed, pressing her to the pillows.

" Be quiet, little Polia. . . . Be quiet, quiet. . . . "

She was suffocated beneath the intolerable weight of this perspiring flesh and the dizzy odour of alcohol. She did not resist, crushed in the shadows ; she could not resist : how could she when this was inevitable and unalterable ?

She did not notice when Badin went away. The dark gulf seemed to be revolving, groaning, and filled with sparks. Somewhere far away, a great crowd howled and roared like thunder. Yes, this was the north-east wind. This was neither rain nor thunder ; it was the north-east wind. Now the sky was dry and transparent, decked with stars in dazzling coloured clusters.

Had Badin been there or not ? Perhaps this was the usual nightmare. Everyone knows that nightmares seem as real as life. Isn't that why they are so dreadful and disturb the soul ? Had Badin been there—or not ?

She lay motionless on the couch, all naked and crushed. Her chemise was pressed like a damp bundle above her breasts and smelt of sweat and of another nauseating odour which she had never known before. For a long time she could not sense her own body, as though she were only a head with no body. Everywhere was void and infinity : the black gulf. Only her head lived, swimming in the unendurable darkness. And out in the darkness was this crashing thunder and the howling of the storm. It was so nice and peaceful : and nothing existed any longer, and time had ceased.

She heard Serge's step approach her door and then stop. Why did Serge approach her door ? Polia heard the steps and her heart beat quickly ; suddenly her blood began to rush through the veins and she was convulsed with wild cramps. Her body hurt dully. Badin ! Yes, his door was in her wall, by her head. He had come and gone. Now there was no terror—there was nothing. And deep down in her heart there was a trembling and a shuddering, and her throat was clutched by hot pain.

Her teeth would not stop chattering. And her heart and her throat burned and hurt. . . .

" Oh. . . ! Oh . . . ! "

She writhed on the bed ; then crawled on to the floor and suddenly lay dumb and still with deadly fright. Again the dense blackness enveloped her. The darkness crawled upon her, pressing upon her like a rock, driving its claws into her.

Almost losing her senses, barefooted, in chemise, she ran out into the corridor. She clutched the handle of Serge's door and pressed against this door, blinded with terror, without being able to take her eyes away from the open door of her own room.

" Serge ! Serge ! Quick ! Please ! Serge ! "

She scratched on the door, pressing close to it ; and, as though in a dream, she felt that the door breathed under her body, but could not open.

And when the door did open, Polia flung herself on Serge's

breast, breathless with sobbing, a little helpless creature with the shape of a child.

Serge's hands trembled and his heart beat fast. He led her to the bed and covered her with a blanket. He poured out a glass of water for her; her teeth chattered against the glass, and little rills of water ran out along her chin.

" Oh, it was horrible, Serge—. It was disgusting ! I don't know what happened, but it was something that can never be remedied, Serge ! "

He drew a chair near to her and sat down. With soft shy movements, he arranged her pillows and stroked her hand, hair and cheeks.

" Now, don't—. Be calm, Polia. I know. . . . If you had called out, I should have forced open the door and strangled him."

" You don't know, Serge. . . . You don't know ! It's impossible to struggle against him. It's impossible to save oneself from him."

" Don't let's talk, Polia. Drink a drop more water and go to sleep. I shall sit by you here and you will sleep. You absolutely must try and sleep. It's the north-east wind. For a long time we have had no north-east wind. To-morrow it will be cool and fresh."

" Serge, dear little Serge, you're so good to me, so near to me. I knew that this would happen, Serge. . . . And I couldn't. . . . I don't know what will happen now, Serge."

He sat near her, trembling with uncontrollable emotion. He had been like this ever since he heard Badin's voice in her room. Then he had felt the floor shake under him ; and with the first roar of the north-east wind everything seemed to turn and whirl about him.

" I knew, Serge dear, that something would happen. Haven't you seen those faces, heard those voices ? ' Have pity, Brothers. . . . Help. . . . Famine. . . . Hunger ! ' And the dice rattling and the violins, in the cafés . . . and the shop windows. . . . The revolution has turned to greed. . . . And this—. It all belongs together, Serge."

" Yes, it all belongs together, Polia. We must pass through this dreadful stage. We must go through it, must go on. . . . Must go through with it, at whatever cost."

She fell asleep with her hand in his ; and, till the dawn, he sat by her without moving, looking at her attentively with mournful affection.

4

SABOTAGE

After Gleb's departure, the work of renovating the factory became feverish. The broken panes in the windows and sky-lights had not yet been replaced ; there were still gaping holes in the concrete walls, fringed with the torn ends of broken cables. In the dim interior, under the light of the electric lamps, echoes resounded from hammers and drills and the clanging of metal.

Two hundred men were working there—the full force now obtainable. The rotatory furnaces needed special attention. The steel shells had to be re-riveted and the fireclay linings re-laid. They had to make new small castings for the crushing machines, the hoist and for the complicated shafting. The mixers were badly damaged and new mechanical stirrers had to be made. They had to replace the whole pipe system. Enormous cylindrical sieves had to be replaced as well as a quantity of auxiliary plant. The least need for repair was in the generators and the Diesel engines which Brynza tended. Brynza lived there and the engines also lived.

Men, blue with dust, were bustling about, climbing on the furnaces, running on the stairways, the scaffolding, the gang-ways, like spiders. Like rats they were gnawing away at the solidified mud in ditches and holes. They were riveting, cutting, sawing iron and copper, entangled in a network of cables, shouting, swearing, spitting mud and choking with dust, a prey to this sudden storm of work.

On the second truck-way the work was going on more peacefully. The rails had been re-laid in various places ; the viaducts were repaired and stones and rubbish were being cleared away.

As before, the factory still stood in dust and desolation. But everywhere one could feel its breathing and the early vibration of its machinery. In the engine-room, the Diesels were already panting day and night.

Every day, Engineer Kleist, grave and severe, made a tour of the whole works. He was dressed all in white and for the first time a repressed smile glimmered in his face. The old technicians and foremen accompanied him attentively as before, and in the same way he gave them low orders, nodding to stress his words. With the workmen, he was dry and taciturn as of old, passing them by without seeing them, indifferent and strange.

Gleb had gone away for a week, but did not return for the space of a whole month. Already in the second week of his absence the work was frequently interrupted, and in the end it stopped altogether. The factory management ceased carrying out the plans which had been approved and stopped the supply of materials. In the Economic Council it was impossible to get anything done. Always the same old answer—Bureau of Industry, Cement Trust, State Planning Commission. . . .

In the offices, the spruce specialists would speak frankly to Engineer Kleist.

" Why don't you drop this fantastic idea, Herman Hermanovitch ? You know that the factory cannot be started again. In fact, what need is there of it ? It's absurd, Herman Hermanovitch. Let us suppose that the factory is going and that the store-sheds are filled with cement. Well, what then ? Where is our market ? There is no market ! Formerly our cement was destined principally for foreign markets. But now ? Construction ? But nothing is being built, and nothing can be built, since there is no capital nor productive capacity. They've stirred things up a great deal here, trying to start it—you must give them credit for that. But they have no strength, no experience, no means for creating new enterprises. And they cannot, when private capital and initiative are absent. They won't go very far with their nationalisation. Willingly or unwillingly, we shall have to apply to the foreigners."

Coldly and gravely, Engineer Kleist listened to the specialists while smoking a cigarette. He did not argue with them, but answered briefly.

" I did not come here to discuss questions of political economy and the general economic system of Russia. I have merely a modest aim : to exact from the management the fulfilment in the near future of our plan of production. Our repairing work has stopped at present owing to the fault of the management."

The specialists were looking at their fingers and hiding their smiles, listening with polite attention.

" The management has nothing to do with it, Herman Hermanovitch. It receives all its instructions from the Economic Council. Will you not apply direct to that institution ? "

These were newcomers, sent by the People's Council of

Economy, but, under cover of apparent loyalty, they were cherishing the past. Kleist too carried the past in his mind, but it had become remote and dead, cremated by the present, and only ashes remained. Between him and these other men no understanding seemed possible. He saw their faces fall at his unexpected reply. In their smiles, there was a hidden sneer, and cowardice and distrust. They thought : " This funny old chap is either too cunning or he has gone off his head in terror of the Bolsheviks."

Engineer Kleist went to the Economic Council. He was received there respectfully, as one of their own people ; and they smiled there in the same significant, enigmatic way, with their gold-stopped teeth. And there was a fixed suggestion in their eyes, just as it was with the factory management.

In his usual cold and grave manner, he explained the reason for his visit ; concisely and clearly as he had done with the factory management. He received the same polite official answers, delivered with a hidden sneer.

" Yes, the carrying out of deliveries according to your schedule has been stopped ; most likely your estimates will have to be revised. You see we cannot go against the instructions of the Bureau of Industry and the Cement Trust. Up till now the necessary conditions do not exist. The Chairman of the Economic Council is a competent and careful man."— They watched him with a little laugh playing in their eyes.— " And has agreed with our report. Everything has been too hurried. What will the Cement Trust say ? There is reason for believing that all this somewhat wild enterprise will not meet with approval in the Bureau of Industry and especially in the Headquarters of the Cement Trust. We are awaiting authoritative instructions."

And now Engineer Kleist walked alone—without specialists and foremen—in the courtyards of the factory, along the truck-way, examining the buildings, the dismantled machinery, the debris of interrupted labour. He was thoughtful, and mournfully struck at the stones and scattered refuse with his stick. In his lonely walks he used to meet only one man, the watchman, Klepka, with his eyebrows and beard flecked with cement.

Gleb returned, his helmet on the back of his head, all dirty and rumpled from the journey, but with clear and wide-open eyes. He did not call home but walked straight to the factory.

He spent a short time there and then, pale with emotion, blind and cursing with wrath, he hurried to the ropeway; everywhere emptiness, rubbish and decay, just as during the days after his return from the front.

Breathless with rage, he rushed to the management offices.

The sleek specialists, in their elegant clothes, rose in astonishment, deafened by the unexpected noise and loud oaths; those who were walking stood still; those who were sitting down jumped up. And those who were writing did not raise their heads, keeping their noses down close to their frozen pens.

From the very threshold, Gleb began to shout, deafening everybody, hurling the words from his very bowels.

"Tell me what bastards have done this bloody thing! I'll smash their damned faces for this treachery! Where's the director? I'll send all these dogs to the Cheka for sabotage and counter-revolution! You thought because I wasn't here you could carry out your old tactics—that without me your dirty tricks would succeed. You sons of bitches, I'm going to hang you all at the end of a rope!"

From room to room he ran, his face congested; he was looking for someone, but saw nobody; knocked the chairs about, swept papers from off the tables and hurtled against people who stood in his way. The girl typists, like pretty dolls, cowered terrified in their chairs, bending their coiffures down to the keyboards of their machines.

And the people stood or sat stupefied and amazed, dumb with shock. When he left them, they looked at each other in panic and raised their hands or their papers to their mouths.

When his mad fit had partly abated, Gleb threw his military coat and knapsack down in one of the rooms and stormed into the director's private office. With the same alarmed amazement—nevertheless, assuming a calm severity—the the assistant director, Muller, received him. His skull was covered with silvery bristles; he had a silver, close-cut moustache and gold pince-nez.

He rose, his gold-stopped teeth glittering, and stretched out a hand to Gleb over the table.

"Why so much noise, Comrade Chumalov? You're swearing so loudly that you'll break the window panes."

Gleb neither sat down nor noticed the outstretched hand. Standing sideways to Muller, he turned on him his face grown thin and burnt with the sun.

" Who gave the order to stop work at the factory ? "

Muller's teeth again glittered. He raised his hands in a gesture of helpless submission.

" Don't play the fool ; speak out straight ! What swine has interrupted all the work here, that was in full swing ? "

Muller, his face suddenly worn and grey, raised his head, the lens of his pince-nez shimmering.

" Firstly, Comrade Chumalov, I must beg of you, be more careful in your expressions. The factory management has nothing to do with it. We stopped the work because the Economic Council has discovered that it is impossible to continue the repairs for lack of the necessary resources and without the sanction of higher economic organs."

" Show me the order of the Economic Council. You bastards have come to an agreement with those wasters in the Economic Council. You thought you'd be able to shuffle the cards behind my back. You thought the Bureau of Industry was going to give me a dressing down and that then you would cut in and win. Go on with your little game, I shall be able to get you all in the net ! "

" What grounds have you, Comrade Chumalov, for making such serious charges against us ? I protest categorically. Without reflecting, you say most offensive things. We're not little children : we can't go beyond the instructions and orders which come from above. We have even been removed from all participation in these affairs. All the stores have been put under seal by the Economic Council and all documents have been taken from the files here by their representative. If you're going to make a row, will you kindly do it, not here, but at the Economic Council."

Gleb bent close over Muller and struck the table with his fist.

" Please don't talk this rot to me. I know all your intrigues perfectly well. I'm not going to leave it at this, for the sake of your beautiful face. My friends, you seem to have forgotten that affair with the Forestry Department ! You're going to learn to your cost at what price this sort of thing can be done—you're going to learn how people are stood up against the wall ! You took me for a fool, and tried to humbug me with the Bureau of Industry. Now I'm going to break your head and your ribs ! Bear this in mind : to-morrow morning the work is going to start again. The renovation must be finished within two months. From autumn on, the factory will be working to full capacity. Have you understood ? "

Muller shrugged his shoulders, smiled confusedly, tried to say something, but his parched tongue choked him.

On the square in front of the Factory Committee offices, the workmen were clustering in small groups, in idle tedium. Some were sitting in the shade against the wall ; others were going in and out ; they were smoking, chattering, and laughing. Gromada was standing on the top step of the portico, in the open doorway of the office, brandishing his bony fists, wearing himself out with the hectic excitement of a consumptive.

" Just so, it's like that, Comrades, only temporary. . . . But we are obliged, as the working-class, to show our consciousness . . . and so on . . . and so on. . . . We in the ranks of the group and of the meeting, and as the Trade Union Council and the Building Workers' Union are our own organisations, we shall know how to defend our own interests and shall hand the matter over to the Revolutionary Tribunal—— And all these swine and sons of bitches will be smashed."

The crowd broke into an uproar of hand-clapping, laughter and shouting.

And now, Savchuk, in a tattered shirt, pushed his way through the crowd like a bull, waving his arms and yelling like a madman.

" They must be crushed—the bastards ! Into the sea with them, the dogs ! Why are you delaying, you fools ? I can't stand it ! "

Gleb ran down the wide steps and was at once drawn in to the mass of dusty, sweaty faces, amid the yells and moist raised hands.

" Here he is, the bastard ! Ah, this is the fellow ! You old scoundrel, you ! Here's the soldier who'll fix up everything. He'll get things into order again ! Ho, the devil took you away in an evil hour ! "

And among these jubilant cries were other voices, morose and stern.

" What's happened, Comrade Chumalov ? What does it mean ? Might as well go to the devil as work in this fashion ! Is it a joke ? We know whose tricks they are ! It's the old gang who dream of the Tsar's rule. They're waiting for their old masters, the dirty swine ! They must all be shot ! No good can be expected from them."

Sweat and tobacco smoke arose in clouds. These crushed bodies and breath were sultry and intoxicating. With his shoulders Gleb pushed them away to the right and the left.

" Comrades, work will start again at full speed. To-morrow morning, when the hooter blows, each will take up his own work. I'll unravel all the plots of these specialists and shall know how to stand them against the wall. I'm going to the Economic Council. Comrades, we shall demand the ruthless punishment of these counter-revolutionaries. At the Bureau of Industry I have obtained approval of all my orders for materials ; fuel has been sent down here with me. We're going to send some men for rivets. One of the first things we're going to do is to start the crusher and the press."

Gleb made a dash to get out of the crowd, but could not succeed. The people were shouting and moving with him across the square, waving their arms, stamping on the concrete.

" Hurrah, for Chumalov ! Toss him in the air ! Hurrah ! "

Savchuk, striking out with his fists, was making his way through the crowd to Gleb and bellowing.

" Gleb, you old heathen ! Gleb ! Let the coopers' shop start too ! I'll smash them——! We'll get the bastards ! "

Gleb waved his helmet over his head.

" Gromada ! Where is Gromada ? Send him over here, Brothers ! Good ! Come on, Gromada ! "

But Gleb did not go straight to the Economic Council, but got out of the droshky at the door of the Soviet Executive.

He dragged Gromada by the arm up the stairs to the second floor. Gromada, exhausted, was snorting, breathless.

" Ah, what a worn-out old shoe you are ! A fine fellow for a campaign ! Come on now, get your breath—get ready for a fight ! "

" You know, Comrade Chumalov, I'm always having these choking fits, but I'll give any specialist forty points and beat him."

" Ha, we're going to turn things over now, damn it all ! Right you are, lad ! You're half dead, but you can shoot like a machine-gun."

As soon as the bewhiskered guard at the door saw Gleb he moved his chair to one side and opened the door for him.

Badin was not alone. Shramm, Shibis and Dasha were in his office.

Dasha glanced at him and her eyes lit up with astonishment and then anxiety and pleasure. But it wasn't pleasure that Gleb saw in her eyes, but something else, something unknown, deep as a sigh ; and it passed through his heart, searing it.

Badin glanced at him absent-mindedly, from under his knotted eyebrows, and then dropped his gaze to the papers which he was turning over with his hairy fingers. He was listening to Shramm.

Shibis was sitting there the same as ever ; one could not tell whether he was bored, was resting or was thinking of some affair of his own of which he could not speak aloud.

Why was Dasha here ? Dasha—with Badin ? Was there anything true in that jest and her enigmatic riddle about the one bed with Badin in the Cossack town ? Had it happened or not ? Why these shadows in her eyes, and this new expression ? Her eyes were dry, round, burning with a feverish heat. . . . Again her soul was like a deep well,—distant and unapproachable. Motia's forgotten words arose in Gleb's memory : " They will not have a common life and a common mind ; they will not share one home and one warm bed."

He did not go up to her ; she remained sitting on one side, looking at him no longer. She was like a stranger.

Shramm sat opposite Badin, unnaturally calm, and spoke in his dull gramophone voice.

" But it was not my fault if there were abuses in the Forestry Department. I fulfilled exactly the instructions of the leading organs. Why didn't the Workers' and Peasants' Inspection notice anything amiss and why have they now come forward with a mass of accusations ? The apparatus of our Economic Council is exemplary and works splendidly they say. And then suddenly it seems that this was no work at all ! It seems now that what went on was practically wholesale robbery. I do not understand this at all and request the most detailed investigation."

Badin looked at him coldly, with the full weight of his heavy eyes, from under his dark frown.

" You don't understand. It's quite clear why you don't understand. The apparatus of the Economic Council is a masterpiece ; its schemes are carried out perfectly. It is just because this machine is such a model that it proves to be the best screen for every kind of crime. You have laid all the work in the hands of elements which are hostile to us. From behind your perfect apparatus you couldn't see the increasing robbery that was going on in the Forestry Department, that the workers were left without bread and clothes and tools and that some of the agents were openly speculating at the expense of the State. You don't understand why every possible kind of swindling conspiracy to seize the people's property is carried out under your own nose ; as, for instance, a short time ago, the leasing of a tannery to its former owner. You can't see or understand that in one of your departments a scheme was worked out for the concession of the cement works, so that they should be taken from the State and handed over to their former share-holders. You don't understand it, but I see in these things the worst form of economic counter-revolution."

Shramm remained in the same state of unnatural tension. His eyes became moist and his voice was hoarse and cracking with exhaustion.

" In the last case you have mentioned, I could only accept the point of view of experts, who proved by actual figures that it would be impossible to exploit the factory during the next ten years. All the documents in this question have been sent to the Centre. I had no right to leave it to the decision of the Economic Conference. Regarding the question of the tannery, the Soviet Executive Committee approved the concession."

Badin showed his teeth and exchanged a glance with Shibis.

" I know that it was authorised by the Soviet Executive. But it was unknown to us that your report was based upon false figures as well as upon men of straw. This matter will be discussed to-day at the sitting of the Presidium."

He took a paper from the table and ran through it quickly.

" Take this, Comrade Chumalova, and go at once to the Communal Administration. They must order that all three houses be evacuated in order to convert them into crêches and maternity homes."

Dasha came up to the table without looking at Badin or Gleb, but Gleb saw an intoxication illumine Badin's eyes for a moment. Gleb clenched his jaws until they hurt, and his ears tingled.

" Comrade Badin ! "

" Ah, there you are at last ! Where have you been wandering all this time, damn it ? Well, let's have your report, please ! Your face looks absolutely baked—I supposed they roasted you well up there ! "

And he smiled amicably at Gleb.

Gleb stood next to Gromada opposite Badin. And he began to speak, sternly, distantly, hard and brief. It came so rapidly and steadily, that it seemed he was not improvising his phrases, but reading them from a paper.

" Comrade Badin, I and Gromada, a member of the Factory

Committee, have hastened here in order to learn by whose order and on what grounds work at the factory has been stopped. There is complete disorganisation there and decay. Such criminal action cannot be overlooked. I would like to know what scoundrel has been breeding sabotage and counter-revolution here! The workers are restless. Such wicked waste is worse than an attack by the bandits. Here's Comrade Shramm; let him tell us how the Economic Council could permit such a crime."

Badin's white teeth shone again in a strangely gay smile.

" I know about that. The Economic Council received a wire from the Centre of the Cement Trust, ordering them to cease work until it should be made quite clear that it would be necessary and practicable to set the factory working again."

" I know whose work that was, Comrade Badin! But now the Economic Council has received a wire from the Bureau of Industry, addressed to the Chairman of the Economic Council, instructing them to take all measures to organise the work of renovation. This question has been discussed back there and I have the documents in my hand."

Shramm said in a strange hoarse voice :

" That is the Bureau of Industry, but there is also the Cement Trust."

Gleb, beside himself with rage, flung up to the table. A nervous tremor beat in his cheeks.

" Comrade Chairman of the Executive : I am putting this question plainly. It is impossible to work in this way. Let us agree if you like that Comrade Shramm is a good Communist— the devil's own best Communist in the world !—nevertheless he must be hauled over the coals for this. This is no joke, Comrades ! We shall speak about this robbery in another place ! But Comrade Shramm never comes near to the workers —there's no doubt about that ! That matter will be laid before the Party Committee. Comrades, there is a plain threat here to our whole economic policy ! Comrade Badin spoke correctly when he said : ' Economic counter-revolution.' An end must be put to this ! The case of the Forestry Department was a comparatively small matter. This one is much more vital. We shall have to come to our senses, Comrades, roll up our sleeves and start a merciless clean-up ! We'll have to have a sweeping-out in all the Institutions. We've had enough messing about with all this White Guard crowd ; it's time to make them feel our fist. I have to inform you, Comrade Badin, that the resolu-

tions which we adopted at our Economic Conference have
been approved; and that our requests for supplies and assistance will be carried out in full. I have obtained these measures
during my absence. To-morrow work will start again and
the Factory Committee will knock the seals off the stores and
will take them under its care. And I'll tell you one other thing,
Comrade Badin: we absolutely demand a new management
staff for the factory. If necessary, we'll carry this question all
the way to Moscow! "

He unbuttoned his tunic and produced a bundle of papers,
which he threw upon the table.

" There are the documents for you. We've had the Bureau
of Industry thrown in our faces all the time, now we're going
to give you Bureau of Industry! "

Shramm's face was deathly pale and his eyes dirty and
glazed like those of a corpse.

Shibis suddenly rose and rushed from the room without any
of his former languor.

Badin again looked from under his deep brows at Shramm;
again he smiled with that strange gaiety.

" Well, and now, Shramm? The Economic Council will
have to sit on the same bench with the Forestry Service, eh?
It makes an interesting picture, now that things have taken this
turn."

In the corridor Gleb ran into Dasha. Most likely she was
waiting for him. Again she looked at him with bright, profound eyes, in which he saw fever and a tortured cry. She
stood before him, calm as usual, tranquil and pre-occupied.

" Gleb, little Nurka is dead. She's already buried; you
didn't come in time. Little Nurka has gone, Gleb. She
flickered away and you weren't there. . . ."

Gleb felt at first as though he had received a terrible blow in
the chest. When this passed, his heart felt swollen to bursting
and he had a sickly feeling in the entrails, as one feels when
falling from a height. He looked fixedly at Dasha and for some
time could not control his breathing.

" How so? But—it's not possible! How? Little Nurka.
. . . But it can't be——! "

Dasha stood leaning with her back to the wall, and Gleb
saw her eyes, suffering, quivering and full of tears.

Close by them, Gromada writhed convulsively in the grip
of a paroxysm of hoarse barking coughing.

Chapter XVI

TARES

I

" OUR HEARTS MUST BE OF STONE ! "

THE purging of the Factory Group was fixed for October 16th
—that is, in a week's time from now. Serge was awaiting this
day with his usual pensive smile, without any emotion or
alarm, or the customary self-questioning which had so tortured him of nights. His only wonder was why he could not
for a moment forget this date : October 16th. He even thought
about it in his sleep.

He knew that this would be a terrible turning point in his
life, and yet his feelings somehow were numb. The great
question was : would he be excluded from the Party or per-
mitted to remain in it ? This question flowed through his
consciousness like a wave of light, irradiating all the cells of
his brain so that they went quietly and undisturbed about their
work. Only at night did there flash up within him strange
images and recollections. There were some curious light
effects : sunlit foliage, sun-bathed children, the sea and the
mountains in the sun ; and then the cries of playing children
or the chirping of crickets.

The bald spot on his head, with its curly border, shone as
usual when he went to the Party Committee or to a meeting.
As always he walked in deep thought, and carried his tightly
packed, shabby portfolio. He was always busy and strictly
performed his daily task. But not for a moment did he forget
October 16th.

During the report of the Presidium of the Party Committee,
regarding the work of the Provincial Centre for Political
Education, Shidky gazed at him with affectionate derision
and laid his hand on Serge's.

" Are you afraid, Serge ? Look out, they'll give you a good
work-out ! "

" Why then ? What for ? I don't feel anything like fear.

It's as though it were something outside of me, which does not concern me. . . ."

" All right, don't worry. We'll defend you. . . . The devil is not as black as he is painted."

As usual, Lukhava was sunk in his chair, his chin on his knees, his eyes and hair glistening.

" You lie, Shidky. You're afraid of this combing-out yourself. And I'm afraid too. I fear nothing and yet I am afraid of this. Serge will be excluded. How have you the power to prevent it ? A former Menshevik—. Hasn't Lenin said that we must turn out the Mensheviks ? "

Shidky banged his fist on the table.

" He won't be turned out. Why should he be, if neither you nor I are ? For what reason would they exclude him ? Menshevik ? An intellectual ? That's nonsense. Those are not motives. We could all protest if this happened. The Commission is working very badly : they're excluding people for doubtful reasons or imaginary ones. During this week already about 40 per cent. of the responsible workers and about the same number of rank and file members have been excluded. Shuk, for instance—a worker, too. The reason : disrupting and fractional work."

" Shuk ! Is he turned out ? "

Serge stretched his head out towards Shidky in astonishment. Yet it was an involuntary action and Shidky's words did not really move him ; just as if the affair was in reality far away from him and of little significance.

Lukhava broke in, unusually calm and firm, and with a certain official quality in his voice.

" The Commission is not obliged to bring all the facts to your knowledge and you have no right to interfere with its work and to criticise its methods. For the excluded, there is only one thing to do : to lodge an appeal."

" All right, but I'm going to act, and I shan't stop short of anything. I shall make a row right up to the Central Committee of the Party. Those who are doing the purging don't know anything about their work. It only leads to the destruction of our organisation. We have ample grounds for protest. I'm not going to drop the matter."

And Shidky slammed his fist upon the table with an oath.

Lukhava laughed and buried his nose between his raised knees.

" You ass ! You too will be excluded for this, or transferred to lower grade work."

" Don't worry : I'm not afraid of anything ! "

Serge noted that Shidky and Lukhava were gazing at him and then at each other with feverish eyes, burning with terrified foreboding.

In the Women's Section, Polia, grown thinner, with tormented eyes, was unable to control the convulsive twitching of her hands and face.

Dasha, big and strong, was seated at the table, writing with difficulty some kind of report. She did not see Serge or Mekhova. What mattered to her their troubles and their conversations ?

With her hand Polia beckoned to Serge, indicating a chair near hers. She looked at him, and then at Dasha, threw a glance at the window, and could not master the nervous trembling of her hands and face.

" Serge, won't you help me to understand all that's going on now ? I've gone completely crazy. Dasha doesn't understand me any more ; she's become very rude and won't speak to me as she used to. Serge, I feel that I am going to be turned out of the Party."

Dasha was silent. She could not hear what Polia was saying.

Serge also was silent. He did not know what to answer. He wanted to be tender with her but could not find the right words. He wanted to say something about himself that was simple but earnest ; however, he was at a loss for a suitable phrase.

" I shall tell them what I see and what I feel. Do you understand ? I'm going to be excluded. . . . That which is going on. . . . Happening. . . . What crucifies me and the revolution. . . . I can't lie to them."

Dasha ploughed the paper with her pen ; then she rested her right hand on the table and raised her head. Under the obstinate brow with its red headscarf, her eyebrows were raised in interrogation.

" But what has happened, Comrade Mekhova. Perhaps I'm too stupid to understand. The work in the Women's Section is going on much better ; we women have learned to speak for ourselves and to act together, no worse than the men. What is wrong then, Comrade Mekhova ? "

Polia shuddered at Dasha's voice and jumped up.

" How dare you say this? Don't you know what's happened? Don't you know that the blood of workmen and soldiers, a regular sea of blood—do you hear, Dasha?—a sea of blood was shed staining the ground; and before that blood is dry we're giving them the ground for markets and cafés chantants? So that everyone can roll together in one filthy heap? You don't know that, eh?"

Serge had never seen Polia in such a violent state before. Her face was like that of a person in a fit: it was congested with blood and her brow and upper lip were covered with a sticky sweat; her eyes were dry and murky.

Dasha again bent over her writing with a smile of indulgent comprehension.

" I thought it was something else. . . . Is it possible, Comrade Mekhova, that you think that everyone except yourself are such fools and idiots?"

" Yes, yes! Fools! Traitors! Cowards!"

Then suddenly Polia became calm, gave Serge a smile which was just a pitiful grimace, clapped her palms to her eyes and began to cry.

" Why didn't I die then, in those days? Dead in the streets of Moscow? Or in the Army? Why did I have to live to know these torturing, shameful days, dear Comrades?"

An irresistible smile began to twist the corners of Serge's lips. He felt unable to breathe. His lips danced. Polia, the window, the walls, swam in a heavy mist. Possibly he was tired. Without doubt he could never support the tears of another. Probably Polia had robbed him of his last strength, that night when she had burst into his room, terrified and broken by the bestial power of the Executive Chairman.

Dasha, standing near Mekhova, her eyes misty, pressed the girl's shoulder.

" Comrade Mekhova, you should be ashamed! Do these tears and nervous attacks prove your strength? You're not a young lady, but a Communist. Our hearts must be of stone, Comrade Mekhova. Let our heart burst, if it must, but we don't want a heart of tears—not a heart of cotton-wool! One's heart must be like flint. . . . Go home, Comrade Mekhova, and calm yourself. You may rely upon me; I have strength for a long time to come yet."

She returned to her place; determinedly she grasped the pen and resumed the dogged scratching of the semi-literate.

Polia, perplexed, looked for a long time at Dasha and then

at Serge ; then silently she sat down. With a harsh frown, she said in an unusually hard and cold tone : " I shall not go any-where. I came here to work ; and I shall work right through to the end."

" Yes, good ! I know you, Comrade Mekhova ; you know this isn't the first time that we've worked together."

Dasha wrote on without lifting her head, smiling.

2

THE PARTY CLEANSING

Mekhova and Serge attended the Party-cleansing at the Factory Group. Serge because he had been specially attached to it and Polia because she had been unable to attend the cleansing in her own group because of illness.

The Group meeting opened in the large hall of the club. A large number of people were present. Non-members of the Communist Party had been invited, and they filled rows and rows of seats. The Communists were in the two front rows and the non-Party workers filled the rest of the hall. The mirrors around the room reflected the crowd in an infinite series, so that it appeared that there were thousands of people present. Actually there were one hundred and thirty. Gleb made the third member of the Cleansing Commission, which sat at the table in front of the stage. A chandelier of fifty electric lights flashed and sparkled with its crystal pendants and chains.

The two members of the Special Commission were strangers. Both wore military coats and caps. One had prominent cheek-bones and was so dark he was almost black ; his brow, nose and chin were dotted with grey warts. It was impossible to know whether he was smiling or in a rage. The other one was gaunt, with a pale face and a beard like a besom. He was con-stantly taking it between three fingers and pulling it. When he sat down he shrivelled up into the smallest possible compass. When he raised his eyes they disappeared under the half-closed lids. When he interrogated a Communist, summoned before him, he did not look at him, but spoke as though he were addressing someone else. He did not seem to look at the Party card belonging to the questioned person, which he would be pressing between his thin stiff fingers.

Serge heard a murmur behind him.

"He's a hard one, he is. He'll grind us to hell. He's going to take our pants down all right! And the other—did you see him? He purrs like a tiger!"

And when the gaunt man called Gromada, Serge could not catch whether it was he who spoke or the man beside him. Again he heard a whisper behind.

"Did you hear that, like a bloody ventriloquist! He'll skin us like an expert."

The whisperer choked with laughter.

Gromada came out of the crowd and leaped up to the table like a hare, stretching out his nose towards the bony man.

Again behind Serge came that sobbing laugh, and the voice could not resist shouting:

"Blow your nose, Comrade Gromada; relieve yourself while you can!"

Whether Gromada's nose was running, or whether he was just scared, no one knew; but he put his finger to his nostril and gave a whistling sniff.

The hall rocked with laughter, and behind Serge a screeching laugh split the air.

Gleb was convulsed with laughter, his cheeks blown out like bellows. The pimples of the first member of the Commission were jumping up and down with merriment. Gleb struck the bell and raised his hand.

"Order, Comrades! Be serious! This is a serious business, Comrades!"

The gaunt member of the Commission was still deaf and immovable. He just pulled his beard with three fingers with a kind of milking motion.

"Comrade Gromada—your autobiography?"

"This is my autobiography, Comrade: a working proletarian, a poor working dog, ever since I was a little child. I need not discuss now how wonderfully we were exploited by the Capitalists. You yourself can see how consumption has got me by the chest, and so on, and so forth. . . ."

And from behind a whisper:

"Ah, he's going it! He's showing his teeth, the son of a bitch!"

"When did you enter the Party?"

"Under the new Soviet regime—making a year."

"And why didn't you enter it before?"

"What apprentice becomes a master before his time? Haven't you ever been an apprentice, Comrade? An apprentice has to go through the mill, and so on, and so forth. . . ."

" I've asked you why you entered the Party so late ? "

" I'm trying to tell you—. I was being danced around in the civil war. Everybody went off their heads in that time."

" Right you are, Gromada ! Go on ! They were all crazy then ! "

" Were you with the Red-Greens ? "

" I wasn't, Comrade, actually with them over the mountains, what you might call . . . but I went up to the mountains, daily, and so forth. . . . I wasn't beyond the mountains. . . . But I didn't make life any sweeter for the White soldiers and the bandits. There was a gang of us with Dasha, putting the screws on them."

" So you were not with the Red-Greens. You preferred to stay at home and wait for good weather, eh ? "

Gromada sensed peril in the questions of this bony man. The questions bristled with spite and facts. This gaunt man was getting all round him with his obstinate questions, and in every word there lay hidden a serpent which was stinging him painfully but invisibly. When Gromada felt this, he suddenly became still and hatred flashed in his eyes. Perhaps the thin man noticed it or he was tired of Gromada. He scribbled something with a pencil and waved him away.

" You may go. Does anyone want to say anything regarding Comrade Gromada ? "

" Gromada ? Oh, Gromada's a trump. He'll give anyone forty points and win ! "

" Next—Comrade Savchuk ! "

The crowd stirred, whispered and began to laugh.

Savchuk, in a long coarse linen blouse without a belt, hairy, in torn trousers and barefooted, walked up, jostling and elbowing the people as they looked wonderingly at him and grasped him by the shirt.

" Heh, you damned cooper ! Be careful there ! "

Savchuk stood morose before the table and, holding his fists apart, began to nod his woolly head.

" Eh, you, Comrade Cleanser, don't trouble me about my life biography ! "

" Why ? It is necessary ; all our examinations are based on it."

" Don't poke into my rotten life. You've got no interest in it. Phew, enough ! I'm a cooper—make barrels. Just now I'm not working at that, because the coopers' workshop at the factory is a muck-heap. But if Gleb—this bastard here—will only shift himself for all he's worth, the saws will begin to hum, and then we'll get some new barrels."

" You have written here that you've beaten someone on the head lately and that you'll land someone else. Whose head have you beaten and about whom are you speaking ? "

Savchuk's face was swollen and the veins on his brow and neck were thick like twisted cords. He stuck his fists further out and his eyes were filled with laughter and anger. Everyone opened their ears. They were hoping that Savhcuk would explode with all his force and that there would be an uproar and some fun. Everyone knew how Savchuk burst out with words like dynamite—straight out, without thinking of consequences. A hoarse laugh rolled in his throat, but did not rise to his hairy face. The rush of blood to his head made it jerk rhythmically.

" I have smashed these dirty bastards and will go on trying to smash them—the villains ! Just new masters and bourgeoisie —gapers and wasters. . . . Over on those seats there are sitting mechanics with whom I've had to fight too. . . . They were driving me crazy with their pipe-lighters, which was all that interested them. There's more than one devil, we must fight him everywhere ! Under the old regime, they used to sit in automobiles, showing off ! And now they're showing off in the same way, hitting our brothers. . . ."

" Who is hitting our Comrades of the Party and the Soviets ? Speak more concretely."

Someone in the back rows was gabbling and hiccupping, then shouted in uncontrollable joy :

" Eh, Savchuk ! Let them know about it ! To hell with all that snuffling crowd ! Show them up."

Again the hall broke out into laughter, which gradually died down into the stillness which awaits something sensational.

Just one last voice, from the back rows again, a voice broken with a cough, bellowing loud :

" Give him one on the jaw, the damn fool ! What's he trying to stuff our heads with anyway ? "

A shuddering sigh passed through the hall ; there was a low murmur.

" You must speak more precisely, Comrade Savchuk. There are many different kinds of heads ; certainly there are some which ought to be broken, but some should be better guarded even than your own. For instance, what about our heads—are they among those which ought to be smashed ? "

" How the devil do I know what's inside them ? You've got the people together here, and you've got them all worried. . . . We've got enough masters and commanders already, enough to pave the streets with ! "

The thin man was blind and deaf. He did not look once at Savchuk.

Gleb rose behind the table, his teeth clenched.

" Comrade Savchuk, stop this bullying and swearing ! Don't you know how to behave ? "

Savchuk pressed his stomach up against the table, his shoulder muscles crawled under his blouse ; the veins in his neck were ready to burst.

" Shut your jaw, you swine ! I'm no loafer, you bastard ! What are you all worked up about ? "

He drowned all voices in the hall with his roaring.

" Don't stop his mouth, Comrade Chumalov. He's doing the job all right ! "

A woman was shouting loudly and walking quickly down the aisle between the seats.

" Savchuk doesn't tell how he's been lapping up home-made vodka and how he's been breaking the bones of his wife Motia. He's such a swine to his wife ; I could strangle him with my own hands ! "

" Yes, all the men are like that—a dirty lot ! The women have to be here and there, with a pot and a bag, ready for a blow, or ready for bed, or ready to feed him ; they must be quiet and bear children every year. The men want to be bosses and play the grand ! They're all the same—the wretches ! "

The women began to scream and riot and wave their hands.

The baited Savchuk turned to the crowd ; under his matted hair his eyes glistened like those of a wolf.

" Fools, you stink, you rotten swine ! "

Laughter. The walls trembled and the chandelier seemed to wink and resound.

Motia ran down the gangway to the thick of the crowd. She was shouting and snarling.

" It's not true ! Not true ! It's a lie ! If Savchuk has beaten me, I've beaten him too." (Laughter.) " The whole lot of you are not worth the sole of Savchuk's shoe. We all have to be beaten, chattering hens that we are—all, without exception ! We have lost our kids, ruined our homes—fools that we are !

We've become a lot of female loafers ! None of us are worth
the sole of Savchuk's shoe ! "

The people had suddenly become quiet, shocked and bewildered. They were deafened by Motia's shrieks ; and the
women and men stared at her with eyes getting larger and
larger.

" And where is Savchuk's sole ; he's barefooted ! "

Motia shrieked angrily, standing and stamping her foot.

" Don't you dare to touch Savchuk ! Yes, Savchuk's the
best of you all ! Don't let them get you, Savchuk ! Savchuk's
afraid of nobody ! He's the best and strongest is Savchuk ! "

Polia shivered and shrank together as though with the
ague. She sat close to Serge and never took her eyes from the
table. Fascinated, she was looking at the gaunt member of the
Commission, and her lips were parted in a smile. But only
her lips : her face was marbled with dark shadows, like that
of a sick person.

Serge was in a confused state of joy and excitement. Wasn't
it all the same whether this joy came to him from within
himself or whether it came from the crowd which sat there
bathed in light ? Joy sang and laughed with a child's laughter
in every cell of his being, and everything—this sweating crowd,
the laughing whispers behind him, the chandeliers with their
clusters of fiery grapes—seemed unusually new, filled with a
deep significance and importance. Everything was reduced
to the primitive, the simple and naked. And the laughing and
whispering, the curiosity of the crowd, and this curious sort
of trial at the table where traps seemed to be set in play—it was
all human and simple, arising from a series of uncomplicated
movements. He need only seize isolated sounds and gestures,
or sometimes the long wave of sighing—and everything became
so clear and diverting ! Isolated instants—torn from life—so
full of lively animal play ! But why did this game, through the
relating together of these isolated instants, become such a great
and complicated process ? This complex process was the great
destiny of mankind ; and is not the destiny of mankind
tragedy ? Father says differently. Perhaps there are single
moments which contain within themselves a whole historical
cycle ? Perhaps the most important is not time—but the moment ; not humanity, but man ?

Why did Polia's ears seem superfluous ? They bloomed like
open petals. When she breathed, her nostrils distended and

became pale at the edges. Her blood pulsated in red drops, pouring through the veins ; and in that blood was pain and anguish. And in that blood is the whole sense and solution of human life, all its joy and all its simplicity.

" Comrade Serge Ivagin ? "

He got up. Took one step, two, three. . . . He stood still. This was all so simple and meaningless almost to absurdity.

He spoke without the least effort. He heard his own voice and saw the crooked nose, hard as a beak, before him. It did not look like skin, but clay mixed with water.

" Was it your brother, the Colonel, who was shot a short while ago ? Did you see him often before he was shot ? "

" I met him twice before ; once at the bedside of my dying mother, and the other time when, with Comrade Chumalov, we caught him while he was signalling."

" Why did you not try to have him arrested after the first meeting ? "

" Obviously there was no reason for it."

" Why didn't you leave the town with the Red Army in 1918 ? Why did you prefer to stay here with the Whites ? Were you so certain you would not be shot ? "

" No, how could I be certain ? I saw no reason to run away ; it was possible to work here ! "

" Ah, you were not a Communist then at that time ? Well, then it's quite understandable."

" What's understandable ? What do you mean by your ' understandable ' ? "

" Comrade, I am not obliged to answer questions. This is not a debate. You are free."

Serge did not go back to his place, but walked between the rows of workmen down the middle of the hall, and it seemed that, side by side, with him and walking towards him, were several other Serges, all with bald patches and misty eyes, looking attentively at him. It seemed he was walking along a moving narrow plank, always down, down. And he could not control his steps, as if it were not he who was walking, but the narrow plank sliding under his feet, giving him scarcely time to keep stepping. Countless faces, rough hands, swimming in smoke and fiery mist, piling up on all sides in a suffocating stuffy heap. . . .

Then suddenly it all disappeared like a vision. He ran out through the open door. There was the marble staircase, with its massive carved balustrade, and the two oak columns on top of which burned the mother-of-pearl lamps. The corridor was empty, full of a singing silence. From somewhere, behind shut doors, came fresh young voices—the Young Communist League.

The Party Cleansing Commission. The gaunt man blind in face and blind in movement, inaccessible in thought, neither smiling nor feeling pain—he seemed to have no lines on his face. Gromada and Savchuk were in his power and Polia, Gleb and Dasha will be the same. They all looked at him anxiously. They all have this terror in their hearts, and he also ; it was twisting in his heart like a worm.

Do questions ever reveal the soul of man ? Are answers to them ever convincing or true ? There are no right questions and no true answers. Truth is that which questions do not invoke, and it cuts right across all answers, having its own direction.

Voices sounded behind the door like rattles ; the cells of his brain were singing like rattles.

As soon as he opened the door he was blinded by red flags and banners ; the walls were blazing with them and white inscriptions flew across their red surfaces like white birds. Everywhere in the windows and the corners, like clots of fire, were mountain flowers.

And the lads and girls were as numerous as the flowers. They were all in shorts, and their arms and legs were bare. You could only distinguish the girls from the boys by their red head-bands and full breasts.

They were in rows, rhythmic movement. . . .

" One—two—three—four ! "

The lines twined and looped, knotting and linking. . . .

" One—two—three—four ! "

Serge watched this music of movement from the door ; he felt the blood welling up into his heart.

" One—two—three—four ! "

Then the moving figures clashed and intermingled, jostling each other and bursting out into laughter and happy cries.

Serge stopped by the door, leaning against the post. He could go no further. The little table beyond the mass of heads and shoulders, with the three heads above it, seemed inaccessibly distant ; and the reflections of the crowd in the mirrors and the lustres was unbearably bright.

Polia stood before the table, looking very small, like a young girl. She did not wear the accustomed headscarf round her yellow curls, and she was breathlessly and painfully crying :

" I can't endure it, because I can neither understand nor justify. . . . We have destroyed and we have suffered—. A sea of blood—famine. And suddenly—the past arises again with joyful sound. . . . And I don't know where the nightmare is : in those years of blood, misery, sacrifice, or in this bacchanalia of rich shop windows and drunken cafés ! What was the good of mountains of corpses ? Were they to make the workers' dens, their poverty and their death, more dreadful ? Was it that blackguards and vampires should again enjoy all the good things of life, and get fat by robbery ? I cannot recognise this, and I cannot live with it ! We have fought, suffered and died—was it in order that we should be so shamefully crucified ? What for ? "

" Don't you think, Comrade, that this lyricism of yours is like that infantile sickness of the left-wing, about which Comrade Lenin spoke recently ? "

The even voice of the tall man was calm and severe, and in comparison the cries of Mekhova sounded like sobs. The dusty, forward-leaning crowd stirred, and leant still further forward, troubled.

" You are a leader of the Women's Section and women's organisations, and yet you speak so thoughtlessly in front of working men and women. That won't do, Comrade."

Polia's lips were trembling and her eyes sank under a flood of tears.

And as she passed down along the aisle, with drunken aimless steps, rows of people stared at her sadly. Some leaned towards her, whispering wheezily.

" Just so, Comrade. . . . The essential. . . . Without rhyme or reason. . . . Yes, for the working man. . . . We always get the same, nothing. . . . The bastards must be smashed . . . smashed. . . ."

" Who has anything to say regarding Comrade Mekhova ? "

A unanimous sigh arose from the crowd ; they shouted discordantly, waving their arms.

" What the devil—! What's the reason—? She's right ! "

" Comrades of the Commission, Comrades of that sort must be thrown out ! If it must be, it must be. That is the New Economic Policy. Only the workers must be treated equally. . . . That should be obligatory, it should be written down."

" Silence ! Is this a barnyard, Comrades ? "

" Comrades ! It's right—. The little woman spoke well about all this inequality."

" I should like to emphasise, Comrades of the Commission, that this little golden-haired Comrade was born too early. As we are not yet at the stage of full communism—. Such little women should be shown the door. . . . Young ladies. . . ."

When the flood of yelling had ceased, and the heads and backs were still, Serge saw Gleb standing up at the table look-ing at the lanky man with the dull gaze of a stunned beast. He was bending over him, trying to say something—you could see his lips and jaws moving—but the member of the Commission did not raise his head, was motionless as a corpse.

Dasha stood in front of the table, her gaze following Mekhova, full of sorrow and fear.

Serge followed Polia into the corridor. Quickly and un-steadily she walked to the exit. Her head was thrown back and lolling from side to side. He called to her shyly and his voice echoed in the empty corridor. But she did not turn round and ran with all her force out of the door.

He returned to the door of the hall, and then he heard for the first time the loud youthful tones of the lanky man's voice :

" Yes, I understand ! Here is a real member of the Party ! This is a real worker and militant for our Party ! Our Party can only be proud of such Comrades. Go, Comrade Chumalova. I wish you every success ! "

And Serge saw the bony man get up from his chair and shake Dasha's hand.

3

AN INSIGNIFICANT ATOM

In his little room in the House of the Soviets, Serge sat till dawn by his little lamp, reading Lenin's *Materialism and Empirio-Criticism*.

Carefully he underlined certain paragraphs in pencil and made illegible notes on the margin. He would get up once in a while to pace diagonally across his room, from the table to the wash-stand, over a dusty, threadbare carpet. Thoughtfully he would smooth his bald patch with the palm of his hand. He was thinking without being able to formulate his thought. In his heart was a confused colour. And loudly and distinctly he kept on repeating in the silence :

"The principle of energy in no way contradicts dialectical materialism, because matter and energy are only two different forms of one and the same cosmic process. Everything lies in methods and not in words. Dialectics are energy. The relations of the elements of universal matter are infinite in form and are subject to laws. In the formula, 'matter and energy,' the word 'and' is the only one about which one can argue. It is static and demands dialectical interpretation. One must think. . . . One must analyse. . . ."

He re-seated himself and took up his book ; again he began to underline sentences and scribble annotations on the margin.

Next door, in Polia's room, was quiet. She was at home. As he came down the corridor he had noticed the electric light inside in her room through the ground glass panel. For a moment he noted an indistinct shadow of a curly head upon the glass. Inclined to enter he had placed his hand upon the door-knob. Then the shadow disappeared. He decided then that he had better not go in to her. If she wanted him, she would knock at the communicating door between their rooms, or would come in as she usually did.

With his book in his hand he went on tiptoe to the door and listened. Polia's room was quite quiet. Not a step nor a living sound. Without doubt she was lying on her bed—lying there with the same look in her eyes as she had had when she walked from the meeting. Perhaps she was asleep, worn out with the excitement of the past few days. It was a good thing if she was sleeping ; she would be stronger in the morning. She was only a little bit tired. So many people are tired nowadays. She only needs rest. She had been happy during the wars ; she had learned to laugh heartily there. She worked strenuously at the Women's Section, and she laughed quite a bit there too. But now came a new stage, and she had sunk under the blow. All she needed was to have rest and to realise things a little. He himself must not sleep ; perhaps she would call him if she needed him, or come to him as she usually did.

The Party Cleansing. The bony face and gramophone voice of the member of the Commission. All this happened a long, long time ago. It was all so insignificant. Could such a tiny fact have any importance in the general process of events ? Not he, but everything mattered ; and he was only a grain of dust in the whole.

Golden and silver moths in fluffy coats flew in through the open window. They circled and beat against the little lamp. Flying out into the middle of the room and humming like a slack violin string, they made the room seem enormous ; and he felt that he was alone and that many unknown changes were ahead of him. He approached the window and looked out into the darkness. It was October, but still warm ; and in the warmth and the dark there were already the odours of autumn decay, of fermenting mould and fallen leaves. Among the shadowed stones of the town (the street lamps were not yet in use), was a deep tranquillity. Only in the distance, at the station, one could hear screaming whistles and trucks rattling like broken glass. And there, beneath the mountains, beyond the bay, shone a garland of electric stars. That was the factory arising to life. One saw scattered points of light on the docks and on the steamers, and heaving flares showed in the water, reflecting these glimmering lights.

There was a moment when Serge fell into a half-slumber, and he saw his father jogging along, barefooted, in torn breeches, laughing merrily.

His father stood before him, his hand on a chair, muttering indistinctly some horrible nonsense. And because this absurd gibbering was incomprehensible, Serge became terrified. He sat paralysed, wanting to get up and to strike his father, but could not. His father was shaking his finger at him, plucking at his beard and laughing gaily.

A dream. On waking, his heart was throbbing violently. Behind the door of Polia's room sounded the deep bass voice of Badin. The iron bed creaked. Polia's voice was torn : she was either crying or laughing. Again quietness.

His heart beat slow and deep, and his blood scared it. Stooping, the veins in his bald scalp and temples swollen, he approached the door. He listened. He stood for a minute with raised fist ready for a blow. Then a cramp seemed to seize him ; his fist dropped slowly and open. Shivering with cold, blue-faced and stunned, with exhausted, weak steps he went towards his bed. He stood a moment listening, and then lay down. Again he rose and listened for a moment. Began carefully and slowly to undress. Switched off the light, covered his head with the blankets and was still.

4

CHIPS

In the morning, at the usual hour, Serge awakened and rose at once. He washed quickly but thoroughly. Towel in hand he stood near the window, which had been open all night. It was cold in the room and a cold shiver ran down his spine, making him feel fresh and braced. The sky was deep blue as in summer and the air was transparent and golden in the distance. The houses below shone in the sun, and the roofs glistened with the morning dew, and seemed blue with the reflection of the sky. On the tops of the mountains above the factory, the snow-drifts were dazzling. Far away in the valley, winding between the quarries and the woods, a goods-train crawled like a red caterpillar. He could clearly distinguish the little square box-cars with their black doors and the gaily revolving wheels. In fiery wreaths the steam was flying from the funnel, and for a long time did not disperse, but rolled over and over in pink clouds. And the smell of the autumn was sweet ; the acrid smell of the earth poured in in invigorating and cool waves. It was healthy, fresh, bright and sunny.

The Party Cleansing. . . . The mirrors with the repeated reflections of the crowd and the chandeliers. His confused and naïve answers. It all seemed so far away and so unimportant ! The blood coursed fresh through his healthy body and he longed for heavy manual work to develop his muscles. Standing at the window he was waving his arms which needed movement : one—two—three—four !

Polia. . . . Like a shadow a dull pain fell upon his heart.

She had not come to him ; she did not need his friendship. This time she wanted to keep to herself what had happened in the night. That was his pain, and his pain only. His pain made her seem nearer and dearer. He would never tell her about his pain, and so she would never know of it. She was strong, knew how to laugh, and would meet him one day with a smile, greeting him like a friend. Dear, dear Polia. . . .

He took his portfolio and went out into the corridor. Polia's door was shut and it was quiet in her room. She slept. Let her sleep. She must rest and calm herself so that she might smile joyously later on.

Arrived at the Party Committee Headquarters, he went into the office of the Party Cleansing Commission.

Although it was early in the morning, the dimly-lit room, with its iron barred window, smelt of cheap tobacco and damp. Several men were standing near the table and their faces were like those of men just convalescent from a severe illness. Two stoop-shouldered men blindly collided with Serge ; they had worked with him in the People's Commissariat of Education ; silently, blindly, like beaten creatures they stumbled through the doorway. Then Serge heard Shuk's shout.

" What we need is some shooting, dear Comrades. Those are the ones who should be chucked out of the C.P.R. What do they know about the working man ? All you do is to look after your own bellies, and to hell with the workers ! How could you clean me out, you swine, when you don't even know my mug ? Have you ever eaten porridge with me ? What are you trying to put across—when you're not worth a damn yourself ! "

The lanky man sat at the table, cold and deaf, wrapped in himself, he was looking at some papers in a voluminous dossier. As Shuk shouted his last words, he raised his eyes and looked intently at Shuk.

" Comrade, if you consider yourself a Communist why don't you show more self-control. I have already told you that——"

Shuk rushed towards him with distorted face and banged his fist on the table.

" Do you want me to say thank-you, you bloody swine, for all the dirt you have done me ? Is that what you want ? I've been watching you long enough, you careerists and profiteers ! I'll unmask you all. You'll get yours in the end ! "

The tall gaunt man remained completely apathetic, as though the words which Shuk was shouting did not concern him at all. He only said indifferently to another comrade who stood near the wall :

" Comrade Nachkassov, look up the papers about Shuk and put them aside for re-examination at to-day's sitting of the Commission."

Again he looked at Shuk with his cold gaze.

" Comrade Shuk, you have now destroyed for good all chances of re-entering the Party. You have amply shown your-self to be a harmful disruptive type. I shall bring up the question to-day of your final and definite exclusion. And if you continue to shout in this way, I shall ask the Comrade on guard to remove you by force. Please leave the room."

And again he began to glance through his papers.

Blinded, his face purple, Shuk ground his jaws. Then he noticed Serge and went up to him as though he sought protection.

" You see what is happening, my dear Serge. Let us watch, observe and learn. . . ."

With a discouraged gesture he left the room.

Tskheladze was standing opposite the table. He rolled his big, bloodshot eyes and gazed fixedly at the papers on the table. His jaws moved continually like a mill, and a thick milky foam was in the corners of his tightly closed lips. Serge had always seen him silent ; one never saw him at work, and a couple of years ago he had been with the Greens, of whom he had commanded a section ; he had been the first to enter the town during the fighting.

He seemed to have brought his eyes up against something pointed ; he shuddered and stepped up to the lanky man. He spread his fingers wide apart and gesticulated.

" Comrade, why are you joking ? Let me see with my own eyes—. What's the use of words ? Let me see the document."

Surprise flashed in the eyes of the gaunt man.

" I have already told you, Comrade : you've been turned out of the Party for intrigue and plotting. I have no time to joke with you. You can lodge an appeal."

Tskheladze froze into his former pose, again his jaws worked.

" Ho, so this is how things are done, Serge, dear Comrade. Look, take it all in ! "

Serge went up to the table and inquired regarding the decision of the Commission. Inwardly, he had known since yesterday that he would be excluded. He did not know why, and if he had put the question to himself he would not have been able to answer. But he was completely convinced.

" Yes, you have been excluded."

" On what grounds ? "

" I cannot read you the report just now. In due time you will receive a copy and you will know the grounds. If you are not satisfied you may appeal."

He did not look once at Serge.

As soon as Serge heard his words, his heart jumped and he felt a swooning nausea invade him. It was not he, but another, saying in a hoarse whisper to the gaunt man :

" You know, this means political death to me. Do you understand that, Comrade ? "

" Yes, I understand. It is political death."

" But what for then ? "

" There were serious reasons."

Serge wanted to go away but could not move his feet from
the spot. They seemed heavier than himself. Outside the
window there was no sun, just a red reflection in the sky. And
he thought, how seldom the sun shines in this damp mist ;
and he saw the blue sky and the blue mass of the station warehouse nearby. He did not know how he walked away from
that table, and did not remember where he had been standing.

Shuk was clenching his fists and laughing bitterly.

" Well, here you are, Serge ; what fine work, eh ? But
Badin remains in the Party ; Shramm remains, Khapko and all
that drunken crowd. Ha, the bureaucrats can sing in glee !
But Savchuk has been turned out of our Group, and Mekhova
and you have been excluded—now it's easier for them ; everything will go well for them now. But I'm going to show them
how the fishermen catch fish ! I shall know how to shake them
up."

Tskheladze shuddered convulsively and again stretched his
fingers out like a fan.

" Comrade, why are you joking ? Why are you speaking
empty words ? Let me look with my own eyes at what you
have written about me ? "

Again there was astonishment in the eyes of the quiet man.
He leaned short-sightedly over the papers and said in a tired
voice :

" Comrade Nachkassov, show Tskheladze the decision in
his case."

Tskheladze with his heavy boots clattered over to the other
table, and the stout member of the Commission showed him a
sheet of a paper covered with writing.

" Here. Read. Can you read Russian ! "

And he pointed with his finger to the middle of the sheet.

" Go to hell, you son of a bitch ! "

Crazily, with mad, burning eyes, Tskheladze stared at the
grey warts of Comrade Nachkassov ; his teeth were chattering
like small shot.

He did not glance at the paper. He struck himself a terrible
blow with his fist behind the ear, and cried in a strident voice
of pain and terror :

" You've cleaned me out   . You've cleaned me out ! I'll
clean you out—! Oh ! "

A shot echoed in the room and it filled with smoke.

Tskheladze lay on the floor. Blood trickled from his pierced skull.

The gaunt member of the Commission sat at the table. His face was grey. His wide-open eyes were like those of a blind man, expressionless.

Serge never knew how he had left that room. When he came to himself he saw Shidky beside him. He was pushing a glass of water between his teeth, shouting and breathing heavily.

" Drink, damn you ! Don't cry like a woman. Understand, everything is not decided here. There are higher organs. The Party Committee will not let the matter go by. They can clean me out of the Party too if they like, but I won't forgive this disgrace."

Serge lay on the sofa, his whole body shaken with sobs.

Chapter XVII

A THRUST INTO THE FUTURE

I

" WE SHALL GO ON ! "

THE re-starting of the factory was fixed for the anniversary of the Bolshevik revolution in the coming November. It was decided to have a solemn sitting of the Town Soviet in the "Comintern" Club in order to combine the historic triumphal anniversary with the first great victory locally on the economic front.

The Party Cleansing was at an end, but the corridors of the Palace of Labour were crowded with sweaty battered people, full of blue smoke, suffocating confusion and patient expectation. The people were collecting together in groups; their sweat-damped hair clung to their foreheads. They spoke in low tones, and looked like sick people.

The Workers' and Peasants' Inspection had been for several days, quietly and unostentatiously, carrying on a strict revision.

As usual, Gleb sat in his private office, with doors close shut, and received visitors from eleven till two. Calm and severity reigned behind his doors.

The apparatus was working, despite its complexity, calmly and powerfully, with a staff just as large as before. Only the elegant technologists were rather paler than before; dazed and with anxious eyes. Among the crowd of employees, bending over books and papers, one could mark no excitement or fear, just as though there were no Workers' and Peasants' Inspection here at all; as though no one knew what it meant, or that an inspection was taking place.

Gleb divided his time between the factory and the management offices. He ran from building to building, workshop to workshop, amidst the dust, piles of materials, the clamour of toil, restraining himself with difficulty from grasping a tool, and himself joining in the work. In the repair-shop he got into a row with Saveliev. He was one of the old workmen, morose, unsociable and silent. He often stopped work for a moment, coughed noisily and spat black thick phlegm. On one of these occasions, Gleb snatched the tool from his hand and pushed him away from the bench with his shoulder.

" What are you messing about here for, damn it! Do you think you're working for strangers ? "

Saveliev, stupefied, stared at him with bloodshot eyes, deprived of breath from his coughing.

" You mustn't waste time to spit here, wink or blow your nose, but only to work. Every second is more precious to us than a whole life ! "

He was shouting and swearing, brandishing the wrench, all feverish. Savaliev pushed him away with his shoulder, shook his beard and spat on his fist.

" And what do you know yourself, you shaven fool ? I've been working at the bench for years. I'm a turner and a fitter and I know my job, God damn it ! And you, why— you're still wet behind the ears ! You're still a weakling kid ! You were still at your mother's breast while I was carrying loads on my back. And here you are swanking like a commander."

" And I—I spit in your old beard ! There's a lot like you, always ready to loaf around and talk about what wonderful workmen they are. All you're concerned about is your own belly ! You don't know anything about the general labour question and production—all that means nothing to you ! "

Saveliev, his fist on high, was bellowing ; he looked like a hairy shaggy old watch-dog.

" Wordy bastard ! Go to hell with you, damned animal ! "

Without stopping their work, the workmen were laughing and yelling with delight.

" Give Chumalov one in the jaw, old whiskers ! Go on ! "

" Hit him in the mug, Chumalov ! Bring the old fellow to his senses ! "

Gleb pulled himself together, threw the tool on to the bench and laughed so loud that it filled the whole workshop.

" Well, what an idiot and an ass I am ! Don't get angry, old pal ! My hands are itching, and I'm mad as a hatter ! "

And off he ran to another department.

The repairing of the furnace and the crusher was almost finished. The ropeway was already working. Wheels were spinning and pulleys shrieked into the mountains. The overhead cable to the wharves, however, was still silent, with its trucks, as it were, frozen in their flight; and the safety-net beneath it red with rust. The white seven-foot clock, in the factory tower, which for three years had been still, again moved its hands; and, at night, lit up by an arc lamp, showed the hour so clearly one could read it a mile away.

In the coopers' shop preparations for work were being made. The work benches were repaired and the rubbish and dirt cleared away. Rivets had been brought from the stores in trucks. Savchuk, perspiring freely, covered with dust, was shouting and swearing—coopers are the best at swearing. He and his mates were hurrying from place to place in the shop, getting everything ready.

Every day Gleb visited the engine-room, and here the influence of the place transformed him. The light was deep blue and still. The window panes, the tiles, shone with cleanliness; the Diesel motors shimmered in black and brass. In the air was a tender singing hum from the pistons and wheels. . . . This severe and youthful music of metal, amid the warm smell of oil and petrol, strengthened and soothed Gleb's being. These gentle songs seemed to re-echo within his heart. Everything beyond those walls seemed insignificant, petty, rubbish which should be thrown away. Only here could one find that which was essential, vital, significant—amid the gentle ringing, and the sighing of these black altars standing so firmly in compact squares. From behind the safety-barrier, he would gaze long at the gigantic fly-wheels, at the broad red belts, running as on wings, and palpitating as if alive. Near the fly-wheels, so illusive and almost alarming in their silence, hot moist air-waves flooded over Gleb's hands and chest. Fascinated, he would lose all consciousness of time, his mind absorbed in this iron flight; and he would stand there, regardless of the outer life, without thought.

Brynza always awakened him from these ecstasies. He would take him by the arm and lead him silently to the immense window, through which he could see the sea glistening infinite, and the aerial spaces between the mountain crests.

Brynza was a different man from the one he had met last spring. True, he wore the same greasy cap like a pancake over his nose; true, there was the same nose sticking out like the peak of his cap; the same grimy sharp cheek-bones and chin, and the brown whiskers like wet rags. But the eyes were now cold and concentrated, shimmering like the nickel and brass of the Diesels. No longer did he shout, but listened attentively to the ringing and whirring of the engines.

Their conversation always started the same way :

" Well, Commander ? "

" Well, dear friend ? "

" Well, and what further ? "

" We shall go on, Brynza ! "

" And we won't break our necks ? "

" What's the matter with you ? Are you off your head ? We'll have to get you into the Party, you old bastard ; that'll put the lid on your piffle."

" Ha, Commander, be off with you and your Party too ! What can I do with a Party when I've got my hands full with the engines ? There's the Party—and here are the engines. I don't understand the Party, but I understand engines. They must work without fail. I've got no time for jabberers—on your way with you, Commander ! "

He stopped abruptly and, with supple, firm steps, slightly round-shouldered, without looking round, he plunged into the dark gangway between the Diesels.

One day, while inspecting the repairs going on in the various dust-covered buildings, amidst the trampling and shouts of the workmen, Gleb encountered Engineer Kleist. The extraordinarily fixed look in the technologist's eyes had already more than once surprised Gleb. They burned with emotion and anxious questioning. Kleist took him gently by the arm and they walked out on to the viaduct. Shoulder to shoulder they walked on to the terrace of the tower where they had met each other on that memorable evening. On their right, down below, the Diesels were murmuring and the dynamos hidden in their depths sang softly. On the roofs of the buildings were crawling the figures of the workmen, small as dolls. Sheet-iron rang out reverberantly ; hammers beat like musketry and drums. The windows of the buildings were no longer black and gaping, but were flashing and coloured—reflecting the blue sky and fiery sun.

The autumn air was clear and singing, saturated with a sun which belonged rather to summer. Seagulls described dazzling white curves and whorls above the bay. Everywhere, in the air and underfoot, and in the actual stones, one could hear an inarticulate subterranean murmur. And somewhere else, nearby, was the shriek of a drill as it bored through rusty iron.

Gigantic light-blue cylinders, the smoke-stacks flying upwards, eighty metres high. Did not their cold throats announce infernal fires that smouldered below ?

Gleb patted Kleist on the shoulder and laughed.

" Well, Comrade Technologist ! Everything's coming all right. When a fool says : ' I have strength ' he is already no longer a fool, but only partly one. Then, if he goes right on, without hesitating, he's an intelligent fool ! We Communists dream like fools, but not so badly after all, Comrade Technologist. On the anniversary of the Revolution, we shall start this huge thing shaking with fire and smoke."

Engineer Kleist smiled strainedly ; he preserved his usual air of dignity and importance. Suddenly he pressed Gleb's hand.

" Chumalov, I beg you to forget the great crime I committed towards you and the other workmen. The remembrance that I once gave up people to death and to torture gives me no peace."

And Kleist looked into Gleb's face with fear and hope ; he could not repress the trembling of his hands, nor could he hold his head straight and still.

Gleb looked him full in the face, his eyes flashing with sharp points. His face suddenly became motionless, obstinate and terrible, like the face of a corpse. But this was for a second only, and then his teeth showed in a smile.

" Comrade Technologist, that was long ago—it's past. In those days we were at each other's throats. But just remember this : if you had not saved my wife at that time not even her bones would be left now. Now you are one of our best workers—a fine intelligence and hands of gold. Without you we couldn't have got anything done. Just see what a wonderful job we have done under your guidance."

" My dear Chumalov, I intend to devote all my knowledge and experience—all my life—to our country. I have no other life except that life with all of you ; and I have no other task except our struggle to build up a new culture."

And for the first time Gleb saw Kleist's eyes fill with tears, through which hitherto unseen depths became visible. And those things that were within his eyes were greater than his eyes, greater than himself.

Gleb pressed his hand and laughed.

" Well then, Herman Hermanovitch, let's be friends ! "

" Right, Chumalov, we shall be friends."

And the Engineer walked away with steady step, leaning on his stick.

2

ASHES

After the Party Cleansing, Dasha no longer slept at home. She had moved to Mekhova's room. She went to live with her after she had received the following note :

"I feel that I am very ill, Dasha, although I walk about, eat and talk, and apparently nothing is wrong with me. But I can neither see nor feel anything. During the daytime I feel like a hunted animal and my nights are one long nightmare. Another day of this, and I feel that I can no longer endure it. No doubt I am really ill. You alone can help me and put me right. As a friend, I beg you to come and live with me, help me to pull myself together and get on my feet. It's midnight now and I'm sitting in Serge's room. I sit in here every night. He's very tired, but brave as ever, and gentle and kind. He looks after me as he would a child. He's prepared to keep awake all night for my sake. When I leave him he doesn't let me go through the corridor, but through the door leading into my own room. I'm afraid Serge will overstrain himself and collapse. A change is taking place in my soul. What kind of change I don't know ; but I do know that if you would only pass a few days with me, everything would be all right again."

And that evening, Dasha, with a bundle under her arm, went away to the town, with the same quick step as when she went about the business of the Women's Section. She returned later to get some bedding, and would not take her evening tea with Gleb.

"Well, Gleb, you can keep house and make yourself comfortable. I'm taking my things now and I'm off."

Gleb stared at her in astonishment, and rose from his chair.

"Another surprise ! But wait, you haven't told me anything about it ? Where are you taking your things ? Where are you going to ? "

"When you have a minute to spare, call in at Comrade Mekhova's. We're going to live together. Comrade Mekhova has got a screw loose—she's got to be repaired and put into working order again."

"And how many days will you be repairing Comrade Mekhova ? "

" I don't know. When the mare is running again then we'll get back into double harness. We must do everything possible to see that Comrade Mekhova does not leave the ranks of the Party."

" Yes, that's true ! They played the fool enough with this Party Cleansing ! "

" Well, I'm off ! But don't expect me back too soon, Gleb. I don't know how it's going to turn out."

They shook hands silently, confused. In their smiles trembled unspoken words ; and eye avoided eye, dimmed by unanswered questions.

They stood silently, smiling, hand in hand, wanting to speak the words that stayed in their throats, but could not.

" Well, I'm going ! "

" Yes, go if necessary."

He saw her off to the gate, and just beyond the gate he took her hand again. All the time they were smiling and silent. And Gleb felt that Dasha was not leaving the house simply, as though she were just going to work or leaving on some mission. This time Dasha was carrying away with her for ever all the past years. Perhaps she would not come back at all ; perhaps, here at the gate, in this last glance of hers, was a regret for the past and pleasure at the thought of a new road. He could not speak to her any more like a master. He could not say : " Dasha, I won't allow you to go. I need you more than Comrade Mekhova does. Without you there is no warm comfortable home, and my bed will be cold and grow soiled."

He had no power to utter such words because Dasha had taken this power from him. This was no ordinary woman standing before him now, but a human being, equal to him in strength—one who had taken upon her shoulders all the burden of the past years. Dasha was not just a wife ; she was a woman with vigorous hands, without her former attachment for home and husband. Now she will go away and perhaps won't come back. She will stay in far-off places and be strange to him like other women. Well, what of it ? Up till the present they had lived in one room ; slept, separately at first, and then together. But not for a moment could Gleb forget the essential thing : the old Dasha was no longer there ; there was another one, a new Dasha, who might go away and never return.

The last thread of their conjugal life was broken. Nurka, their little Nurka had died ; and there had been days when their common sorrow brought them close together, through tears and pain. But these days were like the past days of their love now. The Party Cleansing had come, a period of heavy responsibilities : for him, the factory ; for her, the Women's Section. When they met at tea-time, they felt that Nurka's death broke the last tendril of their life in common. They must shape their destiny differently : there was not time for dreams of personal happiness. This dream had been insignificant, harmful to themselves and to the cause. Then, after the Party Cleansing, Mekhova fell ill ; and the entire leadership of the Women's Section was thrown on to Dasha. And in the Party Committee, when they met her, everyone said :

" Now Dasha's in her place ! It's just as though she had always been at the head of the Women's Section."

And she knew, as did everyone else, that her position as leader of the Women's Section would soon be transmuted from " temporary " to " permanent."

And now, at this last parting with her, Gleb had wanted to say a grave and significant word to her, from his soul. But he could not; he did not know what to say. Yet, if ever, it had to be said now. If not now—never ! And he was afraid to say it : Dasha knew how to listen to him intuitively and wisely, but she always answered him in her own words. And her own words were not those which he wanted ; they brought him too much pain.

" Well, go on, little Dasha. I really don't understand our life together. . . . The devil only know's what's in it. . . . We should have to begin all over again. . . ."

Dasha took her hand from his ; she looked at him appraisingly, frowning.

" What is there to understand, Gleb ? I shall never become what I used to be ; I am no longer the woman for your bed. If you wish you can make some arrangement which will please you. You can get yourself a woman according to your taste and strength. There are plenty of fools in the world ! "

" What the hell—! Why don't you just tell me plainly that you don't love me any more, and finish it ? "

Dasha frowned ; her eyes were dark with trouble.

" Well, and supposing I told you that it is so, Gleb ? Supposing I did tell you that I did not love you any more ? "

Gleb laughed absently and his dry tongue burned his lips.

" Well—then I should say : ' Finish ! Everything has come to an end. Nothing will help now, neither force nor tenderness.' I should suffer alone. . . . But to say that you don't love me, it's all rot——! "

" I don't know, Gleb ; perhaps I don't love any man. And perhaps I love—. I love you, Gleb ; that's true—but perhaps sometimes I love others too ? I don't know, Gleb ; everything is broken up and changed and become confused. Somehow love will have to be arranged differently. . . . Well, I'm off now, Gleb ! "

His mouth was dry and his heart was squeezed with suffering. Behind him, the house : a black empty dwelling full of cobwebs ; and in front of him, the road, along which Dasha would go.

" Go on now, Dasha, or I shall make a scene ! "

Scarcely had Dasha gone a few steps when Motia came out of her gate. She was waddling along like a fat duck, with her enormous belly and full breasts. There were red pimples on her face and blue circles round her eyes which were subdued, tired and serious. She waved her hand before she came up to them and smiled.

" Well now ! So you're starting to walk away, like a spinster now, eh ? You've got one of the best men in the world, and yet you don't want to be a real wife to him. How I'd like to give you a good slap in the face ! A woman ought to bear children, and here she is walking about, the bitch ! And look at her now, trotting along with her bundles, leaving her husband ! I'd like to tie all these good women to their husbands' beds and then give them the order : ' Make some children, you bitches ! That's enough for you ! Sleep with your husbands and have lots of children ! ' Look at my belly ! I'm going to have one every year now, if you want to know. I'm going to be a woman, while you're just a barren magpie."

Dasha went up and put her free hand round Motia's shoulders, laughing.

" And you—you're just a brood hen, Motia ! To look at you one would say : this isn't a woman, just a belly. "

And she patted her on the stomach.

" Aha ! I'll go to your damned old Women's Section. I'll stand up and take my clothes off among you all, and shout : ' Come on, women, bow down, kiss my navel ! ' "

They all laughed together.

Dasha was walking towards the gap in the wall, along the path through the long grass, with her bedding under her arm. Gleb was waiting ; here Dasha would turn and wave her hand to him. She did not turn. Her red headscarf flashed once or twice through the gap, and then disappeared behind the wall. Like this, Dasha went away every day, not returning until late in the evening. Sometimes she left to go out of town staying away days and nights at a time. The Cossack villages had not yet settled down; bandits roamed the mountains and hid in the ravines. Dasha's journeys used to cause him great anxiety.

But now everything was suddenly bare, oppressive and strange; this dwelling, the garden path, the little garden itself, and this wall that separated him from Dasha and which surrounded him like the wall of a prison. What was the good of the empty, musty room now? What was the good of the small garden and the little stone yard? Dasha had gone away with her bedding under her arm; she had gone away without turning her head. She had spoken to him in the language of a stranger. She had gone away, and perhaps would not come back. Dasha was no longer there, and he was alone. Nurka had died. No Dasha. No Nurka. He was alone. A damnable life! It was like the crusher: it broke everything, destiny, habits, love.

Motia was looking at him sideways—like a hen. In her eyes—full of maternity and inward joy—tears sparkled and quivered.

" Oh, Gleb! How sad I feel about you two dear people! What a miserable fate! Dasha is lost from her home. She exists no longer, Gleb. Your little daughter has perished. And you're alone—no family, no warm corner, like a tramp! But don't complain, Gleb. Those who play with fire, themselves get burned. And between you, little Nurka flashed out like a spark. Oh, how I pity you——! "

He turned away from Motia and began to fill his pipe.

" Never mind, Motia, fire is not such a bad thing. When you know which way you're going, when one is sure of one's feet and eyes, you need not be too scared of burns, big or small. We're fighting and building a new life. All's going well, Motia, don't cry. We're going to build up everything, God damn it! In such a way that we ourselves will be astonished at our own work. The time will come. . . ."

" Oh, Gleb, Gleb! You have destroyed your own home! "

" What then? We'll build a new one, Motia! If the old home has been destroyed, it means that the old home wasn't much good. And how are you? When is the kid going to appear? "

She laughed with her eyes only ; joy rushed into her face.
" In a month, Gleb. You know, you're going to be the
god-father—don't forget ! "

" That's fine ! That'll suit me all right, only there must be
one condition : if I see a priest in your house I'll put him into
a truck and send him down by the ropeway to the wood
stores. I'll arrange the festival for you, Motia—we'll make
the hooters howl ! And we'll make an honourable workman
out of your little son."

Motia laughed happily ; and Gleb, instead of returning to
the house, walked down the path towards the factory.

3

NORTH-EASTER

The end of October brought a number of unexpected events.

On the night of the twenty-eighth, Shramm was arrested
and sent at once to the District Centre. The same night, a
number of arrests were made among the technicians of the
Economic Council and the factory management. On the
thirtieth there was great excitement among the Party workers.
Shidky was called to the District Bureau of the Central Committee ; Badin was appointed Chairman of the District
Economic Council. Shibis, Chairman of the Cheka, was sent
to some distant part of Siberia.

These events had been expected for a long time ; one had
spoken about them in an undertone ; there had been rumours
and uneasiness. Everyone had expected these things, the days
had been full of tense expectation. Nevertheless when the
events happened they surprised by their suddenness and their
reality.

Every morning at the usual hour Serge went to the Party
Committee with his untidy portfolio, the bald patch shining
on his head. He walked softly, stooping, his eyes continually
questioning. Every day he carried out punctually and exactly
the Party tasks upon which he was working at Agitprop and
the Department of Political Education. He never missed a
single session, even if his presence was not obligatory. He
spoke to no one about the Party Cleansing and his exclusion,
nor of his efforts to re-establish himself in the Party. It seemed
that nothing was of importance to him except the work
assigned to him. After he left the Party Cleansing Commission,

the day they had communicated to him their decision on his exclusion, he had never returned there. He did not ask any of the Party functionaries to help him, he did not complain. Only his head with its red bald patch and long curls seemed larger and heavier than before ; in his eyes burned, through red moisture, a fever of suffering.

He received a laconic extract from the report of the Party Cleansing Commission which he read with the same attention as he gave to other documents.

ITEM.	DECISION.
Ivagin, Serge Ivanovitch. Member of C.P.R. (B) since 1920. Party card No.......... Former Menshevik. Intellectual.	Excluded as a typical intellectual and Menshevik, with demoralising influence on Party.

Dasha brought him the extract. He was sitting in the Agitprop, working assiduously on the revision of a thesis on the question of Workers' Co-operatives, to be transmitted to the groups. Dasha looked at him closely and searchingly, frowning. For the first time she was wondering about Serge— why was he so calm and indifferent ? Why was he silent ? Was he thinking about something else ?

" Comrade Ivagin, an appeal must be made at once. It's no good just saying ' To hell with them ! ' We must hit hard, immediately, and take the matter as high as possible."

He smiled at her with his moist eyes and took from his portfolio a sheet of paper covered with close writing.

" I have already appealed, Comrade Chumalova. Here is a copy of my appeal. I passed it on to Shidky. The Party Committee is interceding on my behalf."

" If you have any need of a testimonial, Comrade Ivagin, I will write you one in a moment. It's a scandalous abuse. You and Comrade Mekhova cannot be turned out of the Party."

" If you think a testimonial is necessary, Comrade Chumalova, will you write one and give it to Shidky ? "

He rose from his chair, smiling shyly, and held out his hand to Dasha.

" And don't forget for a moment that I'm a Communist, a member of the Party, who must go on working without interruption."

" That's so, Comrade Ivagin; but you must act, stir yourself and not just sit in a chair."

" So far it has not been called for. If it is required, I shall get up and shall go everywhere necessary."

Dasha looked at him again attentively, and again she frowned in wonderment. Then she smiled and quickly left the room.

Polia had recently been sent to a sanatorium. Since Dasha had established herself in Polia's room Serge had not called on her any more. Nor had she called on him or opened the door which communicated with his room. She had forgotten him; and his sleepless nights had vanished from the young woman's memory. He often heard her laugh and resonant voice interweaving with Dasha's. In his lonely room he shuffled up and down in his heavy boots and was sad in his heart. Nevertheless he was happy to hear laughter once more in Polia's room.

Only one thing then was necessary : the Party and Party work. No personal life. What was his love, hidden in unseen depths ? What were these problems and thoughts which tortured his mind ? All were survivals of an accursed past. All came from his father, his youth, the romanticism of intellectuals. All this must be extirpated to the very root. These sick figments of the mind must be destroyed. There was only one thing—the Party ; and everything to the last drop of his blood must be given to it. Whether he would be re-admitted or not made no difference ; he, Serge Ivagin, as a personality did not exist. There was only the Party and he was an insignificant item in this great organism. But that day he was going through his old pain once more.

It was exceptionally quiet in Shidky's room and stuffy. Badin, Gleb, Dasha, Lukhava and Shibis were all assembled there. Serge was nervous at seeing them all there together and foresaw an explosion. All were business-like, serious and cold, and questions were decided without discussion. You could only hear Shidky's rasping voice, reading.

" Are there any objections to the plan ? Then it's accepted. So the final plan for the celebration is as follows : in the morning the various contingents will assemble in their districts——"

Lukhava raised his hand and roughly interrupted Shidky.

" Stop ! We know all that by heart. Get on ! "

Gleb got up and held out his hand towards Shidky.

" Stop, Chumalov. The question has been thrashed out already. There's nothing more to speak about. Shut up ! "

" What do you mean—shut up ? I protest against the clause ' honouring of the heroes of labour.' This must be struck out. What heroes of labour ? What great deeds have they done that they should be in the ranks of the heroes of labour ? That should not be, dear Comrades ! I'm not speaking just for myself. I beg leave to give you my standpoint regarding this——"

"Chumalov, there can be no reservations on this! What nonsense are you talking ? Idiot ! "

Shibis sat as usual, either dosing, resting, dreaming, or thinking of something else about which he would never tell anyone. Badin sat with his chest against the table, silent and heavy ; push against him and he wouldn't move, strike him and he wouldn't feel. Dasha was smiling and her face was flushed. It was as though she desired to cry aloud, as though expectation made her tremble ; as though she expected just one word which would cause an outburst.

His leather clothes creaking, Badin raised his head from his hands and with black, gloomy eyes gazed at Gleb. He leaned sideways from his chair and laid his hand upon Gleb's breast.

"What have you here ? "

With his finger he tapped the Order of the Red Flag.

"Well, that's——"

"Now then, please don't play the part of the austere spartan. If for instance you were Serge Ivagin, a bashful intellectual, your modesty would be comprehensible and real. But it doesn't suit you at all."

The blood rushed to Gleb's face and his eyes moistened. He stepped back away from Badin, stamping his foot.

"Comrade Chairman, I ask you not to advise me. I wish to state once more very strongly that this love of titles and grades has got to be abolished. If we're going to build everything on wooden scaffolding and empty words we shan't do much, God damn it ! I have objected and shall object again to the proposals of Comrades Badin and Lukhava. If it's so precious to Comrade Badin, write ' hero of labour ' on his Party card : and then when he's got this new stripe he can go about giving orders."

Shidky was tapping the table with his pencil ; his nostrils were expanded as though he were trying to tame great laughter which stirred within him.

"Enough, enough, Comrades ! Order ! "

Lukhava looked sharply at Gleb and Badin, and laughed gaily and shrilly like an urchin.

Now Gleb saw for the first time in Badin's darkened eyes an iron hatred. Last spring his eyes had also been clouded, but then it was only vigilance and hostility towards a newcomer's strength. Then it had been curiosity and something else which he could not understand: something heavy and inhuman, which lived in Badin's blood. And as at their first meeting last spring Gleb felt as though he had received a terrific blow.

" Gleb, come to your senses ! Are you crazy ? "

Dasha was looking at him sternly, her eyelids trembling, an appeal in her eyes. When Gleb met her gaze he turned pale : his heart was seared with anguish and fury. Dasha—Badin. Dasha, his wife. . . . She had been with Badin that time in the Cossack village. Bandits in the ravine. . . . The night in one room in one bed. . . . Then Dasha had not been joking. Dasha and Badin. And he, helpless with all his strength.

Shidky showed his teeth and rapped loudly on the table.

" Let's have order, damn it ! Keep quiet, Chumalov ! Everything has been decided and is finished."

Shibis was screwing up his eyes and looking at him silently with a faint smile.

" Sit down, Chumalov ! An experienced member of the Party mustn't play the fool. Sit down ! "

Badin was sitting motionless as before, as though cast from metal, looking darkly at Gleb.

" What's the matter then, Comrade Chumalov ? "

Gleb was panting ; he thrust his hands deep in his pockets ; he could not master his heart : it filled his breast, swelling, bursting, sinking, scorched with blood. He was shivering from head to foot, and his extremities were numbed. Through the window, the sea burned like a fiery soapy bubble ; the air was burning ; a whirlpool of sparks filled the air ; and the sky burned ; the whirling clouds burned too. Everything in his soul must smash with a great thunder and a scattering of all things into dust ! And Gleb, no longer master of himself, raised his fist and shouted with all his strength :

" Libertine ! Son of a bitch ! "

Dasha seized him by the shoulder and her eyes grew green like an owl's.

" Gleb, have you gone mad ? Have you lost your sense, Gleb ? Shame yourself, Gleb ! "

Suddenly they all seemed to become small, perplexed and deafened. Only Shibis sat as before, with half-closed eyes and a hidden smile, drowsy and bored. Badin, with heavy indolence, again leaned forward on the table, and said calmly and coldly, as though discussing business in his office :

" Ah, is that all ? It's a pity that you didn't set a watch on me like the deceased Tskheladze. You'd have learned more then. Even Serge Ivagin knows more than you. Serge Ivagin is here, you know, and he can relate interesting things. But he can't make up his mind to do so because of his shyness about making a scandal. As you see, jealousy is always short-sighted."

Dasha angrily stood between Gleb and Badin. There was neither alarm nor horror in her eyes.

" Gleb has no right to speak this way. Comrade Badin is an exceptionally good and capable worker ; there are very few like him. Gleb is a bit overstrained with work. A devil of a job like getting a factory working—it's quite worth two-pennyworth of fuss now. These damned men—they're always ready to fight over a trifle, but when they're at work they're like iron."

Shidky rose from his chair and his preoccupied look surveyed them all. Serge went towards him, without taking his eyes off him, shaking and broken, wanting to say something but unable to express it. And instead of crying out to Shidky that which was weighing on his soul, he just stooped a little more, waved his hand evasively and walked from the room.

It was cold. The north-east wind was blowing from the mountains, and the air between them and the sea was extremely clear, saturated with the blue of the sky and with the sun. Over the bay enormous ragged clouds floated as though projected from unseen craters. Over the town they seemed to break up and sweep away in fragments towards the brown far ridges of the mountains. Beyond the town, on the slopes, the autumn mist was condensing in the cold, and the crests of the ridge were veiled with mists that rose from the wooded gorges and rocky gullies. Fiery patches blazed on the mountain, floating over the slopes and *arêtes*, vanishing as they reached the gullies and lighting up again on the chalk cliffs. Here, between the mountains and the town, above the bay, was a clear burning blue, and the mountains looked like crystal and the factory seemed blue, with its great square buildings, the smokeless chimneys shooting up like arrows, and its aerial network of towers and cables. Dazzling thick, white snow-drifts of cloud rolled over the defiles surging round the peaks and melting under the sun in the gullies and quarries. The stormy sea was smoking white, like a whirling snow-storm, a mass of dense foam. Between the breakwater and the quays, near the docks, rainbow colours flashed in the air. Against the concrete walls of the docks the waves were flinging up masses of spray, whipping with grey spume the buildings which lay drowned in the russet haze of autumn.

As usual Serge went along the quay, his long curly head uncovered and his hair fluttering like an unshorn fleece blowing into his face and on to his bald patch. The wind howled like the clamour of a mighty mob and was bearing him towards the town; he walked without effort, light-footed. People met him, bent under the force of the wind, but he did not see their faces, only their crushed and flattened hats, and the women's heads with shawls warmly wrapped around them.

Against the stone sides of the docks were Turkish feluccas and fishing smacks, tracing designs in the air with their long masts like spindles.

Shidky had been expecting him to speak and he had not said anything. Why had he gone to the Party Committee when he ought to have gone to the Department of Political Education for a meeting of the Library Commission? Yes, now he remembered: his father was no longer in the library and he did not know where he was living now. Verochka had recently come to see Serge. While speaking, she trembled and did not take her bright brimming eyes off him.

" Serge Ivanovitch, Ivan Arsenitch, he's getting along splendidly! He's such a wonderful man! But he ordered me—. He's ill, Serge Ivanovitch, but he said that you need not. . . . "

She did not turn her child-like eyes from him; Serge did not know whether she was crying or laughing.

" Serge Ivanovitch! If you only knew—. He's dying, Serge Ivanovitch."

And smiling tearfully she had gone away, without turning back when he called her.

Did it matter what happened to his father? The process of selection in life is infallible and unavoidable. Where was Serge's place in the gigantic working-out of history? Perhaps he would be crushed? Perhaps his personality would become steeled like that of Badin, Chairman of the Executive. The impact of these past years had been so strong, and the days had been so ruthless and cruel, that old wounds bled still and every hour new ones were made. Was it not unimportant what would happen to him when every second demanded the full sum of his energy? Work and nothing but work! And when it is grey routine—let it be routine; this was the dream transformed into imperative tenacious toil.

Would he be re-admitted to the Party or not ? It was of no importance : it would not alter his fate. He must work and work only. If he were to be thrown out like garbage, then it meant that this was necessary for the future. He was consecrated to history as an element of strength, an element in the great process. He was united to the whole world, to all mankind, by unbreakable bonds.

The young girl on the ship's deck had passed over his soul like a wave, and remained forever in his heart. Where was she ? But wasn't it all the same : she had gazed on him with a full significant look, and she would never fade in his memory. Then there was Polia Mekhova. She had come to him through her laughter and the fresh courage of her blood. Through the sleepless nights which he had spent sitting at her bedside she had grown into him forever through love, like a grief, a secret joy, an unquenchable fire. And even if Shidky, Shibis and Badin were no longer by his side, nor Lukhava and Dasha. . . . Gleb would stride over the Republic with stony steps, bearing the burden of the heroism of toil. Nothing could change his destiny : he, Serge, was strength, sacrifice, a necessary link in the chain of mighty achievements.

Below the massive wall of the docks the waves were splashing and foaming with green spray. There was a broad landing-place for mooring steamers, and the waves had washed and nibbled at the concrete. There were piles of seaweed, rubbish, shells and dried jelly-fish. Beyond the breakwater, where the dust whirled in the wind, Serge stopped and looked down.

Quite close to the breakwater, washed up against the debris and the seaweed, was lying the body of a new-born child. A red handkerchief was tied around its head, there were socks on its feet, and one could not see its little hands as it had a white cloth tied around it. The corpse was quite new and the little milk-white face was peaceful, quite life-like, as though asleep. It was quiet here between the breakwaters, and the waves, driven by the outer storm, met and broke softly upon each other. Why was the body of this child so carefully placed upon the seaweed ? From where came this suckling with its waxen face ? The warmth of its mother's hand was almost still upon it as could be seen by this scarf, the carefully tied white cloth, and the tiny socks upon its chubby feet. Serge looked at the dead child and could not tear himself away ; it seemed to him that at any moment it would open its eyes and stare at him and smile. From where came this little child, so inhumanly sacrificed, arousing in him such poignant pity ? From a wrecked ship ? Thrown into the sea by a frenzied mother ?

He stood there, unable to turn his gaze away from the little body. Passers-by approached curiously, looked at the corpse and at once continued on their way. They muttered a question to Serge, but he neither heard nor saw them. He stood there gazing without thought, sorrowful, his eyes full of astonishment and pain, and he felt a deep oppressive grief encircling his heart. Then unconsciously he spoke aloud, without hearing his own voice.

" Well, yes. . . . It must be so. . . . That is the very thing. . . ."

4

WAVES

On the landing of the steel-trellised tower stood Gleb, Shidky and Badin, the members of the Factory Committee and Engineer Kleist. But Gleb felt alone amidst the countless crowd below, swelling, swaying, clamouring, covering the ground like a field of sunflowers as far as the eye could reach. They were there—and he was up here.

Right and left in long rows red flags blazed like beacon-fires. And the landing itself glowed with red banners floating from the metal cross-bars. The banner of the Party Group was suspended from the railing by Gleb and with its thick folds and fringe fell down towards the other flags among the crowd below. On the other side, where Badin and Shidky were standing, was the banner of the Building Workers' Union. And below the railings, lower down, on a rich expanse of blood-red bunting immense white letters flashed :

WE HAVE CONQUERED ON THE CIVIL WAR FRONT.
WE SHALL CONQUER ALSO ON THE ECONOMIC FRONT !

It was swarming with heads and shoulders, swaying and tossing, flashing with red headscarves ; or raising dark and pale faces, hats and caps—and everywhere inscribed bannerets waved like red wings. They hid part of the crowd, but behind them were still more masses surging and eddying. On the mountain slope and the rocks, still more crowds and more banners and slogans, like a poppy field. They streamed out of the valley in thousands, higher and higher. In the distance a band was playing a march, and from the depths came the

thunderous clamour of the people mingled with the roar of
the Diesel engines and the clanging of metal. It was impossible
to distinguish the roar of the crowd from the roar of machinery.
Brynza was right: machines and people are one. The masses
cannot be silent. Their life is different from the life of individuals: they are constantly in strenuous movement, always
ready for an irruption.

The day was transparent, autumnal, fresh and bracing. The
far-away points seemed near, as is the case in this season. Gleb
looked at the mountains and at the sky, which was filled with
the hum of an invisible aeroplane; silken white cobwebs swam
in the blue shimmering like mother-of-pearl.

Gleb grasped tightly the iron railing and could not control
the exhausted trembling of his body. His heart was swelling
in his breast until he could hardly breathe. From where came
this multitude? There were already twenty thousand people
here, and still new columns were arriving. There were some
marching nearly a mile away along the mountain slope, among
the boulders and thickets, pouring themselves into the general
mass and spreading higher and higher. In this way the human
mass could cover the whole mountain to the very summit.

Nearby, behind the tower to the right, a regiment of Red
soldiers was standing at ease. Once he had stood so with them.
How long ago was that? And now he was here, once more a
factory worker and, besides, the leader of the Party Group.
The works! What strength had been put into it, and what
struggle! But here it was—a giant, a beauty! Not long
ago it has been a corpse, a devil's mud-heap, a ruin, a warren.
And now the Diesels roared. The cables vibrated with
electricity, and the pulleys of the ropeway sang. To-morrow
the first giant cylinder of the rotary furnaces would begin to
revolve, and from this huge smoke-stack grey clouds of steam
and dust would roll.

Wasn't it worth while that all this countless crowd should
come here and rejoice in their common victory? He—what
was he, Gleb, in this sea of people? No, it was not a sea, but
a living mountain: stones resuscitated into flesh. Ah, what
power! These were they who with spades, picks and hammers,
had cut into the mountains for the ropeway. This had been
in spring, on just such a clear sunny day as this. Then the first
blood was shed. Now the town had wood to burn and everything was ready to start the works. How much blood was in
this immense army of labour! This blood would last long!

The ropeway was working; the steam mill would start soon. The shipyards would open soon. Were there not enough mountain streams to instal power-stations ?

There had been deadly nights and days of war during which he had trembled for his life and thought anxiously of Dasha. How long ago this all seemed, how distant and unimportant ! Dasha—she was not there : she was lost in the crowd and could not be found. Did this matter ? Dasha had been, and was no more. All this was far off and insignificant. And he, Gleb, no longer existed ; there was only an unbearable rapture and his heart which was almost bursting from the flooding blood. The working-class, the Republic, the great life they were constructing ! God damn it, we understand how to suffer, but we also know the grandeur of our strength and how to rejoice !

A roar from the depths of the crowd. The machines roared and the wind in the distant mountains was howling. But this was only the trampling of the crowd and their songs which arose here and there, wordless, intermingling with cries.

" Chumalov ! "

Engineer Kleist stood next to Gleb, pale, stern, grey-haired, with dry, deep-sunken eyes.

" Chumalov, I have never experienced anything like this in my life. One must have strength to support it."

Gleb took him by the arm ; he did not know who was trembling so, he or Engineer Kleist.

" Herman Hermanovitch, no one can vanquish us ! Look ! This is unforgettable ! We are going to salute you as a hero of labour."

Engineer Kleist turned and walked to the other side of the platform.

The crowd was in movement, some forming into groups, the masses becoming more compact. Banners and slogans waved and fluttered. Laughter echoed up from the crowd, and full-throated roaring. The planks shook under Gleb's feet. The myriad heads were cleft here and there showing grey furrows. Caps and red headscarves were flung up in joyous abandon. There was dancing, punctuated by hand-clapping and a staccato recitative. One could see pebbles and stones slipping down the face of the rocks.

Loshak and Gromada were also on the landing. Loshak, made out of anthracite ; his hump, his face and greasy cap. It was the same face as they saw at the Factory Committee, morose, obstinate, scarred ; but his bloodshot eyes opened wider and wider. Gromada, hunched together as though with cold, his shoulder-bones moving under his coat like sharp pieces of wood. His face was yellow and feverish, with starting cheek-bones. He was raising his shoulders to his ears and trembling and convulsed with coughing. Damn the man, what power kept him going, while Gleb felt like a speck of dust amidst this avalanche of humanity? And as for Loshak, the devil himself wouldn't affect him : he had his work cut out to carry the burden of his hump, upon his back and his protruding chest.

" Well, Brothers ? What a hell of a noise we're making, boys ! "

Loshak turned his bovine gaze upon Gleb and pulled his cap over his eyes.

" We're getting on all right, eh ? We've got the factory fixed up and everyone is backing us. I've got to say that much ! "

Gromada waved his arms and it seemed that his bones were rattling.

" That's so, Comrades ! There's no disputing that ! We've done something wonderful—I can hardly stand on my feet for wonderment at the way these working masses are proving their proletarian consciousness, and so on and so forth. . . . Comrade Chumalov—! Ah, if only ! But hell—! Comrades ! Here and everywhere . . . and so on and so on. . . ."

Gleb could no longer stand quietly. He felt like jumping from that height into this sea of heads ; he wanted to shout with all his might, wordlessly, until he had no breath left. Could one endure this ? Here was everything for which he had been living all those past months—here it was, all gathered into one strength.

He walked over to Badin and Shidky, his face convulsed, ecstatic.

Badin looked at him coldly. A black shadow passed wave-like over his eyes.

" It's time to begin, Comrade Chumalov. I shall speak for a quarter of an hour and then you can get down to the heart of the business. And then, immediately, you will give them the signal. We shall have the homage after the hooters have sounded."

Shidky took Gleb by the shoulder and shook him in an intoxication of joy.

" Ah, old Chumalov ! You bloody fool ! But all the same, I'd hate to part from you ! "

Badin, reserved and cold, turned away and walked up to the railings. Again Gleb felt in Badin's iron carriage and the metallic glint of his leather clothing a stern aloofness and a brooding hostility in his eyes. And again his heart shuddered as from a blow.

He took a couple of steps backwards. Below on the high road dense columns with flags were still marching towards them; between the concete walls bands, songs and footsteps thundered.

That was a man beside whom he could not stand. Badin stood alone, his hands on the railing, his shoulders raised. He was looking down on the crowd, the mountain living under this human mass. And in the supple movement of his healthy, active muscles, in the alert poise of his head, there was something of unconcern in his manner, and consciousness of his strength and importance, and the pride of a leader.

" Careerist ! "

Gleb clenched his teeth till his jaws ached. Even now he shuddered at the remembrance of the scene in the House of the Soviets.

Shortly after Dasha had gone away from the sitting, he had called in passing to see how she and Polia were getting on. The corridor was quiet, half-lit and drowsy. The clock had struck eleven. Low intimate conversation could be heard from within the rooms. There was a faint rattling of china and the hissing of a Primus stove. At the end of the corridor was a square patch of light upon the wall. This came from Shibis' room, of which the door stood open.

Behind Polia's door all was quiet. Gleb had not yet knocked when quick, frightened steps came to the door—probably Polia was barefooted—and there was a low startled cry.

" Who is there ? "

And the door opened suddenly, striking Gleb heavily on the shoulder.

" Damn it all ! You'll cripple me if you're not careful ! What a crowd these women are ! "

Mekhova barred the way into the room. She was pale and terrified, her mouth open ready to cry out.

" Gleb ! "

" Well, what's the matter with you, my girl ? Do you think I'm a bandit ? What a touch-me-not ! What made you jump so ? It's a long time since I've seen you. Where is Dasha ? "

He stepped towards her, raising an arm to push her gently

to one side. She changed suddenly, leaned against the door-post and smiled wistfully.

" Ah, Gleb, how startled I get ! Dasha's coming in a minute. After all I've been through, Gleb, I've quite lost myself. It would be better if you didn't come in. . . . Why didn't you stand by me before ? I'm ill, Gleb. Don't come here any more. It would be too painful for me. It is just as though I have been in an accident and am being crushed by the wreckage."

Confused, Gleb looked at her, not knowing what to say. He felt none of his former tenderness or pity towards her : she was too miserable, too helpless. There was nothing left in her of the gay curly-haired girl who had once touched his heart with rapture. The rapture had gone, and Polia with it.

" I must go away, Gleb, to rest and get my strength back. There's something frightful in men. It seems to me now that there's a Badin in everyone of you. Don't look at me like that : it seems that it's not you, but Badin. Go away, Gleb, I beg of you ! We can talk some other time—not now, but later. In other surroundings. . . . Why didn't you give me once what I wanted ? Then perhaps this would not have happened. . . ."

She laughed like a joyous bell, and Gleb recognised in that laugh a tender joy mingled with tears as though in one demented.

" Here's Dasha ! Here she is ! Take him away, Dasha, please, and tell him not to come back again."

Dasha took him by the shoulder and walked him away from the door. Then closed the door carefully upon Polia.

" Now then, soldier, go home ; you've nothing to do here."

And although she laughed, her hand was not friendly but was strange. Gleb felt wounded to the depths ; there was only emptiness and dust within him as in his room at home.

" I see there's no hope of going on together. And you ? It looks as though you'd settle here for good. And things will go badly with me, eh ? You spoil things all right, Dasha. When are you coming home ? "

She trembled inwardly ; it could be seen in her face and eyes, and she bent her brows with suffering. She did not answer at once and, in this brief pause, Gleb saw that there were two forces struggling furiously within her.

She raised her head and her face became like a pale mask. Her red headscarf slipped back, and her eyes shone hard. Even if she had not spoken, Gleb would have known what she wished to say.

" Yes, I am settled here, Gleb. It must be so. It is better
for both of us. We can't live together. We must work out
our lives differently."

Hot blood stormed in his head ; he grew deaf and suffocated
with fury.

" So, now we know clearly ! I could feel it—! We were
only playing the fool. Badin is a worthless scoundrel and a
bandit. I shall fix him when the time comes ! He's gobbled up
both you and Mekhova. Both he and I can't live at the same
time. That's clear ! "

" Gleb, you're nothing but a stupid mad bull ! You don't
know what you're talking about. Go home and pull yourself
together. You must think with your brain and not with your
body. Comrade Badin is no more responsible for this than
you are. Remember that ! Neither you nor Badin have anything to do with it ! "

He turned heavily on his heels and went back down the
corridor. Then he stopped suddenly, remembering that he
had not said the most essential thing.

" Remember this : I'm a homeless dog now. I put all my
soul into the factory. You and the factory have taken all my
strength. We live only with one half of ourselves. . . . I shall
return to the Army."

Dasha came up to him, disquieted ; she smiled kindly and
her eyes glittered with girlish tears. She put her hand gently
on his shoulder and sighed.

" It's not our fault, Gleb. The old life has perished and will
not return. We must build up a new life. The time will come
when we shall build ourselves new homes. Love will always
be love, Gleb, but it requires a new form. Everything will
come through and attain new forms, and then we shall know
how to forge new links."

With bloodshot eyes and a dull pain in his breast, Gleb
turned and stepped down the corridor. Suddenly he stood
stock still : he had come face to face with Badin. He was
standing by the door of his own room and looking at Gleb
with a gloomy mockery. He stood erect, his leather jacket
shining, his hands shoved deep in his pockets.

" Come in here ! You've never been in my room before.
I want to speak frankly with you."

Gleb stood paralysed and could not take his eyes off him.
An icy inward shivering passed through him. Unconsciously
he was fingering his belt, hips and holster.

" You are looking in the wrong place. Your revolver is in its place. Don't worry ; the holster is buttoned up."

And in the other's look Gleb saw the inextinguished flame of hatred. Badin slowly and calmly turned and strode with heavy steps within his room. With every movement the muscles worked elastically at the back of his shaven neck.

Dasha gently took Gleb's hand and led him along the corridor.

" Go on, Gleb. . . . Go on, my darling. . . . I shall come to you. Without fail I shall come. Go and calm yourself. Do you think the question is settled ? No, Gleb, we shall find each other again. But bound by other ties, Gleb ? "

He pushed her away from him and ran rapidly down the staircase.

And now again he saw the blue shaven back of Badin's neck under the flat Kuban cap, provoking him. This damned head was asking to be shot !

Shidky was standing in front of Gleb, his nostrils twitching and trying to hide a smile.

" What's the matter with you ? Are you deaf ? "

He led him to the railing.

The crowd had been settling down, and the clamour of voices was subsiding in expectation. The songs and the music stopped, and the various contingents with their countless heads and banners had streamed in and joined the main body.

Badin was speaking. He spoke for some time, with all his voice and all his energy.

Is it possible to report everything which Badin said ? He mentioned everything necessary for this occasion : the Soviet power, the New Economic Policy, economic reconstruction, Comrade Lenin, the Communist Party of Russia, the working-class. . . . And then he came to the main point :

" And here is one of our victories on the economic front : a great superhuman victory. The re-starting of our factory, of this giant factory of our Republic. You know, Comrades, how our struggle began. In spring, our organised forces for the first time began to strike with hammer and pick, attacking the mountain rocks. Our first blow brought us the ropeway and fuel. Without letting go the hammer, the building workers struck blow after blow, re-constructing life in the machines, in the whole complicated system of these great works. The works are ready for production at full pressure. On this day, the

fourth anniversary of the October Revolution, we celebrate
a new victory on the proletarian revolutionary front. In the
course of the struggle the proletariat produces its organisers
and heroes. Can our working masses ever forget the name
of that fighter, the Red soldier, who gave his life willingly
to the great cause of the revolution, can they ever forget the
name of Comrade Chumalov ? And here we see him, on the
labour front, the same self-denying hero as he was on the field
of battle. . . ."

One could hear no more. It was as if the mountain had
moved from its place and fallen in a dreadful avalanche upon
Gleb, upon the landing and the factory buildings. Rearing,
yelling, din, earthquake ! The high platform was vibrating and
swaying as though it were of wire. Another moment and it
seemed that it would break like a toy and fly through the air,
over this sea of heads, over the banners and the flood of
human tumult. Below, and farther away, the bands blared
brassily.

Gleb, pale and dazed, was muttering strange words which
he could not himself understand. He was choking, brandishing
his arms and laughing uncontrollably. His laughter came not
from within, but through the convulsive distortion of his face.

" Speak ! It's your turn ! Go on ! "

Why speak, when everything was clear without words ?
He needed nothing. What was his life, an infinitesimal speck
in this ocean of human lives ? Why speak, when his voice and
words were not needed here—unnecessary, stupid and insignificant ! He had no words, no life—apart from this tumultuous mass.

His jaw trembled, his teeth chattered. His eyes were blinded,
and the crowd still stormed.

" Go on, man, speak ! Go to it ! "

And he did not know what he was saying ; it seemed to
him that he was talking incoherent, pitiable nonsense. Yet his
voice could be heard to the limits of the crowd, far away on
the mountain slope.

". . . it's not a matter of words, Comrades . . . not a
wagging of tongues. . . . Keep your heads firm on your
shoulders and get the work well in hand. That's how you have
to look at it ! It's no merit when we struggle consciously at the
construction of our proletarian economy—! All of us—!
United and of one mind. If I am a hero, then you are all heroes,
and if we don't work with all our guts towards that kind of

heroism, then to hell with us all ! But there's one thing I want to say, Comrades : we'll do everything, build up everything, and give points to everyone, and be damned to them ! If only we had more technologists like our Engineer Kleist and a bit more of some other things—we'd put it all over Europe in no time. And we'll do it, Comrades ! It must be ! We've staked our blood on it, and with our blood we'll set fire to the whole world. And now, tempered in fire, we're staking everything on our labour. Our brains and our hands tremble—not from strain but from the desire for new labours. We are building up socialism, Comrades, and our proletarian culture. On to victory, Comrades ! "

Again the mountains thundered and burst into a roar of voices and the blaring of the brass.

Gleb remembered as though in a dream how he had grasped a red flag and had waved it three times above the crowd. And the mountains echoed with metallic thunder and the air was shaken by a mad whirlpool of sound. The sirens shrieked —one, two, three !—all together, discordantly, bursting one's ear-drums. And their shrieks seemed to come, not from the hooters, but from the mountains, rocks, crowd, factory-buildings and smoke-stacks. The myriad crowd yelled and thundered with the sirens. They were dancing and leaping there beneath the high platform, on the rocks and mountain slopes, where the banners flashed like wings of fire, and the bands rang like thousands of great bells.

THE END

EUROPEAN CLASSICS

Honoré de Balzac · *The Bureaucrats*

Heinrich Böll · *And Never Said a Word*
And Where Were You, Adam?
The Bread of Those Early Years
End of a Mission
Irish Journal
Missing Persons and Other Essays
A Soldier's Legacy
The Train Was on Time

Madeleine Bourdouxhe · *La Femme de Gilles*

Lydia Chukovskaya · *Sofia Petrovna*

Aleksandr Druzhinin · *Polinka Saks • The Story of Aleksei Dmitrich*

Venedikt Erofeev · *Moscow to the End of the Line*

Konstantin Fedin · *Cities and Years*

Fyodor Vasilievich Gladkov · *Cement*

I. Grekova · *The Ship of Widows*

Marek Hlasko · *The Eighth Day of the Week*

Erich Kästner · *Fabian: The Story of a Moralist*

Ignacy Krasicki · *The Adventures of Mr. Nicholas Wisdom*

Karin Michaëlis · *The Dangerous Age*

Andrey Platonov · *The Foundation Pit*

Arthur Schnitzler · *The Road to the Open*

Ludvík Vaculík · *The Axe*